PRAISE FOR DAN SHAMBLE, ZOMBIE PI...

"The Dan Shamble books are great fun."
—**Simon R. Green**

"A dead detective, a wimpy vampire, and other interesting characters from the supernatural side of the street make *Death Warmed Over* an unpredictable walk on the weird side. Prepare to be entertained."
—**Charlaine Harris**

"A darkly funny, wonderfully original detective tale."
—**Kelley Armstrong**

"Master storyteller Kevin J. Anderson's *Death Warmed Over* is wickedly funny, deviously twisted and enormously satisfying. This is a big juicy bite of zombie goodness. Two decaying thumbs up!"
—**Jonathan Maberry**

"Sharp and funny; this zombie detective rocks! Loved it!"
—**Patricia Briggs**

"Kevin J. Anderson shambles into Urban Fantasy with his usual relentless imagination, and a unique hard-boiled detective who's refreshing, if not exactly fresh. *Death Warmed Over* is the literary equivalent of Pop Rocks, firing up an original world with supernatural zing, bold flavor, and endlessly clever surprise."
—**Vicki Pettersson**

"*Death Warmed Over* is just good plain fun. I enjoyed every minute it took me to read it."
—**Glenn Cook**, author of the Garrett, P.I., paranormal detective novels

"Down these mean streets a man must lurch. . . . With his Big Sleep interrupted, Chambeaux the zombie private eye goes back to sleuthing, in *Death Warmed Over*, Kevin J. Anderson's wry and inventive take on the Noir paradigm. The bad guys are werewolves, the clients are already deceased, and the readers are in for a funny, action-packed adventure, following that dead man walking . . ."
—Sharyn McCrumb

"A zombie sleuth prowls the mean streets as he works a half-dozen seriously weird cases . . . Like Alexander McCall Smith's Mma Precious Ramotswe, the sleuths really do settle most of their cases, and they provide a lot of laughs along the way."
—*Kirkus Reviews* on *Death Warmed Over*

"Anderson's world-building skills shine through in his latest series, Dan Shamble, P.I. Readers looking for a mix of humor, romance and good old-fashioned detective work will be delighted by this offering."
—*RT Book Reviews* (4 stars—compelling page-turner)

"Less-than-scary vampires, hit-man werewolves, witches who sue the publishing company who didn't do a "spell check," and various levels of decaying zombies, monsters, ghosts, trolls, goblins and other creatures (some even human) combine into one twisted, tasty treat!"
—*Stratton Magazine*

"Fast-paced and full of fun characters, adventure, suspense, mystery, and humor—*Death Warmed Over* is the first in a promising new series. Urban fantasy fans should check out this unpredictable and complex story."
—*Sci Fi Chick*

"Funny and entertaining . . . If you are looking for a light, entertaining read, this book is undead from front to back, and a lot of fun!"
—*You'd Only Slow Me Down*

"Part *Chinatown*, part horror comedy, *Death Warmed Over* is entirely fun."
—**Roqoo Depot**

. . . AND FOR KEVIN J. ANDERSON

"Kevin J. Anderson has become the literary equivalent of Quentin Tarantino in the fantasy adventure genre."
—*The Daily Rotation*

"Kevin J. Anderson is the hottest writer on (or off) the planet."
—*Fort Worth Star-Telegram*

"Kevin J. Anderson is arguably the most prolific, most successful author working in the field today."
—**Algis Budrys**

"Kevin J. Anderson is the heir apparent to Arthur C. Clarke."
—**Daniel Keys Moran**

"I always expect more from a Kevin J. Anderson tale, and I'm yet to be disappointed."
—*2 A.M. Magazine*

Also by Kevin J. Anderson

Stakeout at the Vampire Circus
Death Warmed Over
Clockwork Angels: The Novel (with Neil Peart)
Blood Lite anthology series (editor)
The new *Dune* novels (with Brian Herbert)
Hellhole series (with Brian Herbert)
The *Terra Incognita* trilogy
The Saga of Seven Suns series
Captain Nemo
The Martian War
Enemies and Allies
The Last Days of Krypton
Resurrection, Inc.
The *Gamearth* trilogy
Blindfold
Climbing Olympus
Hopscotch
Ill Wind (with Doug Beason)
Assemblers of Infinity (with Doug Beason)
The Trinity Paradox (with Doug Beason)
The Craig Kreident Mysteries (with Doug Beason)
Numerous *Star Wars, X-Files, Star Trek, StarCraft* novels,
movie novelizations, and collaborations

Unnatural Acts

Dan Shamble, Zombie P.I.

KEVIN J. ANDERSON

KENSINGTON BOOKS
www.kensingtonbooks.com

KENSINGTON BOOKS are published by

Kensington Publishing Corp.
119 West 40th Street
New York, NY 10018

All Kensington titles, imprints, and distributed lines are available at special quantity discounts for bulk purchases for sales promotion, premiums, fund-raising, educational or institutional use.

Special book excerpts or customized printings can also be created to fit specific needs. For details, write or phone the office of the Kensington Special Sales Manager: Kensington Publishing Corp., 119 West 40th Street, New York, NY 10018. Attn. Special Sales Department. Phone: 1-800-221-2647.

Kensington and the K logo Reg. U.S. Pat. & TM Off.

ISBN-13: 978-0-7582-7736-7
ISBN-10: 0-7582-7736-9

First Kensington Trade Paperback Printing: January 2013

10 9 8 7 6 5 4 3 2 1

Printed in the United States of America

DEADICATION:

To MICHAELA HAMILTON, at Kensington Books,
who has just the right deadpan sense of humor and all
the enthusiasm and energy of a horde of very, very
hungry zombies.

ACKNOWLEDGMENTS

As an author, I have to treat the undead, as well as various types of monsters, with all due respect. I would very much like to thank Deb Ray, Louis Moesta, and Rebecca Moesta, as well as fans and legal experts Nancy Greene and Melinda Brown, for their insights and added humor. My editor, Michaela Hamilton, at Kensington, showed enthusiasm above and beyond the call, as did my agent, John Silbersack, of Trident Media Group.

Nothing unnatural here at all. Move along. . . .

CHAPTER 1

I never thought a golem could make me cry, but hearing the big clay guy's sad story brought a tear to my normally bloodshot eyes. My business partner Robin, a lawyer (but don't hold it against her), was weeping openly.

"It's so tragic!" she sniffled.

"Well, I certainly thought so," the golem said, lowering his sculpted head, "but I'm biased."

He had lurched into the offices of Chambeaux & Deyer Investigations with the ponderous and inexorable gait that all golems have. "Please," he said, "you've got to help me!"

In my business, most clients introduce themselves like that. It's not that they don't have any manners, but a person doesn't engage the services of a private investigator, or a lawyer, as an ordinary social activity. Our visitors generally come pre-loaded with problems. Robin and I were used to it.

Then, swaying on his thick feet, the golem added, "And you've got to help my people."

Now, that was something new.

Golems are man-sized creatures fashioned out of clay and

brought to life by an animation spell. Tailor-made for menial labor, they serve their masters and don't complain about minimum wage (or less, no tips). Traditionally, the creatures are statuesque and bulky, their appearance ranging from store-mannequin smooth to early Claymation, depending on the skill of the sculptor-magician who created them. I've seen do-it-yourself kits on the market, complete with facial molds and step-by-step instructions.

This golem was in bad shape: dried and flaking, his gray skin fissured with cracks. His features were rounded, generic, and less distinctive than a bargain-store dummy's. His brow was furrowed, his chapped gray lips pressed down in a frown. He tottered, and I feared he would crumble right there in the lobby area.

Robin hurried out of her office. "Please, come in, sir. We can see you right away."

Robin Deyer is a young African American woman with anime-worthy brown eyes, a big heart, and a feisty disposition. She and I had formed a loose partnership in the Unnatural Quarter, sharing office space and cooperating on cases. We have plenty of clients, plenty of job security, plenty of headaches. Unnaturals have problems just like anyone else, but zombies, vampires, werewolves, witches, ghouls, and the gamut of monsters are underrepresented in the legal system. That's more than enough cases, if you can handle the odd clientele and the unusual problems.

Since I'm a zombie myself, I fit right in.

I stepped toward the golem and shook his hand. His grip was firm but powdery. "My partner and I would be happy to listen to your case, Mr. . . . ?"

"I don't actually know my name. Sorry." His frown deepened like a character in a cartoon special. "Could you read it for me?" He slowly turned around. In standard magical manufacturing, a golem's name is etched in the soft clay on the back of his neck, where he can never see it for himself. "None of my fellow golems could read. We're budget models."

There it was, in block letters. "It says your name is Bill."

"Oh. I like that name." His frown softened, although the clay face was too stiff to be overly expressive. He stepped forward, disoriented. "Could I have some water, please?"

Sheyenne, the beautiful blond ghost who served as our receptionist, office manager, paralegal, business advisor, and whatever other titles she wanted to come up with, flitted to the kitchenette and returned with some sparkling water that Robin kept in the office refrigerator. The golem took the bottle from Sheyenne's translucent hands and unceremoniously poured it over his skin. "Oh, bubbly! That tingles."

It wasn't what I'd expected him to do, but we were used to unusual clients.

When I'd first hung out my shingle as a PI, I'd still been human, albeit jaded—not quite down-and-out, but willing to consider a nontraditional client base. Robin and I worked together for years in the Quarter, garnering a decent reputation with our work . . . and then I got shot in the back of the head during a case gone wrong. Fortunately, being killed didn't end my career. Ever since the Big Uneasy, staying dead isn't as common as it used to be. I returned from the grave, cleaned myself up, changed clothes, and got back to work. The cases don't solve themselves.

Thanks to high-quality embalming and meticulous personal care, I'm well preserved, not one of those rotting shamblers that give the undead such a bad name. Even with my pallid skin, the shadows under my eyes aren't too bad, and mortician's putty covers up the bullet's entry and exit holes in my skull, for the most part.

Bill massaged the moistened clay, smoothed the cracks and fissures of his skin, and let out a contented sigh. He splashed more water on his face, and his expression brightened. "That's better! Little things can improve life in large ways." After wiping his cheeks and eyes with the last drops of sparkling water, he became more animated. "Is that so much to ask? Civil treatment? Human decency? It wouldn't even cost much. But my people have to endure the most appalling conditions! It's a crime, plain and simple."

He swiveled around to include Robin, Sheyenne, and me. "That's why I came to you. Although *I* escaped, my people remain enslaved, working under miserable conditions. Please help us!" He deepened his voice, growing more serious. "I know I can count on Chambeaux and Deyer."

Now that the bottle of sparkling water was empty, Sheyenne returned with a glass of tap water, which the golem accepted. She wasn't going to give him the expensive stuff anymore if he was just going to pour it all over his body. "Was there anyone in particular who referred you to us?" she asked.

"I saw your name on a tourist map. Everyone in town knows Chambeaux and Deyer gives unnaturals a fair shake when there's trouble." He held out a rumpled, folded giveaway map carried by many businesses in the Quarter, more remarkable for its cartoon pictures and cheerful drawings than its cartographic detail.

Sheyenne flashed me a dazzling smile. "See, Beaux? I told you our ad on the chamber-of-commerce map would be worth the investment." Beaux is Sheyenne's pet name for me; no one else gets to call me that. (Come to think of it, no one had ever tried.)

"I thought you couldn't read, Bill," I said.

"I can look at the pictures, and the shop had an old vampire proofreader who mumbled aloud as he read the words," Bill said. "As a golem, you hear things."

"The important thing is that Mr., uh, Bill found us," Robin said. She had been sold on the case as soon as the golem told us his plight. If it weren't for Sheyenne looking out for us, Robin would be inclined to embrace any client in trouble, whether or not he, she, or it could pay.

Since joining us, postmortem, Sheyenne had worked tire-lessly—not that ghosts got tired—to manage our business and keep Chambeaux & Deyer in the black. I didn't know what I'd do without her, professionally or personally.

Before her death, Sheyenne had been a med student, work-ing her way through school as a cocktail waitress and occasional nightclub singer at one of the Unnatural Quarter high-end estab-lishments. She and I had a thing in life, a relationship with real potential, but that had been snuffed out when Sheyenne was murdered, and then me, too.

Thus, our romance was an uphill struggle.

While it's corny to talk about "undying love," Fate gave us a second chance . . . then blew us a big loud raspberry. Sheyenne and I each came back from the dead in our respective way—me as a zombie, and Sheyenne as a ghost—but ghosts can never touch any living, or formerly living, person. So much for the physical side of our relationship . . . but I still like having her around.

Now that he was moisturized, Bill the golem seemed a new person, and he no longer flaked off mud as he followed Robin into our conference room. She carried a yellow legal pad, ready to take notes. Since it wasn't yet clear whether the golem needed a detective, an attorney, or both, I joined them. Sheyenne brought more water, a whole pitcher this time. We let Bill have it all.

Golems aren't the smartest action figures in the toy box—they don't need to be—but even though Bill was uneducated, he wasn't unintelligent, and he had a very strong sense of right and wrong. When he started talking, his passion for Justice was apparent. I realized he would make a powerful witness. Robin fell for him right away; he was just her type of client.

"There are a hundred other disenfranchised golems just like me," Bill said. "Living in miserable conditions, slaves in a sweatshop, brought to life and put to work."

"Who created you?" I asked. "Where is this sweatshop located? And what work did you do?"

Bill's clay brain could not hold three questions at a time, so he answered only two of them. "We manufacture Unnatural Quarter souvenirs—vampire ashtrays made with real vampire ash, T-shirts, place mats, paperweights, holders for toothpicks marketed as 'stakes for itsy-bitsy vampires.' "

Several new gift shops had recently opened up in the Quarter, a chain called Kreepsakes. All those inane souvenirs had to come from somewhere.

More than a decade after the Big Uneasy brought back all the legendary monsters, normal humans had recovered from their shock and horror enough that a few tourists ventured into the Quarter. This had never been the best part of town, even without the monsters, but businesses welcomed the increased tourism as an unexpected form of urban renewal.

"Our master is a necromancer who calls himself Maximus Max," Bill continued. "The golems are mass produced, slapped together from uneven clay, then awakened with a bootleg animation spell that he runs off on an old smelly mimeograph. Shoddy work, but he doesn't care. He's a slave driver!"

Robin grew more incensed. "This is outrageous! How can he get away with this right out in the open?"

"Not exactly out in the open. We labor in an underground chamber, badly lit, no ventilation . . . not even an employee break room. Through lack of routine maintenance, we dry out and crumble." He bent his big blunt fingers, straightened them, then dipped his hand into the pitcher of water, where he left a murky residue. "We suffer constant aches and pains. As the mimeographed animation spell fades, we can't move very well. Eventually, we fall apart. I've seen many coworkers and friends just crumble on the job. Then other golems have to sweep up the mess and dump it into a bin, while Maximus Max whips up a new batch of clay so he can create more golems. No one lasts very long."

"That's monstrous." Robin took detailed notes. She looked up and said in a soft, compassionate voice, "And how did you escape, Bill?"

The golem shuddered. "There was an accident on the bottling line. When a batch of our Fires of Hell hot sauce melted the glass bottles and corroded the labeling machine, three of my golem friends had to clean up the mess. But the hot sauce ruined them, too, and they fell apart.

"I was in the second-wave cleanup crew, shoveling the mess into a wheelbarrow. Max commanded me to empty it into a Dumpster in the alley above, but he forgot to command me to come back. So when I was done, I just walked away." Bill hung his head. "But my people are still there, still enslaved. Can you free them? Stop the suffering?"

I addressed the golem. "Why didn't you go to the police when you escaped?"

Bill blinked his big artificial eyes, now that he was more moisturized. "Would they have listened to me? I don't have any papers. Legally speaking, I'm the necromancer's property."

Robin dabbed her eyes with a tissue and pushed her legal pad aside. "It sounds like a civil rights lawsuit in the making, Bill. We can investigate Maximus Max's sweatshop for conformance to workplace safety codes. Armed with that information, I'll find a sympathetic judge and file an injunction to stop the work line temporarily."

Bill was disappointed. "But how long will that take? They need help now!"

"I think he was hoping for something more immediate, Robin," I suggested. "I'll talk to Officer McGoohan, see if he'll raid the place . . . but even that might be a day or two."

The golem's face showed increasing alarm. "I can't stay here—I'm not safe! Maximus Max will be looking for me. He'll know where to find me."

"How?" Sheyenne asked, sounding skeptical.

"I'm an escaped golem looking for action and legal representation—where else would I go but Chambeaux and Deyer? That's what the tourist map says."

"I've got an idea," I said. "Spooky, call Tiffany and tell her I'll come to her comedy improv show if she does me a quick favor."

Sheyenne responded with an impish grin. "Good idea, Beaux."

Tiffany was the buffest—and butchest—vampire I'd ever met. She had a gruff demeanor and treated her life with the utmost seriousness the second time around. But she had more of a sense of humor than I originally thought. Earlier that afternoon, Tiffany had dropped in, wearing a grin that showed her white fangs; she waved a pack of tickets and asked if we'd come see her for open-mic night at the Laughing Skull, a comedy club down in Little Transylvania. Maybe we could trade favors. . . .

I knew Tiffany from the All-Day/All-Nite Fitness Center, where I tried to keep myself in shape. Zombies don't have to worry about cholesterol levels or love handles, but it's important to maintain muscle tone and flexibility. The aftereffects of death can substantially impact one's quality of life. I worked out regularly, but Tiffany was downright obsessive about it. She said she could bench-press a coffin filled with lead bricks (though why she would want to, I couldn't say).

Like many vampires, Tiffany had invested well and didn't need a regular job, but due to her intimidating physique, I kept her in mind in case I ever needed extra muscle. I'd never tried to call in a favor before, but Sheyenne was very persuasive.

Tiffany the vampire walked through the door wearing a denim work shirt and jeans. She had narrow hips, square shoulders, no waist, all muscle. She looked as if she'd been assembled from solid concrete blocks; if any foolish vampire slayer had tried to pound a stake through her heart, it would have splintered into toothpicks.

Tiffany said gruffly, "Tell me what you got, Chambeaux." When Bill emerged from the conference room, she eyed him up and down. "You're a big boy."

"I was made that way. Mr. Chambeaux said you can keep me safe."

After I explained the situation, she said, "Sure, I'll give you a place to stay. Hang out at my house for a few days until this blows over." Tiffany glanced at me, raised her eyebrows. "A *few days*—right, Chambeaux?"

Robin answered for me. "That should be all we need to start the legal proceedings."

Bill's clay lips rolled upward in a genuine smile now. "My people and I are indebted to you, Miss Tiffany."

"No debt involved. Actually, I could use a hand if you don't mind pitching in. I'm doing some remodeling at home, installing shelves, flooring, and a workbench in the garage, plus dark paneling and a wet bar in the basement den. I also need help setting up some heavy tools I ordered—circular saw and drill press, that kind of thing."

"I would be happy to help," Bill agreed.

"Thanks for the favor, Tiffany," I said.

The vampire gave me a brusque nod. "Don't worry, he'll be putty in my hands."

CHAPTER 2

Eager to shut down the illegal golem sweatshop, I went to find Officer Toby McGoohan. McGoo was my BHF, my best human friend, and our lives were closely related, but not in lockstep. Back in college, we'd both wanted to be cops, but my life didn't turn out as I had planned. After a lackluster career on the outside, I set up my private detective business in the Quarter, and I did all right for myself (my own murder notwithstanding).

McGoo stuck with his law enforcement and criminal justice training, became a police officer. And his life hadn't turned out as planned, either. He had never been a rising star. His sense of humor and lack of political correctness had gotten him transferred from a dead-end career on the outside to an even deader-end career here in the Quarter.

McGoo didn't like the assignment, but he made do. As a cop, he believed his job was to enforce the law and keep the peace. "If I was in a quiet, affluent district with a low crime rate, what would I do with myself all day long? Hang out at the doughnut shop and get fat?" Victims were victims, and scumbags were scumbags; it didn't matter that they had fangs or claws. McGoo knew he wasn't going to be promoted to a better job, regardless of how many gold stars he got on his record. He was always going to be a beat cop. So be it.

He made sure I understood the irony. "Who would have guessed it, Shamble? *You* were the one who dropped out of the curriculum, and you're the one who made detective!" It was a joke, but not a very funny one. Most of McGoo's jokes weren't funny.

Where do you find a zombie that's lost its arms and legs?
Exactly where you left it.

His monster jokes were a safe bet. These days, a guy could get in trouble for picking on ethnic minorities, but it was perfectly all right to disparage unnaturals (though it wasn't smart to insult a werewolf in full-moon heat).

McGoo and I often helped each other. He could use department channels off the books to get me details I needed on cases; for my own part, since I didn't wear a badge, I could use unorthodox means to dig up information that he needed. It was a good partnership. We were also drinking buddies.

Our friendship had changed fundamentally once I became a zombie. No surprise there: A *lot* of things changed after I came back from the dead. It was only natural . . . or unnatural.

Around McGoo, I would try to pretend that nothing had happened, for old times' sake. I drank the same brand of beer and sat on the same bar stool, and McGoo did his best to ignore the differences. But when we sat together in the Goblin Tavern, sometimes he couldn't look me in the eyes; instead, he focused on the neat round bullet hole in the center of my forehead (makeup notwithstanding).

Right now, I found McGoo leaving the Transfusion coffee shop, where I knew he'd be this time of day. As a service to the customers, Transfusion had opaque windows so that insomniac vampires could hang out during daylight hours, have a cup of coffee, read a book or work on a laptop. McGoo just liked their coffee. From his gruff exterior, McGoo seemed like the type of person to order coffee strong and black, but he preferred cinnamon lattes (and was ready to deliver a punch in the nose to anyone who called him a sissy for it).

Carrying his latte as if it were a live hand grenade, McGoo saw me coming toward him down the street. "Hey, Shamble!"

"I need a favor, McGoo."

His grin turned into a frown. "Never a good way to start a conversation."

"Consider it job security, some excitement in your life. A good deed for the day."

"I just try to get through the day, Shamble. Wanna hear a joke?"

I cut him off. "I'd rather tell you about an illegal sweatshop, enslaved and abused golems, a black-market souvenir racket. I need you to call in a raid. You'll be glad you did."

For all his curmudgeonly exterior, McGoo took his job seriously. "You aren't kidding, are you?"

"When have I ever lied to you?"

McGoo took a long sip of his cinnamon latte. "You really want me to stand here and make a list?"

"Instead, how about making a few calls, bring in some backup, and bust down a door?" My face wasn't good at expressions anymore, but I made sure I looked absolutely confident. "One condition, though—I get to come along. I have to make sure my clients' interests are served."

"And who exactly is your client?"

"About a hundred oppressed golems. We're going to have a civil rights suit for unsafe and inhuman working conditions, employee abuse, health hazards. You know how Robin is when she gets feisty."

"Sure do." McGoo nodded with a wistful smile. "All right, let me get back to the precinct house, file some paperwork, twist some arms. If I get this rubber-stamped, we should be ready to roll by twilight."

Before they busted down the door to the underground sweatshop, McGoo told me to stand behind the five cops with us. "Just in case there's any gunfire," he said.

"Gunfire? I can handle being shot better than you can. I've already been through the experience a few times." (All but once after I was already dead, fortunately.) Even now, my jacket sported several bullet holes that had been repaired by a not-too-skilled zombie seamstress named Wendy. I could have bought a new jacket, but I rather liked the reminder. Sheyenne thought it lent me character.

"Don't give me more heartburn, Shamble. I ate my last meal at the Ghoul's Diner." Too often, *last meal* was an apt phrase at the Ghoul's Diner.

I hung back. "It's your show, buddy." I hoped we had the correct address. I'd never live it down if I accidentally called a raid on an old witch's bridge club.

When we crept along the shadow-choked alley past a rusty Dumpster, the brownish fumes wafting up made the cops cough and rub their stinging eyes. I saw four rats lying dead on the ground next to the Dumpster, their mouths open, their little paws clutching their throats in agony. I knew this had to be the place where Bill had dumped the toxic hot sauce.

A metal door set into the brick alley wall was marked with hexes and protective spells—standard stuff. Since the Big Uneasy, all search warrants came with counterspells that nullified home-security hexes and protective runes.

McGoo wielded the battering ram with obvious relish. He smashed the lock, pushed open the bent wreckage, and yelled down the stairs. "Police! We have a search warrant!"

The raid team charged down the cement steps into the subterranean levels, trying to outdo one another with their enthusiasm. "Freeze!" "Stop where you are!" "Hands up!" I hurried after them, keeping my .38 in its holster, but I could draw it if necessary.

I heard deep-voiced groans from the underground lair and a high-pitched yelp of panic. "Don't shoot! I surrender!"

The golem workshop was a cesspit—and I don't mean that as a good thing. The place reeked of rot and wet clay, the sour stink of mudflats on a humid summer day. A crowd of clumsily formed, mass-produced golems stood shoulder to shoulder at cramped work stations, applying labels, filling bottles, operating silkscreen presses or thermal package sealers, printing and folding T-shirts, wrapping salt and pepper shakers, boxing up snacks labeled "Certified Unnatural." Crates and crates of finished souvenirs were stacked against a wall, ready for shipment.

Even during the raid, the golems continued to work, trying to meet their quotas. The sound they made was not quite a song, but a low miserable chant that caused the brick support pillars to thrum.

At the far end of the underground chamber, a gold-painted supervisor's chair sat like a throne. The tall necromancer, presumably Maximus Max, sat on the throne and flailed his long-fingered hands. He wore a purple robe embroidered with crudely stitched symbols; I wondered if he had done the embroidery himself. Though I'd never heard of necromancers taking up cross-stitch, I'd seen plenty of strange things in the Quarter.

Max had a long horsey face, as if someone had taken his chin and stretched his head beyond tolerance levels. He was balding, his sparse brown hair in a comb-over that he must have been able to see in a mirror. The center of his forehead sported a third eye drawn in eyeliner. He had been working on a digest-sized book of sudoku puzzles.

"Maximilian Grubb, I have a warrant for your arrest," McGoo said.

He had run the records: Maximilian Grubb, aka Maximus Max, was a two-bit necromancer with a rap sheet of petty crimes. Nothing major, nothing violent—just a lifetime of questionable choices.

Max kept his hands up in surrender, terrified. "On what charge? I've done nothing wrong. I run a good clean business here!"

"One of your workers—a golem named Bill—filed a complaint. And on first glance, I see about a dozen permit violations."

The necromancer missed the point entirely. "You found Bill? I thought he'd gotten lost."

I said, "Bill has engaged the services of Chambeaux and Deyer on behalf of himself and his fellow golems." I looked around the subterranean chamber. "The inhuman work conditions are pretty obvious."

"Inhuman? But they're *golems!*" As the cops put Maximus Max in handcuffs, he remained distraught, babbling excuses. "I'm a reformed necromancer! At least I don't play with dead things anymore. I'm just trying to make a living."

McGoo and his companions ladled out water to the listless golems, who gratefully moisturized their clay skin.

I wandered to the sealed crates of souvenirs ready for shipment, and when no one was looking, I pulled the delivery label off one box. If there was more to this black-market souvenir racket, I wanted to know the details. *The cases don't solve themselves.* I slipped the tag into the pocket of my sport jacket.

McGoo came up to me, shaking his head. He pulled out a T-shirt that showed a cartoon figure of a hairy werewolf who had yanked down his pants to flash his bare buttocks. *Full Moon in the Unnatural Quarter.*

"Scout's honor, I've never seen so much stupid junk in my life," he said. "We're going to impound tons of it for the case— and I mean tons. We'll have to build a separate evidence locker."

"Or maybe you could hold an officers' benefit yard sale," I suggested.

McGoo picked up a black whoopee cushion billed as *Sounds just like a real outgassing corpse!* "When I was a kid, my parents took me on camping trips—it was rainy and miserable and full of mosquitoes, but at least it was a family vacation. Who in their right mind would want to visit the Quarter as a tourist?"

"I guess there isn't any place on Earth too seedy to be commercialized."

As the necromancer was ushered off, his hands cuffed behind his back, McGoo impounded his book of sudoku puzzles as evidence. "Can't be too careful. Might contain potential spells."

The hundred golems were freed, and Bill would be pleased at how this had turned out. Even I was surprised at how swiftly we had shut down the sweatshop. Case closed, justice served.

CHAPTER 3

I intended to celebrate by going on a genuine, long-postponed date with Sheyenne. Unfortunately, Robin overheard me ask her. "Oh, I love Shakespeare in the Park!" Robin flashed me that big bright smile that could always soften my heart, even if it wasn't beating anymore.

"It's Shakespeare in the *Dark*," I corrected her, but the detail didn't matter to her. "The theater troupe is composed mostly of ghosts, with other unnaturals as guest stars."

"They're doing *Macbeth*!" The troupe had originally announced a performance of the comedies *Taming of the Shrew* and *The Merchant of Venice*, but the bloody and murderous tragedies were bigger crowd pleasers in the Unnatural Quarter.

Robin's excitement continued to grow. "Would it be all right if I tagged along? I'll pay for my own ticket, and I'll be no trouble—I promise."

So much for the quiet, romantic date with my ghost girlfriend. . . .

I saw the flicker of disappointment on Sheyenne's face, knowing she would have preferred a semi-normal evening with me, but she smiled. "Sure, Robin. We wouldn't expect you to go by yourself, especially at night, to the Greenlawn Cemetery."

Robin looked as happy as I'd seen her in a long time, and I appreciated Sheyenne for being so flexible. Robin is a partner and a friend, and all-around good company—not your typical fifth wheel. Besides, it wasn't as if she would put a damper on any hanky-panky, since Sheyenne and I could have no physical contact anyway. It would just be a nice night out for the three of us.

Sheyenne showed her genius at innovation, adding spice to our date. Although I couldn't touch her, and she couldn't touch me, she *could* touch inanimate objects. (Don't think about it too much—I didn't make up the rules.) As we passed through the cemetery gates, she slipped a tan polyester glove over one spectral hand and reached out to me. "It takes a fair amount of poltergeist concentration to do this, Beaux, and it won't feel exactly the same, but at least we can hold hands. Sort of."

When I slipped my hand around the fingers of the glove and squeezed, I felt a firm hand inside. It was Sheyenne! "We're like a couple of teenagers."

She batted her spectral eyelashes. "Holding hands isn't enough, but at least it's contact."

"Best I've had in a long time," I said. "This may be a good date after all." She squeezed her fingers, lacing them in mine, and I squeezed back.

Hand in hand, we walked through the wrought-iron cemetery gates, which had a welcome mat on either side.

We arrived just before midnight, still hoping to get good seats. It proved easier than expected, since only a small crowd had gathered for the show. Previously, the Shakespeare troupe had held a matinee performance at 10:00 P.M. for families and children, but they discontinued it due to lack of attendance.

Every time I returned to Greenlawn Cemetery, I had mixed feelings—how could I not? *There's no place like home.* This was where I'd been buried after my murder, where Robin, McGoo, kindly old Mrs. Saldana—and not many others—had come to pay their last respects. Private detectives had clients, but few friends; some unsuccessful PIs didn't have many clients, either.

After the Big Uneasy, one in seventy-five dead people came back as a zombie, while one in thirty returned as a ghost. Even from six feet under, I had beaten the odds. It was one of the first lucky breaks I'd had in my life; I just wish it'd happened *in* my life.

I'd come out of the ground nicely embalmed but caked with dirt, my funereal suit ruined. (I almost never wore it anyway.) One other guy had risen up the same evening, Steve something-or-other. As I'd stood there on the dew-damp grass, trying to gain my bearings, I heard the sound of sod tearing from a nearby grave, seen the dirt move and a questing hand reach up and out, fingers crooked. By now, you'd think gravediggers would have figured out a quick-release exit from the plot. I lurched over like a drunk arthritic, still trying to loosen up my own joints. I reached down to grab my undead comrade by the hand and helped him clamber out of the ground.

We brushed each other off as best we could until we were somewhat presentable. I looked around at all the tombstones and crypts, saw the wrought-iron gates, and pointed. "I think that's the way out."

Still disoriented, we shambled out of the cemetery, getting our bearings. I even gave him my business card, which some-body had placed in the pocket of my burial suit (now, *that's* planning ahead). Steve and I shook hands, wished each other better luck the second time around, and I made my way back to the offices of Chambeaux & Deyer to a still-grieving Robin and the ghost of Sheyenne. . . .

Greenlawn Cemetery had changed quite a lot in the months since. As Robin went off to buy her own ticket for the evening's Shakespeare performance, Sheyenne and I followed other theater fans into the graveyard. Just inside the gate, we passed a small card table manned by a plump woman with cat's-eye glasses. Her fangs were so small it took me a moment to realize she was a vampire. She greeted everyone coming in: "Hello, welcome to the cemetery. Hello, I hope you have a good time."

With all the zombies, ghosts, vampires, and whatnot coming back from the dead, well-meaning volunteers had established a Welcome Back Wagon. I stopped to take a look at their packets and complimented the plump vampire. "Thanks for doing this. I sure could have used a friendly face after I came out of the grave."

The vampire volunteer made a *tsking* sound. "So sorry you had to face that yourself, dear. You didn't get a welcome packet, then?"

"Afraid not."

"Here you go, dear. You deserve one. It's been hard to find sponsors, so the goodie bag has an eclectic mix of useful and, well, *interesting* items. But we're growing every day."

I accepted the packet and thanked her. Drifting beside me, Sheyenne thought aloud. "Maybe we should include Chambeaux and Deyer refrigerator magnets—to let the newcomers know about the services we offer." She was always looking for new business. "New unnaturals often come back with mysteries to solve, or probate and legal issues."

"But refrigerator magnets?" I didn't want to dismiss Sheyenne's suggestion outright, but the recent raid on the golem sweatshop and all those ridiculous black-market souvenirs had given me a jaded view toward commercialization. "Let's think about it. Maybe we can find something classy."

"What else is in the bag?" Sheyenne said.

Rooting around, I found a packet of breath mints (a newly

reanimated corpse could certainly use those), a stale granola bar past its expiration date, a packet of antacids from the Ghoul's Diner, a coupon for a free drink from the Basilisk nightclub (*Premium alcohol and specialty blood types excluded*). I also found the cartoony chamber-of-commerce map of the Unnatural Quarter, and a flyer for Full Moon Escort Services. *Our Ladies Cater to Discriminating Unnatural Clientele. All species accepted.* In fine print, it said, *Succubus available upon request.*

The Quarter had rough edges and a tendency to ignore gray areas of the law. Prostitution seemed more minor than many evils in the changed world, and nobody minded letting ferocious monsters blow off a little steam.

Sheyenne's gloved hand squeezed mine. "Why are you studying that brothel flyer so closely, Beaux?" I quickly put it at the back of the stack.

The next page was even more startling, declaring in bold capital letters: *You Are Damned!* Below that was a campaign picture of stern, cadaverous-looking Senator Rupert Balfour.

"I represent the normal natural humans in this senate district. Monsters might be contained, but they are not forgiven! You creatures may think you can interact with normal society, but sooner or later your true blood will show itself. Good, decent citizens are watching, *and we are ready!*" In tiny letters at the bottom of the page, a sentence read: *Paid for by the Re-elect Senator Rupert Balfour Committee.*

"He's not going to make many friends in the Quarter," I said. Since unnaturals were not allowed to vote, they were not a constituency that politicians bothered to pander to.

I had heard of the man, a grim and humorless blowhard, an ultraconservative senator who demanded enforcement of laws that prohibited "unnatural acts," which he defined as any form of sex among vampires, werewolves, zombies, and the like. The senator looked as if he himself had not had sex of any kind, natural or otherwise, in many years, despite the fact that he was married (to an equally grim, humorless, and unattractive woman). He also looked as if he suffered from persistent hemorrhoids. Or maybe I was making assumptions. . . .

Balfour had garnered publicity on far-fringe radio talk shows, whose hosts called for UFOs to abduct the unnaturals and take them away for medical experimentation (don't forget the anal probes). It was the sort of thing that made most people roll their eyes and regard the man as a joke; the senator's supporters, however, came out of the woodwork and made so much noise that Balfour's proposed Unnatural Acts Act had actually gained some traction.

With our tickets for the festival seating area, Sheyenne and I found a comfortable spot on the green among the tombstones. We managed to get close to the stage, since only about thirty others had come to see the play. I guess there isn't much call for highbrow entertainment in the Unnatural Quarter.

The acting troupe, run by a man who claimed to be the actual ghost of William Shakespeare, struggled valiantly to bring culture to the monsters, though with mixed results. The troupe had built an elaborate stage set that evoked the original Globe Theatre in London, the venue where Shakespeare's plays had initially been performed (probably to larger audiences than this, and with fewer ghosts). The ambitious set was constructed of whitewashed plywood with painted half timbers and clumps of straw to simulate a thatched roof. By special arrangement with the Greenlawn Cemetery outreach committee, the troupe was allowed to leave the stage in place over the summer months.

Robin joined us with her ticket in hand and a stormy expression on her face. "One of those intolerant Neanderthals who works for Senator Balfour is standing there with a sign that says *God Hates Unnaturals.*"

"Only one supporter?" Sheyenne asked. "Not a whole demonstration?"

"Just the one man, and he's being heckled by a bunch of goblins. Normally I'd call them hooligans, but right now I'm tempted to applaud them."

"If it's just one person," I said, "then he looks silly instead of threatening."

Robin allowed herself a smile. "He does look rather silly, at that."

For the start of the performance, a ghost flitted onto the stage, and he was the clichéd image of William Shakespeare from all the history books. He wore a velvet cap, a stuffed doublet, a heavily laced and embroidered shirt, and trunk hose padded to an impressive girth. His face was as painted as any woman's I'd ever seen. All in all, he looked like an overstuffed jeweled-velvet sausage.

"Good ladies and gentle sirs," said Shakespeare's ghost. "Tonight we put before you a play whose name no living actor dare speak. Now dead, we no longer fear such a curse, and so this band of humble players presents the Immortal Bard's *Macbeth*—a tale of witches, curses, and bloodstained hands . . . a story to which every gentleperson here can relate! For this performance, we are also pleased to have as our special guests three genuine witches to portray the Weird Sisters."

From the ticket booth, the lone protester yelled, "God hates unnaturals!" which set up an angry grumbling among the audience. Claws and fangs were bared; hulking shapes rose up and began to loom toward the man, who held his sign like a pathetically small shield.

Shakespeare's ghost defused the situation by calling from the stage, "We thank you for your opinion, sir, and for your amusing performance. All the world's a stage, but this one does not belong to you. If you have not purchased a ticket, I shall ask you to leave."

Two hunchbacked bouncers advanced toward the ticket

booth, and the man seemed to shrink into himself. Senator Balfour's support quickly vanished as the man dashed through the cemetery gates and fled into the night.

"Ah, parting is such sweet sorrow . . . ," Shakespeare's ghost said with comical regret, and the audience tittered. He continued to strut across the stage. " 'Tis a sad reminder. Back in my day, religious zealots labeled all plays the work of the Devil, and my Globe Theatre was burned down. The world has changed overmuch since the Big Uneasy, but alas, not in every way." He cleared his throat. "For tonight, the show must go on. Ladies and gentlemen, ghosts, vampires, werewolves, zombies, and unnaturals everywhere, we present . . . the Scottish Play!"

Robin heaved a contented sigh. I clasped Sheyenne's glove, and we leaned back against a comfortable tombstone to watch the performance.

CHAPTER 4

I didn't expect the ghost of a legendary bank robber to come into our offices, and certainly not to ask for legal advice. But a client is a client.

Alphonse Wheeler had been famous in his day—about twenty years ago—for a series of daring bank robberies that were as much performances as they were crimes, and he'd won over the hearts of the public. Wearing his signature pencil mustache, checkered sport coat, and dapper hat, he arrived at every scene holding a bouquet of flowers. After finishing a robbery, but before dashing to his getaway car, Wheeler would hand a flower to each of the female bank tellers he had just robbed, give them a polite tip of his hat, and escape.

Banks wisely became leery of mustachioed customers wearing dapper hats and checkered sport coats and carrying bouquets of flowers. As a delightful joke on the day before his last caper, Wheeler had paid twenty look-alikes to wander into different banks wearing his distinctive outfit. Twenty-one were arrested, and one turned out to be the real Alphonse Wheeler.

Although he was an independent robber, Wheeler had connections to organized crime. He paid a portion of the stolen money to his criminal masters—he wrote the money off as "membership dues" on his taxes, a deduction that was "disallowed with prejudice" when auditors went over his filings—and kept the rest for himself. After he was thrown in jail, Wheeler refused to turn against his mob accomplices, and he also refused to reveal where he'd hidden his stash of stolen money. He vowed to take the secret to his grave—which he did. Alphonse Wheeler died after two decades in prison.

And now his ghost had turned up at our office door, asking Robin for advice.

Though he had worn a prison uniform for twenty years, Wheeler's ghost chose to manifest wearing his distinctive clothes again. He even brought a bouquet of daisies, which he presented to a delighted Sheyenne. "Beautiful flowers for the lady. I was in lockup for so many years, I'm out of touch with the outside world, but I assume flowers are still appropriate?"

"You assume correctly." Sheyenne sounded like a giggly schoolgirl as she took the flowers. "I remember reading about your exploits when I was a girl—I had a crush on you."

Alphonse stroked a finger along his pencil mustache. "Did you send me a marriage proposal while I was in prison? There were so many I couldn't keep track."

Sheyenne seemed embarrassed. "I was only ten years old."

"And now you've grown into quite a ravishing—"

I cut him off by introducing myself. Robin also seemed immune to his charms, saying, "Mr. Wheeler, how may we be of service?"

He eyed Robin up and down with an intent grin. "That's a wide-open question, my dear. I can think of many types of service a beautiful woman like yourself could—"

Robin remained cool. She preferred to devote her efforts to the innocent and downtrodden, not convicted bank robbers with mob connections. "And if I took you up on your implied offer, Mr. Wheeler, what do you think you could *do?* You're a ghost—flirt all you want, but you can't touch. Now, shall we get down to business?"

"Yes, I suppose so." He cracked his spectral knuckles and drifted over to a seat. "I trust you're aware of my famous career?"

"Your life of crime?" Robin asked.

"Of course we are!" Sheyenne said. "Robin, be nice to the client."

Despite his insubstantialness, Alphonse Wheeler took a seat. "My robberies left me with a nice nest egg, for all the good it did me. I was true to my word, never revealed where I hid the loot, not even on my deathbed. But enough is enough. I'd like to retrieve my stash. After all this time, it's my money, isn't it?"

Robin frowned. "It's money that you stole from a bank, Mr. Wheeler."

"But that was a long time ago, and I'm dead now. Isn't there a statute of limitations or something?"

Robin was trying hard to be patient. "The money never belonged to you, Mr. Wheeler, and you should turn it in. Clear your conscience—don't be one of those restless ghosts. As an attorney, that's what I advise."

"But whose money is it? The insurance already paid the bank after the robberies. No depositor was harmed."

"Then the money belongs to the insurance company," Robin said. "I have an obligation to answer your question, but I also have an obligation to counsel you to avoid criminal activity."

It wasn't the answer Wheeler wanted to hear. He sank deeper into his chair, which rumpled his checkered ectoplasmic sport coat. "What if I just don't tell anybody?"

I had to interrupt. "Mr. Wheeler, your hidden stash is legendary. If you suddenly started waving money around, it wouldn't take a private detective to put two and two together. Somebody would come after you."

"You're all a bunch of spoilsports," Wheeler said, no longer sounding flirtatious. "What happened to the law of finders keepers? Or possession is nine-tenths of the law?" He heaved a dramatic sigh. "I lived in prison for so many years, I don't know what to do with myself on the outside. And being a ghost, there's not much fun anymore at all—as Ms. Deyer so pointedly reminded me. And now you're telling me I can't even spend the money I stole." He lifted himself out of the chair and tipped his hat to Robin. "Thanks for your help, pretty lady— even though I wish you had offered counsel that was more favorable to *me*."

"Come back if you need further assistance," Robin called, and the ghost left through the door without bothering to open it.

I went back to my office to review outstanding cases. I made a call to Tiffany to check on Bill. Now that all of the golems had been freed, he had no reason to remain in hiding, but the buff vamp seemed satisfied with her houseguest. "He's going to stay with me for a while. He's pleasant enough company, and useful around the house. He insists on cooking and cleaning and doing housework and yard work, says he owes it to me, even though I told him that's nonsense. He doesn't leave any chores for me to do."

"Glad to hear it. Want to hire a hundred more golems?"

"No, thanks, Chambeaux. That exceeds my needs at this time."

Bill had been ecstatic that his people were liberated, although it left them jobless and homeless for the moment. I tried to think of some way I could help all those liberated golems, and then I had an excellent idea (yes, I do have excellent ideas occasionally).

I pulled on my stitched-up jacket, took my fedora, and told Sheyenne, "I'm going to the mission. I've got a favor to ask

Mrs. Saldana." I could have used the phone, but I wanted to stretch my legs to keep the stiffness from setting in. Besides, I preferred face-to-face meetings.

Mrs. Hope Saldana, a kindly old woman with unmatched generosity for downtrodden people (or former people), had established the Unnatural Quarter's first soup kitchen and shelter in an effort to improve the lives of unfortunate souls, and even those who didn't have souls. Even though the Hope & Salvation Mission had always operated on a shoestring budget, most of the Quarter's denizens applauded the good work she was doing. I had been her friend, both as a human detective and now as a zombie.

"Mr. Chambeaux, always a pleasure to see you!" She made me think of grandmothers every time she smiled. She offered me a cookie, which I accepted, because one does not turn down gifts from Mrs. Saldana. "What brings you here?"

"Somebody needs help," I said. "In fact, a lot of somebodies."

"Why, that's exactly the reason I'm here—to help."

Rescuing a hundred golems would strain the limits of Hope & Salvation's resources, however. "This is bigger than the usual hard-luck case."

As I described the plight of Bill's friends, Mrs. Saldana's zombie assistant, Jerry, shuffled into the room, leaning on the handle of a push broom that he nudged around the floor. He was a shambler, one of the zombies less fortunate than me—an addict with a taste for brains. Mrs. Saldana had rescued Jerry, and he was a recovering brain-eater, one of her greatest success stories. He had stayed by her side for years, working in the shelter.

Jerry seemed more listless and sluggish than I had ever seen him, however. Without even looking at us, he pushed the broom over to the wobbly old piano Mrs. Saldana used for her church services; she had tried to train Jerry to be her pianist, but he didn't have the aptitude or dexterity to play more than a dirge. Now, seeming mournful, Jerry began a slow and painstaking tapping of the keys. At first, it sounded like random notes, but I managed to identify the melody, "Heart and Soul." At least he had graduated from "Chopsticks."

Before I could ask if Jerry was sick—I had no idea whether zombies could get sick, although I hadn't had so much as a sniffle in the months since I returned to life—Mrs. Saldana held up an extended finger like a schoolteacher. "Oh, I have just the thing for those poor golems! Would you and Ms. Deyer be my guests tomorrow night at a charity banquet? I'm presenting a Humanitarian of the Year award to Irwyn Goodfellow for all the marvelous work he's done in the Unnatural Quarter. It's an evening to benefit MLDW."

While I had heard of the philanthropist Irwyn Goodfellow, the organization was new to me. "What's Mildew?"

"MLDW—Monster Legal Defense Workers. I'm acting director and member of the board. We might have just the thing for those poor golems."

"Robin and I will be there," I said.

It was an excellent idea. A man like Irwyn Goodfellow might indeed be able to integrate the hundred golems into society. Satisfied to have found a possible solution, I finished my cookie and waved farewell to Mrs. Saldana and her zombie helper.

Jerry just leaned against the push broom, looked up, and let out a low moan.

CHAPTER 5

Private investigators don't usually make house calls for initial consultations, but when the madam asked me to come to the Full Moon brothel on an urgent matter, I decided to make an exception. Strictly business, of course.

The Full Moon was a big row house with a full porch, dusty blue siding, and fake shutters on the windows. The two adjacent houses had been condemned and sat empty and available, in case Full Moon decided to expand their operations.

Once I stepped into the parlor, I found myself facing the receptionist, who was all teeth—pointed ones—in a professional smile. She was a slender, slinky wolf-woman who wore only a black negligee and panties that didn't cover much. With a wide hairbrush, she languidly stroked the reddish fur on her arms and thighs. According to the name tag on the reception desk, her name was Cinnamon.

She licked her muzzle. "Girls, we've got a live one—or a dead one. At any rate, it's a customer."

"Not a customer," I corrected her. "I'm here to see a Miss . . . Neffi?"

"Ooh, he wants the madam! Starting right at the top."

"You think he wants to be *laid* to rest?"

Two vampire princesses, a strawberry blonde and a brunette, came out to regard me with their large hypnotic eyes, followed by a pair of pallid and long-haired zombie girls who would have delighted a Tim Burton casting director. The zombie girls introduced themselves as Savannah and Aubrey; the vampire princesses had more flowery names, Nightshade and Hemlock.

The Full Moon was appointed in lavish—or gaudy, depending on your point of view—bordello décor, with an abundance of blood-colored velvet, chaise lounges strategically placed so the girls could lie back and look sexy, overstuffed chairs where clients would relax and have a cigar or sip a glass of their favorite intoxicating beverage. A curving grand staircase led upstairs to a series of rooms. Three of the doors were closed, behind which I heard what might have been sounds of pleasure, of one form or another. Everything about the place suggested "ill repute."

One other girl remained in the downstairs hall, endearingly shy. She was small and waifish with bobbed red hair in a tight perm; her emerald-green eyes showed not the slightest hint of a reptilian slit. She had elfin features and a pointed chin, and her whole demeanor had a little orphan "please hold me and take care of me" vibe that brought out the full-fledged paternal instinct even in a guy like me, who had no paternal instinct whatsoever.

It took me a moment to realize that this was the brothel's resident succubus. Her name was Ruth.

One of the vampire princesses interrupted my thoughts. "You sure you want to see the old lady?" Hemlock was a buxom, ebony-haired beauty in a white nightgown that wasn't much more than a tangle of cobwebs. "A man like you needs someone with youth and vigor, not a dried-up, ancient—"

"Maybe he prefers someone with experience," said a husky

voice as a door opened from a main office adjacent to the main sitting room. "Lots of experience." I turned around to see the Full Moon's madam, Neffi, standing there in all her (theoretical) splendor.

I removed my fedora. "I'm Dan Chambeaux, ma'am. You called me here for an appointment?"

"We have plenty to discuss, Mr. Chambeaux." She gestured me toward her office. "This is business, girls."

"I thought it was all business," said one of the pretty corpse girls.

"When's the last time you had an actual client, Neffi?" huffed the werewolf receptionist, which elicited a chorus of good-natured chuckles from the ladies.

"Don't mind them, Mr. Chambeaux," Neffi purred. "Come into my parlor."

The madam was an unwrapped, well-preserved Egyptian mummy with leathery brown skin stretched tightly over sticklike bones. Her breasts looked as hard as knots on an old log of firewood. Her lips were pulled back to show yellowed teeth in what might have been a smile or just a desiccated rictus. Her eyes were like black lumps of burned-out coal.

Her gray metal business desk was similar to what might be found in any Cold War–era government office; in addition to the in-box and a telephone, the desktop was covered with wide-mouthed jars, pump bottles, and squeeze tubes of skin creams and lotions. As I followed her into the office, Neffi picked up a bottle in one clawlike hand, squirted a dollop of a honeysuckle-scented cream, and rubbed it on the skin of her upper arms.

A four-drawer metal filing cabinet stood against the far wall. A dozen manila folders lay strewn on her desk, each with a name written on the tab. Clients? Or maybe the Full Moon customers put their names on a mailing list.

"Thank you for coming." She let out a brief cackle. "That's a line we use whenever satisfied clients leave: *Thank you for com-*

ing! Not an original joke, but it goes with the territory. Have a seat."

Unlike the plush bordello lounges in the lobby, Neffi's private room had standard office chairs. I was glad the madam intended to treat this as a straightforward interview; Sheyenne was sure to question me about what happened there.

A fish tank filled with dead, floating goldfish sat on a waist-high credenza next to an antique grandfather clock that had stopped ticking long ago. Through an open door in the back of the office, I could see a dim private bedroom with several canopic jars and an Egyptian sarcophagus where Neffi no doubt slept. She also had an actual bed for the occasional discriminating customer, but banker's boxes and stacks of paper were piled on the mattress.

I lowered myself onto the hard chair. My knees felt more stiff than usual today, the result of sitting on the damp cemetery grass during the previous night's Shakespeare performance.

Neffi took a seat behind the desk and folded her clawlike hands together into a macramé of knuckles. On the floor were three small sarcophagi carved in the images of cats. Neffi set one of the ornate containers in her lap and began stroking the carved feline head. "These were my pets in ancient Egypt, mummified and placed in the tomb with me so they could be my companions through eternal life. Even though they weren't restored to life in the Big Uneasy, they're still my beloved cats."

I wanted to get down to business. "Your request was rather vague, Madame Neffi. How can I help you?"

She pulled her chair closer to the desk. "At Full Moon, we're in the pleasure business. It's a necessary service, and unnaturals have needs just like anyone else. Those needs tend to be a bit different, but no less legitimate. We have an understanding with the police department." She picked up several files, glanced at them, and not quite accidentally let me see the names on the tabs. One I recognized as McGoo's watch commander.

"We also cater to human clients who like to take a walk on the dark side—it gives them a thrill, and the girls say humans tend to tip better anyway. You know, when a zombie tells you to keep the tip, you have to be careful what he really means. . . ." She waited for me to laugh, so I did. Just to be polite. It reminded me of McGoo's jokes.

Neffi squirted another blob of lotion and rubbed her hands. "I may not look it now, Mr. Chambeaux, but I was quite a dish in my day. Cleopatra and Nefertiti had nothing on me. Wealthy patrons showered me with gifts, which allowed me to build myself a large tomb, designed by the best interior decorator on the Nile. Gold, lapis lazuli, pearls. When I came back, I had the stake I needed to open this business. I'm a competent businesswoman, and I know how to run the oldest profession—it's been around even longer than I have." She cackled again. "I thought I was all set."

"So why do you require my services?"

"Because I'm being intimidated! The Full Moon has been the target of vandalism, attempted arson, threatening letters thrown through windows. Someone's trying to drive us out of the Quarter, and I need to put a stop to it. Nervous clientele are often limp clientele."

Remembering the pathetic lone demonstrator at the Shakespeare play—*God Hates Unnaturals*—I asked, "Does Senator Balfour have anything to do with it?"

Neffi's expression shriveled up even further, though I hadn't imagined that was possible. "No, not that dickhead. It's organized crime moving in, Mr. Chambeaux. Wiseguys who think they can intimidate a five-thousand-year-old mummy. But they picked the wrong bitch to mess with!"

I was surprised I hadn't heard of it. "Organized crime is trying to move into the necrophilia and prostitution racket?"

"I run a good clean business here, a family business, and I don't want to see it corrupted." She made an angry sound, her vocal cords vibrating until I feared they would snap like frayed cello strings. "This town might belong to monsters, but I'll be damned if I surrender to a bunch of *thugs*." She calmed herself by stroking the cat sarcophagus. "That's why I need private security, around the clock. Does your company have rent-a-goons? I need someone big, ferocious, and intimidating."

I looked down at my average physique, my rumpled and stitched-up jacket. "Chambeaux and Deyer is just me, my lawyer partner, and our receptionist. And as you can see"—I held up my hands—"I'm not all that intimidating."

The old Egyptian mummy considered. "No, you wouldn't project a very frightening presence, unless you were willing to let yourself rot a little."

I don't give up on a client so easily. "Let me ask around. I know people." I rose from the chair, placing the fedora back on my head. "I'll get back to you."

"Thank you, Mr. Chambeaux. And please . . . feel free to stop by anytime. For any reason."

CHAPTER 6

When I returned to the office, Robin was waiting for me, wearing a good business suit, briefcase in hand, ready to head out the door. "Dan, you made it in time! Come with me to the police station. Officer McGoohan is about to interrogate that necromancer. He said we could sit in, and I think it's important for our case. Besides, I want to look that creep in the eye."

"All three eyes," I said, turning around again. "I'm ready."

When Sheyenne appeared in the air, I noticed a flush on her semitransparent cheeks—maybe a twinge of jealousy? "How was the brothel, Beaux?"

"A very nice place," I said. "Professional. Some charming ladies." One glance at Sheyenne's face, and I could see that this wasn't the time or the place for teasing. "I informed the madam that I was unable to provide the services she requested."

"You've got that right! And what services was she after?"

"Protection." I thought of making a wisecrack that every client at an unnatural brothel should use protection, but decided to keep my mouth shut. "It's outside the scope of Chambeaux and Deyer, but I promised I'd try to find someone."

Robin was at the door, holding it open. "Dan, we'll be late. I want to hear how that simpering worm plans to defend himself."

I softened my expression and looked into Sheyenne's big blue eyes. "Spooky, you don't have a thing to worry about. Really." I blew her an air-kiss as I followed Robin out the door, and she blew me one back.

Whoever designed the basic police interrogation room must have been having a bad day. An austere room with cinder-block walls painted white, a table in the middle, several uncomfortable chairs, not much else. You've seen it in every cop show since the dawn of television.

The necromancer Maximus Max sat on one side of the table, miserable. His embroidered purple robes were rumpled, since Max had slept in them in a general population holding cell— and gen-pop in the Unnatural Quarter precinct wasn't anybody's idea of a cocktail party. Max's eyes were red-rimmed and bloodshot; the third eye drawn in eyeliner on his forehead was smudged.

Robin and I entered the interrogation room with McGoo, who had a notepad and a digital recorder, which he set upright on the table. Anxious to get his ordeal over with as quickly as possible, the necromancer looked ready to babble any confession we desired, so long as we let him go. He had already waived his right to counsel and to keep his mouth shut. Robin gave him a baleful glare as she opened her briefcase, removed a yellow legal pad and a pen, and took her seat.

I sat straight-backed and silent, observing, partly for moral support, partly to make the suspect nervous. It was my job.

McGoo went through the preliminaries, noting the date, time, location, and subject of the interrogation, and confirming that Max had chosen not to remain silent. "Maximilian Grubb, also known as Maximus Max, certified necromancer and, judging from your rap sheet"—he pulled out a folder and opened it—"a small-time troublemaker and general nuisance, the type of person who gives me heartburn."

"I'm just trying to make a living, a guy who wants to get by." Max's voice had a persistent whining quality. "It's not easy these days. Tough times."

"We've filed only minor charges so far, but it could get a lot worse," McGoo said. "This is a conversation to obtain more information, even though you've already confessed to plenty. You waived your right to an attorney. Are you certain you don't want one present on your behalf?"

"I don't like lawyers," Max said. "They scare me."

Robin said, "Boo," and he flinched.

As McGoo reviewed the papers, he shook his head. "To be honest, it doesn't look good for you, Mr. Grubb. We've impounded your sweatshop, freed your golem workforce, and confiscated all of your trinkets as evidence."

"But I haven't done anything wrong!" he wailed.

Robin's nostrils flared. "Oh? So slavery is fine with you?"

Maximus Max looked more confused than terrified. "But golems are *made* for work! Would you call me a terrible person for using a lawn mower or a coffeemaker?"

Robin extracted a legal document from her briefcase and slapped it on the table. "As of a ruling seven months ago in the case of *McDowell v. Clay*, golems were classified as unnaturals, and therefore entitled to citizenship in the Quarter. They must be treated as any other citizen and must receive equal protection under the law."

Max opened his mouth, closed it, and opened it again. The second time, words spilled out. "But golems are disposable—they're mass produced! You use a golem until he wears out, and then you get another one."

Indignant, Robin leaned over the table. I could see sparks were about to fly. "Are you comparing those poor golems to . . .

toothbrushes? Golems are thinking beings, not inanimate objects. Your days of using golems as slaves to manufacture tourist garbage are over, Mr. Grubb. Ignorance of the law is not a viable defense."

Beads of sweat stood out on Max's brow, causing the drawn third eye to run. He sniffled. "I was trying to be respectable, and now I'm ruined because the rules keep changing. What's going to be politically correct next week? How can I keep up? I'm just a middleman. I fill the orders and ship them off. The Smile Syndicate runs the gift shop racket inside the Quarter— why not go after them? If there weren't any customers, I wouldn't need golems to make trinkets."

I was surprised to learn that the Smile Syndicate owned the new Kreepsakes souvenir shops. A big conglomerate, the Syndicate kept a low profile, buying businesses right and left, but they did not put their name on neon signs. They had been around for decades, family owned and operated by the Goodfellows. Apparently, the Smile Syndicate had decided that tourism was the Next Big Thing in the Unnatural Quarter.

Several years ago, Irwyn Goodfellow—Hope Saldana's philanthropist benefactor—had publicly and dramatically broken ties with his sister, Missy Goodfellow, who continued to handle the family business. Irwyn wanted to do good deeds with the family fortune, to leave a positive mark on the world; he washed his hands of what he called their "shadowy and underhanded dealings" (although he never gave specifics).

Now Robin shook her head at Max's wobbly defense. "When buying merchandise from an outside vendor, retailers are not obligated to follow the supply chain, nor are they responsible for any violations in the producer's operation. You're on the hook for this, Mr. Grubb. Not the Smile Syndicate."

"But I didn't know it was *wrong* to put golems to work, I really didn't!" The necromancer turned to McGoo. "Can't you cut me a break? Please? You've already taken everything from me. I'm not a bad person, just unlucky."

Robin continued to glare daggers at him, but I whispered to her, "Could we have a private consult with Officer McGoohan outside the room?"

McGoo switched off the recorder and gave a stern warning to Maximus Max. "Don't try to work any spells while you're alone in here. We'll be watching." He pointed to the mirrored wall.

"Oh, I won't—I swear!"

Out in the hall, with the door closed, I asked them both, "How strong is our case, really? Everybody in the Quarter knows that golems are workhorses, designed for assembly lines and menial labor. Max wasn't exactly peddling drugs, weapons, or dangerous magical items. This is going to be a tough sell, especially if the Smile Syndicate decides to defend him with their lawyers." I put my hand on Robin's shoulder. "I'm not convinced the end result would be worth the time and expense of litigating this. We already got what we wanted. Max is shut down and all of Bill's friends are freed."

Robin was tied up in knots. "I want that necromancer punished for abusing those poor golems. I could file a civil rights suit and take him for every penny he has!" She paced back and forth, letting her legal mind take charge over her emotional reaction. "But I doubt he has more than a penny to his name." She lifted her chin and forced herself to look on the bright side. "The most important part is that the golems are liberated, I suppose. We saved them. They can go out and live happy lives now. I'll be able to sleep well at night."

I put my arm around Robin's shoulders and gave her a squeeze.

"Oh, he's not getting away—we've got him on at least ten permit violations," McGoo said. "We'll put him through the wringer.

Scout's honor, Grubb will not be a happy camper when this is all over."

We reentered the interrogation room, and Maximus Max perked up, his eyes filled with puppy-dog hope. "This is your lucky day, Grubb," McGoo announced. "We won't be sending you to prison—not for this. But we might squeeze your wallet dry."

"Oh, thank you, thank you!" Max rubbed his hands, then said in a small voice, "Um, how much is this going to cost?"

"You operated a manufacturing center without the proper permits," Robin interjected. "Your building was not zoned for the production of souvenir trinkets. You didn't register your business. You didn't have regular safety inspections. I could go on, but you get the idea. Each one of those infractions carries a severe penalty and a significant fine."

"If you pay all the fines, you're free to go," McGoo said.

"Oh, I will, even if it takes my last few cents." He swallowed hard. "I didn't know I needed permits for all those things, or licenses, or registrations."

"Sounds like you don't know a lot of things, Mr. Grubb," I added. Robin closed her briefcase and snapped the locks shut with a pronounced click.

"Do your research before you open a business," McGoo warned. "Next time, fill out a form for everything you can think of and file it with the clerk. Pay the required fees. Better safe than sorry. It's a lot cheaper than what you're going to pay now."

The necromancer groaned and swiped a hand across his forehead, smearing his third eye into oblivion.

CHAPTER 7

Even though McGoo and I spent a lot of time together, we weren't sick of each other's company—not yet. Traditionally, or some might say habitually, we met for a beer or two after work. As a private investigator, I've got no time clock to punch, and as a beat cop McGoo worked odd shifts. The Goblin Tavern stayed open twenty-four hours and was a ready watering hole whenever we wanted to kick back and talk. Neither of us had anyplace better to go.

The Tavern wasn't an upscale establishment, but rather a comfortable spot where you could just be yourself, whether natural or unnatural. It had a gleaming wooden bar polished by customer elbows, a selection of multicolored high-end and low-end liquors, potions, and other concoctions made to serve all types of patrons.

I went in early so I'd have time to get ready for the humanitarian awards banquet later in the evening. After having a rough day of his own, McGoo was already on his usual stool, which he claimed was upwind of me, even though I gave off no whiff of decay. "Shamble, you look like death warmed over."

"I take that as a compliment." I took my usual stool beside him. "And you look as sour as always."

We would have had the same banter even if I weren't undead. McGoo and I had been friends since college, and it was a mark of his character that he still treated me basically the same, dead or alive.

I called to the bartender. "Hey, Francine, how about a beer here?" She was busy at the far end of the bar refilling a large jar with pickled eyeballs.

Even though I'm a zombie, I drink to keep up appearances, to give me a sense of normalcy. I like the feel of a cold beer in my hand, the suds in my mouth, the cool taste going down, although I no longer get a buzz regardless of how much I consume. Some zombies suffer adverse reactions when alcohol interacts with certain embalming fluid formulas. They complain of headaches, or their skin turns odd shades of green or gray. Fortunately, I don't suffer from allergies; I just don't feel the pleasant effects anymore.

I looked past the bar to the back office, which was dark, the door closed. "Has there been an Ilgar sighting tonight?"

"I haven't seen Ilgar in two weeks," McGoo said. "After he sold the Tavern, he couldn't get out of this place fast enough."

Ilgar, the original goblin owner, was an unlikely candidate to own a bar, since he didn't like customers, and a successful business generally requires customers. Ilgar used to sit in the back office with his adding machine, running the accounts, ordering blood and liquor supplies, working crossword puzzles—Hell, I didn't know what he did in there all the time. He rarely came out to chat up his patrons behind the bar—a good thing, since Ilgar was a dreary fellow who complained about the business at every opportunity. It was an open secret that he'd been trying to find a buyer for the Goblin Tavern for years, though he pursued the sale only halfheartedly, as he did most things. Recently, however, an amazingly sweet deal had fallen into his lap.

In all my years in the Quarter, I had never seen Ilgar with so much as a faint smile, but on the day he announced the sale of the business he was grinning so widely that his rubbery face stretched back to expose rows of pointed teeth. "Drinks are on the house—for a period of five minutes only. I am retiring and glad to get rid of this albatross around my neck."

The fifteen customers in the Goblin Tavern had applauded politely, some with more enthusiasm than others. Ilgar thought we were congratulating him; most, though, were happy at the prospect of a less dreary owner. And everyone was glad for the free drinks.

"Some big corporation called the Smile Syndicate bought the Tavern. They plan to make it a destination place in the Quarter, a regular stop for tour buses. They might even turn it into a nationwide chain. There may be Goblin Taverns everywhere." Ilgar managed to squash his own joy. "And good riddance to all of it!"

He had gone back into his office and begun clacking on the adding machine keys. Exactly five minutes from the time he'd announced the free drinks, he came out and cut them off.

Now that we'd talked with Max the necromancer that afternoon, I realized that the Smile Syndicate's acquisition of the Goblin Tavern was perfectly in line with their chain of Kreepsakes gift shops: expanding their presence in the Quarter, mainstreaming the monster business. Robin probably saw it as celebrating monster diversity, but something about it didn't sit well with me.

Francine still had her back to me, head bowed as if she were staring at the pickled eyeballs that looked back up at her. "Don't forget about my beer, Francine," I called and turned back to McGoo. "I can only stay for one tonight. I have to get freshened up for a big charity banquet Robin and I are attending."

"Freshened up?" McGoo said with a sniff. "You need a lot of freshening."

"Ha ha."

"What's the big occasion?"

"Awards dinner for the Monster Legal Defense Workers. Mrs. Saldana thinks we might find benefactors for those golems we just freed. Irwyn Goodfellow himself is going to be there."

I looked up, furrowing my brow. Francine was usually more attentive than this, and the Tavern wasn't even busy. She was the best and most longstanding bartender the Goblin Tavern had ever had—a hard-bitten human in her late fifties, though chain smoking and a couple of divorces had added at least ten years to her appearance. She was well liked among the regulars. She chatted with unnaturals, listened to their problems, sympathized with their sob stories, and ladled out advice from her personal store of experiences. Since Francine had made enough of her own bad choices, she liked to say, "I made a lot of mistakes, so you don't have to."

McGoo had finished half of his beer by the time Francine finally turned to me. She hadn't been filling the pickled eyeball jar at all—she was crying. "Sorry, Dan. I'll be with you in a minute." She wiped her eyes, picked up a mug, and went over to the tap. "The usual?"

I had seen Francine pissed off at unruly customers, and she had no tolerance for rudeness, but I'd never imagined her to be an emotional basket case. "What's wrong, Francine?"

"Just not having a good day," she said with a loud sniffle.

McGoo was also concerned. "Francine, we've been coming in here for years. When was the last time you had a *good* day?"

"Not like this. I should have seen it coming." She handed me my beer, and some of it sloshed onto the coaster. "Got my pink slip today. The new owners are letting me go."

"What?" I said. "The Tavern won't be the same without you."

"Tell that to the Smile Syndicate. They've decided that I don't fit their new company profile, that I'm too old and too human to match their demographic." She snorted. "They even had the nerve to be cutesy—they called it their 'demongraphic.' "

I thought of the conglomerate wanting to open similar "fun with monsters" taverns around the country, featuring fake cobwebs, wait staff dressed up as cartoon vampires or werewolves, cheesy items on the menu that made puns on traditional favorites. It would be nauseating.

And one-of-a-kind Francine, with her salty sense of humor and acerbic advice, would never fit in an amusement-park version of the Goblin Tavern.

"New management is advertising for replacements, and they quite clearly say *no humans need apply*." She faced me, placed her hands on her breasts, and pushed them up. "I can pad these, if that's what they want."

"I don't think that's what they want."

She sniffed again and composed herself as three more regulars plodded in. Francine had a lot of regulars, and once word got around, I doubted any of them would be happy.

"Beer's on the house tonight for my old friends," she said to us. "If the new owners don't like it, I've got a few unnatural suggestions for them."

After that, McGoo and I had little to say to each other, both disturbed by the news. The beer was free, and my taste buds were generally deadened, but even so, it tasted bitter.

CHAPTER 8

I'm not the sort of person who regularly attends swanky banquets or black-tie affairs. Even when I was alive I couldn't tell the difference between wine from a $200 bottle or a $20 box. I simply don't frequent those social circles.

So I had good reason to be both excited and intimidated by going to such a glitzy soiree to raise money for MLDW. I wondered if I'd meet the rich philanthropist in person, and if I did, I wondered if I'd say something stupid. . . .

On my way back to the office, I stopped by Bruno and Heinrich's Embalming Parlor, hoping for a quick touch-up before the gala event. Bruno immediately rose to the occasion. "Ooh, big night, Mr. Chambeaux?" He topped off my fluids, powdered my face, and added a bit of color to give the skin a more lifelike appearance; he smoothed over the putty that covered the bullet hole in my forehead and even trimmed my cuticles, buffed my nails, and did a complete executive manicure.

"We must use heavy moisturizers to maintain external hydration. Zombie skin is delicate and damages easily," Bruno said, rubbing lotion on my hands. I thought of Neffi and all her lotions. "Our work is never done. Would you like a foot massage tonight with a pedicure?"

"No time, Bruno." I doubted I would ever find time for a pedicure. On purpose.

I arrived back at the office, as "freshened up" as I was going to get. Sheyenne had rented a tux for me, and I felt as if I were ready for my own funeral all over again (in fact, the tuxedo was much nicer than the old suit I'd been buried in). After I put the strange penguin-suit components together, Sheyenne inspected my appearance and insisted I looked damn fine. She was probably just saying that, but I felt puffed up regardless.

Robin wore an understated pearl necklace and earrings, a sapphire chiffon cocktail dress that looked like a love spell on her, and a smile that, if she had been the one requesting charitable donations, no benefactor could have resisted.

We took Robin's rusty old Maverick, affectionately named the Pro Bono Mobile, and puttered along the streets until we reached the library, where the humanitarian banquet was to be served. Robin self-consciously parked four blocks away so no one would associate us with the battered car. We were, after all, dressed in our finest clothes.

Robin slid her arm through mine and we walked up the steps, moving at my pace. Two red scaly demons stood at the door with the guest list; they wore crimson frock coats, as if they were part of a royal guard. I announced, "Dan Chambeaux and Robin Deyer, guests of Mrs. Hope Saldana."

The demon on the left, with pointy ears and forehead horns, flipped through pages on his clipboard and found our names. He gestured us inside and said in a voice that growled through phlegm, "Pick up your name tags and meal tickets at the reception table."

People and monsters milled about inside the library's main hall, drinking blood, champagne, or sparkling water from fluted glasses. A stack of programs rested on a polished table next to rows of handwritten name tags. After Robin and I chose our meal selections from chicken, vegetarian, or unnatural, I found my name tag, fumbled with my fingers to peel off the adhesive backing, and pressed the *HELLO MY NAME IS: Dan Chambeaux* sticker to my jacket collar.

Sequined gowns, enameled nails and claws, glittering diamonds—it was a heady experience. Thanks to the high bar set by Bela Lugosi, vampires were quite comfortable in evening formal wear, but I had never seen a full-furred werewolf in a tux and tails before. Despite my rented outfit, I felt woefully underdressed.

Mrs. Saldana waved us over. She wore a flower-print church dress and a string of obviously artificial pearls around her throat. "Mr. Chambeaux, Ms. Deyer! I'm so glad you came." We were relieved to have someone to talk to, but she was already bustling away. "Follow me—there's someone I'd like you to meet." Even with my deadened senses I could tell she wore a lot of perfume.

Irwyn Goodfellow was chatting politely with two well-dressed zombies and a troll. Mrs. Saldana came up to him, touched his arm. "Irwyn, sorry to interrupt, but these are the people I was telling you about."

Goodfellow was a big, solidly made man with broad shoulders above a broad chest above a broad but rock-hard waist. His face was square; if anything, his jaw was wider than the top of his head. Bristly light brown hair stood out in a lavish flattop that made his head look like a thistle. His smile was infectious, his grip warm and dripping with sincerity as he took my hand and folded his other hand atop it, giving a firm squeeze.

"Dan Chambeaux, private investigator! My good friend Mrs. Saldana tells me that you and Ms. Deyer have been a great help to her."

"Pleased to meet you, Mr. Goodfellow," I said. "I understand you've been quite helpful to her yourself."

He gave a hearty laugh. "Mrs. Saldana said you and I would get along—we have a lot in common." Goodfellow turned to Robin and graciously gave her a warm handshake as well. "We may have to recruit you to help with the Mildew Society, Ms. Deyer. We can always use volunteers, especially ones with legal experience."

"Always happy to join a good cause," Robin said.

"Good deeds make you feel all warm and tingly inside, don't they?" Goodfellow touched his chest. "I'm thrilled to have a chance to use my family's wealth for benevolent means. So many people and monsters need help. Being named the year's greatest humanitarian—no pun intended—is gratifying, but that's not why I do it. I'm the white sheep of a family with a, shall we say, *checkered* history."

A waiter walked by carrying a tray of drinks. Goodfellow and Mrs. Saldana chose sparkling water. I avoided the blood, considered the champagne, then decided on water myself, too. Bruno had suggested I keep myself hydrated.

Mrs. Saldana was beaming. "I didn't tell you my good news, Mr. Chambeaux. Irwyn has just given the Hope and Salvation Mission a very generous endowment, enough operational funding to carry us through the next five years. It changes everything for us."

Goodfellow looked giddy with his own sense of satisfaction. "You do good work, Mrs. Saldana, and good deeds should be rewarded—that's always been my mantra." When he turned to me, I felt that he was focusing his entire attention, his complete being, on me and Robin. "Now tell me about these golems who need help. The situation sounds dreadful—their plight simply must be addressed."

After Robin explained, Goodfellow shook his head in deep concern. "It's a damn shame, that's what it is. Let me think about how I can apply my money and resources, but I'm a man who acts quickly. I won't drag my feet, and there won't be any bureaucratic problems. We'll help those golems, I promise."

I lowered my voice and got serious. "I'm sorry to mention this, Mr. Goodfellow, but you might have a conflict of interest. Those slave golems were manufacturing souvenirs for the Smile Syndicate's new line of gift shops."

Goodfellow looked deeply troubled. "Smile Syndicate work is all Missy's doing. She's my sister, and I have to love her, but sometimes I'm ashamed of how my family wastes its wealth on selfish gain. Missy and I used to be close, but when I had my epiphany and decided to devote my life to kindness and charity, we had a . . . falling out. She calls me Goody-Two-Shoes, as if it's an insult! She just doesn't understand the joy that fills the heart and soul simply from being a good person."

As the reception continued, Goodfellow excused himself to continue his duty dance, talking with other rich investors or industrialists. Envelopes containing donation checks piled up in offering trays around the hall.

When we were summoned to the banquet by a loud gong, Robin and I found our assigned table, which we shared with two loquacious witches who knew far too much about celebrity gossip, two brothers—full-moon-only werewolves—who bickered and snarled at each other throughout the meal, and an uncomfortable-looking human businessman who said barely a word.

Robin did her best to maintain the conversation through the salad, main course, and dessert. I didn't have much appetite, but I politely moved my food around on the plate. In the back of my mind, I pondered whom I might recruit as private security for the Full Moon, and I also worried about Francine being let go from the Goblin Tavern.

At the end of the meal, we were all treated (if that was the proper word) to a musical performance by a banshee solo artist who had recently had a top-forty single. As she sang, numerous glasses shattered, and audience members squeezed their eyes shut and covered their ears; at least a dozen lost the meals they had just consumed. Then everyone applauded, the banshee took a bow, and the award ceremony began.

Mrs. Saldana looked confident as she stepped up to the microphone, adjusted it to her height, and thumped it with her finger to gain everyone's attention. "Ladies, gentlemen, and others, tonight we are pleased to present an award to a most deserving individual, a man who has selflessly given his time, energy, and, most importantly, his wealth"—she paused for a quick chuckle from the audience—"to help underprivileged unnaturals. He founded the Monster Legal Defense Workers Society, of which I am now the proud chairperson of the board. He gave a generous donation to my Hope and Salvation Mission. He instituted numerous rehabilitation programs and sponsored clothing drives for those newly risen from the grave.

"Not only has Irwyn Goodfellow done many good things, he is also a wonderful human being—and I hope you unnaturals won't hold that against him!" She paused for another chuckle. "One of these days, we'll name a street after him in the Quarter, but for tonight, I am proud to present this plaque."

She lifted a small polished marble slab, like a miniature tombstone, on which Goodfellow's name had been engraved. The audience applauded as the big man rose from his seat. Bowing and nodding to the people at his banquet table, grinning benevolently, he sauntered up to the podium.

"Thank you, thank you all. I don't do this for the awards or the recognition." He lifted the marble slab to admire it. "I am grateful to receive this wonderful plaque, but I see no reason to stop there. Tonight, when talking with the Unnatural Quarter's own private investigator, Dan Chambeaux, I learned of the terrible plight being faced by one hundred formerly enslaved golems. Whenever I hear about monsters or people in need, I just have to do something about it. I was touched by their situation, and I hope you will be, too."

He leaned forward on the podium. "We each have to make at least one small improvement so that the world can be a better place for everyone. I have decided to create an Adopt-a-Golem program with the goal of finding gainful employment for those clay souls. It'll be a charitable and tax-exempt program, and we'll start accepting donations tonight. Ms. Deyer?" He looked around the audience until he spotted Robin. "Would you be willing to do the legal paperwork to set up the project?"

"Of course I would," she said. "Pro bono, of course."

CHAPTER 9

Some news was just too good for a phone call.

On the morning after the charity banquet, I drove Robin's car to the residential area of town, where I found Tiffany's house, a fixer-upper that would always be a fixer-upper no matter how much work she put into it. The shingles were bright and black, recently replaced; Tiffany had probably done the work herself (at night).

The garage door was open, and Tiffany stood inside out of direct sunlight as she balanced sheets of dark wood paneling on two sawhorses. Using a circular saw, she cut the sheets to the proper length. She wore overalls and a tool belt. Bill stood next to her with a stack of two-by-fours balanced on his clay shoulder and a dozen nails in his mouth. Tiffany plucked one of the nails from his lips, snatched a hammer from her tool belt, and with swift sure strokes pounded the paneling onto a support beam.

Because the Pro Bono Mobile's muffler was so loud, they heard me arrive (probably from miles away). As I shuffled up the driveway, Bill grinned at me and two of the nails fell out of his mouth. While the two-by-fours teetered on his shoulder, he bent down to pick up the nails.

I made my announcement. "Good news for you and your golem friends, Bill—we found you all a benefactor."

Bill looked giddy as I described the Adopt-a-Golem program and how Irwyn Goodfellow had promised to help. "And Maximus Max has been slapped with a mountain of permit violations and fines. He'll have to find a new line of work, and he won't bother you anymore."

"Need to find someone to rewrite all those animation spells, Chambeaux," Tiffany said. "Old mimeograph paper fades fast, and I don't want my friend Bill here to crumble into a pile of dirt in the middle of my garage."

"I apologize in advance for the mess," Bill said.

"Not the point, Bill. What did I tell you before?"

The golem was sheepish. "That I'm a person, just like everyone else."

I could see they were getting along well. "Thanks for taking care of him, Tiffany."

"Goodfellow's not the only one who can do good deeds," she said. "Besides, Bill's the perfect houseguest, kind of useful in his own way. He insists on doing the laundry, he cooks, he cleans—and he doesn't get in the way. He puts the toilet seat down, he doesn't make a mess, doesn't play loud music of a kind that I don't like, and he even makes himself useful with my home-improvement projects."

Bill beamed at the compliment. "She calls it a win-win situation. I've never won anything before." He kept smiling, and this time he managed to keep the nails in his mouth when he talked. "Doing a few chores for room and board is a lot better than slaving to make souvenirs. I hope my comrades can find a good situation, too."

"Glad to hear it's working out for both of you. Still, we'll find him a real job and get him out of your hair as soon as possible."

"No hurry on that, Chambeaux. You've got a hundred other golems to worry about. Meanwhile, happy to have him here."

"Tiffany, I'd like to return the favor," I said. "I've got a client, the madam of the Full Moon. She's been having some trouble, needs to hire private security, and I thought of you."

"Rowdy clients?" she asked.

"Outside troublemakers, although I doubt she'd turn down the services of a good bouncer. You'd be a natural for it." I eyed her solid build. "If you're interested, I'll introduce you to Neffi."

As a private investigator, I knew plenty of unsavory types—both monsters and humans with a natural knack for being unpleasant and intimidating. In other words, good candidates to work private security. But if I recommended someone to work the brothel, I was putting my own reputation on the line. I couldn't suggest just any scumbag who liked to growl at suspicious customers; Neffi wouldn't want to scare away potential clients. Tiffany seemed a good choice.

She looked down at the paneling and circular saw. "Although nobody enjoys knocking heads together more than I do, I'm in the middle of remodeling the basement to make it a nice lightproof den. And once I finish that, I've been wanting to take up gourd crafting, unlock my inner creative spirit. I read an informational brochure at the gym, and it sounded interesting to me."

"Could I be a security guard?" Bill asked.

I eyed his big frame. "I bet you'd be good at it."

"Would I get to wear a uniform?"

Tiffany said, "I thought you wanted to make sure your friends got situated first. Besides, I could use your help on some handyman projects."

Bill looked embarrassed. "Yes, my friends should come first. And I will help in any way necessary, Tiffany."

"No pressure," I said. "You know how to find me if you change your mind."

I stopped at the Transfusion coffee shop to pick up a bitter coffee for myself and a cappuccino for Robin. She usually drank tea, but she enjoyed a special treat now and then. Considering our caseload, it never hurt to have a caffeinated partner.

As always, the guy ahead of me in line was rattling off an incredibly complex frou-frou order of something no sane person would drink. What's wrong with just plain coffee? He was a big, bristling werewolf with hunched shoulders and powerful muscles, and in his clawed hands he held a piece of scrap paper; someone with a spidery hand had written down a long and involved order that made the poor teenaged barista's head spin. I rolled my eyes (gently, so they stayed firmly in their sockets).

After he finished his order and paid, the furry guy turned around, and I was startled to recognize Larry, the werewolf hit man who had hunted me during a stolen-painting case not long ago.

"Shamble," Larry growled. "Good to see ya."

"Hello, Larry. I'd shake your hand, but I'm afraid you'd rip my arm off."

I'd recently lost an arm, and though it had been successfully reattached, I had no desire to go through that ordeal again.

"No hard feelings," said the werewolf hit man. "It was business. You were obligated to serve your client to the best of your abilities, and so was I." Larry did not look like the sort of person who would voluntarily drink the high-maintenance concoction he had just ordered, but I made no comment about it.

I put in my order for Robin's cappuccino and my coffee, and the barista looked relieved that I had asked for something comprehensible. While we stood at the bar waiting for our drinks, I considered Larry and said impulsively, "Say, have you ever considered working private security? I've got a client who needs a little muscle, somebody to keep the peace."

Larry's eyes narrowed to slits. "Who is it?"

"The Full Moon brothel. They're being harassed."

The werewolf let out a low howl. "Been there. Nice place, nice ladies. Would be a plum of a job." He shook his muzzle. "But I'm already working as a personal bodyguard."

"For whom?" I asked.

He didn't sound proud of it. "Harvey Jekyll."

My heart sank. Jekyll was the most hated man in the Quarter, and I could imagine he'd need a bodyguard to walk across his own kitchen. But . . . Larry? "I'm disappointed in you. That's the best you can do?"

The big werewolf shrugged. "A paycheck is a paycheck."

The barista called his name, and Larry picked up the tall foamy, half-caff, extra-hot, single pump of vanilla, skim milk, dash of nutmeg, one pack of sweetener, double-sleeved coffee beverage. "This is for him," Larry said.

I was tempted to spit in it, but I doubted the werewolf would let me, even if I asked nicely.

CHAPTER 10

Whether in the Quarter or in the outside world, it's never a good sign when you hear fire engines and wailing sirens roaring across town.

Fires have many mundane causes—cigarettes left burning, kids playing with lighters, or an electric space heater running too close to a stack of those annoying coupon newspapers the mail carrier keeps cramming into your box, even though nobody wants them. In the Unnatural Quarter, though, the cause of a fire is more likely an amateur incineration spell gone wrong, or a pissed-off fire demon who had caught his wife cheating.

At Chambeaux & Deyer we're not ambulance or morgue-wagon chasers, but the fire trucks were making such a ruckus late at night that Robin and I went out to investigate. We could see the orange flames from the windows of our second-story offices. After flitting ahead, Sheyenne returned with a report. "Big blaze over at the Greenlawn Cemetery."

"Was somebody trying to do a Viking funeral again?" Robin

asked. "They need permits for that, and most of the time they're disallowed."

We hurried through the wrought-iron gates and saw that the elaborate theater stage for the Shakespeare in the Dark festival was an inferno. The faux half-timbered walls and the artificial thatched roof crackled as tall flames rose into the air. Curls of smoke wafted toward us with an acrid stench, like the fumes of unkind theater critics getting what they deserved. Humans and unnaturals had gathered to watch the big stage burn.

In case of a demonic fire, the firefighters wore special protective gear—hex-painted clothing and rescue packs—but this turned out to be a perfectly normal blaze. Due to city ordinances to beautify Greenlawn, all fire hydrants had been painted tombstone color and disguised to blend in with the landscape . . . which meant the firefighters had trouble finding them, and by the time they engaged the blaze, the Shakespearean stage was unsalvageable.

Some sluggish zombies shambled into the cemetery, attracted to the bright light and commotion like moths to a flame, but the blaze was extinguished by the time they arrived, so the crowds began to disperse.

"Shakespeare's original Globe Theatre burned down," Robin pointed out. "I can see the irony."

"It's not irony—it's arson," I said, unable to swallow any other explanation. I suspected Senator Balfour's minions were both upset and violent enough to light a match or two, just to make a point.

Next morning, Sheyenne went to make a fresh pot of coffee in the office, even though I couldn't taste the difference between the new gourmet stuff and the tarry residue at the bottom of yesterday's pot. Nevertheless, Sheyenne claimed that brewing coffee made our office smell fresh and homey. I suspected that she did certain things just to remind herself of what she'd once had in life, clinging to a few routine details—making coffee, going out to lunch, taking a walk in the fresh rain. I did the same thing; that was half the reason why I spent so much time at the Goblin Tavern. Since death had left us behind, we clung to the few anchors we had.

Sheyenne was rinsing the pot in our little kitchenette when a young man entered the office. He wore a slightly scruffy camel-colored suit and had rakishly tousled blond hair, a handsome face, and a disarming smile: good-looking in a way that made him seem a natural-born salesman, or a con man. If he was a client, we would help him in any way we could. If he was a salesman, I doubted we were buying.

Sheyenne flitted back out to welcome the visitor, and I heard the coffeepot crash to the floor, spilling water everywhere. The young man grinned at her. "Sorry I missed your funeral, sis."

"Travis!" There was definite shock and alarm in Sheyenne's voice; I couldn't tell whether she was delightfully surprised or angry. She had never mentioned a brother before, but from the similarity in features, it was obvious that they were siblings.

Robin came out of her office, shocked to see the broken coffee urn and the mess on the floor. "I'm Travis." The young man extended a hand to Robin while he looked at me with a hint of intimidation, sizing me up. "Travis Carey."

I had met Sheyenne at the Basilisk nightclub, where she was a singer, and I thought of her by her stage name, although I knew her real name was Anne. "Shy Anne." I sometimes call her Spooky, because that was the first song I ever heard her sing, but I never knew her last name, never asked. Even while she was lying in a hospital bed, in the last throes of the toadstool poison that had killed her, Sheyenne told me she didn't have any family, no living relatives, no one I should contact.

Something fishy was going on here.

I stepped closer to Travis and did my best to loom, just in case she needed backup. "I'm Dan Chambeaux, Sheyenne's employer . . . and very close friend."

Sheyenne hovered there, wrestling with her reaction. I watched a catalog of emotions skim across her face. I wanted to hold her—she needed some support right now—but we didn't have a full-body glove close at hand.

Sheyenne had already told us how she had lost her parents: They were killed by a businessman talking on his car phone—and back then I mean an *actual car phone* installed in his Mercedes with a handset and stretchy cord pulled out. He'd been having an argument about a Chinese to-go order, not watching where he was driving, and the crash had killed Sheyenne's parents on impact.

She'd been just a teenager, forced to take care of herself. She went through a succession of jobs, holding on by her fingernails, learning whatever she could, and never giving up on the chance to make something of herself. I'd always admired her spunk and determination.

She'd worked in the business world before deciding to change careers and go to med school. Money was tight. While working at a nightclub for monsters, she barely scraped by in a tiny apartment in the Quarter, late on the rent, unable to pay her phone bill. All of this she had shared with us.

But she had never mentioned Travis.

"You must have been . . . out of the picture?" I prompted, raising my eyebrows.

"My sister and I had a parting of the ways, but that's all water under the bridge now." Travis kept his attention entirely on Sheyenne. "I would have been here if I could. You know you mean the world to me."

"I know a lot of things, Travis. Do you expect me to forget what you did? I may be dead, but I don't have amnesia." She turned to us, explaining in a huff, "I worked my fingers to the bone to survive after our parents died, trying to make something of myself, but Travis went the opposite direction."

"We had the same goals," he said. "I wanted to make something of myself, too."

"You wanted a shortcut," Sheyenne said, clearly furious. "You looked for the easy way out, and I paid the price for it."

Travis tried his disarming grin, spread his hands. "So I was a little unlucky. I was an entrepreneur, and Fate wasn't on my side."

Sheyenne said to Robin and me, as if her brother weren't there, "His schemes crashed and burned. He lost all of his money, and then he lost other people's money." Her blue eyes were flashing, intense. "I tried to help you."

"Please, let's not rehash this, sis. You should have loaned me the money I needed. I had a line on a big score, and we both could've had a villa in Cancun right now if it had paid off . . . if you'd given me that investment I needed."

Sheyenne huffed. "I was saving to go to med school. I couldn't spare a dime." Robin and I stood there awkwardly, not wanting to be in the middle of a family feud, but I wasn't averse to taking sides. Sheyenne spun to face me. "He stole my money, Beaux. He cleaned out my accounts and then disappeared. I haven't seen him since, until today."

Travis looked flustered. "I was earning your money back, trying to make it up to you. I swear I would have repaid you every cent, but now you're . . . dead. So what's the point?"

Realization hit me, and I said to Sheyenne, "That's why you had to move into that little apartment and take the job at Basilisk? Because your brother stole your savings?"

Sheyenne pressed her pale lips together and nodded.

Travis talked fast and frantic. "I didn't hear about your death until recently, I swear." The term *douchebag* came immediately to mind. "And when I found out you were a ghost, I just had to make amends. I came by to say I'm sorry. You're my sister—we're flesh and blood."

"I'm not flesh and blood anymore," Sheyenne said. "And whatever happened to the big score? Since you *took* the money I didn't lend you, show me my villa in Cancun, and I'll rethink my opinion of you."

Self-consciously, he tugged down the front of his jacket. "That investment didn't pan out due to political turmoil on Easter Island. Nothing I could have predicted."

Sheyenne sniffed. "You stole my money, then you lost it."

"Come on, Anne—I'm your brother, I'm family! We're stuck with each other." He looked so earnest, so pleading. "Look, I mean to make it up to you. I came back, didn't I? I've turned over a new leaf. Give me another chance."

I was ready to give Travis the bum's rush out the door, if that was what she decided. But it was Sheyenne's choice.

She looked uncertain, then seemed to deflate. "I don't want to be one of those vengeful ghosts. I'll bury the hatchet—so long as you know that you really did me wrong."

"I am sorry, I truly am," Travis wheedled. "I just wanted to make sure you're okay, even being dead and all."

"I'm fine. I've learned how to deal with it."

"And . . . I wanted to spend a little personal time in the Unnatural Quarter. Do you think I could stay at your place, just long enough to get my bearings?"

Sheyenne floated in the air in front of him. "I'm a ghost, Travis. Why would I pay rent for an apartment?"

"I guess I didn't think that through." He chuckled nervously and looked at me. "How about—?"

I had a small room upstairs, but it was more claustrophobic than cozy, cluttered with boxes and old furniture. On the rare occasions when I did go up to take a nap, I usually just leaned against a wall for a while. Robin's place, next to mine, wasn't much bigger. She had made it her home, even though she spent little time there, and I had no intention of suggesting that this guy could use it.

"Sorry, Travis, no room at the inn."

Again with the disarming smile, Travis pretended not to be disappointed. "No problem. I'll find someplace else."

Sheyenne rummaged in her desk and pulled out a sheet of paper that we offered for our out-of-town clients. "Here's a list of places you might try. Some of them are dirt cheap."

"Good, I'm sort of living on a budget." Travis smiled at Robin and me again, as if we hadn't just heard all of the ugly details about his character. "It was a pleasure meeting you." He turned to Sheyenne. "And I really want to make amends, Anne." With a final wave, he left.

Sheyenne muttered, "Sometimes family ties are a noose." With great intensity, she busied herself cleaning up the mess of the broken coffeepot.

CHAPTER 11

In spite of her unending, exhausting work at the Hope & Salvation Mission, Mrs. Saldana maintained a sunny disposition. Whenever I went to check on her, I felt rejuvenated by the dose of good cheer that rubbed off from the old woman's halo. Maybe she put special additives in those cookies she made for the unfortunate unnaturals in her congregation, or maybe optimism and good cheer just came naturally to her. She drew genuine heartwarming pleasure from helping those less fortunate; that was the only pick-me-up she needed.

Mrs. Saldana rarely visited our offices, and so when she walked in, accompanied by her more-lethargic-than-usual zombie helper, Jerry, I couldn't help but notice her deeply troubled expression. "Mrs. Saldana, what's wrong?"

"I'm looking for help, and I don't know where else to turn."

I tried to sound brave and reassuring. "Of course you know where to turn—how can we help?" Sheyenne flitted off to make Mrs. Saldana a cup of tea in the microwave, since our coffeepot was broken.

"It's Jerry." She turned her frown toward the listless zombie.

"My poor, dear Jerry. Bless his heart and bless his soul—unfortunately, he doesn't have either anymore."

The zombie just stood there, showing very little reaction. He straightened as if recalling where he was, then he seemed to run out of steam.

Robin joined us. "What happened to him? How can you lose your heart and soul?"

It was a matter of some theological, or maybe nonsensical, debate as to whether unnaturals had souls at all. Zombies did have hearts, though, no matter how withered or nonfunctional they might be.

"He didn't exactly lose them," Mrs. Saldana explained. "He *pawned* them to get money for the mission. We had a rough patch, and I didn't know how we would pay the bills. Dear Jerry managed to get enough cash so we could stay open for business. The pawnbroker paid him extra for an outright sale rather than a loan."

The zombie slurred, "There's good money for a heart-and-soul combo pack."

Deeply troubled, Mrs. Saldana patted Jerry's grimy shirt sleeve. "I didn't realize what he had done—I just thought he was being more sluggish than usual, maybe because of the damp weather. But now that Mr. Goodfellow has given us such generous patronage, the Hope and Salvation Mission has all the money we need. Jerry wants to restore his heart and soul."

"If they're in a pawnshop, you should be able to buy them back," I said.

"We've tried, Mr. Chambeaux, but the gremlin proprietor—a very unpleasant fellow, I must say, and I rarely speak ill of people—has already sold the bundle to another customer. Too late."

I could feel her urgency, but I had to shake my head. "Sorry to say, Mrs. Saldana, but that's the way pawnshops work."

"Then I want to find the customer and offer to buy back the heart and soul, at a premium if necessary. Jerry's worth it to me." She patted his arm again. "But the pawnbroker won't tell us who bought them." Jerry let out a low, phlegmy moan, as decrepit zombies often do. "You can see he's just miserable."

Now I understood why she had come to us. "So you want me to track down who really purchased Jerry's heart and soul and see if I can get them back?"

Mrs. Saldana nodded, but Robin was troubled. "If Jerry pawned the items and understood the terms of the agreement, and if another customer legitimately purchased them, we don't have any legal recourse."

"I'll have a little talk with the gremlin pawnbroker anyway," I said. "That's the best place to start."

Don't get me wrong, I like Shakespeare well enough. I'd read *Romeo and Juliet* and *Hamlet* in high school, got passing grades, but never felt any need to go beyond the "to be or not to be" stage. The main reason I enjoyed *Macbeth* the other night was for the opportunity to be close to Sheyenne, and thanks to the nice glove, we actually got to hold hands. I know that sounds like something a pimply teenager would say, but when it's all you've got, it makes an impression. Apart from that, I wasn't all starstruck by the Bard.

So, to me, Shakespeare's ghost was just another potential client when he came in for a consultation. The ghost stood there in his full ridiculous outfit, complete with stockings, poofy pants, and silly hairstyle. "I am William Shakespeare," he said in the stentorian voice he had demonstrated during the play, enunciating clearly and projecting his words out into the crowd.

"No, you're not," I said.

That startled him. "What do you mean?"

"I mean, you're not William Shakespeare."

He lifted his chin. "Very well. I am the *ghost* of William Shakespeare." He seemed to think I would be impressed.

"No, you're not," I said again. "The Big Uneasy happened only ten years ago. We don't have ghosts from medieval times running around the Unnatural Quarter."

"Not medieval times. It was the Elizabethan Era, the Golden Age," Shakespeare insisted. "And how do you know I wasn't a natural ghost before that? Surely they existed. Vampires and werewolves did."

"Because your performance isn't convincing. A person who lived in the Elizabethan Era or the Golden Age wouldn't ever *call* it that."

"Perchance I learned the term afterward, Mr. Chambeaux." He sounded defensive. "Why are you treating me like a criminal? I want to be your client."

"The two aren't mutually exclusive," I said. "Look, you are not the actual ghost of William Shakespeare, and if you don't start telling me the truth, how do you expect me to help you?"

He seemed flustered, then discouraged. "Oh, very well. It's just a stage name, I admit, but I did have my name legally changed. I *am* William Shakespeare. It says so on my driver's license."

"You have a driver's license?"

Robin joined us for the consultation. "Let's just take him at his word, Dan. How can we help you, Mr. Shakespeare?"

"Someone burned down our stage last night. A very expensive set."

"We saw the fire," I said. "Somebody meant business."

"We're just entertainers, Mr. Chambeaux. My troupe tries to put on a good play for a good cause, bringing culture to the Unnatural Quarter. Shakespeare's plays are eternal. All the more reason for us to bring them to an undead segment of the public. With our Shakespeare in the Dark program, we are doing exactly what the Bard wanted, delivering his works to a much larger audience.

"Our company has applied for grants, cultural subsidies, local sponsors. Alas, the arts foundations tell us they don't have enough money to fund *living* actors and flesh-and-blood theater companies, let alone ours. Their goal, one of them said, is to keep starving artists from genuinely starving and becoming destitute ghost performers like us." Shakespeare frowned in disgust. "But that was nothing compared to the vandals, the arsonists. How could anyone burn down our set, destroy all our props and costumes? We lost everything! That stage was a remarkable replica of the Globe Theatre!"

Robin said, "We enjoyed the performance of the Scottish Play very much."

Shakespeare beamed. "Why, thank you, fair lady. I knew I came to the right place to seek restitution. I'm glad to be in the presence of such a perceptive attorney."

"Wasn't Shakespeare the one who wrote 'First, kill all the lawyers . . .'?" I asked.

"Dan enjoyed the performance as much as I did," Robin interjected. "And that Shakespeare quote is always taken out of context. He never actually advocated killing lawyers."

The ghost smiled. "Thank you—a reader who pays attention!"

"I presume you want help tracking down whoever set fire to your stage?" I asked. "We saw the heckler from Senator Balfour's organization—I wouldn't put it past them."

"Yes, if you please, Mr. Chambeaux. Were we done to death by slanderous lies? My troupe requires the services of a private investigator. While we go through the paperwork, fill out the insurance forms, and hope to reclaim some money from our very expensive set and all those lost props, I want to know who was responsible and bring them to justice."

"If the senator or his minions were behind it, I'll be happy to help nail them," I said, and before Robin could volunteer to do this case on a pro bono basis, I explained our fee structure.

"Alas, I am Fortune's fool." When Shakespeare found his purse and pulled it open to show he carried not a single penny within, l suggested we take our cut from the insurance settlement. I knew Sheyenne would be proud of me.

CHAPTER 12

More and more human tourists were coming to the Quarter, happy couples who strolled down the main streets and peeped into the windows of friendly shops that catered to various types of monsters.

The Timeworn Treasures pawnshop was not one such place.

No one would pass the pawnshop by happy accident. Timeworn Treasures was tucked in a gloomy side street off the gloomy main drag, a dingy and cluttered shop filled with other people's junk. Customers, or victims, slunk down the main street, ducked into the alley when they thought no one was looking, and slipped through the front door to negotiate with the furry proprietor.

I understood that people ran into tough times and had to resort to desperate measures to pay the bills, or get that operation, or buy the shiny new RV they wanted so badly. To me, a pawnshop was a repository of lost dreams, a place where customers surrendered their precious possessions as collateral for high-interest loans, often for pennies on the dollar, hoping to restore their finances in time to retrieve their valuables before someone else bought them. In extreme cases, they sold their items outright.

That was how Jerry the zombie had lost his heart and soul.

I straightened the collar of my sport jacket, tilted back the fedora on my head, and pulled open the door. I hoped the pawnbroker was a reasonable person who would react favorably to a business proposition. That way, I could take care of this quickly and cleanly for Mrs. Saldana.

Unfortunately, the shop owner was a gremlin, the unnatural equivalent of a pack rat who loved to collect esoteric objects for the sole purpose of *having* them. A gremlin pawnbroker wasn't interested in making a profit from buying and selling these objects; he just wanted to surround himself with them. I had seen an episode about gremlins and all their junk on *Unnatural Hoarders.*

After entering the shop, I let my eyes adjust to the gloom. I saw shelf after shelf filled with items on display, arranged in no order that I could discern: used spell books, fat leather-bound volumes as well as the more compact paperback editions; bone china hors d'oeuvre plates and entertainment sets for coven get-togethers; a Maltese falcon with a price so ridiculously high that I didn't dare touch it; next to it, a shriveled and curled monkey's paw that was marked down at a discount: *Special Offer This Week: Only One Wish Left.*

There were racks of moldering old clothes and a jewelry case filled with fashionable rings, necklaces, brooches, and bracelets. Zombies and vampires fresh from the grave often found themselves in a tight financial spot, forced to pawn the jewelry and clothes in which they'd been buried for seed money to start a new unlife. Timeworn Treasures was one of the places they went.

Propped on a high wooden stool behind a chicken-wire barrier sat the gremlin proprietor. He was only about three feet tall, average size for a gremlin, with tiny teeth, a pinched face, and tufts of fur in all the wrong places. He was not a member of the silly fictional species that you weren't supposed to feed after midnight. This guy was an old-school gremlin, the type that liked to hitchhike aboard planes and rip the cowlings off engines or punch holes through wings. After strict airline safety regulations made such mischief a thing of the past, the gremlin had found himself a new career as a pawnbroker.

"How can I help you?" he asked, his voice nasal, his words blurred at the edges as if his lips and tongue were still fighting off the effect of a dentist's anesthesia. "Looking for anything in particular?"

Not bothering to look at more shelves of what the gremlin classified as "timeworn treasures," I fished out my business card. "Actually, I want to see you. Dan Chambeaux from Chambeaux and Deyer Investigations. A client asked me to make inquiries on his behalf."

With small, clawed fingers, the gremlin reached through a gap in the chicken wire, took the business card, and perused it with yellow slitted eyes. He made a gurgling rumble in his throat, halfway between a purr and a growl. I didn't think it was an indication of anger or displeasure, just the fact that he was congested.

He scooted his butt on the small chair, and I could see that his little legs dangled high above the floor and he wore no shoes on his furry feet. He set the card down, as if unimpressed, made a coughing harrumph, then picked up a dirty rag, dabbed it in a jar of silver polish, and began vigorously rubbing an inscribed silver chalice along with its accompanying silver-handled sacrificial dagger. Around him, other silver objects gleamed. Though the gremlin was little, he had bulging biceps, probably from vigorous and constant polishing.

He looked up at me. "Shiny," he said, still lisping. "I like shiny thingth."

At his left elbow, in a large stone stand that might originally have been a birdbath, sat a crystal ball a foot in diameter, marked *Not for Sale*. The gremlin touched the surface of the crystal ball and peered into the transparent depths. "Shiny," he said again. When he removed his finger, he found a smear on the globe's surface, which he rubbed away before heaving a contented sigh.

"Let me tell you about my client, Mr. . . . . uh?"

"Thnaathzhh."

I had never heard such a name before. "Pleased to meet you, Mr. Thnaathzhh."

The gremlin's moist nostrils flared. "Not Thnaathzhh. *Thnaathzhh!*"

"Thnaathzhh," I said again, precisely the same way he was pronouncing his name. In a huff, the gremlin tore a sheet from his receipt book and scribbled on it, *Snazz*.

"Oh, Snazz! That makes more sense."

"Thnaathzhh," the gremlin repeated, working his lips with such determination that spittle flew out. Luckily, the chicken wire blocked the trajectory, so the spittle did not make it to me and my jacket.

"Struggling with sibilants, I see? The sequence of so many esses does sometimes seem silly."

The annoyed gremlin struggled to find a sentence that did not contain the letter *S*. He found a good one. "What do you want?"

"My client is a zombie named Jerry who works for the Hope and Salvation Mission. He pawned his heart and soul here, and he would like to purchase it back."

"Already thold," said Snazz.

"That's what I hear."

The gremlin continued to polish his silver. "Heavy demand on the combo packth, already thold theven thetth thith month."

"Seven sets this month? I was hoping you could tell me who the customer was. I'd make it worth your while." I lowered my voice. "I have some sparkly and shiny things I could pass your way."

The gremlin's eyes lit up. "Shiny..." He sounded very tempted.

He bent over to a credenza next to his stool, worked a combination lock to open the drawer, and pulled out a ledger book nearly as big as he was. He propped it on his lap, taking care to keep the contents out of my sight line. He flipped from page to page, humming, gurgling, until he found the correct entry. "Yeth, I know who bought it."

I contemplated what sparkly or shiny objects I could use for trade. Snazz seemed like the sort of person who might even be delighted with strips of aluminum foil.

"Won't tell you." The gremlin slammed the ledger book shut. "Not worth it."

"I haven't even made an offer yet."

"Thtill not worth it."

Either the intractable gremlin had a well-defined sense of business ethics, or he was genuinely afraid to divulge the identity of the purchaser. Why would anyone want Jerry's heart or soul in the first place? I tried a different tactic. "You said you've sold seven combo packs in the past month. All to the same customer?"

"None of your buthineth."

"Actually, it is my business, Mr. Snazz. I'm a private detective, and this is a case."

"*Private* meanth I don't have to anther your quethtionth. Thith ith a pawnshop. Buy thomething, or go away."

I could see that traditional negotiation would get me nowhere. If McGoo got a warrant, the pawnbroker would have to reveal the purchaser, but even though McGoo and I kept a running back-and-forth of favors, I didn't have a legitimate legal reason to request a warrant—Jerry had pawned his heart and soul, and someone had purchased it. No crime committed.

Still, I needed information from that ledger book. Maybe, I realized, if heart-and-soul bundle packs were such a hot commodity, I could spot the avid collector if I kept an eye on Timeworn Treasures.

To be polite, I perused the objects on the shelves. On one of the high displays, I actually found a coffeepot to replace the one Sheyenne had broken when her brother Travis made his surprise visit. I didn't even want to imagine the dire circumstances that would drive a person to pawn a *used coffeepot* for cash.

But when I offered to buy the coffeepot for the price marked on the tag, the pack-rat gremlin couldn't bear to part with it. "Thank you anyway, Mr. Snazz." I tipped my hat to him, then walked out the door.

As I stuck my hands in my jacket pockets, I found the delivery paperwork I had snagged from the golem sweatshop: the address of the warehouse where the souvenir doodads were to be shipped. Even though Bill the golem and his companions had been freed, and Irwyn Goodfellow had already put Robin to work drawing up the papers for his Adopt-a-Golem charity, I sensed there was more to the case. And I was disinclined to be thrilled with the Smile Syndicate's expansion into the Quarter.

By now it was sunset, and since I was out anyway, I decided to snoop around the warehouse. The cases don't solve themselves. A detective has to organize information, put the pieces together, and come up with viable answers.

But first I had to collect the pieces.

CHAPTER 13

It was a nice night for a stroll. A dank mist curled up from the sewers, a full moon rode high overhead, bats flitted about in charming mating dances. The Quarter's business district was hopping with nightclubs, blood bars, garment shops, red-light massage parlors, and restaurants that catered to specific clientele. I was surprised at how many wide-eyed humans strolled along, taking in the sights, anxious but thrilled. Was this the new trend in date nights?

In one shop, a big sign in the window had a little smiley face drawn beneath it: OPENING SOON. The unlit neon sign said KREEPSAKES, FINE GIFTS AND SOUVENIRS. The sign maker had even managed to include a TM after the logo. Another annoying chain brought to you by the Smile Syndicate. I cringed to imagine what they would do with the Goblin Tavern once they "improved it for a wider audience." Further evidence that the Big Uneasy wasn't the only civilization-threatening apocalypse people should have been worried about.

Okay, the Unnatural Quarter had never been a nice place, but I didn't see *this* as an improvement. What was next? Would the Greenlawn Cemetery or Little Transylvania search for a corporate sponsor like those castrated sports amphitheaters now called Hemorrhoid Cream Park or Disposable Douche Field? I shuddered at the thought.

Leaving the bustle and groan of downtown, I made my way to the warehouse where the golem-made souvenirs were stored, a blocky building with a loading dock. Bright security lights flooded the area, shoving away the comfortable gloom. The cracked parking lot sported a fringe of weeds that struggled up through the asphalt while avoiding the actual flower bed area around the building. Could be they used a landscaping-curse service that kept the weeds away. Dim after-hours lights shone through the barred windows; otherwise the warehouse seemed empty.

A long string of incomprehensible zombie graffiti marred the side of the blank wall. You could always tell zombie graffiti because the spray paint started out with complex symbols, then degenerated into gibberish. When the undead tagger lost track of his thoughts, the letters would peter out into drooping, half-hearted squiggles.

I peered inside the nearest window and could see stacked crates of souvenirs marked as *T-Shirts, Knick-Knacks, Ashtrays, Place Mats, Novelty Snacks.* One entire row held plastic-wrapped packages labeled *Bobbleheads.* McGoo thought the unnatural bobbleheads were hilarious, zombie and skeleton dolls whose heads popped completely off if you bumped them too hard.

Hearing a car, I turned away from the barred window to see a white pickup truck with an amber flashing light on top. An old human security guard climbed out, holding a big .38 in both hands, which he pointed straight at me, trying to aim for the head. His arms trembled. "What are you doing there? Go find some other alley to curl up in. You can't sleep here."

I was offended. "I'm not homeless. I've got a good job."

"Then why is your jacket all patched up like that?"

I brushed at the black threads that repaired the bullet holes. "I've been told it adds character."

His pistol kept wavering, and I supposed that if he fired enough bullets, he might actually hit me by sketching out a wide target circle. "Can't you see the signs—No Trespassing?"

Actually, I hadn't seen any signs. I looked around. "Where?"

The old security guard muttered a curse under his breath. "Damn, I meant to put those up." Then he raised the gun again. "Still, there's no trespassing. Were you vandalizing the place?"

"No, just window-shopping. I meant no harm." I kept both hands up. Security guards had every reason to be jittery in the Unnatural Quarter; at least the Smile Syndicate didn't require him to wear a red shirt as part of his uniform. I lowered my voice. "You sure you're getting paid enough for this?"

The old man's voice was a hoarse squawk. "A job's a job— and I get hazard pay."

"And health benefits?"

"Funeral benefits, too." He waved the gun. "Now, move along."

I moved slowly. This guy had an itchy trigger finger, though he didn't appear to have good aim. "I won't cause you any grief. I'm a private investigator. Is this warehouse owned by the Smile Syndicate?"

"Says so right on the door, and that's who signs my pay-checks."

"That's all I wanted to verify."

He scrutinized the business card I offered him, then his shoulders slumped in relief. "Sorry to be so jumpy."

"No harm in caution."

Before I left, I offered to help the old guard, whose name was Phil, tack up the No Trespassing signs in prominent places around the warehouse.

* * *

The next morning, after picking up notes on other inquiries to make during normal human business hours, I left the Quarter and found the glass-and-steel headquarters of the Smile Syndicate. Since these people were buying my town from the sewers on up, I wanted to know more about them.

The Smile HQ receptionist, Angela Drake according to her nameplate, gave me a look of contempt as I presented myself and asked to see Missy Goodfellow.

"Do you have an appointment?" Angela said.

"Do I need an appointment? Consider me a goodwill ambassador from the Unnatural Quarter, since the Smile Syndicate is expanding into so many local businesses."

Again, Angela was not impressed. "Goodwill ambassadors don't usually come from the low-rent mortician's district."

"We are talking about the Unnatural Quarter," I pointed out, then added, feeling a little defensive, "and this is a damned good embalming job."

Angela was dour, with gray circles under her big brown eyes. Her cheeks were sunken, and it seemed as if she wore anorexia as a badge of honor. I saw tattoos on her neck clumsily covered with thick makeup; her earlobes and nostrils showed the dimples of half-healed piercings. Her nails were painted a bright pink, and her hair was a determinedly average mouse brown, cut short (apparently with hedge trimmers).

I identified the type: Angela had probably been a sour-tempered second-wave Goth with black nails, black hair, and a shitty attitude—not as any kind of personal statement, but because her friends did it. After the Big Uneasy and the mainstreaming of the Unnatural Quarter, however, Goth trappings had become perfectly normal, so she gave up the affectations, hid the remnants in the workplace, and waited for some other popular trend that she could copy.

Or maybe I was imagining it all.

I tried a different tactic. "We're working with Missy Goodfellow's brother, Irwyn, on another matter. I met him the other night at a MLDW Society charity banquet, when he received the Humanitarian of the Year award."

From behind me, a snippy voice said, "Knowing Goody-Two-Shoes doesn't gain you any clout with me."

Missy Goodfellow was tall and slender, dressed in a pristine white pantsuit. Her hair had been dyed a bright yellow, the goldenrod color of a smiley-face sticker. She was pretty in a cold-bitch way, and her expression had the effect of tightening sphincters all around.

She continued, "The Smile Syndicate is a for-profit business run by professionals, not some Easter Bunny operation trying to raise the ghost of Mother Teresa."

I'd never heard the Easter Bunny and Mother Teresa invoked in the same sentence before.

I manufactured a smile. "I found your brother to be a pleasant and dedicated man. Doesn't his good work bring respect to your family?"

"Irwyn is the laughingstock of our family, and our father is probably rolling over in his grave," Missy said, then muttered, "Good thing we added the extra seals and locks to the crypt. We've cut Irwyn off completely from Syndicate day-to-day operations. He can waste his share of the money however he likes, so long as he has no connection with the company." She regarded me with a haughty frown. "I would ask how I could help you, but *helping* is not on the agenda today, Mr. . . . ?"

"Dan Chambeaux," Angela answered for me.

I extended my hand. "Pleased to meet you, Ms. Goodfellow."

"The pleasure is all yours." She made no move to take my hand.

I soldiered on. "Recently I helped liberate a hundred illegal golems who were manufacturing souvenirs for the Smile Syndicate. I wondered if you had any comment on that?"

Her expression remained stony beneath her bright yellow

mop of hair. "The Smile Syndicate is about to open a line of gift shops, and we obtain product from numerous vendors. That inventory comes from private contractors, and we have no idea where or how the items are made." Missy rattled off the explanation so rapidly and cleanly that she must have rehearsed it in front of a mirror.

"And you're not at least surprised to hear it?" I asked. "Not sympathetic to the plight of downtrodden golems?"

She found a speck of lint on her white blazer, plucked it off, and held it between two fingers. She extended her hand toward Angela, who scrambled from behind the desk, relieved her boss of the offending lint, and deposited it in a trash can beside her desk.

Missy turned back to me. "Would you rather we bought our souvenir items from child-labor organizations in Third World countries?"

"Are those the only two options?" I asked.

"Mr. Chambeaux, the Smile Syndicate sees great commercial potential in the Unnatural Quarter. We have followed all appropriate laws and ordinances, and we hope to be good neighbors as well as equal-opportunity employers to our monster friends. Angela, please give Mr. Chambeaux a coupon for a free appetizer at the Goblin Tavern, valid once we reopen it as a family-friendly establishment."

As Angela rummaged in the top drawer of her desk, I said, "Thanks, but no thanks. The place just won't be the same. You're already letting our favorite human bartender go."

"Marketing feels that a monster bartender will better fit the needs of the customers," Missy said. I doubted she knew that Ilgar the original goblin owner had already tried that with a succession of unnaturals, but Francine was the only bartender who had lasted more than a week.

But I'd had enough fun for today. I had accomplished my

intent: I'd met Missy Goodfellow, sized her up, seen the place. I doubted the company would make any sloppy legal mistakes, but sooner or later I was sure one of my cases would point back to them.

As I left Smile HQ, Angela called after me in a chilly voice, "I hope your day is a sunny one."

CHAPTER 14

Sheyenne's brother graced us with another visit. My excitement was immeasurable because devices had not yet been invented to detect such minute amounts.

Travis had found lodgings, or at least found somebody to let him use a shower; he was freshly washed, his hair still wet and slicked back, his cheeks smooth from a close shave. Even I could smell the liberal amount of cologne he had applied. Robin, who did not have a deadened sense of smell like mine, wrinkled her nose, but tried to be pleasant.

Travis had brought doughnuts as a gesture of goodwill, but Sheyenne wasn't impressed. "I'd rather you paid back the money you stole from me. What am I going to do with doughnuts? I'm a ghost."

He turned to Robin and me, grinning. "I thought maybe your office mates would enjoy them."

"I can't taste much anymore," I said.

"Too much fat and processed sugar," Robin said.

Travis took a jelly doughnut for himself and enjoyed the treat, making a powdery mess everywhere.

Sheyenne busied herself brewing a fresh pot of coffee, using a new urn that Robin had picked up from a normal thrift store, since my negotiations with the gremlin pawnbroker had been unsuccessful.

"Remember when we used to go out for Halloween, sis?" Travis was good at that charming-and-disarming thing, but Sheyenne had obviously had a lifetime of seeing it all before. "How about when you were in eighth grade, the last year we went trick-or-treating together? I dressed up as a hobo, rubbed coffee grounds all over my face, took some old clothes, and you . . . you were an Arabian princess, right?"

"That year I was a witch," she said. The coffee started brewing. Her voice was wistful. "Pointy hat and all, and a magic wand with a star on the end." She caught herself and her voice grew hard again. "We were just kids, of course. So innocent. In fact, the whole world was innocent." As if against her better judgment, Sheyenne gave a wan smile and offered a memory of her own. "Remember when you were about to get beaten up in the fifth grade?"

Travis frowned. "I was always getting beaten up in fifth grade."

"Not when I was around. I took care of it, and I took care of you. I remember two bullies said you had stolen someone's lunch money, and they threatened to beat it out of you, said they would shake you upside down until the money fell out of your underwear."

"Yeah," Travis said, "then you came in like hell on wheels and saved my ass."

"I was so mad at them for accusing my brother of stealing!" Now she stopped, and a contemplative expression crossed her face. "*Did* you take that kid's lunch money?"

He seemed embarrassed. "What does it matter now? Look how much has changed. The last time we were together and really close was at Mom and Dad's funeral. I was younger than you, didn't understand the seriousness of what was going on—I knew they were dead, but didn't realize all the other things that were going to change. You did, though—you knew how important it was, and you promised me that we had to stick together, that we would take care of each other. You said it was going to be all right!"

"Then I guess I lied," Sheyenne said. "That makes us even . . . oh, wait, you lied more than once."

"I'm still your brother, and families should stick together. It's just you and me with Mom and Dad gone."

Sheyenne hovered before him, beautiful and translucent. "In case you haven't noticed, I'm gone, too."

Travis's eyes had that puppy-dog look. "And I'm sorry I couldn't be there for you."

Sheyenne laughed, a bitter glissando. "You were *never* there for me."

"I'm here now," he said, avoiding the money question. "I'd make amends if I could, you know that."

"Do I?"

"I was wondering if . . . all those family keepsakes, the photos and whatever else . . ."

I saw all the anger go out of her, replaced by chuckling disappointment. "Now it all makes sense. You tracked me down to see if there's any inheritance."

"No, no! But I really don't have any photos of Mom or Dad, or you. No keepsakes, mementos. I've lost everything over the years. You know what a scatterbrain I am."

"I know what a *con man* you are."

"I thought you said you were going to bury the hatchet, sis."

"Yes, but I didn't say where."

As I awkwardly eavesdropped, I thought of the sour resentment Missy Goodfellow had shown toward her philanthropist brother, and I hoped that Sheyenne's relationship with Travis hadn't degenerated so far. Sheyenne flitted back and forth, a restless ghost; the two of them had a far too complicated relationship to fit into simple pigeonholes. Finally, she grumbled, "Well, I don't have much, just a few boxes in storage. I've got a few student loans I could leave to you, though."

Travis let out a lame but hopeful chuckle. Sheyenne turned to me. "Beaux, would you come along with us to the storage unit? I'm not sure I want to do this alone."

"I'll be there for you, Spooky." I pointedly repeated what her brother had said. The difference was, Sheyenne believed me.

Chambeaux & Deyer kept a small unit in the Final Repose Storage Complex. We stored old case files there, banker's boxes filled with client records, solved crimes, incriminating photographs, interview transcriptions, expired coupons.

After Sheyenne's death, I'd gone to her apartment to retrieve her remaining possessions. At the time, I stored everything even though she had no close relatives. (An understatement, I now realized.) I had been able to put everything she owned into three boxes—a depressingly small encapsulation of an entire life.

But Travis was her brother, and I supposed the family mementos would mean something to him. If Sheyenne was willing to give them to her brother, it was none of my business. Their relationship was more twisted and complex than most of my cases.

In its agreement, the Final Repose Storage Complex had a long list of prohibited items, most prominently "No Storing of Bodies Allowed." Some of the undead had trouble paying the rent for a larger place in the Quarter, so they might be tempted by the cheaper lodgings of a storage unit.

There were also restrictions against cursed artifacts without proper safety interlocks, and any hazardous objects connected to black magic and necromancy. There had been a recent accident in a different storage complex—an ancient flesh-eating plague was released when a scurrying rat knocked over a clay Sumerian urn. Afterward, the local authorities cracked down and imposed strict regulations on potentially dangerous items placed in storage.

Previously, we had been allowed to access our unit whenever we liked; now each tenant had to sign in at the front office, and the manager was authorized to (was in fact *required* to) inspect and maintain a list of specific items stored there. Since Chambeaux & Deyer investigations merely kept boxes of customer and case files, we were probably the most boring tenant in the complex.

As we drove to the Final Repose, Travis was sunny and smiling, chattering away with childhood reminiscences. Sheyenne allowed herself to participate, gradually warming up to her fond nostalgia.

We arrived at the front office, which according to a handwritten sign on the door was Under New Management. When we entered the cramped office, I was surprised to see that the new manager was the disgraced former necromancer Maximilian Grubb. He smiled automatically at Sheyenne and Travis, hoping for new business, then recognized me and recoiled in alarm. "*Now* what have I done? Are you trying to ruin me again? I don't have any golems working here—this is just me!"

His frantic reaction raised my suspicions, so I pressed him. (I couldn't help it; an occupational hazard.) "And have you filed all the proper paperwork? Publicly disseminated a list of every unusual and possibly dangerous item kept in these units?"

"I th-think so," Max stammered. He was pale, and the third eye drawn on his forehead seemed cruder than before. A digest-sized booklet of sudoku puzzles sat on his little desk. "What else do I need to do? I'm t-trying to run everything right. I've gone straight."

"Did you file a specific permit for each type of item?" I asked, making up the requirement out of thin air. "If something goes wrong, the authorities need to know whom to blame."

"I'll do that, right away, I promise!"

"That isn't why we're here, Beaux," Sheyenne said, and I realized she must be anxious to be done with this obligation. "We need to get into our storage unit."

"Oh, you're *tenants!*" Maximus Max said. "I only recently acquired this business as an investment. I'm still getting to know my longtime customers."

Sheyenne's brother thrust his hand forward. "Travis Carey, pleased to meet you!" I was afraid they were birds of a feather.

"You won't be seeing Mr. Carey again," I said. "We're here to access our things." I signed on the clipboard and marked down our unit's number, then added an edge in my voice. "But we'll be watching closely to make sure you follow all rules and regulations."

"I plan on it, Mr. Chambeaux. I've turned over a new leaf, I promise!"

Leaving a flustered Max in his office, we went to our unit. I fished the key from the pocket of my sport jacket, opened the padlock, and rolled up the metal door. Inside, the cement-floored unit was dusty, with plenty of cobwebs and spiders (at no extra charge). A black-and-yellow salamander scuttled in its drunken waddling gait along the floor and ducked through a hole into the adjacent unit.

Sheyenne's possessions were on a separate shelf from the case files. Travis and I pulled the three boxes into the middle of the unit and lifted off the covers. I stood back while Sheyenne and her brother picked through her clothes and found family documents, old letters from her parents, and a scrapbook full of photos of Sheyenne as a little girl, shots of her mom and dad, family vacations they had taken together. Travis was in a few of them, but not many.

"This is . . . all?" Travis said.

"All that remains." Sheyenne picked up a photo of the two of them dressed up for Halloween.

It was a somber time, but Travis could not hide his interest in two gold necklaces, an antique cameo pendant, a few rings— the extent of her mother's remaining jewelry. Travis picked up the necklaces. "This could really help me out, sis. I've run up a few gambling debts."

"Big surprise." Sheyenne sounded more disappointed than angry. "Take them. Do whatever you want. I don't need them anymore."

Travis brightened inappropriately. "You're the best sister in the world!"

"Yes, I am. I wish you'd figured that out earlier."

With a rapid gesture of a man accustomed to magic tricks, Travis pocketed the jewelry, after which he no longer seemed interested in the scrapbooks or photos. "Why don't we just leave the rest of it here? Since I don't have a permanent place to stay, better to keep the family photos in storage for safekeeping."

CHAPTER 15

That evening, I went back to the Greenlawn Cemetery alone so I could prod through the charred remains of the Globe Theatre set. The theatrical stage had been built from cheap and flimsy materials: papier-mâché, plywood, colored paper, and dyed fabrics. Now it was a sodden mess of ash and scraps—nothing salvageable whatsoever. The firefighters had been thorough and enthusiastic when they quenched the blaze. A complete and total loss.

Shakespeare had given me a detailed inventory of the possessions lost in the blaze, including hard-to-find Elizabethan costumes, large Comedy and Tragedy masks for the play, and antique furniture, not to mention the set itself. The ghost had also tallied the performance money they'd previously earned per show, so as to estimate loss of income. It was a dismal amount, however, and I could see that the theatrical company definitely needed those arts grants (or, preferably, bigger audiences). If we could prove malicious arson, the haunted acting company might generate some sympathy and enough donations to keep themselves going—provided they could afford to build another set.

With my shoe I nudged a blackened piece of sheetrock, hoping that some brilliant revelation would scuttle out. A crime lab would have to run a chemical analysis to determine whether a fuel or accelerant, or a carelessly tossed cigarette butt, had been used to start the blaze. I had little doubt that this was an intentional fire set by someone who wanted to harm the Shakespearean company. But I needed proof.

The cemetery was a popular place, and I hoped someone or something might have seen a shadowy, sinister figure lurking among the crypts and tombstones after dark. (Although how would a witness be able to tell a sneaky arsonist from the perfectly normal shadowy and sinister figures that lurked in the cemetery?) I needed someone with a sharp eye for detail.

The dusk shadows were lengthening, but it wasn't yet dark enough that nocturnal monsters had ventured out to run their everynight errands. I moved from crypt to crypt, looking for broken seals and open doorways, calling out "Hello?" as I peered inside. Cemetery addresses were incomprehensible to me: plot and tombstone numbers, rural crypt delivery.

I was looking for Edgar Allan, a simpering troll who co-opted unoccupied crypts and rented them out on short-term leases, although he had no legal right to do so. He had set up his real estate headquarters office in one of them.

All the signs outside the stone door were a dead giveaway, each one sporting a logo of the real estate agency, a smiling photo of the troll's gray and drawn face, and a phone number. *Cheerful service—alive or dead!*

The scaly simian creature had moved a pair of office-surplus metal file cabinets and a desk into the crypt, installed a telephone, and set up a metal bookshelf that held three-ring binders marked *Recent Listings.* Sooner or later he would get his own website.

The first time I'd blundered into the tomb, hoping to get away from Larry the werewolf hit man, the troll wasn't overly glad to see me. In fact, Edgar Allan's burly partner Burt—an evictions specialist—had threatened to throw me back onto the cemetery lawn, flat on my face. Now, though, we were old friends, and Edgar brightened to see me darkening his doorway.

"Mr. Chambeaux, how can I help you with your real estate needs?" He rubbed his gnarled gray fingers together. When he shook my hand, his palms were dry and dusty. (I had expected slimy.) "Do you need more of my business cards? Have you handed them out to your clients?" He pulled open a desk drawer and yanked out more cards.

"I've still got plenty, Mr. Allan. Just here to ask some questions. For a case."

"Happy to cooperate—I help you, and you help me, right? Never underestimate the power of networking."

"I'll do what I can," I said. "I've been hired to investigate the recent fire here."

"My, that blaze drew quite a crowd. In fact, if those Shakespeare plays attracted audiences that large, the actors wouldn't have any financial troubles, if you know what I mean." The troll raised his lofty, scaly eyebrows.

"The crime-scene investigators will be doing an analysis, but I think the best chance for solving this case would be to track down a witness. And since you're usually here, and you always keep your eyes and ears open, I was hoping you might have noticed something or someone."

Edgar Allan settled back in his seat and pulled out one of the binders of recent listings. He pretended to distract himself as he pondered, but he turned the binder in my direction, flipping from page to page, showing off properties zoned for private businesses, small offices, even a new business park. He had already suggested that we move Chambeaux & Deyer Investigations to a brightly lit, carpeted office complex, but I thought our dingy old second-floor digs had character.

"Hmm, let me see. . . ." The troll turned another page while I stood there not moving, patient; zombies are good at that. Finally, Edgar Allan said, "Honestly, I did see a few figures running around, but didn't pay much attention. By the time the fire started and people came to watch the show, I was too busy handing out business cards. Wouldn't miss a great promotional opportunity like that."

I wasn't surprised, but I kept my hopes up. "And where's Burt? Is he wandering the crypts at night?"

"Burt went to Transfusion to get coffee. When he comes back I'll ask him—and I'll also put out the word among my tenants. They always spy and gossip about each other anyway. Hmm, this fire might be the impetus for us to start a neighborhood watch in the cemetery." The troll's lamp-like eyes brightened. "Are we in any danger? I thought the fire was a one-time thing."

"I have my suspicions of who might be responsible, and I doubt they're done causing trouble." I didn't have any proof, however. I needed to learn more about Senator Rupert Balfour and just how far the man was willing to go to ensure passage of his Unnatural Acts Act.

CHAPTER 16

When the madam of a brothel says she needs you right away, it's usually a sales pitch, maybe a special advertising promotion or an extension of the Very Happy Hour pricing. But I could tell from Neffi's tone that she was dead serious. Normally the old mummy's voice sounded like crackling dried papyrus, but on the phone I detected an undertone of fear.

And she was really pissed.

"If you don't find me security soon, Mr. Chambeaux, I'm going to call in the army, or maybe the army of the night, to surround this place with tanks and bazookas. It wouldn't be good for business, but at least it would keep my girls safe."

It was the middle of the night, and I had gone back to the office to get some work done. Sheyenne was there, also working (and, I think, still unsettled by her time with Travis in the storage unit that day). She had forwarded me the phone call. "I'll have a full protection crew for you tomorrow, Neffi," I promised. I already planned to attend the Adopt-a-Golem job fair. "What happened?"

"Better come down here and see for yourself."

I headed out the door, telling Sheyenne I was off to the Full Moon brothel. Not the sort of thing you usually say to your girlfriend, but I was distracted.

The withered old mummy was waiting for me on the front porch with the door wide open. Nightshade and Hemlock, the vampire princesses, stood together, talking intently. They still wore their sexy negligees, but they had removed their makeup in the hour before sunrise; one glance at them au naturel and I shuddered to think of waking up next to them. Cinnamon the werewolf was brushing her face, running a long tongue over her teeth as if she just couldn't turn off the animal-magnetism sell job. The succubus, wide-eyed and waifish with her tight baby-doll perm, remained inside the shadows of the parlor, trying to keep out of the public eye. Her emerald gaze met mine; I could see she was frightened, and she looked so vulnerable.

Indignant and fuming, Neffi strutted back and forth. Her attitude would have made even a harpy cringe. She snapped at me with the sound of a neck bone breaking, "Mr. Chambeaux, we've had another threat." She wrapped her gnarled arm possessively around mine, then lashed out at the vampire women and the two zombie girls who had shuffled out to see what was going on. "Don't just stand there, ladies—tear down those posters! Make a bonfire and invite all the unnaturals. We'll have a marshmallow roast and show everyone how we react to intimidation."

"But Neffi," said Hemlock, the strawberry-blond vampire, "I thought you wanted to keep this for evidence."

"I want those despicable posters gone. Mr. Chambeaux has already seen them."

"Actually, I haven't seen anything yet," I pointed out.

"Then take a look . . . but that's just the window dressing on the disaster."

The two vacant houses on either side of the Full Moon had

been plastered with Senator Balfour's posters decrying brothels in general, unnaturals in general, and unnatural brothels in particular. With my sharp detective's eye, I noted that the headlines on two of the broadsheets contained typos, but Senator Balfour's activists more than made up for their lack of literacy with large capital letters in an extra-bold font. Several posters demanded *Pass the Unatural Acts Act Now!* (complete with misspellings).

"This wouldn't be the first place I'd look to rally support for the senator's bill," I said. "You're telling me that his people posted all these when no one was watching? Shows a lot of balls."

"If they show their balls again, I'll cut them off," Neffi said. "Most people are more interested in what goes on *inside* the Full Moon than in the rest of the neighborhood."

Savannah and Aubrey, the zombie girls, began pulling down the posters, while the vampire princesses wadded them up and made a pile in the front yard, taking Neffi's bonfire suggestion seriously.

The mummy madam looked concerned. "Come in and have a look at the rest. It gets worse."

Inside the brothel, she led me up the curved grand staircase to the lavishly appointed rooms where the ladies did their business. Someone had thrown bricks through the black painted glass, shattering the darkened windows. Shards lay strewn over the comforters on the brass beds.

"Intimidation, pure and simple. The ladies can't use these rooms now. What if this had happened during broad daylight? All that would be left is a pile of ash and a scorched comforter— and I'd have to hire new ladies."

"I see your point." I felt truly concerned now. Would Balfour's activists go this far? "There's a big difference between vandalism and attempted murder."

I recalled the clueless and inept heckler at the Shakespeare in the Dark performance. If the senator's people had burned down the theater set, they had already gone further than protesting, but this was another giant leap from arson.

"To tell you the truth, the senator's minions may not have had anything to do with this. I think the mob is trying to twist my arm—and with these old joints, it is not an easy arm to twist." Neffi held up her brown petrified hand, bent her elbow. "Come, let me show you the worst."

Inside her office, Neffi paused to steel herself. Someone had broken into her private quarters, found the three carved sarcophagi that held the mummified remains of her pet cats. Two of the three had been smashed on her desk, the gauze-wrapped kitties crumbled to dust and fluff, the third one left intact, either as a taunt or a threat.

"Gone," Neffi whispered. "Even the best taxidermist in the Quarter can't put them together again. Who would do that to poor innocent pets?"

"They didn't do it to the pets, Neffi. They did it to *you*." If organized crime was involved, this was the unnatural equivalent of leaving a horse head tucked in her sarcophagus.

"They want to scare me out of business. It's not going to work!"

It was time, I decided, to take this case a lot more seriously. I called McGoo and asked if he could increase the visible police presence around the Full Moon until I could arrange for private security. He said, "That's ironic, Shamble, since unnatural prostitution is still technically illegal."

"Would it help if I asked you to do it for me, McGoo?" You can't keep spending favors unless you earn them back, but my account wasn't empty yet.

"Marginally. But you have to promise to laugh at my jokes from now on."

I hesitated. "All of them?"

"Most of them."

"Some of them," I agreed. McGoo realized it was the best he was going to get, so he left it at that.

"What's the difference between a werewolf and a poodle?" Yes, he was going to make me pay for the favor.

"I don't know. What?"

"If a werewolf starts humping your leg, you'd better let it finish instead of kicking it away."

So I laughed, because I had promised, although I had an odd image of Cinnamon in my head.

At daybreak, when part of the Quarter awakened and the other part crawled back into their darkest holes, I decided to get all my mummies in a row and find out as much as I could about Neffi, just to make sure I had the full story.

The Metropolitan Museum wasn't technically open to the public at dawn, but I had an inside contact. Once upon a time, before the Big Uneasy, patrons would go to the museum to look at the butterfly collection, the gem and geode displays, the dioramas of human civilization, the stuffed wild animals in supposedly natural poses, the hall of dinosaur bones. Lately, the big draw was the original tome of the Necronomicon, the ancient spell book that—through a combination of a rare planetary alignment, the phase of the moon, and a homely old witch's paper cut that had provided the requisite drop of virgin's blood—had sparked the reality upheaval that gave birth to all manner of creatures formerly relegated to ghost stories and paranoid imaginations. The museum dioramas, the insect display cases, even the dinosaur bones, now took a backseat to the creepy stuff.

When I gave my name to the security guard at the door and told him I was a friend of Ramen Ho-Tep's, the man looked skeptical. "Like I haven't heard that one before."

I was puzzled. "What do you mean? He was a client of mine. I know him well."

Again, the guard was unimpressed. "Do you know how many groupies hang around the delivery doors just trying to get his autograph?"

"Uh . . . no, I don't. How many?"

"A lot," the guard said. "He was the Pharaoh of all Egypt, you know."

"Yes, I've heard that before. Tell him Dan Chambeaux is here—I'd just like a word."

"You'd better not be wasting my time." The guard left me standing outside the museum's side entrance. I continued to smile pleasantly at him, holding back my own comment that this guy was wasting *my* time. A few minutes later he opened the door again, looking both surprised and humbled. "What do you know? He says come on in. It's your lucky day."

"Right."

Robin and I had helped Ramen Ho-Tep in his suit to be emancipated from the museum, on the basis that he was a person, not property. Since Mr. Ho-Tep, the Pharaoh of all Egypt, was a significant draw in their Ancient Egypt wing, the museum resisted letting him go his own way. Eventually, we reached a resolution, and now, with his regular dramatic readings, Ramen Ho-Tep had become something of a star, and his weekly performances of "Egypt through the Eye Sockets of Someone Who Was Really There" had even been featured on a national news program.

When I went into his dressing room, the mummy rose to his feet, glad to see me. "Can I get you anything? Coffee? Jellied larks' tongues? I shall summon my slaves."

"That won't be necessary, Mr. Ho-Tep. Just a quick question—I'm hoping you can shed some light on one of my cases."

Ramen Ho-Tep was looking well. His laundered and bleached

bandages had a stiff clean-linen appearance, and his dust-dry sinews and skin had plumped up again (just like any other ramen when soaked in water).

"The wealth of my knowledge is yours for the asking, Mr. Chambeaux. I was the Pharaoh of all Egypt, and I am generous to my friends."

"I've been hired by another Egyptian, with whom you may be acquainted. She's experiencing some trouble."

"I am concerned for all of my subjects," Ho-Tep said. "Who is this person and how may I help?"

"She's another mummy, maybe from a different dynasty. Her name is Neffi. She runs the Full Moon."

Even behind all those bandages, I could see Ho-Tep's expression pull into a pinched grimace of distaste. "She's most definitely a slut, Mr. Chambeaux. No two ways about it. There was nothing between us whatsoever. Just gossip."

Playing it cool, I said, "You know her, then?"

"Knew her—a long time ago. She used to think she was the scarab's knees. Had quite a reputation, that one. But she wasn't as lovely as she wanted to think. She painted herself up more than my sarcophagus, and she always used too much myrrh."

"So . . . ," I ventured, sensing a lot more there than mere hostility, "you two had a little thing going?"

"Not much of a thing," Ramen Ho-Tep said. "Not at the rates she charged! She wanted me to build a pyramid for her, just to show my appreciation, but I wasn't her honey daddy. Plenty of other fish in the Nile."

"Somebody's been harassing her," I told him, "apparently trying to drive the Full Moon out of business."

"Neffi?" He sounded alarmed, and he didn't even try to hide his concern. "Is she all right?"

"Unharmed, but worried. Someone smashed two of the jars where she kept her mummified pet cats."

"Oh, no! Not poor Socks, Whiskers, and Blackie!"

Ramen Ho-Tep had been a cat lover himself. His own pet, Fluffy, was preserved and on display in the museum.

"I shall have to send her my condolences, uh, as a professional matter," he said. "If there is anything that I, as pharaoh, can do to help you solve this case, Mr. Chambeaux, I'll do it. A fiend who would commit such a heinous crime must be punished."

"If I think of anything, I'll let you know, Mr. Ho-Tep. Thanks for the background information."

The mummy seemed rattled, but not so much that he forgot to give me two free passes to Saturday's show. I thanked him and left.

CHAPTER 17

As a man who devoted his wealth to charitable causes, Irwyn Goodfellow did not scrimp when it came to his grand openings. To launch his program to help the rescued golems, Goodfellow hosted a lavish reception and job fair in the Unnatural Quarter community center.

Gratified that the pieces had fallen so smoothly into place, Robin and I wouldn't have missed it. I intended to do my part by contracting four or five of the burliest golems for security work at the Full Moon.

Mrs. Saldana busied herself at various tables where the golems could meet prospective employers. At the reception desk she set out clipboards so that any interested inhuman-resources staff could request golems with specific skill sets (to the best of my knowledge, golems started out as blank clay slates, but they were easily trained).

The homeless golems milled about, fully hydrated now, so that they shed no dust on the furnishings. They gathered the courage to walk up to likely patrons or employers, introduced themselves, struck up conversations. Each golem had his name etched at the base of his neck, and by now Irwyn Goodfellow's volunteer staff had told them who they really were.

Some wore elegant tuxedoes and carried trays of drinks or hors d'oeuvres to audition for jobs in the service industry; some wore chauffeur's uniforms, while others offered to be rented out for straightforward manual labor. Golems weren't picky and tended to be model employees.

Tiffany was there in a clean work shirt and jeans, standing next to Bill, who rarely left her side. His face flexed into a smile when he saw us. "Isn't this wonderful? My people have a chance now for worthwhile lives, an opportunity to be productive in a meaningful way. And we don't have to work for an employer who treats us like dirt!"

I didn't point out that golems, by definition, were made out of dirt.

Tiffany said, "We're here to offer moral support. Bill's going to stay with me for a while, and he's been . . . generally useful." She smiled at him, showing her fangs; if a golem could have blushed, Bill would have been scarlet.

I said, "With a recommendation from you, Tiffany, I'm sure Bill will find an employer who'd be happy to have him. And we'll get all of the other golems taken care of. In fact, I'm hiring some golems for the brothel security job I told you about."

Bill said, "Security would be a good profession for me, and I can heartily recommend any of my friends."

The job fair had a happy buzz of optimism, and I was sure that by the end of the event, many of the downtrodden golems would have decent jobs. Golems continued to talk to potential employers, extolling their skills and interests, but soon heads turned and conversation stopped. An uncomfortable hush rippled through the room.

At first, I saw Larry the werewolf bodyguard. He entered with shoulders squared, his hirsute chest puffed up, and walked with an awkwardly feigned "I'm tough, I'm bad, and don't mess with me" attitude. In his wake came Harvey Jekyll, completely bald, with simian features and a scowl indelibly stamped on his face, which made him look as if he ate too much mustard.

I looked at him, and he looked at me and Robin. There was no love lost between us. I muttered, "What the hell is he doing here?"

Robin does occasionally hold a grudge—despite the way I paint her, she isn't a complete saint—but she also has a pragmatic streak that goes over my head. "He's probably trying to hire some household staff. I doubt anyone else would work for him."

"Larry does," I said, "and he's none too happy about it."

Jekyll was a maniacal, murderous madman, and even in the Unnatural Quarter that wasn't always a good thing. As a human, he had concocted a nefarious scheme to exterminate unnaturals with a line of deadly hygiene items, but we had foiled him. Jekyll was sentenced to death by electric chair, and then, in an irony appreciated by no one (least of all Harvey Jekyll), he came back as an unnatural himself and hated every minute of it. The ride on Sparky, Jr. had not improved his disposition. Even my untrained eye could tell that he needed a better embalming job, but he probably could not afford one after losing his entire fortune to his ex-wife Miranda.

I looked around the room, avoiding my nemesis. "Come on, I want to hire some of these guys for Neffi before Jekyll gets to them."

Even though golems are made from the same general mold—especially the ones mass-produced by Maximus Max—Robin and I signed up the five most intimidating clay figures to work as bodyguards, bouncers, and doormen for the Full Moon. With five never-sleeping, ever-vigilant goons positioned around the building, I doubted Senator Balfour's troublemakers would bother the brothel anymore. Even organized-crime wiseguys would think twice.

After we filled out the paperwork, a simple employment agreement that Robin had drawn up for the job fair, each golem's mimeographed animation spell was transcribed onto more permanent paper, and we sent their employment forms over to Madam Neffi.

Smiling with satisfaction, Irwyn Goodfellow walked among the golem candidates and prospective employers—all smiles, laughing, in his element. He said hello to us and thanked Robin for her legal help in setting up the Adopt-a-Golem program.

Since Irwyn was in a good mood, I took the opportunity to fish for more information. "I appreciate that you're helping these liberated golems, Mr. Goodfellow. It helps to atone for how they were forced to make souvenirs for the Smile Syndicate."

He frowned. "It's a full-time job to atone for all the bad work Missy does. I wish she would soften her heart."

"I had the pleasure . . . well, let's just say I *met* Missy yesterday," I said. "She disavows any responsibility for the items they sell in their gift shops, claims to know nothing about it."

"Oh, she knows where the souvenirs came from, but you'll never prove it," Irwyn said. "She's set her sights on expanding into the Unnatural Quarter. She's a lot like our father, Oswald Goodfellow." He let out a concerned sigh. "I wouldn't be surprised if my sister eventually wanted to own the whole town."

"Looks that way, with the line of gift shops. She's already purchased the Goblin Tavern and intends to open up a nationwide chain."

Irwyn's expression fell into a frown. "Now do you see why I have little to do with my family? There's so much good work to be done, so many people in need. With my share of the inheritance, I do have a lot of money, but it only goes so far. Nevertheless, my name is *Goodfellow*, and I'm trying to live up to the literal definition of the word, rather than my family history."

Now that I had met his sister, I wondered how Irwyn had fallen so far from the tree.

Accompanied by her listless zombie, Mrs. Saldana joined us. She carried a clipboard, pleased with how many golems had already been hired during the reception. Her expression was worried, though, and she held Jerry's arm possessively. "Mr. Chambeaux, I'm on tenterhooks. Have you made any progress in Jerry's case?"

"Oh, dear," Goodfellow asked. "Is something the matter?"

"I'm looking into it." I turned back to Mrs. Saldana. "I went to Timeworn Treasures and talked with the gremlin pawnbroker. He's not much of a businessman—he loves his possessions so much that he doesn't want to part with any of them. But he did sell Jerry's combo pack, as well as quite a few others. Someone's been buying them up, but he won't tell me who."

"What would anybody do with extra hearts and souls?" Robin asked.

"People will collect anything." I still regretted getting rid of my collectible superhero action figures for a few bucks at a garage sale.

Jerry let out a low, bubbling moan, and Mrs. Saldana put a hand to her mouth in dismay. "I wish we could do something."

"I'll keep pressing, don't you worry—I'll find out something," I said. "Snazz keeps his records in a big ledger book, and I assume the information is in there. Maybe if I tempt him with a few shiny things, he'll let me have a quick look at that ledger. Don't give up hope yet."

"Oh, I never do, Mr. Chambeaux."

We were all interrupted when the ghost of the famed bank robber Alphonse Wheeler appeared with great fanfare, wearing his checkered jacket and stylish hat. He carried a bouquet of flowers in one hand and an overstuffed duffel in the other hand.

"Hello, hello!" Alphonse said. "The MLDW Society is doing wonderful work here—what a worthy organization! It makes my heart melt. Let's have a round of applause for Irwyn Goodfellow and all of the Monster Legal Defense Workers."

Everyone clapped, except for Alphonse Wheeler himself, whose hands were full.

"What's he up to now?" I asked Robin, suspicious already. When Wheeler was alive and robbing banks, he had been quite an attention-getter. This was just the sort of thing the bored and restless ghost would do before causing trouble.

"I'd like to give the MLDW Society my personal support, put my money where my mouth is. I've just come into quite a large stash." He shrugged. "I found it, couldn't say where it was from." He handed Robin the bunch of flowers, then unzipped the duffel to display wads and wads of cash.

"That's your stash of stolen money, Mr. Wheeler," Robin said. "I already told you, the cash doesn't belong to you."

"Who can say where I got the money? Maybe it fell off a truck. But instead of using it for my own selfish needs, I want to donate it all to the Monster Legal Defense Workers."

Everybody cheered and whistled. Hope Saldana looked especially delighted.

"I'm happy to accept the donation, Mr. Wheeler," said Irwyn Goodfellow. "We can place it in our holding accounts to continue our good work. In fact, it will go a long way to help pay for my new zombie rehabilitation clinic that opens in a few days."

Wheeler was beaming. "By all means, use it for that purpose!"

Robin cautioned in a low voice so as not to dampen the buzz of excitement, "The insurance companies will come after this, claiming it's theirs."

"Maybe," I whispered back to her, "but they'll look like fools if they try to take it from a charity."

Instigated by Bill and Tiffany, the hundred golems let out three cheers, in an eerie, perfect unison, for Alphonse Wheeler and Irwyn Goodfellow. Then, although I'm not sure they realized the humor or the pun, they sang a boisterous chorus of "For He's a Jolly Good Fellow."

CHAPTER 18

In order to help Jerry the zombie, I decided to keep an eye on Timeworn Treasures. Actually, two eyes, since both of mine still remained firmly attached in their sockets.

I had asked McGoo for a favor, to make up some reason to flash his badge and demand a look at the pawnshop ledger book while I happened to be standing next to him. But favors only went so far—unless I could provide evidence that some kind of crime had been committed, McGoo had no basis for a warrant. Jerry had voluntarily pawned his heart and soul, and Snazz could sell it to anyone he liked. He was under no legal obligation to reveal the purchaser no matter how nicely I asked.

But I could still watch the store.

At an outdoor café conveniently located across from the pawnshop's shadowy alley, I bought a cup of coffee, the special extra-bitter blend, took a seat, and watched the pedestrians go by. The café had introduced a new two-sided menu—one for unnatural tastes and one for human tourists.

At the table next to mine, three tourists chattered about the everyday sights in the Quarter; the woman took photos of every werewolf, vampire, or zombie that wandered by, while her two companions studied the cartoony chamber-of-commerce map and a guidebook as if it were one of those star maps to the homes of Hollywood celebrities. The photographer waved at me and took several photos; her camera was enormous, far larger than was practical or necessary. She encouraged her two companions—husband and brother, presumably—to stand next to me and have their photos taken. Enough of that, and I shooed them away. I was in the middle of a discreet stakeout.

Across the street, a new adult novelty boutique had opened up, featuring items for natural, unnatural, and combined tastes. The shop was named Unnatural Acts, a deliberate jab at Senator Balfour's crusade. *Safe, Fun, Unusual.*

For the grand opening, the adult-shop owners had strung black crepe paper around the door, filled black helium balloons, and set out colorful reflective pinwheels that remained motionless in the forlorn hope of a breeze. A blackboard advertised the daily specials, toys that sounded like torture devices, the usual assortment of whips, spiked collars, and manacles that you would find in any traditional adult novelty shop, as well as a list of items that, I had to admit with some embarrassment, were complete mysteries to me.

Now, I'm well preserved and still capable—at least judging by my morning stiffness in the usual place, as well as a lot of additional places—but since I can't even touch my ghost girlfriend, I don't have much opportunity anymore. I wasn't the target audience for the Unnatural Acts boutique. . . .

The coffee was terrible, as advertised. I finished it and ordered a second cup. The nosy tourists dashed off to chase after a tall horned demon who strolled past and entered an electronics store.

I kept my eyes on the pawnshop alley, and I didn't have long to wait. Unfortunately, Travis Carey was not the one I'd expected to see on my stakeout.

Sheyenne's brother came by with a bounce in his step and a grin on his face, still wearing the same natty jacket, without a care in the world. He ducked down the alley carrying a small paper sack and entered the pawnshop without a hint of hesitation, as if he'd been there before and knew exactly what he was doing.

I was disappointed, saddened, and angry on Sheyenne's behalf, but not particularly surprised. I had no doubt that the sack contained the gold necklaces, rings, and other jewelry she had given him as family keepsakes. Travis said he had gambling debts and people were after him for money. I wondered if he had retreated to the Quarter to get away from brass-knuckled debt collectors.

As I sat there stewing, I debated whether or not to tell Sheyenne. If Travis did pawn the jewelry, maybe I'd dip into the Chambeaux & Deyer petty cash fund and buy the items back for her—if Snazz was willing to part with them.

All of this nonsense was a mystery to me. I didn't have any brothers and sisters. My dad left us when I was eight years old, my mom worked two jobs just to make ends meet, so I rarely saw her. All the stress, and all the smoking, had put her into an early grave. And those were the days when there wasn't even a chance that someone might come back.

After years of warm-sentiment greeting cards, heart-aching holiday specials, and sappy songs, I'd been brainwashed into believing in the joys of having close family ties, but I'd never understood them, not really. Now, knowing everything that Travis had done to Sheyenne and how she felt about it, I couldn't understand why people got completely irrational when it came to idiocy committed by family members. People will roll their eyes and sigh, tolerating stupidity from a relative that they would never accept from a stranger or business partner. Supposedly, you have to put up with it because they're *family;* you have to love them unconditionally.

That sort of sentiment might sound great on a greeting card, but it didn't make any sense to me now. Travis was a jerk by any possible definition.

Suddenly I heard a commotion up the street, drums banging and a squawking brassy noise—a vuvuzela? Not a peppy sound like a parade, but more like a funeral procession (although in the Unnatural Quarter, funeral processions and parades often served dual purposes). A group of normal humans who looked passionate, yet entirely humorless, marched along like an old-fashioned temperance rally, holding up signs that said GOD HATES UNNATURALS, each one hand-lettered and featuring a variety of misspellings. Other signs in the procession proclaimed PASS THEE UNATURAL ACTS ACT NOW!

They handed out leaflets—or tried to. Occasionally, human tourists accepted the flyers; very few unnaturals did. Grumbling complaints and raucous catcalls followed the protesters as they came down the street. Their target, the Unnatural Acts adult novelty boutique, must have been a sharp stick in the senator's eye. How could he resist bringing his minions here?

At the head of the procession was the man himself—tall, with a pale face, lantern jaw, and permanent scowl, as if it had been chiseled onto his visage by a gravestone artist. Balfour's appearance reminded me of photos I had seen of H. P. Lovecraft, except this guy wasn't nearly so handsome—and Lovecraft was by no means a handsome man. A frumpy and equally unattractive woman whose facial muscles seemed incapable of performing the complex act of smiling accompanied the senator—his wife, presumably. If they had been scuffed up and their clothes moldered, Senator and Mrs. Balfour could easily have passed for a pair of zombies.

The procession came forward, causing quite a spectacle, and stopped on the street in front of the café, turning their ire toward the adult novelty boutique. They blocked my view of the alley, and I could no longer see the pawnshop. The ever-increasing crowd of unnatural hecklers made it even more difficult to see, but since the senator's minions were likely responsible for the arson at the cemetery, I decided to pay attention to them as well. I liked working on multiple cases at once. Senator Balfour's intolerance, coupled with his incitement to violence, was something to watch.

The drums and vuvuzela continued to make a racket until the group faced the front of the adult shop. Senator Balfour raised his head, looking proud and arrogant. The alleged music fell silent. "This place is an abomination!" he called. "I should have it burned to the ground."

Like the Shakespeare set? I found the threat interesting.

Two of Balfour's minions popped the black balloons and yanked down the black crepe paper while a third paused to not-too-subtly read the specials listed on the blackboard sign. The camera-happy tourists took numerous photos of the proceedings.

The boutique proprietor came out, looking indignant. "Here now, this is my place of business! Buy something or move on."

She was a mousy, overweight woman—apparently human, but you never could tell. She looked to be in her early forties, not the type you would expect to own an adult novelty store, but people led all sorts of double lives.

One of Balfour's followers tried to hand her a leaflet. She responded by handing him a catalog.

"Your pandering to base instincts disgusts me," Balfour said.

The woman sized him up, then spoke directly to his wife in a loud but conspiratorial whisper. "I can help, truly. We have instructional videos, special oils, role-playing gear. I have an Elvira costume that will fit you . . . or your husband."

Senator Balfour looked flustered. The horned demon had emerged from the electronics store, assessed the situation, then indignantly vomited out a steaming glob of phlegm that burst into flame upon contact with the air. He had excellent aim: The tumbling glob struck the open mouth of the vuvuzela and tunneled inside with a glurp of greenish smoke. The player yelped and dropped it on the street.

"You are damned!" Senator Balfour called. "That goes without saying."

"Then why bother saying it?" howled a werewolf, to much tittering and chuckling.

Sheyenne's brother had come out of the pawnshop, empty-handed now, and he accepted one of the leaflets from a protester. He read the inflammatory words with great interest and stopped to listen to the senator. One of the protesters came up to the outdoor tables of the café and set leaflets at every place. I pocketed one to put in the file.

Balfour continued his rant. "The Unnatural Acts Act has garnered much support in the senate, and we're going to pass it soon. Then everything will change." Balfour raised his fist. "You thought the Big Uneasy was a dramatic shift? This'll be the Big Crackdown."

A ghost called, "Boo!"

"Go back to the rock you crawled out from under!" shouted a vampire.

Senator Balfour pointed his finger at the vampire heckler. "*You're* the one who crawled out from under a rock." Not the snappiest comeback I'd ever heard.

The vampire was baffled. "I didn't crawl out from under a rock."

Next to him, a zombie said, "I did."

"This is a free country," Balfour said. "We have every right to let it be known that we do not approve of unnaturals."

"We have our right to free speech, too," slurred a ghoul. Next to him, a decrepit and fragrant shambler zombie pulled off an ear and threw it at the senator, striking him in the face to peals of laughter.

Balfour reacted with disgust, and other zombies began hurling body parts. One even sacrificed a hand, which struck Balfour's wife in the chest and, through reflexive action, clamped down on her left breast. She screamed and slapped at it.

McGoo and two other cops showed up then. "Here, now, Senator, maybe you should protest somewhere else. How about finding a neighborhood where people want to hear what you have to say?"

"We're perfectly within our rights," Balfour said to McGoo. "Officer . . . ?"

"McGoohan, sir. Toby McGoohan. I'm just trying to keep the peace in the Quarter."

"You're a human, and you serve in this cesspit?" The senator still had a mark of ooze on his cheek from where the orphaned ear had struck him.

"At least until I get a promotion, Senator. Now, please move along. You made your point, and you're not going to win any converts here." McGoo pointed down to the vuvuzela that had been ruined by demon spit. "And pick that up. I'll cite you for littering if you leave it there." Greenish steam from the volatile demon phlegm continued to bubble up from the instrument's opening, and I doubted it would be playing any more "music."

As the crowd broke up and the hecklers realized the show was over, I lounged back in my seat at the café. Travis had already disappeared down the street. In the commotion, however, I'd missed another customer who slipped into Timeworn Treasures—now, as she left the shop, I recognized Angela Drake, Missy Goodfellow's anorexic assistant.

Unlike Travis, Angela looked furtive as she hurried out of the alley. She wore sunglasses and a scarf over her mouse-brown hair. I knew who she was, but I couldn't tell whether she carried anything. I stood up to get a better look, but Angela vanished in the crowd of protesters and tourists.

Missy Goodfellow's assistant at the pawnshop? That raised another set of questions entirely.

CHAPTER 19

Although Chambeaux & Deyer does good work and tries to make sure every client is satisfied with our services, we don't have many repeat customers. Who needs a private eye more than once? Still, we maintain a close relationship with our former clients, and sometimes they come back to visit. Just because.

The Wannovich sisters, Mavis and Alma, were both witches, pleasant and generous ladies, a little lonely. According to Mavis, her sister had a soft spot for me—call it a weekend crush. I try not to fraternize with my clients, and I had no romantic interest in Alma, and not just because she had been transformed into an enormous sow.

The Wannoviches were one of our gold-star cases; from a legal perspective, Robin had achieved exactly what the clients hoped for. The witches had suffered disastrous consequences from an attraction spell gone awry, caused by a misprint in a spell book. Alma—who hadn't been all that attractive in the first place, judging by the photos Mavis showed us—was turned into a pig. The sisters had sued Howard Phillips Publishing, and the parties eventually reached an unusual settlement. Although Alma was not (yet) restored to human form, the two women accepted positions with the publisher. Mavis was now a senior editor there, while Alma spent her days rooting through the slush pile.

The two dropped in for a visit in the late afternoon. Mavis, a hefty woman who wore a black witch's dress and pointed hat over a mop of black hair like steel wool, extended a paper plate covered with cellophane wrap. "I brought cookies." She looked at me with a smile. "Especially for you, Mr. Chambeaux."

The plate of flattened patties looked unappetizing. The witches might be good at making exotic potions and casting unusual spells, but they weren't proficient in the kitchen. I also suspected that they might have added a few special ingredients from the magical pantry to soften me up—or harden me up—for amorous intentions. I didn't need zombie Viagra, nor did I have any intention of becoming the Wannoviches' zombie plaything. I wanted to keep our relationship on a professional level.

"We've come with good news," Mavis said as she passed around the plate of cookies; Sheyenne carried it into the office kitchenette. "We're introducing a new line at Howard Phillips Publishing, calling them Penny Dreadfuls, at a special price of only $5.99. Adventures for the unnatural audience, although we'll distribute them widely across the country."

Alma snorted with excitement and paced around the front offices. Mavis grinned at me, and I saw that her teeth, although still crooked, had recently been whitened. "You inspired our very first release, Mr. Chambeaux. It's going to be a detective series about a zombie private investigator and his bleeding-heart human lawyer partner, who solve cases and defend the rights of monsters everywhere."

"Sounds . . . familiar," I said.

"We're calling it Shamble and Die Investigations. Do you get it?" She giggled. "A play on your names."

"Yes, we get it," Robin said. "I'm not sure . . ."

"Oh, it's only loosely based on your exploits, but we'd still like to have your permission? And Mr. Chambeaux, of course, is the heroic main character, a brave detective who won't let even death stop him from solving crimes. We expect it to be a best seller."

I couldn't imagine who would want to read such a thing. "Are you pulling my leg, Mavis?"

"Oh, my, that would be dangerous, Mr. Chambeaux. Speaking of which, how is your arm? I hear it was detached during the fight against Harvey Jekyll."

"All pieces are back in place." I raised and lowered my arms to demonstrate, flexing my wrist and forearm.

Mavis continued. "I assure you, it's no joke—well, there will be humor in the stories. The Penny Dreadfuls are entertaining stories, not dreary, socially meaningful tracts targeted toward women's book clubs."

"Glad to hear it," Robin said, still uncertain. "I suppose."

Sheyenne drifted closer. "And who's going to write it?"

"We already have a ghostwriter," Mavis said, still delighted. "And that's why we're here."

I raised my eyebrows. "A *ghost* writer? Really?"

"Actually, she's a vampire," Mavis said. "An aspiring writer who's thrilled to be part of the project. We can't put her name on the cover because it's going to be told in first person, and the readers have to think it's truly written by 'Dan Shamble.' But we'd like the ghostwriter to speak with you, shadow you on a few cases, listen to the way you talk, pick up details. It's the best way to get a sense of realism."

"That wouldn't be appropriate," I said, although I couldn't give an actual reason why.

Robin, with her legal expertise, did that for me. "Our cases are confidential, Mavis. Our clients remain anonymous unless they choose to go public. Having an observer would breach the attorney-client privilege."

"And there is an element of danger in our investigations." I plucked at my sport jacket to show the stitched-up holes. "I've been shot and disassembled myself."

The sow sat down on the carpet with a loud snort, and Mavis was obviously disappointed.

Sheyenne, always business oriented, looked on the bright side. "We think it's a delightful idea, Mavis, but if Howard Phillips Publishing is going to sell our stories, Chambeaux and Deyer will have to receive some sort of compensation."

"Compensation?" Mavis said. "Well . . . of course. But these novels are merely inspired by the work of Mr. Chambeaux and Ms. Deyer."

"And without that inspiration you wouldn't have much of a book series."

"No, I don't suppose so."

Sheyenne looked over at me with an appreciative smile. "I'm not suggesting a cut of the royalties, because your books could well generate additional business for us. . . . I was thinking of your own special skills. What if you were to perform a regular restorative spell on Dan? Once a month or so, just to freshen him up, keep him in good shape. And emergency fixes, as needed."

I rolled my shoulders, bent my reattached arm. "I wouldn't mind that."

"Restorative spells are rather difficult, and they require a great deal of preparation. They take a lot out of us." Mavis looked down at her sister, who snorted a lengthy sentence. "Oh, but if we need to do an emergency fix, I suppose that means something exciting must have happened." She ran her eyes up and down my form. "We would like to keep Mr. Chambeaux fully functional."

"If I stay fit and mobile, then I can keep working on new cases," I pointed out.

"Or, as we call them, *sequels*," Mavis mused. "Very well, it's a deal. If you can find time for us, and our ghostwriter, in your schedule, then we'll agree to perform regular restorative spells. Just to keep you limber and intact."

"All right, but work comes first," I said. "The cases don't solve themselves."

Alma snorted, and her sister jotted down notes. "Ooh, that's a good line."

Chapter 20

The Pattersons were a cute couple, a nice couple. They had been married for six years and were still very much in love; I could tell by the way they treated each other—not sappy public displays of affection you'd see from a gushing new couple, but with an obvious sense of *partnership*. They moved together, finished each other's sentences, were very much on the same page.

As they came into the Chambeaux & Deyer offices after scheduling a first-available appointment (Sheyenne fit them in at the end of the day), I could see they were upset and nervous. My heart went out to them immediately—mixed couples never had an easy time of it.

Walter Patterson was a vampire, and his wife Judy was a werewolf, one of the full-time hairy-faced lycanthropes.

"I'm fed up with this crap!" Walter said. "It's not *right,* and I'm sick of turning the other cheek."

Judy leaned forward, nuzzling his pale cheek in an attempt to calm her husband. "We were told that Ms. Deyer might be able to help us. We don't have a lot of money, but we thought the nature of our problem would interest you."

Robin said, "Your message said something about discrimination?" She led them to the conference room, and I tagged along. The Pattersons seemed eager to tell their story to as many people as possible. I had other plans—but not until much later that night.

Robin, with her yellow legal pad, began to compile a case file. Walter Patterson had been a plumber before he was turned into a vampire, and Judy worked in an insurance office. She'd been putting in a few hours of overtime on the wrong full-moon night and had gotten scratched by a drunk werewolf staggering out of the Goblin Tavern (the bartender before Francine didn't always know when to cut his customers off). The two met as unnaturals, fell in love, got married. The Pattersons were strictly middle class, but they worked hard, scrimped and saved, and chased after their own version of the American Dream.

"It took us four years to put together a down payment," Walter said. "I even worked day shifts, without hazard pay. But we finally set enough aside, got ourselves a real estate agent, and decided to buy a home of our own."

"A nice place with white siding, black shingles on the roof, a little yard," Judy said. "Maybe a place for kids to play." She sounded wistful.

"We love to throw Halloween parties," Walter added. "We had it all planned out. At first, our real estate agent tried to interest us in crypts or haunted houses, but we wanted a normal home, someplace outside the Quarter. I don't think Mr. Allan knows the suburban market very well."

I had to give the troll real estate agent points for ambition, if nothing else. "Did he do something wrong? Do you need to file a complaint with the Real Estate Board?"

"Oh, no! Mr. Allan is very earnest, and he has our best interests at heart. It's . . . it's . . ." Judy burst into tears.

"It's the other people." Anger grew in Walter's voice again. "We picked out our dream house, a rancher at the end of a cul-de-sac. Good school district, not much traffic, even a bike path nearby. But the neighbors protested. They don't want our kind there. Apparently, a mixed-race couple simply isn't welcome in the suburbs."

"Or any unnatural couple," Robin said.

Walter's hand clenched. His forearm muscles were well developed, no doubt from his years as a plumber. Tears ran down the fur on Judy Patterson's face, and she wiped them furiously away with a clawed hand. "Don't you think it's hard enough for a vampire and a werewolf to overcome the difficulties? We feel like Romeo and Juliet sometimes." She heaved a growling breath and shuddered.

Walter said, "We even went to see that play at the Shakespeare in the Dark performance a month ago. I didn't know it had such a sad ending! Not much of a crowd pleaser."

"He hasn't even seen *West Side Story*," Judy said in a quiet voice.

"Next time I see Shakespeare's ghost, I'll pass along your complaint," I said.

"What exactly have your neighbors done to harass you?" Robin pressed, getting back to business.

"Protests, picket signs, intimidation. They made it very plain they intend to run us out of the neighborhood," Walter said.

"*If* we ever close the mortgage," Judy added. "Mr. Allan says he's never seen anything like it in all his years as a real estate agent. Simple permits were denied. Our loan application was 'lost'—repeatedly. Our first two mortgages were turned down, even though we have excellent credit and clearly qualify according to their guidelines."

The vampire was working himself up and flashed his fangs as he raised his voice. "It's housing discrimination, and I know that Senator Balfour is behind it. His people have latched onto our case, and they're all brave and snooty now that it looks like he'll push through his Unnatural Acts Act."

Judy reached out a furred hand to touch her husband's pallid, cadaverous one. She extended her black claws and traced them along the back of his clenched fist. "We're just everyday people. We're good citizens. We pay our taxes. We just want the same rights as everyone else."

Robin's dark eyes were flashing, and I could sense her anger rising as well. "This is appalling—and the case is clear. I am offended on your behalf. We'll take care of this garbage. They're not going to get away with it."

Though she was black, Robin hadn't been battered by such blatant discrimination. Her parents owned a nice house in the suburbs and lived a normal upper-middle-class life. Even so, she had always been passionate about civil rights and helping anyone less fortunate. When she went into the legal profession and saw the prejudice and unequal treatment that monsters faced after the Big Uneasy, she'd found her calling in life. I think her parents would have preferred her to have a career in patent law or become a wealthy corporate attorney, but there was no swaying Robin once she set her heart on something. I knew that full well.

"Does that mean you'll take our case?" Judy Patterson asked.

"With pleasure," Robin said. "I'll need copies of your paperwork, your financial records, the forms you filed, the denials you received. There are federal laws against housing discrimination. We have a potential suit against the homeowners' association and also against the lenders for violating the Equal Housing Protection Act. If everything is as you say, it's a clearcut case, and I'll file several discrimination suits on your behalf by tomorrow morning. I'll stay up all night if I have to."

CHAPTER 21

Even though the Goblin Tavern wasn't the same under the new management, McGoo and I kept meeting there, at least for the time being. We were creatures of habit.

When I arrived, McGoo was waiting for me on his regular stool, already well on the way to finishing his first beer. He must have had a rough day, too—as usual. I glanced at my watch—only 7:10. He saw me, raised his mug. "I got a head start, Shamble."

"I can see that, but I'll catch up." I worked my way onto the stool next to his, but something wasn't right. I sniffed, realized that someone had cleaned the bar surface and stools with lemon wax. Francine never did that. When I raised my hand to call out for the usual, I stopped myself, remembering that our favorite bartender was no longer there. Instead, I saw a portly man in a tweed business suit, so cheery that his demeanor practically screamed, "My doctor upped the dosage of my antidepressants, and I'm fine now!" He came over, exuding friendliness.

"Welcome, welcome to the new Goblin Tavern! I hope your day is a sunny one." He had a ready handshake, whether I wanted one or not. I just wanted a beer. "My name is Stu—I'm the new manager here. Still reviewing applications for a new bartender."

Five seats down the bar, three gaunt and decaying zombies sat hunched with their elbows on the bar, their heads sunk down into their chests. One of them said in a gurgling voice, "Are you a human, Stu?" When the new manager happily nodded, the zombie continued, "Mmm, I *like* human stew." The bartender kept the smile fixed on his face, so as not to offend the customers.

"Could I get a beer, please?" I said.

"Certainly, sir." Stu stood at the tap and rattled off the selections, which had increased, mostly light and foreign beers. Francine had never asked what type of beer I liked. I picked one. Stu delivered the mug and said, "If there's any way I can make your visit more enjoyable, please let me know."

I held the beer in my stiff hands and felt a sadness come over me. "You could hire Francine back. That would be a good start."

I meant it as a quick snide comment, but McGoo piped up. "For once, I agree one hundred percent with Shamble." Several of the other monster patrons also called out their support for my suggestion.

Stu was flustered, and I think we hurt his feelings; he was trying so hard. "I'll, uh, forward your feedback, but that decision was made by Smile Syndicate management, high above my pay grade. Until we get a genuine monster replacement, you'll just have to satisfy yourselves with me."

Down the bar, the decrepit zombies raked sharp fingernails along the wooden surface and gnashed their jaws together. "We'll take what's offered," one said. Stu scuttled over to the cash register and kept himself busy as far from the zombies as possible.

McGoo glanced at them, leaned closer to me. "What do you

call a zombie with no brains?" He didn't wait for me to guess. *"Hungry!"*

Remembering my promise to him the previous night, I laughed politely.

He and I talked about our days, traded ideas and information about various cases. "I bumped into Maximilian Grubb yesterday," I told McGoo. "Did you know he's managing a storage unit complex now?"

McGoo finished his beer and ordered another one. "I wouldn't be surprised if he was selling encyclopedias door-to-door."

"Encyclopedias? Nobody uses physical encyclopedias anymore."

He shrugged. "Maximus Max doesn't seem to be ahead of the curve."

I heard a chorus of cheers and catcalls from the other side of the room, where a group of vampires was playing darts. Ilgar, the previous owner of the Goblin Tavern, once had two pool tables there, but after an unfortunate accident involving a broken wooden cue stick and a vampire's chest, he had removed the pool tables out of consideration for his customers. Now the vampires were throwing darts with great enthusiasm, if little accuracy, at a new board onto which they had pasted a photo of Senator Rupert Balfour's dour face. Some of the darts struck in the general vicinity of the bull's-eye, while others fell far short, several feet below the senator's head. Since that would have been the approximate location of his crotch, the vampires considered it a score nevertheless.

I realized I hadn't been listening to what McGoo was saying, then realized that he wasn't interested in the conversation either. Both of us kept looking around the tavern, saw how it had been cleaned and redecorated, but not improved in any way. The real cobwebs had been cleared, to be replaced by kitschy strings and plastic spiders—as if real unnaturals, or anyone with eyes and a brain for that matter, couldn't tell the difference. Framed photos of Bela Lugosi, Boris Karloff, Vincent Price, Lon Chaney (both Senior and Junior), and the great Tor Johnson had been mounted on the walls next to Peter Cushing as Van Helsing (someone had already drawn a mustache on his face) and Christopher Lee as Dracula, in addition to the Toxic Avenger (as himself). People were supposed to believe that the autographs were real.

As the night wore on, the clientele increased, mostly unnaturals coming into the Tavern out of habit, as well as a group of wide-eyed tourists. I finished two beers, but didn't taste either one. McGoo ordered a third, not because my conversation was so scintillating, but because he didn't have any incentive to move. He was off duty and had to go home, which was neither convenient nor appealing since he lived outside the Quarter.

Even though he spent most of his day here, McGoo kept a small apartment where "normal people" lived, and clung to it as a matter of pride, although he wasted a lot of time commuting. I'd once asked him, "Why don't you just find an apartment here?"

"No nice places."

"My flat upstairs from our office is nice."

"No, it's not. When's the last time you actually *saw* your place?"

"Well, the flat itself is nice—I'm just a bad housekeeper."

"No, the bad housekeeping just hides the fact that the place is a dump. Besides, *you* moved into the Quarter and look what happened to you."

"My address didn't have anything to do with some creep shooting me in the back of the head."

"Everything's a factor."

He had a long ride home, and I didn't want to stay in the Tavern any longer, thanks to some unofficial, and more than slightly illegal, business of my own that I had to take care of.

He and I swung off our stools at the same time. "Better get going." McGoo glanced at his watch. "Nine o'clock, and I've got a delightful evening ahead of me at home, doing nothing in particular. What about you, Shamble?"

"Oh, nothing much," I said; McGoo didn't need to know that I planned to break into Timeworn Treasures. We both sighed.

"I hate to say this, Shamble, but we might need to find another watering hole. The Tavern just doesn't have the right ambience anymore."

As we went to the door, Stu the bartender waved and called out a cheery "Thanks, come again—and I hope your day is a sunny one!"

We hit the street, and McGoo and I went our separate ways.

CHAPTER 22

A good private eye needs to develop a variety of informants from all walks of life. He also requires a keen mind to compile thousands of diverse details, and a well-honed sense of intuition to put the pieces together and find the answers to mysteries.

It also helps to have skill with a lock pick.

The alley in front of Timeworn Treasures was dark and gloomy, per city ordinance. Legislation for the comfort of unnatural citizens mandated the removal of bright street lights in certain zoned alleys and side streets. Some impatient unnaturals had taken it upon themselves to smash the offending lights before city workers could get around to removing them.

A faint mist burbled up from the sewers, which made me think that the subterranean dwellers were having a barbecue down there. The Quarter's real night life would get hopping in a few hours, but right now the pawnshop was dark and closed. Snazz had no set business hours; apparently, he worked among his treasured items whenever he liked, which made sneaking inside rather difficult. I was pleased to see the Closed sign hanging in the door next to a flat plastic clock: "Will Return At . . ."

with the hands set to 12:00, although there was no indication whether that meant midnight or noon.

Ducking along the shadows—which was perfectly normal behavior around here, so I attracted no undue attention—I huddled against the locked door, removed my tool kit, and attempted to dissect the lock. I fumbled one of the picks and dropped it to the ground. No one noticed the noise. I retrieved the tool and went back to work.

Before being shot in the head, I was quite nimble, but zombies have trouble with dexterity. (You don't see many zombie trapeze artists, for instance.) Still, I knew what I was doing, and all I required was patience; after so much practice during my regular life, I had muscle memory—the occasional rigor mortis notwithstanding.

I eased the door open, careful not to jangle the customer bell. I expected the hinges to squeak, as is the time-honored tradition, but they were brass hinges, and the gremlin pawnbroker, with his fixation for all things shiny, had polished and oiled them. The door glided open, and I slipped inside with only the slightest tinkle of the bell overhead.

My eyes adjusted to the gloom. This would be a quick in-and-out. I needed to get to the front of the store, work open the combination-locked drawer that held the ledger, find the information I needed, then slip back out with no gremlins the wiser. What could be simpler? A zombie's heart and soul were at stake.

Moving through the pawnshop, I was surrounded by the sinister curiosities Snazz had collected over the years. It was indeed a treasure trove, if you like that sort of junk. The price on the slightly used monkey's paw had been marked down yet again; maybe the gremlin wanted to get rid of it after all (no surprise, given the poor industry safety record of such items). I crept toward the front counter and its chicken-wire barrier.

A tingling sensation went up my back, and my uncooperative skin crawled. I sensed someone watching me, but when I turned around, I saw that it was only a jar of preserved eyeballs floating around and directing their gazes at me. Nothing to worry about. Since they couldn't tattle on me, I let them look all they wanted.

I worked my way down the aisle, listening for movement, worried that the gremlin might sleep inside the shop, but nothing stirred. A thick spell book, written in blood and bound in human skin, gave off a dim phosphorescent glow; it was one of the Howard Phillips Publishing special limited editions.

On a row of shelves I saw a pile of new acquisitions, which were stacked without price tags. As I squinted into the dimness, I was surprised to discover costumes, theater props, and the traditional smiling and weeping masks that symbolized Comedy and Tragedy in Shakespearean plays.

I did a double take. Shakespeare's ghost had insisted that all the props perished in the fire, but apparently the arsonist had decided to make a quick buck as well as make a point . . . which didn't sound like Senator Balfour's minions. At least now I could recover the lost props for the theater troupe, help them get a fresh start. A bonus.

But I could do that during the pawnshop's normal business hours. I wouldn't need to steal them now. Since I could prove that the props were stolen property, I could even get McGoo on my side, if Snazz proved intractable again.

As a matter of fact, if I were going to steal anything, I'd retrieve the family jewelry that Sheyenne's brother had pawned. The very thought made my blood boil. Travis damn well better use the money to get himself out of trouble—and then get himself out of the Unnatural Quarter for good, so he didn't bother Sheyenne anymore. . . .

But I'm not a thief. Much as I disliked the gremlin, technically Snazz had done nothing wrong. He had acquired the items honestly, and I have my own code of ethics (let's not count the breaking and entering). I merely wanted a glance at the ledger—no harm, no foul—before I melted back into the night. Snazz would never know, and I could get on with the process of getting Jerry the zombie back to his former vivacious self.

I moved into the deeper gloom at the back of the pawnshop. On the counter, I saw the basketball-sized crystal ball in its ornate birdbath-shaped holder, sparkling with reflected light. A set of antique bookends had been knocked sideways and lay on the countertop. Snazz's old coffee cup, proclaiming him to be *World's Best Gremlin,* was also tipped over, its pencils and pens scattered everywhere, several of them on the floor. The chicken-wire barricade had been torn loose.

Behind the counter, I found Snazz, dead—and not from natural causes.

When you discover a body, especially a murder victim, several thoughts go through your head. First is a burst of paralyzing surprise. Because the pawnshop was so quiet, I hadn't expected to find anyone there at all, and if I did encounter the pawnbroker, I would have made some excuse, had a conversation, worked something out. But you can't have a conversation with a dead guy.

Snazz lay sprawled there, tufts of yanked fur strewn around, his slitted eyes bulging, tongue lolling out between pointed teeth. His little paws were extended upward as if still trying to fight off an assailant. . . .

The second thing that goes through your mind is fear. You wonder if maybe the killer is still around. So I drew my .38 and cautiously looked from side to side. I was sure I would have heard someone slipping away, or an assailant stalking me. The pawnshop remained silent, even though the shadows seemed even darker now.

The pawnbroker beside me had obviously been strangled; I could tell from the crushed fur around his throat, the cocked angle of his head. Judging by the scattered objects on the counter and around the body, there had been a struggle—not surprising, since victims tend to struggle when they're being strangled.

The third and perhaps most important thing that goes through your mind is the sensation that can only be character- ized as "Oh shit, I'm in trouble now!" I had broken into the pawnshop. I was trespassing. Someone might have seen me slipping down the alley. I'd probably left fingerprints. It was no secret I had told Mrs. Saldana that I intended to get information out of Snazz, one way or another.

I could have run, done my best to wipe off the fingerprints, and hoped that I left no mark. When someone eventually found the gremlin's body, no one would think to interrogate me—at least not right away.

I didn't like those odds, though. Instead, I pulled out my phone. My best bet would be to stay where I was, report the crime, and come clean. I slanted things in my favor, though. I called McGoo directly.

Shortly after I called, I realized I'd miscalculated. Blame it on panic, which makes a person do stupid things, or maybe residual effects of the bullet hole through my brain. If I'd been thinking straight, I would have worked open the combination lock in the gremlin's credenza, found the ledger, gotten the in- formation I needed, and *then* called in the crime.

Too late now.

Hurrying, not sure how much time I'd have before the cops arrived, I bent over the credenza lock, spun the dial back and forth, pretending to be a safecracker, but the gremlin had kept this as well oiled and polished as everything else in the pawn- shop. I kept trying to get the drawer open, realizing this was a big risk to take for a pro bono case.

On the fifth try, I still couldn't get the lock open. I turned to

Snazz's glassy eyes. "You aren't going to offer any help, are you?"

Then I heard the sirens coming, and I knew I wouldn't get the drawer open in time. I made a halfhearted final attempt, then wiped my prints off the lock and stood up, trying to make myself look as harmless and innocent as possible.

McGoo arrived with the first batch of police. He must have been halfway home, but he had rushed back to the Quarter when he received my call, radioing for backup as he came. The cops entered Timeworn Treasures with guns drawn.

"Hands up! Stay where you are!" one of the cops growled—a rookie, I imagined.

McGoo walked in beside him. "Calm down. He's the one who called it in."

"He's still under arrest! This is a murder scene."

"I didn't kill him," I said.

"That remains to be proved!"

"Oh, don't go overboard," McGoo said to the rookie. "He's already *been* a murder victim. I very much doubt he's a murderer." I wasn't convinced that logic would hold up in court.

"If I killed Snazz, why would I have stayed here and reported the crime?" I asked.

"To remove suspicion," said the rookie.

"And did it work?" I turned to McGoo.

"Scout's honor, Shamble, you're a real honorable guy. On the other hand, an honorable guy wouldn't have broken into the pawnshop in the first place."

"I'll make it up to you by solving the crime," I promised.

"That should about do it," McGoo said.

Chapter 23

In one of those "saved by the bell" moments, my phone rang. The rookie cop pointed his revolver at me, as if my cell phone were a concealed weapon. I ignored him and answered the call.

The urgency in Sheyenne's voice was palpable. "Beaux, get to the Full Moon right away! There's an emergency—it's Travis! He's in bad shape. An ambulance is on its way, and I'm going now."

"Travis at the Full Moon? Spooky, what happened?" But she had already hung up. I turned to McGoo. "I've got to go to the brothel." That wasn't what he'd expected me to say.

The rookie cop kept his gun pointed at me. "You can't just leave, mister. You're a murder suspect! What if you skip town?"

"Officer McGoohan will keep an eye on me. Come on, McGoo, I might need your help. I think somebody's hurt. No time to lose." What are BHFs for?

McGoo decided that sounded preferable to a gremlin homicide. "I had a car cruise by there a few times today, as you requested, but I've been meaning to check out the Full Moon in person—strictly for professional reasons, of course."

"Of course," I said.

He barked at the rookie cop. "Lock down the scene and call in the evidence techs. Meanwhile, I'll keep interrogating the suspect. He's got a lot of explaining to do."

By the time we got to the brothel, the ambulance had arrived with flashing lights and full siren, Code 3. Crowds of onlookers gathered in the streets, and the scantily clad vampire princesses struck poses; they didn't look overly concerned, nor did the sleek-furred werewolf Cinnamon. The Full Moon's new golem security guards stood like statues. So this wasn't a security issue.

Neffi stood outside on the sidewalk, her face even more withered and pinched than usual, annoyed rather than frightened by the ruckus. "Can we take care of this as quickly as possible?" she asked the emergency medical technicians. "These are my peak business hours."

The EMTs hauled a gurney through the large front doors and down the porch steps. A weak-looking gray-skinned man lay on the stretcher, his cheeks sunken, his eyelids fluttering. He seemed drained and shriveled. At first, I thought it was an old mummy customer who had overextended his abilities with one of the vigorous ladies. Then I realized it was Sheyenne's brother.

I rushed forward. "Neffi, what the hell happened here?" McGoo did his best to keep up.

The madam clenched her sticklike fingers into a gnarled fist. "Damned fool got in over his head. We warned him. Ruth isn't for just anybody."

Sheyenne's ghost appeared over the crowd and swooped toward the stretcher as the EMTs loaded it into the back of the ambulance. "Travis! What have you done now?"

He couldn't respond. He looked utterly and completely spent, but thankfully still alive.

That was when I saw the emerald-eyed, waifish succubus

sitting on the porch, her back against the rail. Her shoulders were racked with sobs. "I didn't mean to!" She began weeping. "I'm sorry! I didn't think I was getting carried away. Why does this always happen to me?"

"I told you," Neffi said to her in a stern voice, "never overestimate human customers. They're fragile."

Ruth moaned. She looked absolutely miserable.

The back doors of the ambulance slammed shut. The EMTs hopped inside and fired up the lights and siren again—I think they liked to draw attention to themselves—and roared off toward the hospital. The golem security guards waved goodbye to them.

Keeping poor Ruth back and out of sight, Neffi hustled the other girls out onto the street. "Go talk to the onlookers—there's a whole crowd of potential customers. See if you can make new friends."

Sheyenne appeared before me, distraught. I told her, "Go after him, Spooky. You should be with your brother. I'll follow as soon as I can."

"Thanks—I really need you right now." Her translucent expression was an atonal symphony of anger and deep concern. "Travis better have a good explanation for what he was doing there." She flitted off.

McGoo watched her go, then turned to me. "Does she really need someone to explain things to her?"

"She'll figure it out. Too soon, I suppose." My heart was heavy, because she would also figure out where penniless Travis had gotten the money to hire a succubus rather than using it to solve his problems.

Neffi turned to McGoo. "Don't let this color your opinion of my business, Officer. It's just one girl. And that young man—he'll be just fine, if he gets a restorative spell soon enough. I'll even pay for . . . part of it. Maybe we don't need to fill out the paperwork? We can just forget about this whole thing." She stroked McGoo's arm. "I could give you a special discount. Some of our ladies love men in uniform. *I* certainly do."

"As tempting an offer as that may be," McGoo said, "I am on duty."

"You told me you were going home for the night," I said.

"You called me back. How much more trouble are you going to cause in one night, Shamble?"

"That's what friends are for."

Neffi had an edge to her voice as she reprimanded the succubus. "Any fines I have to pay are coming out of your cut, Ruth. It's hard enough to find clients willing to hire you, but I kept you on as a specialty item. Now how are you going to earn your keep?"

Ruth continued sobbing. "I'm sorry!"

My heart went out to her. "Neffi, it's not her fault. Travis is the one who made the mistake—I have no doubt about that. He makes a lot of mistakes." I turned to McGoo, reminding him of the harassment the Full Moon had been suffering. "Let's see how Travis recovers at the hospital before we make a big incident out of this. They don't need any more trouble."

McGoo frowned. "If the man wants to press charges, I'll have no choice but to follow up, but I suppose I can put this on the back burner ... for now." He added in a pointed tone, "You're right—a murder investigation should have higher priority. Now, are you going to tell me what you were doing in the pawnshop with a dead gremlin?"

"I didn't expect him to be dead. In fact, I was hoping not to see him at all."

"Beside the point, Shamble."

"The cases don't solve themselves. I needed to have a look at the ledger book Snazz kept in the credenza behind his counter—as a favor to Mrs. Saldana."

McGoo let out a disbelieving sigh. "So you made yourself a prime murder suspect for something that's not even a paying case?"

I answered sarcastically, "Yes, McGoo, I would feel a lot better about finding a dead body if it weren't pro bono work." I sighed. "I risked a lot, but it was for a good cause. Do you think I could have a look at that ledger, just a quick glance, while you're processing it into evidence?"

He looked at me in disbelief. "You've got balls, Shamble! If I hadn't interceded, you'd be in jail right now." He shook his head, hardened his expression. "No, you can't have a look, not until it's released from evidence, and not until you're cleared of the murder rap."

I decided to ask again later. Now wasn't the time.

Neffi strolled among the crowd with her ladies. Many of the spectators shrank back after having seen the man hauled out on a gurney; others, though, seemed intrigued, like a squirrel showing inappropriate curiosity about a rattlesnake. The mummy madam made light of the incident. "That shows my girls are enthusiastic and vigorous, if nothing else! Don't let this little disturbance scare you off. Is anybody man enough to have a try for himself? Fifteen percent discount until dawn, certain conditions apply."

I turned to McGoo. "I'd stay, but I promised Sheyenne I'd meet her at the hospital."

I had planned on a quiet night breaking and entering at the pawnshop, looking up a name in a ledger, and going home satisfied. Now I was potentially framed for a murder, and Sheyenne's brother was in the hospital.

I was supposed to be solving cases, but more often than not I spent my time cleaning up messes.

CHAPTER 24

Travis remained on life support, holding on but not improving. He looked like a human washrag made out of skin and bone that had been wrung vigorously dry, then given an extra twist for good measure. I couldn't imagine how sweet, emerald-eyed Ruth could have done such a thing. Her despair and guilt were obviously genuine. A succubus was a succubus—what else was she supposed to do, write greeting-card sentiments? No, I laid the blame for the dumb decision on Travis.

If he recovered, he would probably brag about his "wild night."

I sat vigil with Sheyenne's ghost as she stayed with Travis, and I felt a poignant sense of déjà vu, reminded of when I had remained at her bedside in the hospital, refusing to leave as the toadstool poison killed her. The memory of that awful time was enough to make even a zombie shudder.

Since it was clear the doctors couldn't help him, I called Mavis Wannovich. She was happy to help, said she'd be pleased to use her witchery for the benefit of my clients and friends. I didn't point out that Travis Carey was neither client nor friend, and I knew that in return the Wannoviches and their ghostwriter would want to interview me about the Shamble & Die Penny Dreadfuls. I decided to call this my first month's compensation. One of those "emergency fixes."

When the two witch sisters arrived at the hospital, the staff balked at letting them enter. Per hospital policy, large sows were not allowed in the patient rooms, even though Mavis insisted that her sister was a thoroughly hygienic pig and probably carried fewer germs than the other visitors or patients in the facility. Alma squealed, ready to engage in antisocial behavior by defecating on the clean hospital floors, which would not have helped their case.

Fortunately, I arrived before the situation got out of hand. "She's here for a patient's treatment. I requested her services for the man in 554W."

"What sort of services?" asked the charge nurse. "She's a witch!"

Mavis said with a sniff, "I do have some medical experience."

"You're a witch doctor?"

"I prefer 'Practitioner of Alternative Medicine.' " She held a pot filled with a smelly concoction. "And this is just what the doctor ordered."

"No doctor ordered that!" the charge nurse insisted. "Insurance won't cover it."

"Don't worry, I've authorized it," I said.

The nurse placed herself in front of me. "And who are you?" She took a closer look and said, "You're on the wrong floor. The morgue is on the basement level."

I pulled out my wallet, flashed my PI license and Detective Society membership card. "Private investigator for the patient." I took Mavis's arm before the nurse could respond. "Come on, I'll show you to Travis's room." Walking with great confidence, I led the Wannoviches around the charge nurse and then down the corridor.

The normal treatments hadn't helped Travis at all, and few if any medical schools offered curricula that included treatment options for succubus exposure. Sooner or later, I was sure that would become common practice for medical centers near the Quarter.

We dodged patients in ill-fitting geometric-print hospital gowns who were shuffling along with walkers or holding IV poles—not a horde of shambling zombies, but post-surgery patients.

Mavis said, "I only had time to create a general all-purpose restorative spell, not one of the gourmet specialty items. I hope that's all right."

"He doesn't need a gourmet spell," I said. "And he doesn't need to get well too soon or too easily—he won't learn his lesson unless he's hammered over his thick head with it."

"Oh, one of *those* types." Mavis nodded. Alma snuffled and snorted, and her sister translated. "Alma wants to know if he's cute."

"Not your type—not for either of you."

Sheyenne's ghost lingered beside her brother's bed while he lay in a coma. He still looked gray, motionless. She perked up to see the Wannovich sisters.

"Neffi said he needs a restorative spell, Spooky," I told her. "They brought one."

"Who ya gonna call?" Mavis held out the ceramic pot. Her sister wandered to the other side of the bed, snuffling at the heart and blood-pressure monitor.

With great care, Mavis unscrewed the cap on the clay pot to reveal a bubbling, fuming cup full of noxious goo. "We rub liberal amounts of this restorative unguent inside his nostrils, on top of the tongue, around the gums." She smiled. "For added efficacy, it's even recommended we apply it in suppository form."

I felt queasy. "This isn't how you plan to restore me every month, is it? As part of our deal?"

"Oh no, your restorative spell will be much easier. He's in far worse shape than you are."

"That's saying a lot, considering that I'm dead."

Mavis leaned forward slowly and with great relish, letting the fumes roil near Travis's slack, gray face. Suddenly, his eyes flew open, and he took a huge gulp of air. The cardiac monitor bleeped an alarm; his blood pressure jumped up fifty points, and he squirmed in the bed, trying to shrink from the foul-smelling pot. He sat up wide-eyed, his lips trembling. "Get that away from me! Get her away!"

Mavis took a step away from the bed, satisfied. "That does it."

"You mean you're not even going to apply the stuff?" I admit I was disappointed, though I didn't really want to be around for the suppository part of the procedure.

"As I said, it's a powerful restorative spell. The mere threat of having this in one's orifices is usually enough to give the patient-victim all the energy he needs."

"Thank you so much, Mavis." Then I added, very advisedly, "I owe you one."

"Oh, we'll be calling soon." She tipped her pointed hat to me and led her sister back out into the hospital corridors. As they left, I heard her suggest to Alma that they should stop at the hospital cafeteria's all-you-can-eat salad bar before they went home.

Sheyenne's delight to see her brother recovering lasted only a few seconds before her reaction set in; she'd been stewing most of the night. "Travis, Mom and Dad are dead. *I'm* dead! Isn't that good enough for you? Why would you want to kill yourself like that?"

He tried to make a joke. "Can you think of a better way than death through sex? Coming and going at the same time."

She slapped him, and her hand went right through his face. "I thought you were desperate! You said you had no money. How could you pay for something like that?"

Travis turned his head on the pillow, tried to withdraw into the bed. The silence hung for a few moments, until I spoke up. "Sheyenne, you already know where he got the money."

Sometimes when you love somebody, you don't want to see what's staring you in the face. It's that voluntary blindness when it comes to family members. She gaped at her brother. "You *didn't!* You pawned our jewelry to spend the money in a *brothel?*"

"Not all of it," he said in a very small voice.

"I don't believe this, Travis! Even after I'm *dead* you're still jerking me around!"

"Look, I'm sorry." He weakly raised his hands. "She was so pretty and . . . I got carried away. I didn't think it would turn out—"

"Just stop at 'I didn't think'!" Her spectral form glowed brighter as her fury became incandescent. "I—I need to leave before I say something I will regret for the rest of my . . . forever. I don't know why I bother."

In disgust, without even a glance at me, Sheyenne departed straight through the solid wall. I was required to leave by more conventional means, but not before I turned my most baleful glare on Travis. And zombies have a knack for baleful glares.

"I'm tired," Travis muttered; it sounded like a whimper. "Leave me alone, I need to rest."

"Normally I don't get involved in family matters," I said in my most threatening tone, "but if you mess with Sheyenne, I promise I'm going to get *very* involved."

At my undead pace it was difficult to storm off, but I did the best I could.

CHAPTER 25

At noon, McGoo invited me to attend the autopsy of Snazz the gremlin, as his personal guest. VIP seats. It's great to have friends in the right places.

I arrived at the thick metal door at the rear of the morgue, and the fidgety ghoul attendant asked for my ID, compared it with the approved names on his clipboard, and checked me off the guest list.

Inside, McGoo lounged in a hard plastic chair, holding his usual cinnamon latte. "Hey, Shamble, how many ghouls does it take to wallpaper a room?" Before I could stop him, he said, "Depends on how thinly you slice them."

I looked around the morgue. "What are you trying to do, make all the corpses get up and walk out of here groaning?"

"You never appreciate fine humor."

"Hmm, I haven't heard any in a long time."

The murdered gremlin was laid out on a stainless-steel slab. All around us, tables were cluttered with Bunsen burners and bubbling beakers filled with colored liquids, differentiation tubes, glass and metal coils. I actually felt my hair stand on end from the static electricity in the air: A Jacob's ladder buzzed and snapped with a rising electrical arc; a plasma ball flickered with tentacles of contained lighting. Since it was a sunny day with no thunderstorms in the forecast, the lab's skylight was closed, the lightning rods withdrawn.

The coroner, a small-statured and frenetic man with skin the color of spoiled milk, was completely hairless, except for the obvious and out-of-place toupee in the middle of his scalp; I fought down the urge to stare at it. He was working with flasks of chemicals, hunched over bubbling test tubes. He gave me a quick nod of greeting. "My name is Victor."

"Of course it is." Weren't all mad scientists named Victor?

"Dr. Archibald Victor," he added.

McGoo leaned close to me. "Emphasis on the *bald*."

The coroner went back to mixing his concoction, poured a blue liquid into a flask, whereupon it foamed and turned red; he added another chemical, which made greenish brown smoke erupt. After the roiling bubbles subsided, Dr. Victor poured the mixture into a coffee mug and took a long gulp, letting out a sigh of satisfaction. Remembering his manners, the coroner turned to us. "Would either of you like an energy drink?"

"Not me, thanks," I said.

McGoo lifted his cinnamon latte. "I'm fine—let's just get on with it."

Dr. Victor rattled a metal tray close to the gremlin's cadaver on the slab. With building anticipation, he gloated over his selection of scalpels, bone saws, icepick-like temperature probes, spreaders, and silver pans; he showed so much enthusiasm for the shiny objects that I was sure Snazz would have approved. The coroner also had a pad of paper that looked like a game score sheet. He hummed as he got to work, pulling out empty bottles, test tubes, and jars.

"Specimens, specimens, specimens," he said as he trimmed

some of the gremlin's fur and put it into a plastic bag. He ran a metal implement around Snazz's rubbery gray lips, inspecting the teeth. He poked a cotton swab into the gremlin's ear. He counted fingers and toes, wrote down the numbers. With obvious glee, he picked up a scalpel and a bone saw to expose the skull. "And now for the cranium and the brain."

I looked at McGoo. "Do you think his brain had anything to do with it?"

"Not at all."

We had spoken in hushed whispers, but now I raised my voice. "Excuse me, Dr. Victor, but my best guess is that the victim was strangled."

The coroner was startled by the interruption. "And have you spent any time with the body?"

"Yes, I have."

Dr. Victor took up his magnifying glass again and bent over the crushed fur and disjointed larynx at the gremlin's throat. "Why yes, yes, it appears so—definitely, I would say. The victim was definitely strangled to death. Definitely." He sniffed. "And now for the cranium and the brain." With deft movements, he sliced the skin in a neat circle all around the top of the gremlin's head, peeled off the scalp, then set to work on the skull.

McGoo sipped his latte again. "There's no rushing these things."

By the end of the autopsy, I had learned more—much more—about gremlin anatomy and internal organs than I'd ever wanted to know. Heart, lungs, kidneys, spleen, stomach contents—Snazz's last meal had been corn flakes—bladder and its urine for additional testing, toenails snipped off and placed in separate vials. I knew there was a black market in unnatural bodily organs that certain sorcerers used when casting obscure spells. Any number of mad scientists—or just unorthodox collectors—had standing orders for particular body parts, especially brains, though I wasn't convinced that gremlin brains were in particularly high demand.

Most importantly, the coroner thrust the long, sharp temperature probe into the center of Snazz's liver, took readings of the body core, made his calculations. "There we have it. Time of death between seven ten and seven fifteen last night."

"Sounds awfully accurate," McGoo said.

"Yes, yes. Gremlin livers are like stopwatches. Very easy."

I looked at McGoo. "I was with you in the Goblin Tavern last night. We didn't leave until nine."

"Looks like you've got an alibi, Shamble." McGoo sounded as relieved as I felt.

"That's proof that I didn't kill the gremlin."

Dr. Victor blinked up at me; his eyes were extremely large, as if frozen in a permanent look of startlement. "Of course you didn't kill the gremlin. You're a zombie. He was strangled. Therefore, you would have left flakes of dead skin all over his throat. No sign of that."

"You could have told us that from the outset," I said.

The coroner sounded indignant. "I didn't know it was a question." He turned back to poking and prodding around the numerous organ specimens he had just collected. The perspiration on his scalp had caused his toupee to slither halfway down his forehead.

I said to McGoo, "I'm off the hook."

"Off the hook for the *murder*, Shamble. I'm still pissed off about the breaking and entering."

"Are you going to arrest me for that?" That would put a damper on my day.

He sighed. "I have too much pain-in-the-ass paperwork to do already. No need to add more to it."

"So, does that mean I can have a look at that ledger now?" I knew I was probably pushing him too far.

"Evidence techs are still testing it, nothing released yet. But what exactly are you looking for? I might be able to sneak a peek."

"Sales of several heart-and-soul bundle packs, particularly the one belonging to Jerry, Mrs. Saldana's zombie helper. Snazz wouldn't tell me the name of the purchaser. We're trying to buy it back so he can be his old self again, as a favor to her."

He groaned. "For Mrs. Saldana? All right, I'll see what I can find."

CHAPTER 26

After the autopsy, and being cleared of murder, I returned to the office just in time for Harvey Jekyll to come in and try to hire our services.

Robin was at her desk, having worked all night long. At dawn, she had filed a housing discrimination action on behalf of the Pattersons, sent out a barrage of press releases, made contact with the housing authorities. She was already drawing a lot of attention, and she was just getting warmed up.

Back at my desk reviewing case files, I kept kicking myself for not getting a look at the pawnshop ledger before I reported the gremlin's murder. That would have saved me a lot of trouble. What had my hurry been? Snazz wasn't going anywhere, and a few extra minutes wouldn't have made any difference in scheduling his autopsy.

I also needed to contact faux-Shakespeare about the theater props that I had found in Timeworn Treasures. Even though that was good news for the actors, the pawnshop crime scene was locked up tight, and the ghostly troupe couldn't get their property back until it was released from evidence. Nothing I could do before that.

Our door swung open, and the bristle-furred Larry the werewolf stepped inside, scanned our offices with slitted eyes as if assessing threat potential, then gestured with a clawed hand. "Clear, Mr. Jekyll. You can come inside."

Harvey Jekyll sauntered in, a gnomish man that no gnome would ever claim as a relative. He had a wrinkly scalp, large owlish eyes, fidgety fingers, and black burn spots around the back of his head and across his brow, permanent reminders of his ride on Sparky, Jr.

It's not an exaggeration to say that Harvard Stanford Jekyll was one of the men I loathed most in the entire world.

The moment he set foot through the door, Jekyll acted as if he owned our offices, but since his financial ruin and subsequent death sentence, he wasn't in a position to buy much of anything. Nevertheless, it took a while for ingrained attitudes to change.

"Unimpressive." Jekyll frowned in disapproval. "I expected Chambeaux and Deyer to have more elaborate offices."

Robin stood next to me, coiled and furious. "We don't have extravagant tastes."

I put a hand on her arm, and she jumped. "Breathe, Robin," I said quietly, then raised my voice. "What do you want here, Jekyll? I hoped we'd never have the displeasure of your company again."

Larry prowled our offices, circling the perimeter with his biceps bunched, fangs bared, claws exposed, trying to look like a tough guy. That was what he got paid for, I suppose.

"I'd prefer not to be here myself, Chambeaux. How's the arm, by the way?"

"Reattached and perfectly functional." I made a fist. "Care to see for yourself?"

Jekyll ignored this. "Good, because we might need your

services, although my current problem falls more under Ms. Deyer's purview."

"I'm not interested in taking your case," Robin said.

"Really? That's ironic. *Now* who's practicing discrimination?" The comment startled her, and Jekyll talked quickly. "I saw your recent filing on behalf of the Pattersons, and I wish to file an identical one for my own circumstances."

"What could you possibly have in common with that nice couple?" I said.

"I have encountered exactly the same problem. I wish to move away from the Unnatural Quarter to a pleasant residence out of town. I don't feel welcome here anymore."

"That's an understatement," Larry growled under his breath.

"I, too, applied for a mortgage to buy a small home in the suburbs, and I, too, was turned down. I've been shunned."

"Not used to that, are you?" I smirked. "How are you going to make the down payment or afford our fees? I thought Miranda took every cent in your divorce."

"She did," Jekyll said. "But I've made other investments since. Now, from a legal perspective, wouldn't you say I have as much right to a home in any neighborhood I choose as the Pattersons do?"

Robin said in a flat, emotionless voice, "All of my efforts are taken up with the Pattersons. I really have no interest in your case, and since I represented Miranda in her divorce, it would be a conflict of interest."

Jekyll snorted. "So the law only applies to people you like? For shame! There are few enough lawyers willing to represent monsters in the Quarter that you have to bend a few rules in the name of justice. I've heard your crusades and passionate speeches about equality—I guess as an attorney you're as believable as a politician when you make promises. And I've had problems with politicians letting me down as well."

"I hope that was your peculiar way of saying goodbye," I

said to Jekyll. Robin was more furious and confused than I'd ever seen her.

"Very well. I've presented my case. Think about it, Ms. Deyer—and think about who you are. It wouldn't look good for your cause in the press if I were to point out that you practice discrimination yourself, despite all your talk. Come on, Larry. I'd like to stop for a coffee on the way back home."

The werewolf bodyguard bristled. "A to-go coffee, boss. It's the only way I can keep you safe."

Jekyll sighed. "Very well, it's probably best. I'll wait in the car."

Larry followed him out the door, but the werewolf turned back to me and spoke in a quick, low voice. "That private security job you talked to me about, Shamble—is it still open?"

"Sorry," I said, "it's already been filled by a few rent-a-golems."

"Damn! Missed my chance." Larry loped down the hall after his boss.

CHAPTER 27

The five new golems working security at the Full Moon loved their new jobs. One pair stood in front of the porch steps; two others patrolled the perimeter, walking like windup clay soldiers to prevent Senator Balfour's minions from tacking up derogatory flyers; I didn't see the last one.

The golems wore smiles on their crudely fashioned faces and recognized me as I approached. "Mr. Chambeaux, good to see you!"

"We can't thank you enough," said another.

One got carried away in his excitement and disarmingly, but ill-advisedly, clapped me on the shoulder. I felt as if I'd been hit by a linebacker, but I managed to keep my feet. Golems are strong.

"Any more trouble since last night, boys?" I asked.

"Been quiet since the ambulance left—too quiet, in fact. Most of the Full Moon clientele slipped out the back door or ducked through windows as soon as they heard the sirens."

"People can't tell the difference between an ambulance and a police siren," I said.

I plodded up the steps, walked across the creaking porch, and opened the ornate Victorian front door. The fifth golem stood like a statue inside the reception parlor, doubling as a hat rack, if necessary; his name, etched on the back of his neck, was Mike.

Cinnamon was brushing her fur at the reception desk again. The zombie ladies and vampire princesses sat around a table playing cards and looking bored. Neffi paced back and forth in the customer-less lobby, but the girls seemed deaf to her grumbles.

I decided to take an unusual approach and called out with as much cheer as I could manage, "Good news!"

The mummy madam turned her coal-black eyes in my direction. "What's good about it? We haven't had a single client, not even after I announced my special discounts last night. I'm going to have to take out radio ads, offer two-for-one specials . . . hmm, but that'll only attract the kinky customers."

"They're just spooked—they'll come around. The good news is, Travis Carey is recovering in the hospital. I arranged to have a couple of witch friends perform a restorative spell."

Neffi still wasn't overjoyed. "Good, he'll bounce back full of energy and ready to lawyer up. What are we going to do, Mr. Chambeaux?"

"He won't press charges. In fact, I expect him to leave the Quarter before long." There really was nothing left for Travis here; he had said goodbye to his sister's ghost and immediately squandered what meager inheritance Sheyenne had left. No good could come of him hanging around. I'd make sure he understood that.

A ghost in a checkered jacket and stylish hat flitted through the closed front door, tipped his hat, and turned around to open the door from inside. He returned to the porch so he could snatch up the bouquet of daisies he had left there. "Hello, ladies!" Alphonse Wheeler was certainly cheery.

"At least this time you're not bothering any paying customers, Mr. Wheeler," said Neffi. "No competition today."

The bank robber looked around the parlor, surprised. "And these adorable and ravishing women have no company whatsoever? Lucky me." He noticed me standing there. "Apologies, Mr. Chambeaux. You obviously have first pick."

Aubrey the zombie girl clumsily shuffled the deck, spilling cards all over the table, then scooped them back into a pile. Nightshade and Hemlock each drew cards.

"Mr. Wheeler is a frequent visitor, but never a paying customer," Neffi said.

Wheeler grinned. "Not through lack of trying. I used to be quite a ladies' man—I was rather randy in my life. I had frequent-guest cards with three different escort services from Nevada to Rhode Island. But now, being a ghost"—he spread his hands, looking forlorn—"I can look, but not touch. Admittedly, looking upon such beauty is its own reward, but I do find it discouraging." He let out a long sigh. "It's depressing to be a horny ghost. The spirit is willing . . ."

"I know how you feel, Mr. Wheeler," I said. Sheyenne and I faced similar challenges in our love life.

"At least I'm out of prison—for all the good that does me," Wheeler said. "For two decades I dreamed about being back on the outside, but this afterlife business isn't all it's cracked up to be."

I spotted Ruth standing shyly in the hall. Her large emerald eyes were shadowed; she had been crying. "I'm sorry," she said again. "It's all my fault."

"It *is* your fault." Neffi's voice was always harsh since her vocal cords were dried and sinewy. "But it's that dimwit customer's fault just as much." She turned to me. "He did sign a waiver. I can prove we warned him about the succubus. We explained the dangers and the safety procedures. All conjugal relations are *at your own risk*. Generally, we don't recommend humans spend time with Ruth. I tell them again and again." She cocked her head, put her hand on her hip, and put on a performance, speaking in a nasal, bad Jack Nicholson imitation. " 'You want Ruth? You can't handle Ruth!' But they don't listen, that man in particular. He filled out a new-client card and everything, and I can tell you this—I filed it right in the blacklist folder. Travis Carey is no longer welcome at the Full Moon."

Ruth sniffled. "But I'm not going to get any more customers, not after this. What am I going to do? How do I make a living?" The girl was quite sweet.

I took a few steps closer to her. "It'll be all right. Look at me—I'm dead, and I'm still optimistic that things will turn out for the best."

"We don't run a charity operation here," Neffi said to Ruth. "Your take was always smaller than the other girls'. We kept you on because of the novelty, but this is the last straw. If you don't earn money for the establishment, then I can't keep you around. I have to cut you loose. Sorry. It's business."

Ruth began trembling and sniffing. Tears ran down her cheeks to her pointed chin and dangled there like little diamonds in the parlor lights. She slid down the wall, folding her knees until she sat on the floor.

"Give her another chance, Neffi," I said. "Hold off for just a little while. See if things turn around."

"They won't turn around," Ruth said. "I never wanted to work in a brothel—I just wanted to be loved, but I'm poison to anyone who loves me. Even for daredevils, the thrill wears off after a while. Then where am I?" She spread her hands. "And now even the brothel won't have me! This really sucks."

"That's supposed to be my joke." Nightshade threw down her hand of cards and raked in the money from the pot.

"I'll still spend time with you," said Alphonse Wheeler. "It's not as if I can do anything else with the girls."

Neffi said in a hard voice, "We charge clients to spend time with the girls, Mr. Wheeler, whether or not they can get it up. Can you pay for the privilege?"

"If only you had asked me a few days ago, but I don't have my stash anymore."

"Thanks for trying, Mr. Wheeler," Ruth said with a sniff.

I turned back to the mummy madam, very much wanting to help the poor succubus. "Give me a few days to figure out something for her."

"All right, Mr. Chambeaux—I owe you a favor," Neffi said. "A small one."

I retrieved my fedora from Mike the golem hat rack, and left, already putting my detective skills to good use.

CHAPTER 28

Irwyn Goodfellow never seemed to tire of doing good deeds, and I couldn't keep track of all his charitable projects. Fortunately, Chambeaux & Deyer received a high-end engraved invitation for his gala ribbon-cutting ceremony at his new zombie rehab clinic, Fresh Corpses. Sheyenne and I attended, although Robin stayed in the office, swamped with casework for the Pattersons.

The plastic-and-leather surgery facility specialized in restorative operations for zombies who had lost body parts, articulated joints, or large sections of musculature or skin. A team of skilled surgeons, morticians, seamstresses, and upholsterers offered community service work for the free clinic. Zombies could shamble in with no questions asked. Skilled wood-carvers and animatronics specialists who were laid off from Hollywood (when studios could simply hire a real monster, why spend a large budget on special effects?) provided prosthetic limbs and replacements for the less fortunate undead.

In front of the whitewashed clinic, an engraved granite block read: ALL WELCOME. Irwyn Goodfellow stood behind a podium at the entry. "It brings me such great joy to do this. Zombies need no longer be afraid to come out in the daylight. Fresh Corpses has fifty beds and a complete staff to take care of your needs."

"Cute nurses, too?" yelled one of the zombies in the audience.

"Beauty is in the eye of the beholder," Irwyn answered—by which I knew he meant *no, the nurses are not very attractive*— but he used this as a springboard to continue, "And you are all beautiful people, no matter how badly you may be falling apart, no matter which choices you made in life or death. You deserve a second chance, or a third chance. Nobody's keeping score. This privately funded clinic will make you whole again so you can be productive citizens."

Hope Saldana stood beside him and spoke into the microphone. "On behalf of the Monster Legal Defense Workers, we officially declare the Fresh Corpses facility open! It will help zombies with their physical needs." The old woman's voice cracked as she looked out at Jerry, who stood where she had propped him. Alas, restorative surgery would not help Jerry with his missing heart and soul.

Even with Snazz murdered, I hadn't given up yet on discovering who had purchased the bundle pack from the pawnshop. McGoo would get back to me soon; a simple glance at the ledger book, and then I could go make the new owner an offer he couldn't refuse, or at least we could start bargaining.

A wide red ribbon was stretched from one lintel post to the other. Mrs. Saldana offered a large and very sharp pair of silver scissors to Irwyn. "Would you like to do the honors, Mr. Goodfellow?"

He pushed them back toward Mrs. Saldana. "Please, after all the fine things you've accomplished in the Unnatural Quarter, you should be the one to do it."

While she loved to help unfortunates, Mrs. Saldana did not

like to be the center of attention—except when she was leading hymns or sermonizing to her patchwork congregation. Despite her obvious embarrassment, Goodfellow raised his voice. "Ladies, gentlemen, and genderless creatures—please give a round of applause to Mrs. Hope Saldana, acting director of the MLDW Society, who has worked tirelessly for years at her Hope and Salvation Mission."

The gathered zombies moaned out a cheer and began applauding—some so vigorously that their wrists bent at unfortunate angles.

"Oh, all right." She took the scissors and sliced the ribbon in half, as if she were snipping a particularly tough umbilical cord. The streamers fell to each side.

Irwyn opened the front door with an extravagant gesture. "Come inside for the reception, everyone."

Sheyenne and I entered Fresh Corpses, along with the inexorable crowd of shambling undead. In the foyer of the restorative clinic, a piano had been set up. A vampire pianist cracked his knuckles, smiled at us all, and launched into a jaunty theme. He wore a white tuxedo jacket and pants encrusted with rhinestones and sequins. As he played, his fingers were a blur, his sharp nails tickling (and scratching) the ivories. The rhinestones and sequins caught the light from the chandeliers above in a dazzling display that blinded me.

As the crowds came in, Goodfellow welcomed them all. Servers—many of them newly hired golems—walked around carrying trays of drinks or hors d'oeuvres. The zombies sniffed at textured lumps of grayish white matter, then discreetly set the hors d'oeuvres aside when they discovered the snack was, in fact, shaped tofu instead of real brains. Goodfellow had declared the clinic to be a "brain-free zone." One entire wing of the facility was a lockdown, closely monitored withdrawal ward for addicts, so that zombies could kick the habit.

The doctors and nurses acted as tour guides, taking potential donors as well as likely patients around the facility, showing the beds, the various leatherette selections for skin replacement, the putrefaction-freshening spa, embalming-fluid top-offs, and exercise room, where there would be weekly yoga and Pilates sessions to keep the zombies limber. The staff members were especially proud of their high-throughput ventilation and air-freshening system.

Sheyenne and I signed the guest book, picked up brochures that described how Fresh Corpses was funded by the benevolence of Irwyn Goodfellow (though private donations were cheerfully accepted). Irwyn shook my hand vigorously but was careful not to do any damage; my reattached arm still suffered a few twinges. He seemed to be in his element, thriving on the attention and adulation; doing kind deeds was like a jolt of endorphins to the man. Missy Goodfellow, on the other hand, was noticeably absent.

"Now that I've met your sister, Mr. Goodfellow, it's obvious that generosity doesn't run in the family," I said. "Did some angel loan you a halo? How did you get bitten by the philanthropy bug?"

Sheyenne looked at me as if my questions were rude, but Irwyn took no offense. "I wasn't bitten by a bug . . . rather, I was nearly crushed by a falling piano. I didn't think people really used pulleys and winches to haul pianos up to fourth-story windows anymore, but there I was, walking down the street, when it came crashing down in one big discordant note. Missed me by only a few inches."

"And you took that as a sign?" Sheyenne asked.

"No, I saw it as a threat. It wasn't an accident, you see—I didn't need to hire a private investigator to figure that out. My father, Oswald Goodfellow, was a high-ranking member of the mob, though more of a distant uncle than an actual godfather.

He had plenty of blood on his hands, and money in the accounts, mostly illegal stuff, that formed the foundation of the Smile Syndicate.

"I was being raised to follow in his footsteps, a rotten apple falling not far from the tree. But when he tried to crush a rival's church bingo racket, the other mobsters decided to send him a message by dropping a piano on the head of his heir apparent. Fortunately for me, it missed.

"My father insisted on getting revenge, but to me it was an epiphany, like a born-again conversion. Falling pianos can do that. From that point on, I wanted nothing to do with the syndicate money, the corruption, the violence. I vowed to do *good* things with the family fortune. Since my sister and I inherited all the money very shortly thereafter, I could do what I liked with my share."

"How did your father die?" Sheyenne asked.

"Oh, he died quietly in bed—someone smothered him with a pillow. The killer was never caught . . . it might have been Missy." He shrugged. "But since she's family, who am I to point fingers?"

Sheyenne gestured around the zombie rehab facility. "So all this money originally came from criminal activity."

"And now it's being put to good use. All shady Smile Syndicate operations are out of my hands and off my conscience— and I am a better person for it. Sometimes it's hard, but I'm a man dedicated to my charities and my good works. Missy, on the other hand . . . well, at least the company accountants are happy with her. She's been reaping plenty of profits these days."

My phone rang, and I excused myself, stepping aside while other visitors spoke to Mrs. Saldana and Irwyn Goodfellow. "Hey, Shamble," McGoo said. "I had a look at that pawnshop ledger, but can't find any mention of hearts or souls. Just a lot of junk."

I blinked. "No record at all? But Snazz told me himself he had sold seven sets already, and we know for a fact that Jerry pawned his heart and soul there."

"Nothing listed, Scout's honor."

The evidence techs had combed the crime scene, dusted for fingerprints, taken all the necessary photographs, gathered and stored any items they considered useful. McGoo suspected a few interesting items had also found their way into the pockets of the evidence techs, but he couldn't prove it. "We've got what we need from the pawnshop, and we expect to release the items to the next of kin soon enough."

I was sure they must have missed something. "Then can I have a closer look?"

"Maybe. If no one else claims it."

"I've got dibs."

He laughed. "That's not how the law works, Shamble."

For now, I could see about getting the theater props back to the Shakespeare troupe. It would be nice to close one case at least.

After I pocketed the phone, I found Sheyenne drifting beside the vampire piano player, who was reveling in his cheerful performance. She had always liked the lounge lizard music at the Basilisk nightclub, and now she sang along with her knock-'em-dead voice. As they finished a song, Sheyenne leaned closer and asked him, "What's with the rhinestones and sequins? I don't see any sideburns, so it's not an Elvis impersonation."

I said, "He looks more like Liberace."

The pianist showed his fangs in a grin and kept playing. He didn't miss a beat as he answered, "Neither. I'm just part of the minority that thinks vampires should sparkle."

CHAPTER 29

That afternoon, when Sheyenne and I got back to work, Robin was holed up in her office. She looked noticeably rundown, still wearing yesterday's outfit, her eyes bloodshot. I'm certainly not one to talk about somebody else's rumpled, drained, or bedraggled appearance, but I was immediately worried about Robin.

When I asked why she'd been losing sleep, she said, "I'm wrestling with my conscience, Dan, and it's a knock-down-drag-out all-star wrestling match."

That was quintessential Robin. I recalled her various clients, wondered what could be bothering her so much. "Which case is it?"

"Not a case I have yet . . . but one I need to take."

From across the office, Sheyenne groaned. "More pro bono work?"

Robin shook her head. "No, this client can pay. . . . I just don't like him—Harvey Jekyll."

"You're not seriously considering taking his case," Sheyenne cried.

"I have to. He's right, I'm sorry to say. That man has the same legal difficulties as the Pattersons. I should be taking the same moral stance against discrimination. How can I say he doesn't deserve justice simply because I despise him? Even scumbags deserve the safety net of the law."

"Jekyll's broken enough laws. He was executed for it," I pointed out.

"But not in *this* matter. He's as much an innocent victim as Mr. and Mrs. Patterson. He may be a cretin, but *I* don't have to be. I prefer to take the high road."

"As long as it doesn't lead you over a cliff," Sheyenne commented.

"I'm going to tell him in person." Robin sounded very brave, then her voice grew smaller. "Would you come with me, Dan?"

Going to visit Harvey Jekyll was far down on my after-death bucket list, but this was Robin, and she had asked a favor. "Whatever you need—I'm there."

I'd been to Harvey Jekyll's mansion during JLPN's heyday, back when he was still human. (That's merely a biological designation, with no editorial comment on the quality of his soul, or whether he even had one.) As the CEO of Jekyll Lifestyle Products and Necroceuticals, he had owned a large estate with guard dogs and an entire security team.

Then he'd lost everything.

Harvey Jekyll now lived in a small apartment in a run-down 1970s-era complex, the sort of place rented by starving students who saved their pennies so they could move away from there as soon as possible. Now Jekyll had gotten back on his feet enough that he longed for a home in the suburbs, and he had hired us to help him get it. On the bright side, if we succeeded, at least Jekyll would be out of the Quarter.

Robin and I stood before the apartment complex; it wasn't

hard to identify Jekyll's mailbox and front door, since they were the only ones covered with globs of hurled mud, excrement, rotten tomatoes, and other fluid stains that I couldn't identify. Larry stood at the front door with a bucket of soapy water and a hard-bristled scrub brush, rubbing away at the stains. The pungent pine scent of the cleaning solution only made the foul goop smell worse.

He looked at us, curled his black lips back to reveal long canine fangs. "Come to harass Mr. Jekyll like everyone else does?"

"Maybe a little bit, if it comes up in conversation," I said.

"That's not why we're here," Robin said. "I wanted to discuss his case."

Larry let the scrub brush drop into the bucket of gray soapy water. I asked, "Do you get hazard pay for that?"

"Mr. Jekyll says it's part of my job." The bodyguard let out a low growl. "The employment agreement defines my job as private security and lists all the tasks I have to perform in detail. But at the end, another clause says 'and other duties as assigned.' The boss insists that includes scrubbing shit off the front door."

"You should have had a lawyer look over the agreement," Robin said.

"I thought lawyers were scary, until I started working for Mr. Jekyll," the werewolf answered. He let us inside. "Hey, boss—Chambeaux and Deyer are here to see you."

The apartment was austere, and the drapes—blankets tacked above the windows—blocked most of the light. Cinder blocks and plywood served as makeshift bookshelves. The end tables were orange crates that held mismatched lamps. The coffee table was a large cable spool. The only artwork on the wall was a kitschy print of big-eyed zombie puppies painted by the famed ghost pop-culture artist Alvin Ricketts.

Other pieces of salvaged furniture were strewn with electrical components, gadgets, and countless spare parts dismantled from old motors, stereos, and television sets.

Jekyll looked up from his work and regarded us with owlish eyes. His lips drew back in a sneer, as if he expected some sort of provocation from us, but then he smiled. "Ah, I knew you'd come around, Ms. Deyer. Honorable people are so predictable. That's what makes villains much more interesting."

Robin screwed up her courage. "You caused me to do a lot of thinking, and I've decided I will indeed file your antidiscrimination complaint, just as I did for the Pattersons. Provided you have a sufficient down payment and meet the other standard loan qualifications, there is no legal reason why you should be denied the right to own a home in any part of the city you choose."

"My feelings exactly," Jekyll said.

I looked at all the junk strewn on the work table, wondering if any of it had come from the Timeworn Treasures pawnshop. Maybe he'd stolen it from the pack-rat gremlin? How I would have loved to pin Snazz's murder on Jekyll, get him convicted and executed all over again—permanently this time! But that wasn't likely. I didn't see any connection.

"Our services aren't free," I said. "How do you plan to pay our retainer? I thought Miranda took everything in the divorce, and that was after the company collapsed because of the scandal. How can you afford to buy even a modest house?"

"And pay the bills," Larry growled, "including my salary."

"I've had to reinvent myself." Jekyll rummaged among the electronic debris on the table. "I took a self-help seminar, learned how to meet my inner potential. I looked at everything I have to offer and figured out how I could use it to make a living. Follow a new dream."

He poked at his hand and forearm, pinched his cheek. "Short-term, I just want to afford a better embalming job. It was never done properly after my visit to the electric chair." His skin did have a greenish sheen, the color and consistency of spoiling meat.

I've heard that a second embalming after the fact is quite an unpleasant process, like going through an adult circumcision. "I highly recommend you try it," I said.

"My main priority is to leave the Quarter and all those bad memories behind. You saw the vandalism to my door and mailbox. It happens every day, no matter which security systems I put out, no matter how often Larry patrols."

"A couple of poltergeist hooligans," Larry explained. "They're hard to catch."

"Ever since my demise, I've tried to keep a low profile, become a recluse," Jekyll continued. "But they won't leave me alone. You can understand why I just want to have a fresh start, go to a normal neighborhood, live like a normal person."

I had to point out, "You're dead, Jekyll, and a wannabe mass murderer. You left *normal* in the rearview mirror a long time ago."

Robin inspected the inventions strewn all over the table. "And what is all this?"

"I thought you'd never ask." Jekyll smiled. "I may have lost everything else in the scandal, conviction, and execution, but I didn't lose my intellectual genius. I commercialized one of my inventions. You may remember the ectoplasmic defibrillator that I developed at JLPN? A way to defend against criminal ghosts and spectral practitioners of corporate espionage?"

I remembered it all too well. Sheyenne had nearly gotten fratzed by his dangerous device.

"We intend to market it for security purposes among naturals, people who are afraid of home invasions or hauntings, spectral harassment. The defibrillator is a sure way to take care of the problem."

"Why not use it to get rid of the poltergeists harassing you?" Larry growled. "It sure would make my job easier."

"That can't be legal," Robin said. "Your device has no other purpose than to murder ghosts."

Jekyll chuckled. "Murder ghosts? Are you listening to yourself? Naturals want to feel safe. It's just like owning a handgun. And if the ghost doesn't bother people, then the ghost has nothing to worry about." He justified himself with more enthusiasm than our question warranted.

"There are laws against setting up automatic lethal devices for home protection," Robin said. "You cannot use lethal force unless you are in fear for your life from an intruder."

"I guarantee you, most of my customers would be in fear for their lives. And if a ghost is, by definition, dead, then this device cannot be considered *lethal*. It harms no living being."

"Splitting hairs," I muttered.

"With the best of them!" Jekyll said. "I look forward to any legal challenges. I have good backing." He patted one of the devices, a large speaker-type grid hooked up to two car batteries, and I was very glad Sheyenne had stayed back in the office. "This baby is going to make my fortune back. My main investor is a powerful man who very much wants the ectoplasmic defibrillator on the market. Any roadblocks will be cleared away quite tidily."

"And who is your main investor?" I asked, though I had a strong suspicion. Normally I wouldn't expect a businessman to reveal such information, but Harvey Jekyll loved to gloat over his success.

"I may be back from the dead, but I'm still well connected, Chambeaux. It's Senator Rupert Balfour—perhaps you've heard of him?"

CHAPTER 30

When the sole heir of the gremlin pawnbroker came to tidy up the estate, she engaged Robin's services as a lawyer. "My name is Alice, and I'm here to discuss the liquidation of all unclaimed materials in Timeworn Treasures and the dissolution of the estate of my late brother Snazz."

Alice was only about three feet tall, no taller than her brother. She was older than Snazz, the tufts of fur going gray and permed in a no-nonsense wave with the bluish tint that beauty parlors apply to old-lady hair. She wore too much inexpertly applied mascara around her large eyes, and the frumpy housedress made her look matronly even for such a diminutive creature. She came into our offices carrying a practical black snap purse with a chain strap, and she wore unremarkable, sensible shoes. Preceded by a strong waft of a common drugstore perfume, she stepped up to Sheyenne's desk like a schoolteacher demanding attention from the class.

Robin came out and introduced herself with a concerned expression on her face. "I'm sorry for your loss, Miss Alice."

"Me, too," I added. "He didn't deserve—"

"Moving on," Alice said. "My brother and I chose different life paths. We were never close, although his death now brings me back into his life. I assume, Ms. Deyer, that you can take care of all of the necessary paperwork?"

"A clear Last Will and Testament will simplify the process, although if you are the only heir and the estate is uncontested, we should be able to transfer ownership without complications. Will you be taking over Timeworn Treasures? All of the assets and collateral-secured loans are your responsibility. The business may have clear title—"

"Oh, heavens, no!" Alice said. "I spent an hour in the place this morning, but had to leave. I just couldn't stand all that dust and mildew. I sneezed for five minutes even after I came back out to the fresh air of the alley. No, I wish to sell the business, liquidate the assets, and use the money to enjoy my own life."

I remembered the wonderful, exotic, and occasionally frightening objects on the shelves inside Timeworn Treasures. Snazz could have had a lucrative business if he'd been more willing to part with some of those treasures.

"He had a thriving shop, Miss Alice," I said. "You could make a go of it."

"No, thank you, sir. I don't need all that clutter. I want to simplify my life. I have a pension, some conservative investments, and a frugal lifestyle, but I want to travel and see the world. Anything I can't fit into a suitcase is merely a bother." She paused with a wistful smile.

"I do have two cute poodles as pets, but they're very low-maintenance. I acquired them from a taxidermist." She opened her purse, rummaged around in the neatly organized contents, and plucked out a photograph of two dogs mounted on stands in perfect poses, heads turned up, tails frozen in mid-wag.

"Very cute," I said.

Alice retrieved the photo of the poodles after we had adored them sufficiently, inserted it into her purse in its proper place, then snapped the clasp shut. "I want to wash my hands of Timeworn Treasures. Simplify . . . simplify. Minimize hassles, reduce overhead." She clucked her tongue against her pointed teeth. "My brother used to collect the most inane things. A psychological problem, I believe. When he was a boy, he used to have a collection of lint."

"Lint?" Robin asked. "Why would anyone collect lint?"

"Heaven only knows. By the time we were teenagers, he had gathered three large boxes of lint, until one day our parents threw them out. Snazz wallowed in despair for weeks. The last time I talked with him, he was still moaning about the collector's market and how much money he could have gotten for that lint."

I didn't want to ask, so I didn't.

I was, however, surprised Alice had come to us, considering that I had found her brother's body, but she brushed the worries aside. "I looked in the business listings, and there aren't many certified and wide-ranging legal offices in the Quarter. The Better Business Bureau had no complaints on record against Chambeaux and Deyer, and that's good enough for me." She raised her mascara-caked eyelids in a question. "And I understand from the police department that you've just been cleared of all suspicion in the murder?"

"Yes," I said. "The autopsy confirmed—"

"Good, that's settled, then. Moving on. I'd like to take care of matters as quickly and efficiently as possible. I expect the evidence technicians will finish their work soon, so that I can retrieve my property and liquidate the assets."

"We can get you a release from the police department, ma'am," Robin said. "And once I take care of the appropriate transfers and paperwork, you should be free to dispose of your brother's possessions."

"Oh, I won't merely dispose of them, even though the items are mostly junk. No, I intend to have a large auction as soon as possible. Anyone who wants the items can purchase them for the highest bid."

I realized this might be my best chance. "Your brother kept a detailed sales ledger. I went to the pawnshop on the evening of his tragic death because I was trying to learn who had purchased a few particular items. I would be grateful if you'd let me have a look at those records."

Alice held her purse in front of her and regarded me, all business. "Certainly, Mr. Chambeaux. The ledger will be for sale, along with all the other items. You are perfectly welcome to bid on it, and should you make the highest offer, I'd be delighted to help you out."

Even Sheyenne was surprised and disappointed by her hardline stance, but gremlins are not known for their compassion. "It's for a good cause, Miss Alice. You could really help—"

"Moving on," the gremlin said. "My brother may have had the business, but he wasn't much of a businessman. I, on the other hand, believe favors are a sloppy and inefficient way of getting things done. We will do this properly, everything in order. You can help me with this, Ms. Deyer?"

"Yes," Robin said, sounding less enthusiastic now. "I'd be happy to."

"Good. I have my eye on a Mediterranean cruise. If my brother hoarded enough to pay for a nice trip, then I will consider our sibling rivalry to be water under the bridge." She snapped open her purse again, took out a card with her contact information, and gave it to Sheyenne for the new-client file. Alice filled out the formal paperwork, signed the contract, and paid a small retainer, then bustled off to get her fur done at the beauty shop.

CHAPTER 31

I had never been to a bank robbery before, but there's a first time for everything. Sheyenne and I heard police sirens as we strolled down the street that afternoon. Squad cars roared by, followed by an overloaded van from the Special Response Unit. Sheyenne and I had gone out to lunch at the Ghoul's Diner; I didn't need to eat often and Sheyenne couldn't, but we enjoyed having a moment of nostalgic normalcy nevertheless.

She seemed more emotionally clingy lately. The traumatic experience with Travis had shaken her, I think, and she was also concerned (though she wouldn't admit it) that I'd been spending so much time at the Full Moon. I couldn't deny that I remained preoccupied by the plight of the forlorn succubus Ruth, but if I went out of my way to insist that Sheyenne had nothing to worry about, my very earnestness would only make her worry more. It was a no-win situation for me, so I left the issue alone.

As the squad cars squealed up to the front of the Trove National Bank, the commotion drew us—and everyone else in the Quarter, it seemed—like a magnet. It's not smart to rush toward what is obviously a dangerous situation, but it's instinctive. Besides, since I was a private investigator, a bank robbery could well be business-related.

The Trove National Bank is the primary financial institution in the Unnatural Quarter, locally owned and unnaturally operated. Many of the old-guard unnaturals had large stashes, as well as valuable antiques and gold-plated magical items that they kept in safe-deposit boxes.

The name of the Trove National Bank sounded like a witty play on words, implying vaults filled with sparkling treasure, but in actuality the name came from the founder, Bernard Trove, a human businessman with long-out-of-style muttonchop whiskers and very good investment sense.

With guns drawn, cops had surrounded the building and blocked the exits. I could hear a loud schoolbell-type alarm that made the windows rattle. I saw McGoo standing there, his sidearm drawn and aimed at the bank's main entrance. We worked our way toward him. "What's going on?" I asked, the most obvious question I could think of.

"Robbery in progress. Hostage situation, too. It's Alphonse Wheeler, back to his old habits. He came into the bank wearing the same old jacket and hat—even brought the bouquet of flowers. At first the tellers thought the robbery was a joke, but then he fired a few shots into the ceiling. A couple of vampires had rented the floor above for a coupon-clipping service, and they weren't thrilled about the gunfire. They phoned it in."

"There's got to be some mistake," Sheyenne said. "Mr. Wheeler's a nice man—he wouldn't rob a bank." Then she caught herself. "Oh, of course he would."

"Bigger question is why," I said. "He has no use for the money. He just gave his entire stash to the MLDW Society."

"We can ask him after we arrest him," McGoo said.

News vans arrived. Reporters turned their cameras toward

the stymied police, the silent front door of the bank, the continually ringing alarm.

The back doors of the Special Response Unit van flew open, and two hard-looking human cops worked their way out and unloaded boxy equipment that looked like stereo speakers, which they set up with the flat panels facing the entrance of the bank. The second man erected a tripod, then unfolded mesh butterfly petals of something akin to a satellite antenna.

The police chief yelled, "All right, get everyone back, especially the ghosts. Let us do our work."

"You better leave, Sheyenne," McGoo said with an expression of concern on his face. "There could be a ripple effect."

I didn't recognize the equipment, was surprised the department had a budget to buy large high-tech gadgets. Sheyenne beat me to the question. "What is all that?"

"A new acquisition—high-powered ectoplasmic defibrillator designed for emergency situations like this."

"One of Jekyll's zappers?" I asked.

"He's got the patent," McGoo said, "and these things are supposed to be effective against violent ghosts. Senator Balfour presented it as a gift to the department, and the chief accepted it."

The very idea sent a chill down my back. Sheyenne was even more upset. "No, you can't just use that on Mr. Wheeler!"

"Not my call," McGoo said. "But Wheeler won't talk, and he won't come out. He's got hostages. We've already verified that he's the only ghost inside, so there won't be any innocents harmed."

Sheyenne got that determined look on her face—I think she'd been learning it from Robin. Before we could stop her (not that we could if we'd tried), she flitted forward, ignoring the shouts of the policemen, and drifted straight through the front door of the bank.

"You can't turn that zapper on now," I said to McGoo.

His face had gone pale. "Shamble, get her out of there! This is a crisis situation."

"You think Spooky listens to me?"

The police chief was clearly flustered. He was eager to test the department's new toy, and Sheyenne had just spoiled his opportunity. Trying to demonstrate that he was in charge, the chief took up the bullhorn. "Now, you come on out of there. We haven't got all day." I couldn't tell if he was talking to Alphonse Wheeler or scolding Sheyenne.

"No!" Wheeler called out, his voice audible even above the ringing alarm.

"Give us a minute," Sheyenne shouted, also from inside the bank. "We're having a conversation here."

The Special Response officers looked impatient now that they had set up their ectoplasmic defibrillator. Just to be safe, I walked over and tore out the power cord.

"Hey, what do you think you're doing?" said one of the men.

"Making sure you don't get itchy fingers on that power button. That's my girlfriend in there."

Both officers said something that made even my dead ears burn, and then set about reconnecting the cable. So I unplugged the second cord for good measure.

Sheyenne soared back out through the bank's front door amidst a chorus of shouts and cheers from the onlookers. Smiling, she drifted right up to me. "It's a tense situation in there, but Mr. Wheeler says he'll talk. Beaux, he's agreed to let you come in and negotiate—you and only you."

I wasn't thrilled at the prospect. "I'm not a hostage negotiator."

The chief was also miffed, but McGoo said, "May as well try, Shamble. What's he going to do, shoot you?"

"I'll do it, on the condition that *you* stay far back." I pointed to Sheyenne, then added to McGoo, "And you make sure those guys don't start blasting with the defibrillator."

"You got it, Shamble." McGoo walked over and yanked out the cables the Special Response officers had just reconnected.

"Only Chambeaux—nobody else!" Wheeler called. "And approach the door slowly!"

"That's my primary speed these days," I said as I moved forward in my stiff-legged gait. I needed to put in some time at the All-Day/All-Nite Fitness Center to limber up again.

Wheeler opened the bank's door for me, waving his gun offhandedly at the three tellers and four customers who were still inside the lobby. He looked depressed, not the jaunty and cheerful man I had met previously.

"You're having a bad day, Mr. Wheeler."

"The worst—and just one of many." He closed the door behind me and waved the gun at my chest.

I pointed to the repairs in my sport jacket. "Let's not resort to threats. I've been shot before, and in my line of work it'll probably happen again. That gun isn't going to scare me off. How about instead you tell me how we can wrap this up? Do you have a list of demands?"

He seemed surprised. "That's the best you can do as a negotiator?"

"I'm an amateur. You asked for me, so take what you got. Now, what seems to be the problem?"

He looked deeply sad, blew out a long imaginary exhale. "So now you're my psychiatrist?"

"Private detective. That's my calling in life, and I'm trying to figure out what you have to gain by robbing a bank. Makes no sense to me."

"At least it's something I can *do*." The ghost let out a low moan. "There's not much else. I spent so many years in jail that I don't know how to handle unlife on the outside. And now that I'm a ghost, I can't enjoy a good meal, can't taste a good drink, can't make love to a pretty lady. When I first came back, I bought a three-hundred-dollar bottle of wine, poured myself a glass—and all I could do was look at it."

"Bummer," I said. "But what are you going to do with the money anyway? It makes no sense."

"I don't need to *do* anything with it!" He waved the gun around, making the tellers cringe; the hostages put up their hands in surrender. "I just want to *have* it."

"That's kind of pointless."

Wheeler groaned again. "Story of my afterlife. They're just going to put me in jail again, but no jail can hold me. I'm a ghost!"

Apparently, Wheeler didn't understand the true danger he faced. "They don't plan to put you in jail—they're going to defib you," I said. "Judges have gotten a lot harsher since that poltergeist terror spree a few months back, and Senator Balfour is pushing to impose extreme punitive measures on any unnatural who steps out of line. You know that. They already have the equipment set up outside."

Wheeler grew a little more transparent. "Really? But I wasn't going to hurt anybody. I just needed to make sure that I can still rob a bank."

"All right, consider the bank robbed," I said, pointing around at the lobby. "You proved you can do it. Now hand me the gun, and we can let these people go. Don't you have a bouquet to hand out?"

He brightened. "Why, yes I do! It's my trademark."

I plucked the gun from Wheeler's spectral hand, and he, didn't even seem to notice. He was much more interested in passing out flowers to the tellers and, for good measure, he gave one to each of the hostages as well. Finally, he let out a miserable sigh and addressed his victims with a forlorn expression. "Sorry, everybody."

Then I opened the bank's front door and led him out to the waiting police.

CHAPTER 32

The Quarter has restless spirits, vengeful members of the undead, hormone-juiced and short-tempered werewolves, and vampire family feuds that have lasted for centuries. Even so, I sensed even more unrest than usual around here—it seemed there was something in the air.

I knew about the protest at the Goblin Tavern ahead of time, since Robin had cooked it up herself. Hard-bitten Francine was too proud and her feelings too hurt to beg for any intervention, but after I grumbled to Robin about how unfairly the Smile Syndicate was treating our favorite bartender, she took the crusade to heart. (Maybe subconsciously I had hoped she'd do exactly that.)

Since Francine was due to stop by the Tavern that night to pick up her last paycheck, her regular customers had gathered there to show our support. I found it heartwarming to see how many turned out. What a crowd!

Robin had arrived half an hour earlier to organize the protest. Following the incident at the bank, Sheyenne and Robin had spent the afternoon making picket signs to be passed out among the zombie, vampire, and werewolf customers who frequented the Goblin Tavern. Normally, the customers just came to the Tavern to rehydrate themselves and socialize, to grumble about their common problems, or to reminisce about old times. They weren't a rabble-rousing bunch, but Robin had whipped them up with the slogans on her signs.

Boycott the Goblin Tavern!

Francine Is the Tavern's ♥ And Soul!

Another said Shame on You, Smile Syndicate with a frowny face drawn below the words.

McGoo arrived at the Tavern at the usual time, expecting to meet me for our usual beer, but when he saw the growing mob, he tipped back his cap and said, "What is all this, Shamble?"

"A lot of us want Francine back. Care to join the movement?"

McGoo didn't hesitate. "Give me one of those signs." Robin handed him one that said We Can Drink Somewhere Else.

Stu, the corpulent and too-good-natured new manager of the Tavern, came out, looking surprised and distraught. "What is this? Why are you all here? I don't deserve this—what did I do?"

"You fired Francine," a once-a-month werewolf growled.

"But you'll have to take it up with Missy Goodfellow," Stu said. "That was part of the corporate restructuring—a management decision."

"You're the Tavern's manager," I pointed out. "Bad decision."

Stu was so flustered he looked as if he might burst into tears. "Please, let me make it up to you all—a gesture of good faith. Free pretzels for everyone!"

"Francine *always* put out free pretzels," said a zombie. "And other snacks."

"All right, other snacks, then. I want the Goblin Tavern to be a friendly place where you can all feel at home."

188 / Kevin J. Anderson

"Most of us hang out at the Tavern because we *don't* want to be reminded of home," a vampire said, eliciting a chorus of snickers. "We want it to feel like *the Goblin Tavern,* and it isn't the Tavern without Francine."

"Bring back the real cobwebs while you're at it," said a ghoul, puffing on a long cigarette.

Stu turned to uniformed McGoo for help, but my BHF just gave him a stony expression and pumped his WE CAN DRINK SOMEWHERE ELSE sign up and down.

"I don't know what the Smile Syndicate will do to me if sales go down," Stu said. "If monsters don't hang out here, the whole charm of the place is gone. Please, how about..." He reached deep within himself and dredged up a last resort. "How about a free round of drinks for everyone?"

The monsters muttered, looked at one another, growled and sniffed. Many were tempted. Two zombies began to shamble toward the door of the tavern, but Robin said in a sharp voice, "Stand firm, all of you! Hold the line!"

"Could you serve us drinks out here, so it doesn't interrupt our protest?" asked the ghoul, finishing his cigarette. Stu seemed to consider the idea.

Then a large bus drove up with a rumbling engine, coughing fumes of gray-blue exhaust, even though it looked like a sleek modern coach. A bright logo on the sign said U. Q. TOURS, SEE THE BEST OF THE WORST IN THE UNNATURAL QUARTER.

Humans filled the seats, a bunch of rube tourists wearing golf hats or bright scarves and sunglasses, even though it was nearly dark. Their faces pressed against the windows, gaping at the unexpected scene.

"Oh, no!" Stu wailed. "It's our first tour bus—not now!"

A few bus routes carried sightseers around in luxury air-conditioned coaches so they could watch the monsters in their unnatural element. The big player was the Gray Skin Line, but U. Q. Tours had just begun a special twilight tour, on which all patrons would stop at the Goblin Tavern and have a complimentary drink (price included in the cost of the package).

Stu had been ecstatic about all the new business. Personally, I thought it was another death knell for the real character of the Goblin Tavern, and I intended to get a copy of the bus schedule just to make sure I was scarce whenever a busload of tourists was due to come in. According to the advertised route, the buses would also stop at strategically placed Kreepsakes gift shops, where the guests would have the opportunity to buy special mementos of their tour.

Now, however, as the passengers saw the ferocious-looking protesters boycotting the establishment, the driver chose the better part of valor. He slowed enough to let the tourists take photos through the windows, then the bus roared off.

Stu ran after it, waving his hands. "Wait, wait! This is just part of the show—a slice of real life in the Unnatural Quarter!" He kept running. "Please!"

Then the guest of honor herself showed up, astonished to see her regulars there in a show of support. Francine put a hand up to her mouth as she read the signs. "All this, for me?"

"Just making our feelings known, Francine," I said. "The Goblin Tavern can't replace you."

Tears began pouring down her face. "I'm touched. I kinda hoped you might have a little going-away party for me, but . . . I never expected this." She sniffed, lowered her voice. "Do you think it'll do any good?"

To be honest, I wasn't sure Francine *wanted* her old job back, considering the corporate ownership, but she had worked for miserable bosses before. Ilgar the goblin had never been a model employer either.

Robin put an arm around the older woman's bony shoulders. "We're fighting for what's right, Francine. There are laws against workplace discrimination."

"Thank you, thank you all." She sounded choked up. "I don't know what else to say."

Stu came back, his shoulders slumped in despair at having failed to bring the promised customers in. Robin decided to make him even more dejected. "Francine, now that you're here to see this . . ." She marched up to the new manager of the Goblin Tavern. "Your bartender was fired without cause. Your no-humans-need-apply solicitation for replacement employees is blatantly discriminatory. On her behalf, I'm filing a wrongful termination suit against you, sir, as well as an antidiscrimination suit."

When she handed him a folded legal document, he looked as if she had just placed a rattlesnake in his hands. "But . . . I'm not the owner—I can't be sued!"

"You're the manager, you're named in the suit, so you're served. Just to be fair, we're also serving Missy Goodfellow and the entire Smile Syndicate board as co-defendants."

Stu looked as if someone had told him his birthday was canceled. He shuffled back into the Tavern and closed the door. I didn't doubt that he was going to pour himself a very large drink.

"I guess we'll need to find a new place to have a beer, McGoo," I said.

"Too bad. I really needed one tonight." McGoo seemed unduly troubled. During the commotion, I had not noticed his reticent expression, but now it was plain as day. He hadn't even tried to tell me a joke. Something was definitely wrong.

"Worse day than usual?"

"I might have to choose a new place for everything, Shamble. What would you think if I got transferred out of the Quarter? Promoted and sent to a new precinct, out among normal people?"

I blinked at him. "I'd say you were out of your mind. Who would ever promote *you*?" I meant it as a teasing comment, but it was also a stalling tactic while I tried to wrap my head around what he had said. "Are you serious?"

"Why is that so impossible? Think of all the recent successes I've had. My record's looking pretty good."

"Partly because we help each other. That's what friends are for, right?" I said. "How did you manage to be considered for a transfer?"

"It's Senator Balfour," he said, glum again. "He wants me to talk with him, use my inside knowledge to point out any scandals that'll make the Quarter look bad. Embarrassments, heinous crimes—anything that he can label an Unnatural Act. He wants to pick my brains."

Next to me, a sunken-eyed and ripe-smelling shambler perked up. "I'll pick your brains."

"Hey, do you mind? It's a private conversation!" The zombie shuffled off, and McGoo continued, "If he gets that law passed, Balfour wants to crack down like a giant hammer—and the vote's coming right up. If I help the senator gain a big victory, he promised to see that I'm reassigned to a human area."

The idea made me sick inside. I couldn't believe my friend would cooperate with such a vile man, but I also knew McGoo had no other chance at being transferred out of the precinct. He had never been happy with his assignment here.

"So what are you going to do?" I asked, afraid of how he would answer.

"After that bank robbery nonsense this afternoon, I was sorely tempted. But after much thought, I've decided that I like Senator Balfour even less than I like being here. I'll call the senator back and tell him to shove his offer up his ass—preferably with a wooden stake. He's going to have to find himself another patsy."

CHAPTER 33

At the All-Day/All-Nite Fitness Center, Tiffany had worked up a sweat—which was unusual for her. She wore a loose ash-gray sweat suit and a pink sweatband to push back her dark hair. She didn't use the cardio monitor, which was useless for a vampire anyway, but I could tell she was straining hard.

In my trips to the gym, she frequently intimidated me with her offhanded physical feats: the number of reps she performed, the amount of weight she lifted, how she could make the elliptical hum like a jet engine. I never attempted to keep up with her, merely tried to do enough of a workout so I didn't seem a complete wuss by comparison (and in that, too, I failed miserably).

I had a hard time maintaining a conversation while I was wheezing, though Tiffany never seemed out of breath. Tonight, she ran on the treadmill with the incline set to Everest mode, as fast as the motor would allow. She thundered along as if all the forces of Van Helsing were after her.

I took up the treadmill beside her. "Hi, Tiffany."

"Chambeaux," she acknowledged and then, as if to impress

me for some reason, she started to run even harder, intent on her workout.

Minding my own business, I looked up at the row of television sets mounted on the wall, half of which were tuned to competing news channels; one showed a women's gossip show that ran in the late hours (after the Big Uneasy, kaffeeklatsch chitchat programs were no longer the domain of early-morning TV). One set showed an old rerun of *The Munsters,* which seemed very quaint and nostalgic now. The good old days.

I selected a beginner's program, and the treadmill moved at shamble speed. I shuffled my legs to keep up, loosening my muscles. I was lucky to have received a top-notch embalming job, unlike the botched and amateurish process Jekyll had undergone; nevertheless, aches and pains came with the territory. Per Robin's suggestion, I had started taking glucosamine joint supplements, but I didn't notice any improvement. Once I got warmed up, I could move with a speed and dexterity close to my normal pre-death rate, but warming up was the tough part.

With a loud gasp of achievement, Tiffany ended her program, dropped the treadmill speed to cool-down rate, and caught her breath. Now she was ready for conversation. She turned and flashed her fangs at me. "You know, Chambeaux, Bill is definitely bad for me."

"What did he do?"

"Too much, far too much—and I don't dare ask him to stop." She patted her butt. "I've gained five pounds already. I'm not used to eating like that—I usually just grab a preserved blood pack from the fridge, but Bill plans some extravagant dinner every single day. My house is spotless, every dish is cleaned and put away within five minutes of when it hits the sink. He does the laundry daily, and he even irons my work shirts. *Irons* them, Shamble! I feel like a princess. He says it's only right to help me out, for everything I've done for him."

I nudged up the speed of the treadmill. "Sounds like criminal activity for sure. Should I have McGoo arrest him?"

"Not complaining, Chambeaux, and not ungrateful either, although maybe I should send him to work as an intern in *your* offices for a week, just to get even."

I chuckled, hoping she wasn't serious. "Golems are created to serve. They do whatever work they're told to do, and they take instruction well. If you don't want Bill to be such a busybody, then just tell him so." I looked down at the treadmill; I had gone an eighth of a mile already. Tiffany had just done five miles—at a full run. "In fact, give him some lite recipes, or have him watch healthy cooking shows. He can prepare meals that won't make you gain weight."

With a frown, Tiffany wiped sweat from her face. "Then they wouldn't taste so good. You should try some of the meals, Chambeaux. That golem's a gourmet cook—blood sausage, blood sauces with fresh-killed meat and fowl dishes . . . even blood oranges, though I told him that's just a variety name. I'll have you over for dinner sometime."

"The good food would be wasted on me. You could just tell Bill not to cook for you at all."

"No, I'm willing to put in a few extra hours at the gym to burn off the calories. It's worth it. Seriously, I'm more concerned because I think Bill's bored. He's used to working all the time, but I don't have enough for a full-time assistant, butler, and chef to do. He's not my slave."

"Maybe you should have let him take that security guard job," I suggested.

"I've got him applying for other positions as a night watchman. I gave him a glowing letter of recommendation, so let's hope he gets hired. Those other hundred golems flooded the job market."

She grabbed a towel, wiped her forehead, rubbed her armpits, and draped the towel around her neck before she headed toward the weight stations. I looked down: The treadmill said I had gone a quarter of a mile now. Making progress.

On the television, a news broadcast caught my attention—and my heart turned into a deader weight in my chest. Senator Rupert Balfour had summoned the media for a press conference. At the podium, as he lifted his long chin and began his important (to him at least) announcement, the other unnaturals in the fitness center stopped working out. Many booed or howled at the hated man.

"Ladies and gentlemen, humans all—I bring before you a tragic example of the evil to be found in the Unnatural Quarter, a clear indication of the danger these supernatural creatures pose to fine, *normal* people. You'll see why my Unnatural Acts Act is desperately needed to stop the depraved activities that tempt our good citizens."

I wondered what the senator was talking about now. Maybe too much caffeine in Transfusion's espresso? He had already done his best to shut down the adult novelty shop.

"Listen to the heartbreaking story of a poor injured man who has suffered abominably from the vile acts of these unnaturals. He nearly died from what they did to him, and he's here to tell you about his pain and suffering."

So, Balfour had found another patsy after McGoo had refused to cooperate with the senator in digging up dirt on the Unnatural Quarter. I stared at the screen in disbelief as Sheyenne's brother Travis stepped up to the podium. He appeared weak and forlorn, his eyes shadowed (it looked like makeup to me), and he spoke in a quavering voice. "An evil succubus nearly killed me. I survived only through the purest luck, and I've just now recovered enough to tell you the truth about what goes on there."

"Luck?" I yelled at the unresponsive TV. "*We* got you out of there! And it was a restorative spell that snapped you out of your coma."

Travis told a grossly embellished tale of the chamber of horrors that was the Full Moon brothel. He described vampire women luring naïve and innocent victims, like himself, into their sexual web, then he painted a ludicrous picture of the ferocious and demonic succubus who had nearly stolen his life force.

Sweet, waifish Ruth?

"I just stopped at the place to ask directions, and I barely got out alive," Travis lied. "Please, join me in calling for action to help Senator Balfour bring safety and justice back to society. We want the world restored to what it was—it's the only way humanity can survive. We can't mainstream the monsters. I urge you to support the senator in passing the Unnatural Acts Act. Thank you."

He wiped his eye to indicate tears, though I didn't see any on the screen. I wondered how much Balfour had paid him, and I feared that this "token innocent victim" might be the nudge those last fence-sitting senators needed to vote for his bill.

I canceled the treadmill program and got ready to go back to the office. I knew Sheyenne was going to be furious.

Chapter 34

Immediately after the news conference at which Travis told his shocking, and entirely fictional, story about being abused by a succubus at the Full Moon—which only increased the chill that normal people felt at the very thought of unnaturals having sex—Senator Balfour called a late-night vote behind closed doors and finally coerced enough senators to pass the Unnatural Acts Act.

Sheyenne was livid to learn of Travis's betrayal, and I had to calm her down before she plunged into a poltergeist fury. She hadn't seen her brother since storming out of his hospital room, and we all hoped not to see him again.

Without delay, Robin requested the complete text of the Unnatural Acts Act in order to study the new law, line by line. When the delivery service arrived at our office, a man in a dusty brown uniform wheeled in a handcart laden with a stack of paper four feet high, bound in a single yawning comb-clip.

"As ordered, ma'am." The delivery man wiped sweat from his face, turned his cap around, and handed Sheyenne a clipboard to sign. "One copy of the Unnatural Acts Act. Lots of reporters have requested them. You're lucky you got yours first."

I stared at the gigantic document. It would have taken me the better part of a year to read an *adventure novel* that long, and this was a piece of exceedingly dull legislation written in governmentese.

"I'm sure my brother studied every word before he supported the Act," Sheyenne said in an acid voice. Knowing Travis's role in Balfour's shady victory, she was fuming; I could almost hear all the foul names she was silently calling him.

Robin stared at the mountainous document in dismay. "There'll be job security for lawyers like me for some time to come."

Sale tables filled the alley in front of the Timeworn Treasures pawnshop, piled high with a random assortment of odds and ends. *Estate Auction: Everything Must Go!* Alice the gremlin had meticulously checked the price tags, marked some items down for a quick sale, then left the larger pieces for the auctioneer.

While Robin remained buried alive in the new legislation, I took spending money from the Chambeaux & Deyer accounts and went to the auction, dead set on purchasing Snazz's ledger book. McGoo had found no heart-and-soul listings at all, but I was convinced he'd missed something. I wanted to study every entry, looking for some sort of code the pawnbroker might have developed. I figured that others besides Jerry might want their bundles back.

I realized that the ledger would be advantageous in other cases as well, specifically because it would list who had pawned the theatrical company's props before burning down the stage. I had left messages to tell Shakespeare that the pieces had been found, but I hadn't been able to reach him—ghosts were often hard to track down, and he was busy rebuilding the stage for a comeback performance. Once the items were released from evidence, though, and available for reclaiming, I made sure the troupe knew about it. Several of the ghost actors had promised to come to the estate auction, where I suggested they could buy back their props for a song.

After the fire, Shakespeare in the Dark had received numerous donations, and a construction crew comprising both humans and ghosts had begun to rebuild the stage for a new production of *The Tempest*. The acting company promised to come back with a vengeance—not necessarily a good choice of words. I had seen numerous *Tempest* broadsides tacked up around the Quarter, most of them strategically placed over the top of Balfour's *You Are Damned!* flyers. I still hoped to prove his minions had been behind the arson.

Alice the gremlin had set up a cash box and metal folding chair at the front table. As customers paid cash for smaller items, she plucked off the price tags and took their money. Several wide-eyed human sightseers perused the titillating objects, picking up baubles or leafing through battered paperback copies of out-of-print spell books. The gullible tourists always paid full price without complaint; more seasoned residents of the Quarter tried to haggle, even though Alice rarely negotiated.

A troll expressed interest in the slightly used monkey's paw and argued price for five minutes. Alice wouldn't budge. "It's a hard-to-find item and very powerful."

"It's been used—there's not much left! One wish?" the troll said with a disparaging tone. "And these things are notorious for going wrong. It's not worth half of what you're asking."

Alice held the paw in her paws. "Look at the workmanship. It's an antiquity. You don't find these on a discount store shelf."

The troll took out a coin purse and opened it without letting Alice see how much money he had. "I just don't think it's worth that much. I really wish you'd bring your price down."

Both of them froze at what the troll had inadvertently said, staring at the monkey's paw as they waited for something terrible to happen. Alice quickly said, "Oh, all right. I'll take two dollars off, but that's my final offer."

"Two dollars?" the troll said. "Why would I want the thing now? You just used up the last wish."

"That wasn't the last wish. *I* was holding the paw, not you, and I'd already made up my mind to drop the price."

The troll did not look convinced, but he couldn't resist the reduction in price. He plucked out the appropriate number of ancient gold coins from his purse. "If this doesn't work, I'll be back wanting a refund."

She made a *tsking* sound through her pointed teeth and indicated a hand-lettered index card by the cash box: *All Sales Final*. Grumbling, the troll took the monkey's paw and went away.

One precocious young human boy picked up the pieces of a shattered amulet and studiously tried to line up the runes and put the amulet back together. In alarm, Alice scuttled over and swatted the pieces out of the boy's hands. "There, now—It's not a toy!" She found the boy's mother and scolded, "Please, control your obstreperous child." The alarmed parents whisked the kid away.

I spotted Sheyenne's pawned jewelry locked in a case for high-end items, but priced for immediate sale, not to go to auction. That was another important purchase I intended to make today, but first I had to get the ledger book.

Though harried, Alice looked pleased with the number of customers. Many of the items had already vanished from the quick-sale table. I waited while she finished a transaction, and she greeted me. "I want you to thank Ms. Deyer for moving so promptly on the paperwork. She's made this possible. I don't know how to express my gratitude . . . except by paying your bill, of course."

"You could thank me by letting me have a look at the ledger book," I said.

"It'll be the third item up once the auction starts. I think there'll be a lot of interest in that particular item," Alice said.

"Really? In a sales ledger?" I had already found the book on the auction table; its covers were held shut with a plastic security band.

"I sincerely hope you win it, Mr. Chambeaux. I'll be rooting for you."

"I just need to look at one entry. And you can still sell it afterward."

Alice was having none of it, though. "Moving on."

Two ghosts from the acting troupe, dressed in full Elizabethan costume, purchased the theater masks, props, and costumes. They seemed quite happy to have the items back.

"Oh, Mr. Chambeaux!" I turned to see Mavis Wannovich in her full black gown and pointed cap walking alongside her sister. "Alma and I came to see what bargains we could find, but I never pictured you as the sort to frequent yard sales."

"It's an estate sale," Alice corrected, closing the metal cash box.

"What's the difference?" I asked.

"Higher-quality debris."

Mavis sidled closer to me while Alma went over to snuffle at items on the various tables. "Next month we'll have a very nice restorative spell for you, but I'm glad we could help your friend in the hospital."

"He wasn't my friend," I said. Especially not after his latest stunt. "But thanks for helping him all the same. I knew I could count on you both."

The witch said, "We still need to chat about your work as a private eye, provide the gritty details for our ghostwriter, tell us about some interesting cases that you've wrapped up. I left a message with your receptionist yesterday—perhaps you didn't get it?"

"I haven't had a chance to call back," I said. "And Sheyenne had a particularly rough time last night. Family troubles. I've got a crazy caseload . . . but I will talk with you, I promise."

"A detective's life must be so exciting—shall we set up a time now?"

Before I could make an excuse, Alma snorted with excitement to get her sister's attention. The sow had put her trotters up on a table that held the large crystal ball in its birdbath-sized holder. "Ooh, what a wonderful crystal ball!" Mavis found the signature of the magician artisan at the bottom of the ornate holder. She turned to the gremlin. "What's the price?"

Alice hurried over to the table, sensing a sale. She talked at great length about the antique and magical quality of the item, while Mavis insisted that she was quite familiar with various models of crystal balls. They dickered, but closed the sale, and the witches went home, happy with their acquisition.

After a glance at an antique windup clock on one of the quick-sale tables, Alice declared it was time to start the auction.

She had hired a long-bearded wizard to conduct the process. He was well practiced in rattling off a dizzying stream of staccato syllables—a talent he had gained from years of mumbling incomprehensible spells and reading incantations backward— which made him a skilled auctioneer.

The higher-end patrons had already scoped out the large items, jotted notes, made phone calls, checked online listings, and subtly tried to guess which other customers might be their competitors for individual pieces.

The first item up for bid was a rusted iron maiden with a solid oak case; the sharpened tips supposedly still contained blood from victims of the Marquis de Sade, who was something of a folk hero in certain parts of the Quarter. The iron maiden came with a certificate of authenticity, although one of the bidders disputed the provenance (probably to diminish the bids), insisting that the style of the iron maiden firmly placed it in the period of the Spanish Inquisition, not the Marquis de Sade. A tall blond vampire, who looked more like a surfer than a bloodsucker, won the auction.

The second item was a plain-looking willow wand, said to contain great magical powers. Purportedly, the wand had been used by Merlin himself, although to me it looked like a switch that an old-fashioned schoolteacher would use for rapping the knuckles of unruly students.

The wizard auctioneer expected high opening bids, but did not get them, so he waxed poetic about the magic wand, describing in detail the numerous household uses a lucky bidder could find for it. When there were still no bids, his descriptions became more gushing, purple prose extending far into the ultraviolet. Still, no bids. In disappointment, he scratched his long gray beard and set the magic wand aside. "Very well, we shall come back to that one later."

When he pulled out the pawnbroker's ledger book, I shuffled closer to the front of the crowd.

"And here, we have a book . . . no spells inside, as far as I can tell. Just a list of items and numbers." He peered through his round spectacles at the words, then straightened. "Ah, it's the business records of the pawnshop! Hours of fascinating reading, I'm sure. A primary-source historical record for anyone who wishes to do research. Or . . ." He gave a goofy grin. "Do we have any tax auditors out there? This ledger could contain very interesting information."

The unnaturals hissed and grumbled, and the wizard auctioneer noticed that no one had laughed at his joke. The threat of a tax audit just wasn't funny.

"All right, then shall we start the bidding? Who's interested in this lovely ledger book?"

I raised my hand, offered a bid serious enough to scare away casual interest. "Fifty dollars. I'll take it." When I got my hands on that book, I could solve two cases in less than an hour.

"Ah, we have fifty dollars," the wizard said.

"I'll take it for a hundred," said another voice in the back.

I turned, as did many of the other unnaturals. I was astonished to see Missy Goodfellow's assistant, Angela Drake. "A hundred," she repeated.

"That doubles the bid—one hundred, from the young woman in the back." The wizard picked up the willow wand beside his podium and pointed toward Angela. The unnaturals dove aside just in case the wand misfired . . . but it emitted not even a spark of magic.

"One fifty," I said. Angela had discreetly gone in and out of the pawnshop during the tumult of Senator Balfour's street protest; I wondered why in the world she would want the ledger. Possibilities occurred to me in waves.

I did not like the way Missy Goodfellow conducted business. What if the Smile Syndicate was using the pawnshop for moving stolen merchandise, or as a front for drug operations— even selling illegal souvenirs? No telling what else I could find in the ledger. It might be a gold mine. Now I wanted it even more than before.

Angela looked at me as if I were a rank amateur. She glanced at her watch. "My time is worth more than this dickering. Five hundred for the ledger book."

The unnaturals gasped, and I let out an involuntary groan. Five hundred dollars? To solve one pro bono case and an arson case for which the ghostly client might or might not be able to pay? There must be something very important in that book. I needed to have it.

"Seven fifty," I said. Sheyenne and Robin would both be

horrified, but from the look on Angela's face, I knew she would never let the item go.

"A thousand," she said with barely a second's hesitation.

I decided to let her have the ledger. I guess I'd have to solve the cases some other way—but I'm a detective; that's what I do.

The wizard waved the useless wand again. "Sold! To the woman in back."

Angela produced a wad of bills and paid in cash so she could take the ledger book with her immediately. I thought about offering her a hundred dollars just for a quick look at the entries, but Angela would never go for that.

She walked past me, cradling the book close to her chest, and said with a sniff, "No need to air dirty laundry outside of the family." Now I knew the Smile Syndicate was doing something underhanded.

I tried to accept defeat with good grace, though I don't think I managed it.

So as not to go away completely empty-handed, I used the money to purchase Sheyenne's jewelry. That made me feel good, a gesture I had to make for her, though I doubted it would quench her anger toward her brother.

CHAPTER 35

Once Robin started applying pressure on behalf of the Pattersons, she became an absolute pit bull. She did not include Harvey Jekyll's case in her remarks or filings, deciding her best strategy was to achieve a victory with the *likable* couple first before she muddied the swamp.

In only a few days, Robin had filed an anti-discrimination complaint, sent out press releases, and generated a fair amount of publicity (and sympathy) for the Pattersons. Not only did the mortgage bank agree to review the previously declined application, but in a remarkably quick turnaround they relented and offered a loan with an expedited closing date, since the couple had been trying to purchase their dream home for months now.

The homeowners' association held an emergency meeting so that Walter and Judy Patterson could present impassioned pleas, expressing their desire to have a nice, quiet life in a nice, quiet neighborhood. Sitting with her clients and smiling, Robin followed their statement with, "Walter and Judy Patterson are such a nice couple. Don't you think they'll make good witnesses in a discrimination lawsuit?"

Apparently agreeing, the homeowners' association withdrew their bogus objections to having a werewolf and vampire couple in the neighborhood; they also paid a monetary concession to get the couple to drop their case—not a huge settlement, but enough to cover most of the Pattersons' moving expenses.

Delighted, Robin told them to pack up the moving van for their home sweet home. I think, deep in her heart, Robin would have preferred to fight the case all the way, just to establish a legal precedent. However, she could still reference it as an example in her similar fight for Jekyll's rights.

"Dan, you're coming with me. The Pattersons and their moving van are heading off to the house, and we should be there for moral support. I've already alerted the local police and requested protection or crowd control if necessary." She glanced out at the dingy buildings of the Unnatural Quarter. "Things might get ugly out there."

We took Robin's battered Pro Bono Mobile to Meadow Shadows, the quaint subdivision where the Pattersons had bought their dream home. As our car puttered along, gasping and wheezing like an asthmatic mummy, I wasn't convinced we would make it out to the subdivision. We had to park two blocks away because of the growing crowds.

The cul-de-sac was already a circus of reporters and policemen (who weren't necessarily supporters of unnatural rights). Since Meadow Shadows was outside the Quarter, McGoo had been unable to help us.

Tiffany agreed to show up as a concerned citizen, accompanied by Bill (maybe as practice for his security job applications). Their presence was something, at least, but not an overwhelming show of support. Harvey Jekyll and his bodyguard Larry arrived incognito, to see what sort of difficulties he might face once he moved out to the suburbs. They hung at the edges of the crowd.

Robin and I made our way to the nice ranch house just as the moving van arrived with Walter and Judy Patterson and all their possessions.

Emboldened by the recent legislative victory, ten of Senator Balfour's moronic minions were picketing with their GOD HATES UNATURALS and KEEP THE FILTH IN THE SOUWER signs. They formed a human cordon across the road to block the moving van, but the police herded them aside long enough for the truck to drive through before the cordon re-formed, now preventing the van from leaving the cul-de-sac. That might have made the situation even worse, I thought.

Robin and I pushed our way forward to meet the married couple as they swung down from the cab. Mr. and Mrs. Patterson wore work clothes, ready to haul boxes inside and set up their household, but they cringed from the howls, insults, and catcalls that came from the angry crowd.

Robin turned to shout at the spectators. "This couple has every right to live here. Shame on you all."

"Shame on *you!*" said one of Senator Balfour's supporters. "God hates unnaturals, but He loves Meadow Shadows subdivision!"

"Go home!" yelled someone else.

Judy Patterson took her vampire husband's hand, lifted her snout, and faced the angry mob. "We *are* home!" Although she wanted to bare her fangs and claws while her husband glamoured them all, Robin had advised the Pattersons to take the high road. They spoke with respect instead of anger, and the media recorded every bit of it.

Mrs. Patterson gestured toward the house with a furry hand. "We'll pay property taxes, we'll maintain the landscaping, and we'll do everything we can to be good neighbors."

Mr. Patterson added, "This has long been a dream of ours.

My wife and I are very happy to be living together in our new home."

A small number of spectators applauded; a large number didn't. As soon as the Pattersons opened the front door, a professional-looking man in a black business suit and narrow tie stepped up the sidewalk to meet them. The guy-in-tie handed over a folded sheaf of papers. "Mr. and Mrs. Patterson, consider yourselves served. You are hereby in violation of the Unnatural Acts Act. This is a summons with charges pending. Senator Balfour intends to see that this matter is prosecuted to the fullest extent. Our legal teams are already preparing their briefs."

"Violation?" Judy Patterson said. "What violation?"

Robin took the summons from him, unfolded the papers. "This is ridiculous! They're just moving into a house. They've qualified for a mortgage, and they have just as much right to be here as anyone else."

"No, I'm afraid they do not," said the guy-in-tie. "The Unnatural Acts Act makes it patently illegal for any person to 'live with an unnatural in a conjugal manner,' and they just publicly admitted to doing so."

"But we're married!" said Mr. Patterson.

The business-suited man cleared his throat. "According to the Act, your marriage is not recognized either, because marriage is specifically defined as one *human* man and one *human* woman."

The spectators began to shout and howl. The guy-in-tie turned away, walked down the sidewalk, and melted into the crowd.

Tears rolled down the fur on Mrs. Patterson's face. "It's like a stake through my heart," Mr. Patterson said.

"Don't you worry," Robin said, then yelled for the media. "I plan to fight this—just as I fought to get the sweatshop golems freed, and as I'm fighting discrimination against the *human* bartender at the Goblin Tavern!"

The police dispersed the crowd, and I noticed that Harvey Jekyll had slunk away with his werewolf bodyguard shouldering spectators aside.

Tiffany and Bill tried to cheer the Pattersons by pitching in to unload the moving van, but it didn't help much. We all carried boxes inside, hoping to encourage the unnatural couple, and eventually, as Mrs. Patterson unpacked the kitchen utensils, the protesters got bored and drifted away.

CHAPTER 36

After his bank robbery stunt, the ghost of Alphonse Wheeler did not want to await his trial or sentencing. In fact, he didn't even bother to hear the formal charges; Wheeler volunteered to pay his debt to society, promised he would save the taxpayers the legal costs of a drawn-out courtroom trial, and surrendered himself for voluntary imprisonment.

Realistically, for ghosts, all imprisonment is voluntary, but even so it was a nice gesture.

The penal system worked tirelessly to improve methods of spectral incarceration. While effective lockup methods had been instituted for garden-variety unnaturals such as zombies, vampires, and werewolves (both the monthly and the full-time types), criminal poltergeists and convicted ghosts posed the biggest hazard. Mediums and exorcists offered stopgap spirit-containment measures, but most of those didn't work.

With the momentum of his Unnatural Acts Act, Senator Balfour had announced that solving the ghost-felon problem was his next crusade, advocating that the only punishment a ghost criminal deserved was a clean and straightforward disin-

tegration, an eternal death sentence. He had already commissioned numerous ectoplasmic defibrillators from Harvey Jekyll
and was ready to use them.

"It is the only compassionate method," Balfour had said,
not sounding the least bit compassionate. "We're helping those
troubled ghosts go to the light."

Wheeler did not contest the fact he had committed a crime
and needed to be punished. He promised to remain inside the
jail for whatever sentence the judge decided to impose, provided it wasn't eternity.

When Robin, Sheyenne, and I visited him in prison, Wheeler
seemed comfortable and right at home, far less anxious than
when we'd first met him in our offices. His ghost now manifested with a prison uniform instead of his checkered jacket. He
liked the familiarity of incarceration and said he looked forward to making new friends.

"I'm sure you'll fit in, Mr. Wheeler," Robin said, as we sat
across from him at a plain metal table in the community room.

Muted conversations blurred together at other tables. I saw
a vampire woman holding hands with a convicted vampire
felon, telling him that their request for conjugal visits had been
denied.

A werewolf raised his voice, pounding his fists on a table.
"But if they're not twelve *werewolves,* then it's not a jury of my
peers!" His public defender cringed and told his client to calm
down.

A bored and skeptical attorney took notes as a zombie covered with gangbanger tattoos insisted, "I swear, I just found the
stuff! It wasn't mine! I was going to give it to charity." He
glanced over at Alphonse Wheeler. The translucent robber gave
him a thumbs-up. "Yeah," the gangbanger zombie continued,
"I was going to donate it to MLDW so they can keep doing
good work."

These were the cases we *didn't* take on at Chambeaux & Deyer.

Wheeler leaned closer to us and said, "I want MLDW's resources to go toward helping people like that. As for me, I'm in here for the duration . . . unless I decide to escape. Wouldn't that be exciting? Alphonse Wheeler, legendary bank robber, in a great prison break?"

"It's not all that exciting if you can just walk through the walls anytime you like, Mr. Wheeler," I pointed out.

"Don't take all the fun out of it for me." He leaned back in his chair. "Let me get serious for a moment. You've helped me, and I want to return the favor. Now that we're here, with no one eavesdropping, I should warn you. . . ."

Robin, Sheyenne, and I gave him our full attention. When a ghost feels the need to deliver a dire warning, it's a good idea to listen.

"Word gets around the Quarter—I know the cases you're working on, the sweatshop golems you freed, the antidiscrimination suit against the Smile Syndicate and the Goblin Tavern, the murder of the pawnshop gremlin. I even heard you bid against Missy Goodfellow's assistant at the estate auction, and before that you stopped by Smile HQ to talk with Missy?"

"Just introducing myself," I said.

He narrowed his eyes. "You don't know the can of worms you've opened. Who do you think I used to work for in the old days? I robbed banks and gave half of my money to Oswald Goodfellow just to keep him happy." He looked intently at all three of us. "The Smile Syndicate might have a pretty logo and a cute name now, but trust me—they're still the mob. Don't let Missy Goodfellow's sweet face fool you."

I pictured the cold ice queen with the dyed goldenrod hair. "I never actually thought of her face as *sweet.*"

Wheeler rested his elbows on the table, though he miscalculated and sank partly through. "Believe me, the Smile Syndicate is filled with the sort of people who have kitten-drowning contests and wear coats made of baby seal pelts."

Robin gasped. "Monsters!"

Wheeler shook his head. "No, just humans."

The guard informed us that the visit was over, and we rose from our chairs. Wheeler drifted up, ready to be escorted back to his cell, and he lowered his voice to say one last thing. "Don't tell Missy I warned you. I may be here in prison, but that doesn't mean I can't get shanked—if anybody figures out how to do it."

"We'll keep your advice in mind, Mr. Wheeler," I said.

Thinking of the sinister harassment Neffi had encountered at the Full Moon—the threats, the broken black-glass windows, the smashed cat sarcophagi—I wondered if the Smile Syndicate was trying to move into more unnatural activities than the Goblin Tavern and kitschy souvenir shops. I definitely wasn't smiling at the thought.

CHAPTER 37

I found myself heading back to the Full Moon again, although this time my reasons weren't quite as clear cut, certainly nothing that would have convinced Sheyenne. I told myself that many threads of current cases tangled in and around the brothel, and if I were to dig through Neffi's client records, I would find clues to various mysteries. (At the very least, the information would be fascinating.)

My main reason for going there, though, was to check on the sad succubus whose life seemed to be falling apart. I wanted to make sure Ruth was all right, to see if she had found alternative employment. I tried to tell myself she wasn't my problem—I barely even knew her—but I wanted to take her under my wing, see that she lived happily ever after. *Somebody* deserved that.

My feelings were altruistic. I was just being an upstanding citizen, a Good Samaritan. Nothing wrong with that. I was convinced I hadn't been the target of some kind of succubus glamour.

Probably not, at least.

It wasn't the sort of problem I could discuss with Spooky.

When the golem doorman led me into the parlor, the languid negligee-clad ladies called me by name—which, in itself, was not a good sign, a reminder of how frequently I stopped by. I told myself it was all business, only business. Neffi's office door was partially closed, and the unwrapped mummy madam pored over her ledger books; file drawers were open as she added up her accounts. She had been glum ever since the vandals smashed the sarcophagi that preserved two of her mummified cats.

Cinnamon was doing her nails; I didn't see either of the zombie girls, but one of the upstairs doors was closed. Heavy shuffling sounds came from the room; Aubrey and Savannah were either rearranging furniture or engaged with a very large client, and I didn't want to know which.

"I'm here to see Ruth," I said.

"My, aren't you the brave man after what happened?" The werewolf kept filing away with an emery board.

"Not like that. Just worried about her."

"You're sweet on that succubus, I think," said the raven-haired vampire princess. "No need to feel embarrassed, especially not here. We're very discreet."

If my feelings were that obvious, maybe I was fooling myself after all.

"He sees her as much as Wheeler's ghost used to," said Hemlock.

"Wheeler is in jail now," I said.

"For as long as he wants to be." Nightshade tittered. "For now, she's all yours. Ruth!"

"That's not what I meant," I said, embarrassed. Fortunately, having embalming fluid instead of blood makes the flush hard to see.

The green-eyed succubus came shyly out from a back room

and smiled at me. "I was just packing up my things, Dan. Time to be moving on . . . though I don't have any place to go."

Hearing our voices, Neffi emerged from the office, crossed her sticklike arms over her chest. "Unless you've come to tell me about the case, I'm going to have to start charging you for your time with Ruth." Her face looked even more pinched than usual, although I doubted anyone else would have noticed. "She's not earning us any money."

Ruth looked deeply hurt, and I felt the need to come to her defense. "I can solve the problem if I get more information." I tried to sound as professional as possible. "I'll see if Irwyn Goodfellow can help Ruth. He found jobs for all the liberated golems."

"Yes, he did," said Mike, the doorman golem.

I smiled at Neffi. "But I don't know Ruth's job qualifications . . . other than being a succubus, I mean. And there's not much of a market for that these days."

"Not anymore," Neffi agreed. "And I've got nothing personal against her. I just can't afford the insurance anymore. With a succubus on staff, my premiums hit the stratosphere. Go ahead, see what you can do—but don't take too long." She went back into her office and closed the door.

Ruth had taken a seat on one of the red velvet lounges. She pressed her knees together, folded her hands primly on top of them, and gazed at me. "Some people think it's enjoyable to be a female avatar of sexual desire, libido incarnate." She sniffled. "But it's not as much fun as you might think, considering the cost. Vampires suck the energy out of their victims, too." She gestured to the two voluptuous undead princesses. "But they can restrain themselves."

Nightshade spread her lips and tapped a forefinger on her long white fangs. "Precision tools, that's what these are."

"Maybe I should just go find a nunnery somewhere," Ruth said.

Cinnamon barked a laugh. "That wouldn't solve the problem—a place filled with sexually repressed virgins? Libido is libido."

"You're probably right." Ruth sighed. "I really like flowers. I'd like to work in a florist's shop, but everything withers when I touch it."

I wondered what I was doing. I felt myself weakening. If I looked at Ruth's sad face any longer, I might end up inviting her to move into my spare room above the Chambeaux & Deyer offices, and that would not be a good idea, no matter how innocent my intentions. Not a good idea at all.

Suddenly I felt awkward and needed to leave. "I'll, uh, bring it up with Mr. Goodfellow the next time I speak with him. Keep your chin up. We'll figure something out." I hurried out the door without saying goodbye.

The moment I got back to our second-floor offices and planted myself behind the desk to study case files with a great deal of feigned attention, Sheyenne knew exactly where I had been. Maybe she could smell some lingering incense from the brothel lobby or a recognizable perfume used by one of the ladies. More likely, she could read the guilty expression on my face.

She drifted in front of me, beautiful, blond, and translucent—all I had ever wanted, and I wanted her more now that I could never touch her again. What was I doing?

Sheyenne wasn't angry. She didn't argue with me. . . . I could have handled that. No, she looked *hurt,* and that was far worse. "You're spending a lot of time at the Full Moon—more than you spend on any of our other pending cases."

"There's a lot going on, Spooky. I just needed—"

"Beaux, come on. I'm not a kid. I've been through a lot, being poisoned to death and all. You and I can't pretend that we've got a normal relationship, or that it will ever be normal again." I saw her shudder, which, in the ghost, manifested itself as a flicker in her image. "I know that even dead men have needs. Maybe you should go visit one of the girls at the Full Moon, get it out of your system. I'll always be here."

"It's not what you think," I insisted, then realized that I was insisting too loudly and too quickly.

She continued. "If not that cute little redhead succubus, then one of the zombie girls must be your type? Or a vampire?"

"Honest, I'm not tempted," I said. "It's strictly business."

All men have found themselves faced with choices, knowing that absolutely none of the choices is the right one. It's the lady or the tiger—except the lady has a submachine gun and the tiger has rabies. This was one of those situations.

Fortunately, Alice the gremlin walked through the office door at that precise moment—and ended up costing us hundreds of dollars. I couldn't have been more relieved.

Snazz's sister still wore her frumpy housedress, clutched the small purse in front of her, and was cool and professional. She had applied too much lipstick and wore perfume that smelled a lot like mothballs.

With a silent sigh, Sheyenne drifted back to her desk as I went to meet the gremlin's sister. A gulf of unfinished business hung in the air between us, but Alice didn't seem to notice. Under her furry right arm, she had tucked a plain black ledger book.

"You may be interested in a discovery I made, Mr. Chambeaux." She set her purse on the corner of Sheyenne's desk, then held out the black ledger. "While cleaning the pawnshop to rent to a new customer, I discovered loose floorboards under the front display case. I should have known to look there ahead of time. Snazz always had a hiding place for his furry porno magazines when he was younger. I found a second ledger, one that appears to record all transactions." She opened the cover. "I know how much you wanted to have the other one. If you match the final bid, I can sell you this alternate copy."

She had my full attention now, but she wouldn't let me touch the book.

"Missy Goodfellow's assistant already bought the original ledger," I said.

"My brother kept two sets of books, one for show and one with the real information. Standard shady business practice. I have every reason to believe that *this* is the accurate record."

I wasn't surprised. In fact, after working for the Smile Syndicate, Angela Drake should have known that questionable businesses kept two sets of books.

"I believe the bid was for a thousand dollars, Mr. Chambeaux?" Alice said, her eyes twinkling.

I felt a heaviness in my chest.

"That was never a serious bid, Alice. I was just provoking Angela into raising her price. I can go back to the"—I swallowed hard—"seven fifty that I offered, since I no longer have exclusive access to the information."

"Seven fifty was not the final bid, Mr. Chambeaux."

Sheyenne interrupted. "Mr. Chambeaux already made you hundreds more by bidding against Angela Drake. He inflated the price you received, and this money is just gravy. Five hundred is all we're willing to pay. Since the auction, we've made great progress in solving these pending cases, and any information in the ledger is no longer as relevant as it was. In fact, in another few days we're likely to solve the cases, and then we won't need the ledger at all."

"But this book contains the correct and accurate information!" Alice insisted, sounding flustered at Sheyenne's tough negotiation.

"Moving on," Sheyenne said sweetly. "Do you want the five hundred or not?"

I definitely wanted to see the information there, but I tried not to show my excitement. Sheyenne, fortunately, was a better and tougher haggler.

"Very well," Alice said. "That amount will allow me to upgrade my cabin on the cruise."

"I'll write you a check," Sheyenne said.

After the gremlin sister headed off to the Trove National Bank to cash the check, I picked up the black ledger and let out a long sigh. I said, with all the sincerity I possessed, "I don't know what I'd do without you, Spooky."

She took the ledger book out of my hands. "I'll go over this and analyze the information. I'm good at details like that." She looked at me with her spectral blue eyes. "And you just keep thinking about how much you need me."

CHAPTER 38

When Mavis Wannovich called, Sheyenne acted as the moat dragon. She covered the phone with her insubstantial hand, which I wasn't sure would muffle the sound. "Beaux, Mavis wants to come into the offices and talk with you in person. She sounds insistent."

Just then, Francine burst through the door, grinning and frenetic with energy, puffing a long cigarette. "Wait until you hear what just happened!" She took a quick drag. "I got my job back! Stu said I could be his bartender again! He even brought me flowers, a box of chocolates, and a carton of my favorite cigarettes."

I said to Sheyenne, "Please tell Mavis I've got another client right now, but I'll be in touch—honest." Mavis was probably getting anxious for her vampire ghostwriter to get started on the Shamble & Die Penny Dreadful detective novel. "I promise she can have all the time she needs, but it'll be a few days."

As Francine danced with far more exhilaration than I had ever seen her show, Robin cautioned, "I hope you didn't agree to anything in writing. The Smile Syndicate is trying to butter you up so that you'll drop the charges."

Francine was not allowing any rain on her parade. "Stu did butter me up. That's all I wanted—to be appreciated."

"Your customers appreciated you, Francine," I said. "You're the best bartender we ever had."

She reached out to pat my cold hand. "I know you appreciated me, dear. That show of support was the most touching thing I ever experienced—but it didn't make me vindictive against the Goblin Tavern, just made me want my job back even more."

Robin was feisty, crossing her arms over her chest. "Not good enough. We can still go after them for punitive damages. The Smile Syndicate caused you emotional distress, and there's the few days of lost wages. And tips! Discrimination against humans by humans is just as bad as people who are prejudiced against unnaturals. We can set a precedent."

Francine finished her cigarette with a long drag. "Thank you for everything you've done, Ms. Deyer. Your passion makes me short of breath!" She coughed twice and looked around for an ashtray. "But I've got what I want, I really do. Stu offered me a raise, covered my back wages, called the whole misunderstanding a 'paid leave of absence.' I'll be back behind the bar tonight. He does want me to wear a new outfit, a black dress and a cobwebby hat, so I fit in better. He's trying for some sort of Elvira look. Maybe the customers will believe I'm a zombie after all."

"But we can fight this further!" Robin said.

Francine continued to look uncomfortable, but Robin was blinded by moral outrage, so I had to intervene. "We have a satisfied client, Robin. Our efforts got Francine her job back. She doesn't want to change the whole world. It's okay to take the win and do a victory dance."

Robin drew a deep breath, calmed herself. "I'm sorry, Francine.

I've just spent the past two days reading that heinous Unnatural Acts Act, and it makes my blood boil. I'll have plenty of fights coming up." Her expression softened. "I'm very happy for you, Francine. Congratulations on getting your job back."

"McGoo and I will see you tonight, Francine," I said. "I promise."

"The first round is on the house!"

Robin went back to her office to keep working on multiple challenges to Senator Balfour's Act. She had been up all night reading through the mountain of obtuse legal language, writing new notes for every offensive paragraph she found. Without too much trouble, she had tracked down unnaturals willing to serve as examples of specific individuals who would be harmed by certain provisions in the Unnatural Acts Act, so that she had legal standing in her efforts. She had already filed eleven separate suits, and she'd only just finished going through the preamble.

Robin did secure an injunction that allowed the Pattersons to stay in their suburban house, pending the outcome of her challenge to the charges filed against the couple for "living together in a conjugal manner." By extension, Robin was also demanding the right of her client Harvey Jekyll to move into the neighborhood of his choosing. Fortunately for Jekyll—in a legal sense at least—he was not involved in any sort of romantic relationship, natural or unnatural.

Sheyenne, meanwhile, reviewed the new black ledger book from Timeworn Treasures. Using a wooden ruler, she went down the columns of entries, sales figures, and names. McGoo hadn't found any relevant listing in the "public" copy of the accounts, but I felt the right information might be in this book.

When Sheyenne looked up, she wore a strange expression on her translucent face. "You'll want to see this, Beaux. Just found the notation for the Shakespeare theatrical props."

"Maybe we can wrap up that case," I said. "Who's the thief?"

"We can't guarantee he's a 'thief,' " Sheyenne said, "but he is the person who pawned all the props." She touched the line. I leaned over to see the printed entry:

Wm. Shakespeare (Ghost)

"He pawned his own props?" I said. "Well, that raises a few suspicions."

"Look at the date. Not only did he pawn the masks, wardrobe, and props—he did it the day *after* the fire."

Since other cases had been popping lately, I hadn't been giving Shakespeare daily progress reports, but he wasn't exactly pestering me for results, either. In fact, he'd dodged my last attempts to contact him. I had assumed the troupe was busy preparing for the *Tempest* production.

The ghostly actors rehearsed their lines daily, and Shakespeare had advertised widely for an unnatural guest actor to play the part of Caliban. From what I'd heard, he had plenty of auditions—too many—but he finally settled on an appropriately large thespian ogre. Thanks to publicity generated by the fire that burned down their stage, the troupe would have a large crowd for their comeback performance, including many supportive ghosts.

Now, however, I knew Shakespeare had been far from honest with me, and that pissed me off. Being a private investigator was enough of a challenge under normal circumstances; I didn't need my own clients to make a job more difficult. It happened all too often.

Fuming, I grabbed my fedora and jacket. "I'm going to have a few words with Mr. Shakespeare out at the Greenlawn Cemetery." Then I turned back to Sheyenne. "Good catch, Spooky. Thanks for finding that."

She had flipped to a different page in the ledger book, and

she had a glow of excitement about her. "Oh, you don't want to leave just yet—this may be even more important."

She had discovered the entry for Jerry the zombie's heart and soul, with a special asterisk by it. Then other lines, similarly starred, on previous pages. "Heart-and-soul combo packs were a hot item at Timeworn Treasures, just as Snazz said. More than twenty bundles sold." She paused. "And all of them purchased by the same person."

Sheyenne closed the black ledger book with finality, making her announcement as if she were a cinematic detective announcing the solution to a case. "It was Angela Drake—using Smile Syndicate funds."

CHAPTER 39

Shakespeare's ghost could wait—I knew where to find him and his acting troupe, and I could pose my questions later. Instead, I was off to Smile HQ to have a few words with Missy Goodfellow's assistant.

The headquarters building was clean, modern, and professional-looking, completely aboveboard and respectable; it looked like any other office complex. No doubt, Missy's accountants filed the proper (or at least proper-looking) tax forms, permits, and annual reports.

I might have thought Angela was buying up hearts and souls for her own private collection—a strange hobby, but who am I to judge? However, Snazz had deliberately indicated that they were purchased with Smile Syndicate funds. I intended to get some answers.

Admittedly, I didn't present the most professional appearance when I passed through the sparkling glass and metal doors. I'd had a rough few days: My jacket was rumpled, and I was due for another freshening-up at the embalming parlor. Before Missy's assistant could throw me out, I intended to hit her with my discovery—and then we'd have an entirely different type of conversation.

But Angela Drake wasn't at the front reception desk.

Instead, I saw a harried-looking older woman with short curly hair, large out-of-style glasses, and a timid attitude toward her computer that made me think she still considered it a "newfangled thing." She flinched as I came forward. I don't know if she was overwhelmed by the job or reacting to my undead status.

The phone rang and she seized it, hunted and pecked around the switchboard buttons until she found a blinking light to poke, and said, "Smile Syndicate, how may I make your day a sunny one?" At least she had memorized the right greeting. "No, I'm afraid our lightbulb supply is in perfect order, but I will leave a message for Ms. Goodfellow in case we desire to upgrade."

After she hung up, the receptionist turned to me and forced a smile, but she seemed out of practice. "How may I help you . . . sir?"

"Where's Angela Drake? I'd like to speak with her."

"I'm sorry, sir. Ms. Drake is . . . no longer with us."

Since Alphonse Wheeler had warned us about the nefarious activities of the Smile Syndicate, I suddenly imagined that Angela had been murdered, her body hidden, the evidence covered up so she couldn't reveal the information she knew. "What happened to her? Is she dead?"

The older woman flushed. "No, sir! She simply left the company. I'm just a temp, filling in for the interim."

The phone rang again, and she grabbed it as if it were the cavalry coming to her rescue. "Smile Syndicate, how may I make your day a sunny one?"

I stood there, unmoving—*looming*, you might say. It made the receptionist nervous, but that wasn't a bad thing. I waited as she made clumsy chitchat with the unsolicited caller until finally the person on the other end hung up. She turned back to me. I hadn't moved, but now I leaned closer. She tried admirably not to wince or draw back, clearly afraid that her nostrils might be assaulted by a wave of stench from the grave, but I had taken care of my basic hygiene duties. If anything, I smelled like fresh-as-spring soap.

"I need to talk with Angela," I repeated. "Where can I find her?"

"I . . . I wouldn't know, sir. And I'm not allowed to give out former employee information."

"Then I'd like to see Missy Goodfellow."

The temp stammered, and a voice interrupted me from a side doorway I hadn't even heard open. "There's nothing we can help you with, Mr. Chambeaux." If anything, Missy's hair was even more shockingly yellow than the first time I'd seen her. Her pantsuit was so dazzlingly white it reminded me of a toothpaste ad.

"I need to ask Angela a few questions. It's for an interesting case."

"All of your cases are interesting to you, I'm sure, but Angela is unavailable. She's been transferred to Tasmania and is quite out of touch. She has gone to work in a wilderness sanctuary for the devils."

"Convenient," I said.

"It was her life's dream." Missy's smile was so brittle that it would have broken into a thousand pieces if she'd sneezed.

"Not a very traditional dream," I said.

"Angela was not a traditional woman. And I'm afraid I cannot help you, either."

"I haven't even asked my questions yet."

"I wasn't going to encourage you, due to my complete lack of interest."

"We could talk about it over lunch," I said. Looking at her pristine, spotless white pantsuit, I suggested, "I know a place that serves all-you-can-eat barbecue ribs."

"No, thank you, Mr. Chambeaux. I don't eat red meat. And I don't dine with corpses."

Time to make her more uncomfortable. "It's about purchases made at the Timeworn Treasures pawnshop. The sales records indicate that your assistant used Smile Syndicate money to buy numerous heart-and-soul bundle packs, including one that belongs to a zombie named Jerry, who is my client."

Now Missy looked disturbed. "I'm quite certain you have no proof of that."

Not exactly the outright denial I had expected from her. "I'm quite certain I do. Angela acquired one set of the pawnshop books during the liquidation auction, but I've obtained the second set—the *accurate* one."

A dark cloud crossed Missy's expression. The phone rang again, and the receptionist was so intent on listening to our discussion that she didn't think to answer it for three rings. Missy glared at her, and she scrabbled for the phone.

"I should have known that gremlin would keep two sets of books. It's standard business practice, after all."

"Not in my business," I said.

Missy gave me a withering look. No sunshine there. "Any *serious* business, Mr. Chambeaux. But as I said previously and repeatedly, I'm afraid I cannot help you. I don't have the hearts and souls you're after."

I put a light tone into my voice. "Then I'll just have to keep digging."

"Be careful it doesn't turn out to be your own grave."

"Been there, done that," I said.

"I have nothing to hide, Mr. Chambeaux," Missy insisted. "Now I have to get back to work." She turned back to the door that led to the inner sanctum of offices. At the last moment, she remembered to add, "I hope your day is a sunny one."

CHAPTER 40

Since I hadn't gotten anywhere with the Smile Syndicate, I headed back to the Unnatural Quarter to track down the ghost who called himself Shakespeare. On the way, I received a call from the real estate offices at the Greenlawn Cemetery. "While you're out and around, Mr. Chambeaux, could you please stop by the crypt? I'd like to show you something."

I envisioned a binder filled with snapshots of rental properties, attractive alternative offices for Chambeaux & Deyer Investigations. Edgar Allan the troll didn't seem to understand that we liked our somewhat seedy digs in the somewhat seedy part of town. Location, location, location.

"We're not in the market for acquiring property right now, Mr. Allan."

"I'm not always about work, you know," said the troll in his thin voice. "You asked me to contact you if I had any further information about the arson here in the cemetery."

Well, better late than never! "You said you didn't see anything."

232 / Kevin J. Anderson

"*I* didn't, but Burt did. He often roams the grounds late at night."

"I was already on my way over," I said. "I'll be there in a few minutes." Before I confronted Shakespeare, I wanted to gather as much information as possible.

Inside the vacant stone crypt, the troll and his burly assistant were waiting for me. Burt had a stack of For Rent and For Sale signs, along with the logo of the real estate agency. "Cheerful service—alive or dead!"

"Ah, there you are! Perfect timing." The real estate agent rubbed his hands together as he stood up from his desk. "Burt was just about to go out and mark a few properties. Would you like to join him? You could chat on the way . . . and have a look at the options while you're at it. It wouldn't hurt to see what's available. No obligation."

"Maybe some other time—I have another appointment here in the cemetery," I said. "What exactly did you see on the night of the fire, Burt?"

With a voice as thick as hardening epoxy, Burt the evictions specialist said, "I like to walk the cemetery grounds at night. Clears my head."

I didn't know how much Burt had in his head that needed clearing. "You mean, like a security guard? Does Greenlawn pay you for that?" Maybe I could get a job application for Bill the golem.

"Neighborhood watch," Burt said as we stepped outside the office crypt. "I like fire, and I wasn't far from the theater stage when I noticed the first flames. I saw who lit it, but he vanished before I could catch him."

"Burt doesn't usually let people get away," said Edgar Allan. "Special circumstances."

"Can you tell me what he looked like?"

"He was a ghost," Burt said, then proceeded to describe William Shakespeare in perfect detail.

On the other side of the Greenlawn Cemetery—in a large expansion area marked as the site of future graves, complete with a sign saying DON'T WAIT! GET YOURS NOW!—I saw the mostly rebuilt theater stage, with construction teams, a couple of golems and zombies with work belts and hammers, hauling two-by-fours or sheets of plywood while ghostly actors directed the operations. A large new sound system boasting tall speakers added a more modern touch to the mockup of the Globe Theatre.

Burt pointed. "There's the guy right now. Don't know why he's rebuilding the whole stage when he burned it down in the first place."

I was sad but not surprised, since all the clues had been pointing to that answer, but I still didn't understand why. "Thanks, Burt. I needed to have a talk with him anyway."

Edgar Allan scuttled out from the crypt door and gave me something. "Could you hand him my card, if you find a way to slip it into the conversation?"

Shakespeare didn't see me coming. When two of the spectral actors called him over, and he saw the look on my face, he *knew,* but by that time he couldn't avoid me without fleeing in panic. He probably guessed what I was going to say before I spoke a word. The ghost paled, turned more translucent, but at least he didn't vanish out of existence, though he plainly wanted to.

For the time being, I kept my voice down so the other actors didn't hear. "I know you're responsible for the arson, Mr. Shakespeare. A witness saw you light the fire, and I have pawnshop records showing that *you* sold the theatrical props that you claimed were lost in the blaze."

"Oh." He sounded embarrassed. "Are you sure we can't pin this on some of Senator Balfour's crazies? Or even leftovers from the Straight Edge movement?"

"No, Mr. Shakespeare. It was you."

He let out a long sigh. "You cannot blame me for trying. Given the uproar about the Unnatural Acts Act, I was hoping to ride on that publicity, smear a little more mud on some bad people who deserve it."

"I agree they deserve it, but they've done enough genuinely despicable things—we don't need to make up additional ones. You hired me to solve the crime of arson, and I did." I couldn't keep the annoyance out of my tone. "I expect our bill to be paid in full."

"Are you going to turn me in to the police?" he asked. "That would ruin us—and our big comeback performance is in two nights. Please let me explain first."

"I'm listening, but your words may fall on dead ears."

"I did it to attract attention to our plight, to generate larger audiences. The *real* crime, Mr. Chambeaux, is that unnaturals no longer appreciate the works of Shakespeare. Since the fire, though, we've received so much sympathy. Patrons have opened their purses, and donations flowed in more than ever before. And with the insurance money—"

I cut him off right there. "There's not going to be any insurance money. If you burned the stage down yourself, that would be insurance fraud. You'll withdraw your claim immediately."

"Oh, you're absolutely right—I'm forgetting about modern law. But there's been no fraud committed, yet. I, uh, tarried overlong in filing the insurance claims. Those forms are so complicated, and I've been too busy and distracted." He waved his hands to indicate the stage set. "This effort requires the fullness of my attention, not simply the stage, the wardrobe, and that complicated new sound system, but also the casting, the rehearsals, the temperamental actors. And the show is day after tomorrow! *The Tempest* is a most intricate play, and it was an immense challenge to write—I had to develop my literary skills to the fullest before I wrote it."

"I thought *The Tempest* was Shakespeare's very first play," I said.

The ghost seemed even more embarrassed. "We are performing a revised version—the author's preferred text. Howard Phillips Publishing is going to issue a new edition of the script, complete with critical commentary from the online reviews." He paused, still worried whether I would have him arrested. "And since my theatrical company owned the original stage, I'm allowed to burn it, aren't I? Legally? I admit my words were . . . somewhat misleading, but is that an actual crime? Must you turn me in to the authorities?"

"The donors you mentioned—if you actively solicited their donations, then that's fraud, which is a felony."

"No! Not at all, they just came forward. I didn't seek them out."

"You wasted my *time*, Mr. Shakespeare. I could have been working on other cases, solving *real* crimes for *real* clients."

"It was for a good cause, truly. Please don't ruin it now. *The Tempest* could turn everything around for us. Is there not some kind of detective-client privilege? Our big performance is coming up, and I've myriad things to do. All the world's a stage, but I can't seem to finish even this little piece of it."

I was disinclined to be sympathetic, but he seemed sincere. Besides, Sheyenne did love the play. "I might reconsider, if I got two free tickets."

"Absolutely! Front row seats on opening night. You are my special guests—it'll be a show you'll never forget."

I wasn't sure about that, but considering how much Sheyenne's feelings had been hurt—not just by Travis but by me as well—I wanted to make it up to her. I'd take her out on a nice date. Not good enough to heal all wounds, but it was a start.

CHAPTER 41

The next day, Tiffany and Bill stopped by the office, bubbling with excitement. "Can only stay a minute!" said the vampire. "Bill wanted to share the good news."

The golem's clay face was stretched into an absurdly large grin. "Got a job!"

"Congratulations, Bill," I said. "Doing what?"

"As a security guard. I wasn't so sure about the job at first, considering my previous work making stupid souvenirs in an underground sweatshop. But I think I'll be good at it."

Tiffany smiled, showing her fangs. "Bill, you're good at whatever you do."

The golem seemed embarrassed and explained to us, as if we were concerned about his priorities, "And I promise I'll still have time to keep Tiffany's house in shape."

"Sounds like just the right job for you, Bill," I reassured him. "A security guard spends most of his time standing around like a statue, anyway."

"I'm good at that," Bill said.

Robin sounded concerned. "Just be careful. Security guard in the Unnatural Quarter is a high-risk profession."

"He lives for danger," Tiffany said, and I could detect no humor in her comment. "We're off to get him his uniform. He'll look impressive in dark blue. Also, remember not to make plans for this Saturday night—all of you. That's when I'm doing my comedy act at the Laughing Skull. Bring your friends. You promised you'd come, and you promised you'd laugh."

"We didn't promise to laugh," I objected.

"But you will." Tiffany's comment sounded like a threat. *"You will."*

Mountains of papers were stacked on the floor of Robin's office, legal volumes spread out on the desk, and a brand-new box of yellow legal pads from the office-supply store was already half-empty. I stood in her doorway, admiring—and intimidated by—the sheer volume of work she had tackled.

The direct line rang in her office, and she worked her way around the desk to answer it. I watched her face fall. "Calm down, Mrs. Patterson! Just tell me about it. Slower. Wait a second, I'm going to have my partner get on the line."

She motioned for me to pick up the other extension, and she continued, trying to sound calm, but her eyes were wide. "At the moment, you're on solid legal ground, Mr. and Mrs. Patterson. I filed vigorous appeals, and there's been a stay. You're allowed to remain in the house during the proceedings. No one can take you out of there."

"But these people aren't reading legal documents, Ms. Deyer!" said Walter Patterson on the other line.

His wife continued sobbing. "Balfour's people are barbarians! They vandalized our house, spray-painted the most horrible slurs on the garage door. They smashed our windows."

Mr. Patterson picked up the story. "They threw bunches of

garlic and wolfsbane through the picture window in our living room! How can we live in the house now? We'll need to replace the carpeting, fumigate every room. I'll have to rent a new coffin. My favorite one is ruined."

"And they scattered garlic all around the house, as well as a circle of salt—as if that's going to prevent us from leaving!"

"We're not leaving," Mr. Patterson said, defiant.

I could see that Robin was a thunderstorm ready to break. "I will use every possible weapon to fight for your rights, I promise. It's time to blow this whole matter wide open. No more sitting quietly. We're not the ones who took this to the next level."

The Pattersons still sounded shaky as they thanked her and hung up. Robin launched herself out of the office with such fury on her face that she made even Sheyenne flinch. "That's the last straw! I've been drafting a choice little letter for all the bloggers, papers, and TV stations. This is the excuse I've been waiting for. I'm going to call a spade a spade. Balfour's a bigot, and he's inciting violence—we have evidence of that. He can no longer hide behind his radical stupidity."

Even though I'm not usually the voice of reason, I cautioned, "Don't go off half-cocked, Robin. Whenever you write an angry letter, let it sit for a day, so you can cool off, get some objectivity, then reread the letter."

"Justice can't wait around for a day," Robin said. "I'm a lawyer, I know what I'm doing."

I couldn't talk her out of it, and I did want Senator Rupert Balfour eviscerated in public, although I suspected his rotten organs were not fit for even a mad scientist's experiments.

I asked McGoo to pull strings to arrange police protection around the Pattersons' house, even though it wasn't his jurisdiction. I was worried that some nutcase extremist with silver bullets or wooden stakes would take matters into his own hands.

Robin spent hours composing her angry press release that exposed Senator Balfour's despicable activities, then distributed her posting as widely as possible, not only to various media outlets but to popular social-networking sites and bulletin-board discussion groups frequented by unnaturals.

She seemed immensely pleased with what she had sent out— I could tell from her edgy smile and the contained energy with which she moved about the office. Although she wouldn't let me read the text ahead of time, I found it on our website. I didn't disagree with a single word she wrote, but I think my eyeballs blistered after reading the flaming invective.

CHAPTER 42

Knowing that Angela Drake had bought the heart-and-soul combo packs didn't help me retrieve them, since she had vanished. Missy Goodfellow categorically denied possessing the items, and she certainly wouldn't give me access to her financial records so I could double-check.

But a dead end wasn't going to stop a zombie private detective.

That evening I retraced my investigations, which brought me back to the vicinity of the Unnatural Acts adult novelty shop. A frown creased my face. The store was shut down, and yellow tape crisscrossed the door. Senator Balfour's obnoxious flyers covered the outer wall like leprous growths. I noted that they had now registered their *You Are Damned!* slogan as a trademark. And they still didn't know that *unnatural* had two *N*s.

An official notice had been tacked to the center of the novelty shop's door: CLOSED, PENDING PROSECUTION UNDER THE UNNATURAL ACTS ACT.

When the legendary creatures returned in the Big Uneasy,

there had been quite a panic—which was understandable—but as I observed this spread of intolerance toward monsters who just wanted to live and let live (for the most part), I wondered whether the world really was coming to an end. . . .

I entered the pawnshop alley to see that the Timeworn Treasures sign had been taken down, the windows painted over, and a large Commercial Property For Rent sign placed in each one, complete with the smiling face of Edgar Allan. *Cheerful service—alive or dead!*

Alice had wasted no time washing her hands of her brother's shop, sweeping everything under the rug, and heading off on her Mediterranean cruise. I imagined her lounging in a deck chair in the warm salty air, tanning her fur as she cruised around the Greek isles . . . or maybe hiding from the sunlight and spending all hours hunched over a slot machine on the casino deck.

The cruise sounded like something I'd like to do with Sheyenne someday, a chance to spend more time alone with her. I hated for her to think I was no longer interested just because she was a ghost. You have to make some concessions in order for a relationship to work.

Standing in the gloomy alley in front of the closed pawnshop, I was so preoccupied with my personal problems that I didn't notice the two demon goons closing in until it was too late. A private detective is supposed to be observant, picking up tiny details missed by the police or evil criminal masterminds. Even so, I did not see the hulking things before they were right up on me. For all their scales, horns, and poisonous fumes leaking from their nostrils and mouths, demons somehow manage to tiptoe quite well.

"Dan Chambeaux," gargled the larger demon as purplish brown vapors curled out of his fanged mouth. "We need a word with you."

The slightly smaller demon next to him chuckled with a

huffing sound like a badly tuned engine. His breath looked like diesel fumes. "Yeah. Strong words."

They blocked the alley, and I faced them. "How can I help you boys?"

The two demons were of the "hired thug" variety, certainly not management material. Large and imposing, with faces and bodies covered with scaly plates and sharp protrusions, they looked like the result of an unintended pregnancy between a porcupine and a crocodile—and *that* was not a porno clip I wanted to see under any circumstances.

The foremost demon had blazing scarlet eyes, and his partner's were orange, denoting lesser intelligence (or lesser meanness, I hoped). I was sure I would find out soon enough. "If you're looking to rent the storefront here, I can put you in touch with the real estate agent."

The red-eyed demon grabbed me by the front of my shirt, wrinkling my jacket as he shoved me against the alley wall. His clawed hand was the size of my head. My fedora fell off onto the ground.

"Careful with the hat!" I said.

The orange-eyed demon stomped the fedora flat.

"Stop sticking your nose where it doesn't belong, Chambeaux." The purplish brown fumes wafting out of his mouth stung my eyes like acid—maybe it *was* acid—and I couldn't keep myself from coughing. Not exactly the most dignified response I could have made.

"Could you be more specific?" I managed. "I'm a detective—it's my job to stick my nose in things."

The big demon lifted me into the air, letting my legs dangle beneath me, then swung me around and slammed me against the opposite wall of the alley. He chuffed, "Ooh, that's going to leave a mark."

"I've been told it adds character." Actually, because I have embalming fluid rather than blood, bruises don't show, and I can withstand a lot of battering, not that I enjoy it. Even if the bruises weren't visible, however, lumps and broken bones could still be very unsightly.

The demon tossed me to his partner, who turned me upside down and dropped me to the street, as if they had invented a new game called "Pass the Zombie."

I picked myself up. I knew I was damaged, some pieces broken, and my clothes were definitely torn and dirty. The orange-eyed demon stomped on my fedora again for good measure, though it was already flat.

"Just watch yourself," said the larger demon, leaning close and exhaling again so that I couldn't breathe without burning my nostrils.

"You've got a bad case of the vapors," I said.

"Stop poking into Goodfellow matters, if you know what's good for you," said the less intelligent thug. "The Smile Syndicate doesn't like it."

"Really?" I shook my head to clear it. "Missy told me she has nothing to hide."

It was the wrong thing to say, but then I often do that. The scarlet-eyed demon was annoyed that his partner had blabbed the Goodfellow name. They propped me up and used me as a punching bag, hammering away at my chest and face, tearing my jacket (which was going to need several more stitches—as would I).

"If you don't learn your lesson, maybe we'll go twist the head off your lawyer friend," the red-eyed demon said. "Like unscrewing a lid off a jar."

His companion chuckled. "The lid off a jar!"

They left me in a rumpled heap before strutting away, whistling a cheerful tune. "Let's go celebrate," said the big demon.

The orange-eyed partner trotted along beside him. "Can we? Can we?"

I lay there for a long time, feeling a thousand aches, hoping I could be patched up, but knowing I was no longer quite so well-preserved. I work hard to maintain my condition, but it doesn't help when a couple of supernatural bullies target you for your lunch money. I would have preferred that they just gave me a wedgie.

It took a long while to get back on my feet, a little bit at a time. I straightened my limbs, checked the damage—mostly superficial. Fortunately, I knew a good cosmetic artist. Rather than being frightened or intimidated, as the demons had intended, I found myself growing really angry.

I retrieved my fedora. I poked and prodded like a master sculptor, or just a kid with modeling clay, to reshape it into a semblance of a hat. Eventually it looked as much like a fedora as my suit jacket looked like a suit jacket, and I looked like a dead man walking.

I already disliked the Smile Syndicate's practices, the golem souvenir sweatshop, their line of overpriced and intrusive gift shops, their acquisition of the Goblin Tavern, how they had treated Francine, and the fact that they—for whatever reason— had acquired Jerry's heart and soul. Missy Goodfellow was behind the harassment of the Full Moon, I was sure of it. Her goons must have smashed the windows, broken the cat sarcophagi.

Missy had hired those demons to beat me up, *and* her thugs had threatened Robin. She had crossed a line, and I intended to expose whatever Missy was doing, whatever she was *hiding*, whether or not it was directly related to one of my cases.

As a private detective, I might not have a lot of muscle, but I do have brains. Missy Goodfellow was playing dirty—and I could do the same.

It was *on*.

CHAPTER 43

I shambled back to the office to clean myself up and change clothes, hoping to hide the most prominent bodily damage and wardrobe malfunctions from the ladies. Robin was in her office with the door mostly shut, burning the midnight oil (although it was barely 9:00 P.M.) as she went over the Unnatural Acts Act. As of that afternoon, she had gotten up to Tome-Section VII, so she still had a long way to go.

I slipped in as quietly as possible, but there was no getting past Sheyenne. Something about her ectoplasmic ears gives her excellent hearing. "Beaux! What happened?"

"The Quarter isn't a nice place to live anymore," I said. "No wonder the Pattersons and even Harvey Jekyll want to get out of here."

She whisked off to get a wet washcloth from the kitchenette and returned to dab my face. I could feel her ghostly hands through the moist rag. At some other time it would have been a pleasurable intimate experience, but now the main sensations came from all the new lumps around my face and forehead.

"Who did this?" Sheyenne said. "Who do I need to kill?"

"You want to end up in ghost prison like Alphonse Wheeler?"

"At least I'll be in good company, and I'll feel satisfied."

A couple of my teeth were loose, and I needed to have them glued in securely. Maybe when I met with Mavis Wannovich to brainstorm about their line of zombie detective novels I could get next month's restorative spell a little early. (Apparently she had called the office yet again, sounding even more anxious to talk with me.)

"Missy Goodfellow sent a couple of demon thugs to complain about my digging into Smile Syndicate business," I said. "If she's this bothered, I must have touched a nerve."

"I'm going to go all poltergeist on her ass," Sheyenne vowed. "I'll find a piano somewhere and drop it on her head, just like the one that missed her brother. I think someone went after the wrong Goodfellow."

I glanced at myself in the mirror and looked at the dirty, rumpled, and damaged sport jacket and the dirty, rumpled, and damaged fedora, all of which went well with my dirty, rumpled, and damaged body.

My thoughts and my conscience were in a spin, as if inner demons were still playing Pass the Zombie with me. The Unnatural Quarter had gone to hell in a handbasket, and now the handbasket was falling apart. With the Smile Syndicate expanding into the Quarter, and Balfour's Unnatural Acts Act threatening to repress unnaturals in their most basic daily activities, it would only get worse.

I had the sense that the windmill we were tilting at was about to collapse and fall on top of us, but I didn't intend to stop, and Robin would never stop. We weren't going anywhere. Even so, in a derailed train of thought, I felt I needed to do something right away, something good, for a person who didn't have anybody else helping her.

I went to the safe in the wall behind Sheyenne's desk. It took me three tries with clumsy fingers (I think one was broken) to get the combination right. I withdrew a stack of bills, most of our petty cash fund. "There's something I need to do."

"Where are you going?" Sheyenne asked.

I pocketed the wad of bills. "To the Full Moon." Presumably for the last time. I was already down the stairs and out on the street before I realized what a stupid thing that was to say to Sheyenne.

It was nearly midnight when I arrived, and Mike the door golem let me into the parlor and took my hat. Due in part to a massive coupon mailing Neffi had launched, the place was hopping: half a dozen natural and unnatural clients making nervous chitchat with the ladies. Two of the doors upstairs were closed.

Neffi seemed pleased and relieved that business had returned to normal. The withered unwrapped mummy languidly leaned against the door to her office and bedroom. "No waiting over here, boys, if you're looking for someone with experience."

Conversation in the parlor paused for an instant before everyone went back to talking with the other girls.

Neffi saw me enter. "Mr. Chambeaux, you certainly are a frequent sight, though not much of a customer. Is that about to change tonight? Treat yourself?" She eyed me up and down with her burnt-ember eyes. "You look like you've had a rough day at the office."

"Not just at the office. I'd like to see Ruth, please."

The stretched, petrified brown skin covering Neffi's skull bent back in a smile. "It's about time you made up your mind. This is Ruth's last night."

"Has she found another job?"

"Don't know, don't care, but she's on her own as of dawn." She whistled a piercing note, like a hyperactive kid tooting on a broken flute. Ruth came out of the back room, looking small and defeated. She'd been crying, though her green eyes still caught the attention of everyone in the room. When she saw me, she brightened.

I pulled the wad of bills from my pocket. "I've got something for you."

Naturally, that was the exact moment Sheyenne's ghost drifted through the door, her face already angry and hurt. She took in the scene with a glance. "Why couldn't you be honest with me, Beaux? You're worse than Travis. At least his lies are so clumsy he might as well not even try."

Before she could flit away, I said, "Wait, Spooky! I want you to see this."

She hovered, held there by a thread of feelings for me, a thin thread that was likely to snap like a cobweb any second.

Ruth withdrew quickly, confused. "I don't want to cause any trouble. I've already—"

I handed her the bills. "This money is for you to take a bus out of town. Leave the Full Moon, set up a new life for yourself. I want you to have a clean slate." I turned to Sheyenne. "She didn't mean to hurt your brother."

"I never blamed her for Travis," Sheyenne said. "He's always been his own worst enemy. But you . . . you keep coming here."

"Chambeaux may keep coming here, but he never does any . . . *coming* here." Neffi cackled. "Never once hired any of my ladies. He might as well be a piece of furniture, like Mike over there."

The golem's clay face formed itself into a grin as he stood holding my hat over one upraised hand.

"It's the truth," I said. "Cross my heart."

At that moment, somebody called in a bomb threat, which distracted us all.

Cinnamon had taken a break between clients. She answered the phone, then sat staring and growling until she slowly hung up. "There's a bomb in the brothel—and it's set to go off in fifteen minutes."

"A bomb?" Neffi demanded. "Which one of you brought a bomb in here?"

"I didn't," said a hunchback and a ghoul in unison.

Cinnamon's fur stood on end. "The caller said he was sending a warning from Senator Balfour—out of the goodness of his rotten little Grinch heart."

Already skittish from being in the unnatural brothel in the first place, the human customers bolted out the door as Mike waved a polite farewell.

I started yelling. "Everybody evacuate! We need to clear the building."

The mummy madam was enraged. "If there's a bomb here, we need to find it right now!"

Hemlock and Nightshade pounded on the closed doors where the two zombie girls were currently occupied. "Come on, we gotta go!"

Aubrey's muffled voice came from behind the door. "Just about finished!"

I looked at my watch, saw it was almost midnight—happy hour, the busiest time at the Full Moon. Someone had planned this well.

"We can't risk searching the place," I said to Neffi. "Get everyone out into the street. It's too dangerous."

"Fifteen minutes is fifteen minutes, if the timer is accurate," Neffi insisted. "We're going to look, and you're going to help me. Girls, all of you—search your boudoirs for anything that looks like a bomb."

None of us was an expert in explosives, but I hoped a ticking time bomb would be obvious. We yanked red velvet cushions off the sofas, looked in the drawers of the front desk.

Ruth and Sheyenne went together to search the back rooms. The two zombie girls poked their heads out of their rooms upstairs. "Nothing here—all clear."

"It could have been a prank call to disrupt our business," Neffi said. "That'd be par for the course for Senator Balfour."

"Can't risk it." I looked at the madam. "How could someone get in here and plant a bomb?"

"We had a big night, more customers than ever before. Too many people to watch every minute." Neffi overturned a wastebasket, looked behind a potted cactus. "But you can ask the girls—everyone who came in tonight left a satisfied customer. Do you think Balfour's fanatics would go that deep undercover?"

I admitted it didn't seem likely. Considering how much they despised monsters of all kinds, posing—and performing—as a randy client with one of the unnatural ladies did not seem like their style.

A few minutes later, Sheyenne appeared before me, her face urgent. "I hear a ticking sound—it's coming from back there!"

We turned toward Neffi's office and the bedroom beyond. "That's just my grandfather clock," the madam said. "Wait . . . that stopped a year ago."

"No, this is something else," Sheyenne insisted. "I can hear it."

I did mention that she has good hearing for a ghost.

We followed her into the office, past the metal file cabinet, past the fish tank with dead fish, the silent grandfather clock, and into the old mummy's bedchamber. Sheyenne circled the room, pausing at the bulky gold-encrusted sarcophagus where Neffi slept, the rocking chair, and finally she zeroed in on the last intact cat-sized sarcophagus.

"It's here! And it's ticking."

"That's Whiskers," Neffi said. "Whiskers doesn't tick."

Then I spotted the yellowed package of a withered mummified cat tossed unceremoniously behind the rocking chair. "I think *that's* Whiskers."

Sheyenne slowly opened the cat coffin to reveal a small bundle of dynamite sticks wrapped with wires and duct tape, fastened to an old windup alarm clock. The hands were only a few minutes away from midnight.

Mike the golem stepped up to the office door, and as soon as Sheyenne revealed the bomb, he clomped forward and picked up the bundle of dynamite. "Let me take that. I'm just a golem." He plodded away, carrying the bomb as it ticked inexorably toward its midnight detonation.

I ran after him. "Wait, Mike—when that explodes, it'll destroy you."

"That's my job. Better me than anyone else." He stepped out the door to where the other four golem guards had taken position, keeping customers from entering.

"I've got a better idea." Sheyenne swooped after him and snatched the bomb out of the golem's arms. "A simple explosion isn't going to hurt a ghost at all."

Before I could argue with her (not that I had much of an argument to make), Sheyenne dashed through the open front door and rose into the air. I'd never seen her move that fast, but she was unfettered and motivated.

"That was nice of her," the golem said as we all stepped out into the night to watch where Sheyenne had gone.

Ruth came up beside me, looking into the sky with admiration. Sheyenne had vanished with the bomb, swooping over the building tops. "Good thing your girlfriend was around."

Neffi agreed. "We don't get many ghosts at the Full Moon. Can't provide services for intangibles, other than as spectators."

The succubus looked away. "I think it's best if I take this opportunity to leave. I'll go to the Hellhound bus station, take the red-eye out of town, and ride wherever the ticket takes me. Thank you for everything you've done, Dan, but I don't want to cause any more trouble. I told Sheyenne what a nice guy you are . . . but if I'm around, she'll always have her doubts." With that, Ruth hurried down the sidewalk, carrying a suitcase that she had already packed.

I decided it was best not to give her any more than a quick goodbye. At the moment, I was more concerned about Sheyenne, even though I knew she wouldn't be vulnerable to a bomb blast. Still, the thought was unnerving.

At the stroke of midnight, a flash of light appeared far away, and a second later we heard the thump of an explosion. I wondered how far Sheyenne had made it, or where she was trying to go. Resounding cheers came from the few lingering Full Moon clients and the golem guards.

When Sheyenne returned, I was so elated to see her that I threw my arms around her in a large air–bear hug, despite the fact that neither of us would feel it. She was excited, her eyes filled with ectoplasmic adrenaline. "You should have seen it, Beaux! Missy Goodfellow's going to have a big mess to clean up."

"Missy? What did you do?"

"Remember that warehouse where they store all the souvenirs for her gift shops? It was closed down for the night, but coincidentally, that's where the bomb landed right before it went off. Silly little Kreepsakes scattered everywhere."

I laughed, imagining the scene. I took even more delight in imagining the expression on Missy's face when she learned of it. I sure hoped that she hadn't stored her collection of pawned hearts and souls there.

Sheyenne muttered under her breath, "That'll teach her to send goons to beat up my boyfriend."

I took her arm in mine (or at least I tried to), and we left the Full Moon together.

CHAPTER 44

McGoo showed up at the offices the next day, as I figured he would. Exploding bombs had a way of attracting attention.

"You here to get a statement about the bomb at the Full Moon?" I asked.

"Technically, yes." His expression grew serious. "Mainly, I wanted to make sure you were all right."

"Thanks," I said. I still felt disheveled and tired. Even for a dead guy, I'd had a rough day and night.

McGoo stood inside the reception area by Sheyenne's desk and regarded me with a stern look, but couldn't hide the relieved smile behind his stony expression. "You always get yourself in trouble, Shamble. When are you going to stop making extra work for me?" He shook his head at my more-battered-than-usual appearance. "Even on a good day, you look like hell—but now you look like you're from the Ninth Circle of Hell."

"You don't know the half of it." I wasn't going to tell him about being roughed up by Missy Goodfellow's demon goons earlier that evening, and I had grudgingly decided not to turn in Shakespeare's ghost for burning down his own stage.

He brightened. "Oh, and also—why'd the vampire get fired from the blood bank?" I groaned even before he answered. "For drinking on the job!" Then I couldn't help laughing.

"And what does a vegetarian zombie say? Graaaaaaaiiiins!"

"You've overstayed your welcome, McGoo. Sheyenne and I will give you any details we can, but Madam Neffi and her girls will be more helpful. Cinnamon was the one who received the bomb threat—the caller said it was a warning from Senator Balfour."

"Nothing would make me happier than to nail the senator with this," McGoo said.

"The new adult novelty store was shut down," I said. "Locked and sealed up with an injunction tacked on the door."

McGoo gave a somber nod. "I predict that's only the first in a long line of dominoes to fall. It's only a matter of time before they shut down the Full Moon, too. His minions think they have a free pass now that the Unnatural Acts Act is law."

Robin came out of her office. "Not if I can help it. I've been writing legal challenges to stop the Act in its tracks." She looked drawn and haggard enough to be impersonating one of the undead. Robin had consumed a full pot of coffee, freshly brewed in our new pot, even though she didn't usually drink coffee. In circumstances like these, however, chamomile tea wasn't going to be sufficient.

"All this makes me very nervous, Shamble," McGoo said. "The Quarter just isn't as friendly a place as it used to be." And that was saying something, coming from him.

After McGoo left, I gave a wan apologetic smile to Sheyenne. "With all the excitement yesterday, I forgot to mention that we have free passes to Shakespeare in the Dark tonight. Want to see *The Tempest* with me?" I held out the tickets. "Front row seats."

She took the tickets and smiled at me, still a little uncertain. "Another try at a real date?"

"Exactly—just you and me this time, some quality time together." I lowered my voice, felt awkward. "Spooky, you know there was nothing between me and that succubus. I just felt sorry for her, like a big brother."

"I knew she wasn't your type, Beaux . . . but a girl gets worried when her boyfriend finds excuses to keep going to a brothel day after day."

"Not excuses—business reasons."

Robin retreated to her office. "I'm staying out of this one."

Travis sauntered through the door and made our day even worse. After he had hurt Sheyenne—repeatedly—and then become the poster child for Senator Balfour's crusade against unnaturals, I couldn't think of any persona more non grata in our offices. Oddly, he seemed oblivious to his own sliminess. Smiling as he entered, he pretended to be everybody's best friend. "Hey, sis! It's been a long time. I just wanted to say hi."

Sheyenne gave her interpretation of the old cliché *if looks could kill.* "What are you doing here? You've already pawned the last of our family heirlooms, and I don't have any more money for you to rip off."

Travis reacted with clumsily feigned shock. "That's not very nice, Anne! You're my sister. Can't I stop by just to see you?" He noticed the tickets in her hand. I thought he turned pale—and I'm an expert in seeing people turn pale. "Ooh, Shakespeare in the Dark. You're not one for that highbrow stuff—when did you get so snooty?"

She stuck the tickets in the desk drawer. "Dan and I are going on a date. He's taking me to the play—alone, without any extra company."

"Well, la-di-da. Why don't you go out with me instead? We can talk this out, resolve our differences."

Sheyenne stared at him in disbelief. "Are you kidding me? I watched you at the press conference! You're a sock puppet for that vile senator. What did he pay you? And how can you stick up for him, after his people planted a *bomb* at the Full Moon to kill all kinds of unnaturals—and humans, too?"

"Senator Balfour didn't have anything to do with that," Travis said quickly.

"One of his minions called in the threat," I interrupted. "Sheyenne and I were there when it happened."

Travis's expression of indignation looked far more genuine than his previous smiles. "You know, I wish somebody *would* blow up that place. The Full Moon is a cesspool of unnatural acts. That succubus almost killed me!"

"Only because you went to her!" Sheyenne snapped. "You did it to yourself. You signed the waiver. You were warned, but you went ahead anyway."

He sniffed. "Doesn't matter. I should have been protected from myself. I can't be required to know all the inherent hazards of unnaturals."

Sheyenne floated directly in front of him, in his face. "*I'm* an unnatural, Travis, whether you like it or not."

He looked hurt. "Don't you realize how embarrassing that is to me?"

"Sorry I came back from the dead and inconvenienced you," Sheyenne said with bitter sarcasm. "Maybe if you'd been at my funeral you could have told me how you really felt. I forgot what a self-centered, deceitful brother you are, all the crap you've pulled over the years. I want you to leave and never come back. You're dead to me."

"Dead?" Travis bristled. "Hah! You died first. Family's supposed to stick together, but I don't need you anymore. You dug your own grave, now bury yourself in it! Have fun at your stupid Shakespeare play." He slammed the door on his way out.

CHAPTER 45

After the bomb at the brothel, Robin's anger toward Senator Balfour was so great it overshadowed even her loathing for Harvey Jekyll, who was now her client. That afternoon, she called Jekyll into our offices to sign some paperwork for his case.

Still shaken by the confrontation with Travis, Sheyenne kept herself distracted and busy by flitting back and forth to the courthouse filing injunctions to stop enforcement of the Act, then scheduling numerous hearings, traveling so much that I considered adding "courier service" to her already lengthy job description.

She was gone when Jekyll and his bodyguard arrived, so I had to take care of the social niceties. When I offered them beverages, Larry asked for a beer, which we didn't keep in the office; Jekyll asked for a sparkling water, but we were out, having given the last one to Bill the golem.

Heavily caffeinated but exhausted, Robin led Jekyll into the conference room. "I am determined to get you into your house in the suburbs, Mr. Jekyll. The Patterson case establishes a precedent, and their appalling treatment from the neighbors can only sway sympathy, though it's going to be an uphill climb, considering your track record."

"I am no stranger to appalling treatment, and much less accustomed to sympathy," Jekyll said. "I read your amusing treatise against Senator Balfour, by the way. It must have hurt his delicate feelings."

"He needed to be exposed. Momentum is building against him. I can feel it. We'll have the whole Quarter on our side. As of an hour ago, I've filed seventeen challenges to various provisions in the Unnatural Acts Act, and I'm just getting warmed up. I plan to keep Senator Balfour's staff busy twenty-four hours a day. He won't be able to move forward on any aspect of the Act without facing opposition. We'll get it repealed—and your case will help the cause."

"Oh, good," Jekyll said with dripping sarcasm. "I always wanted to be a bleeding-heart crusader for unnatural rights, since the unnaturals have been so kind to me." His small hand curled itself into a fist like the legs of a spider sprayed with insecticide. "Why do you think I'm so desperate to move out of the Quarter?"

Sheyenne flitted through the office door with stamped copies of the documents she had filed. She appeared less unsettled now, more corporeal, but when she saw Harvey Jekyll in our conference room, she grew bothered all over again. I was definitely looking forward to taking her out to the Shakespeare play and getting her away from the tempest around the offices.

Jekyll drew a deep breath, calmed himself. "Life isn't fair, either before or after death. My psychiatrist says I should accept the situation and move on. As the song says, I will survive." He leaned forward, his narrow shoulders hunched, his bald scalp wrinkling with enough furrows to plant weeds in. "On the other hand, I won't lose sleep to see Senator Balfour slapped. He deserves as many headaches as he's caused me."

"But Balfour is one of your investors in the ectoplasmic defibrillator business," I said.

"Oh, he's much more than that. Balfour used to be one of my Straight Edge buddies." He looked at us, and I admit I wasn't surprised by the revelation. "Now he won't give me the time of day."

Larry furrowed his snout. "Don't you have a watch, boss?"

Jekyll ignored him. "The senator stopped taking my calls on the basis that it's not his policy to speak with unnaturals. The nerve! He sent me a notice that my membership in Straight Edge has been revoked. We'll see about that!"

"I thought Straight Edge had been dissolved and disbanded," Robin said.

"It is, for the most part, but we still have a group medical plan, and there's an annual get-together." He shook his head. "I can't believe Rupert would do this. He knows who I am . . . and I know damned well what he is."

"If he's such a bad partner, maybe you should stop making ectoplasmic defibrillators," I said.

"Business is business. In fact, I'm paying all my outstanding bills because he just purchased two industrial-size defibrillators. He says he needs to protect himself against ghostly backlash from the Unnatural Acts Act. My defibrillators could disintegrate an entire army of angry ghosts if they came after him."

"Ghosts aren't the only ones out to get him," Sheyenne said. "Every unnatural hates his guts."

"This is just his opening salvo—any unnatural will do."

"*You* were always good at killing large numbers of unnaturals all at once, Jekyll," I said, remembering his previous genocidal plans.

He looked annoyed. "Yes, Rupert consulted with me. Normally, I'm willing to lend a hand to my friends, but I no longer count the senator among them."

"We gotta go, boss," Larry said. "Dentist appointment."

Jekyll sighed. "I wish you'd set up these things on your own time."

The werewolf picked at his fangs. "We can stop for coffee on the way." That seemed to make Jekyll happy.

After they left the offices, another man entered, wearing a suit off the bargain rack and a thin black tie. I realized I had seen this guy-in-tie before at the Pattersons' house. All business, the man handed Robin a folded packet. "Ms. Deyer, this is for you. I hope you enjoy it. You're served." He briskly walked away down the corridor.

Frowning, Robin unfolded and scanned the document. First her expression fell, then her eyes blazed, as she flipped the pages. "Balfour's playing hardball." She handed the papers to me. "He's slapped me with a defamation and libel suit and filed a complaint with the State Board of Professional Responsibility to get me disbarred."

Sheyenne said, "That's ridiculous."

The troubled look on Robin's face, though, told me that from a legal perspective, the suit was far from ridiculous. Some phrases from her vitriolic press release, which she phrased as actual fact, might have crossed the line. "Ambulatory wad of phlegm" stood out in my mind.

"Looks like I'm going to be working late again," Robin said. "More briefs to file, and now I've got to write up an Answer to his Complaint."

"We're here, Robin, whatever you need."

Sheyenne tried to hide the frown on her translucent face. "We can go see a different performance of Shakespeare in the Dark, Beaux. We don't have to go tonight."

I had forgotten it was time for us to leave, and Sheyenne and I really needed close time together, a night doing something *normal* for a change. "No, I promised you we'd go. The acting troupe has been through a lot, and this is their big comeback.

We need to be there." The crowds would already be arriving as night set in, and I was glad we had reserved seats. There would be a lot of ghosts at the event.

Suddenly, something clicked in my mind. Travis had reacted with visible alarm when he saw that Sheyenne had tickets for the play. Why wouldn't he want her to be there? Why would he care?

The ticket presales had been high. The Greenlawn Cemetery would be crowded with half the ghosts in the Unnatural Quarter, coming to support the spectral company. And Jekyll said that Senator Balfour had just purchased two industrial-strength ectoplasmic defibrillators powerful enough to eliminate a spectral army . . . or disintegrate a whole crowd of ghosts gathered in one place.

Sheyenne saw the expression on my face. "What is it?"

"First they tried a bomb, but this is a hell of a lot worse," I said. "Change of plans!"

When I explained my suspicions, Robin gasped. "And the Unnatural Acts Act is currently in force, with provisions that humans can take any actions whatsoever against unnaturals! The senator will wrap himself in the law! It's a slippery legal slope: You can't murder a ghost, which is, by definition, already dead."

"He won't murder those ghosts," I said, "because we're going to stop him."

CHAPTER 46

As we raced to the cemetery, I called McGoo. "Bring backup to the Shakespeare stage right now! I don't have proof, but I think Senator Balfour is going to attempt a mass disintegration of all the ghosts there."

McGoo did not hesitate. "If there's a chance to implicate Balfour, I'm there. I'll call out the squad cars and meet you."

As Robin, Sheyenne, and I charged through the cemetery gates, I tripped on the welcome mats. I had been trying to shuffle less in my step, but right now I was distracted. At least I didn't do a face-plant into a gravestone. The Welcome Back Wagon vampire with cat's-eye glasses tried to hand me another plastic bag full of goodies, but we hurried past.

Unnaturals were already crowding the cemetery. Hundreds of ghosts had gathered around the tombstones, picking the best spots in the festival seating area. Vampires sat in lawn chairs they had brought. At any other time, I would have been pleased to see that the audience was so large—at least Shakespeare could afford to pay our bill. A disastrous tragedy would ruin the evening.

We elbowed through the line as more ghosts streamed in.

The hunchback taking tickets glared as Sheyenne, Robin, and I bulldozed past. "Hey, you can't just—"

"Private detective," I yelled. "The police are on the way."

Since this was supposed to be a quiet, romantic date, I had hoped to catch the warm-up act with Sheyenne, but it was already in full swing. To the delight of the early-bird audience, three particularly limber zombies juggled a set of shrunken heads, bobbing up and down, passing the heads back and forth in a blur, like a macabre shell game. Towering speakers on either side of the stage blared out peppy music, set to a volume high enough to make the tombstones vibrate.

Then the final piece clicked into place. That big sound system could easily hide a pair of industrial-strength ectoplasmic defibrillators.

"They're in the speakers," I said. "The defibs are in the speakers!"

Sheyenne cried out, "There's Travis!"

Up near the stage, I saw a man who looked like her brother; he wore a fake mustache and a bright yellow shirt with the words *Stage Crew* silkscreened on the back, but he wasn't fooling us. She flitted forward much faster than I could have run even if I weren't so stiff.

As the opening act finished, the zombie jugglers tossed the shrunken heads out to lucky audience members, then ran off the stage.

Robin said, "We've got to get these ghosts out of here, now."

I drew my .38, pointed the gun into the air, and fired off three shots. "Evacuate immediately! This is an emergency!" I could have shot the speakers, but too many unnaturals were crowded up close to the stage. Some of the crowd listened; the others thought it was just theatrical effects and part of the show.

Robin kept shouting. "You'll all be disintegrated! What are you waiting for?"

We could never get the entire ghostly audience to safety fast enough if Travis was ready to activate the defibs. I fired twice more into the air. Some ghosts began wafting away, alarmed; others stopped at the ticket booth to ask for a refund. I had no idea what sort of range an industrial-strength ectoplasmic defibrillator had. I heard the yowling sirens of squad cars as McGoo brought backup to the cemetery, and the noise added to the panic.

Shakespeare came out onto the stage to calm the crowd, but I ran forward, waving my hands. "Get out, everyone out—especially the ghosts!"

He saw me, decided to take me at my word; if you can't trust your private detective, who can you trust? He spoke into the amplification system. "Everyone, please remain calm—and run like hell!"

The crowd ran like hell.

Sheyenne pulled herself up in front of her brother, outraged. "You've done stupid things in your life, Travis, but what do you think you're doing?"

"A good deed—and you weren't supposed to be here!" He backed toward the sound-system bank, holding a remote control pad that I guessed would activate the pulsing generators built into the speakers.

"You want to disintegrate the ghosts in the audience?" Sheyenne placed herself directly in front of him, drifting just out of his reach. "Well, I'm here—go on, do it if you hate unnaturals so much. I'm one of them."

"Just *leave*, sis!" His voice trembled. "This is something I've gotta do. The senator saved me when I needed it most."

"You wouldn't need to be saved if you didn't keep screwing up! Go ahead, throw the switch, if that's what you really want. You've always resented me for being practical and successful. You can't stand it, can you? Do you think your life will be better by disintegrating all these innocent ghosts? Will your conscience be clear?"

Travis wrestled with himself; his lower lip trembled. It wasn't exactly the approach I would have used, but Sheyenne knew her brother better than I did. She stayed right there, glaring at him.

"I can't disintegrate my own sister," he finally said, dropping the trigger remote.

I took matters into my own hands, just in case Sheyenne's little pep talk backfired. While they faced off, I got to the speaker and, using my zombie strength (which is actually overrated), tore out the electrical cables connected to the sound system. A yelp of feedback spilled out of the speakers before they went silent.

Squad cars pulled up by the Greenlawn gates. McGoo led a charge of blue-uniformed policemen into the cemetery where they careened into the mob of fleeing vampires and zombies. In the swirl of evacuating unnaturals, I caught a glimpse of Edgar Allan trying to hand out business cards; he nearly got trampled underfoot.

When he saw the approaching cops, Travis's eyes widened, then he broke down. "I don't want to go to jail. Senator Balfour told me he'd set me up with a new life and a new job far from here, if only I'd do this one thing! But I . . . I couldn't throw the switch, even before I saw you, sis. I swear, I wouldn't have done it!"

I didn't believe that part, but Sheyenne looked torn. "You're part of a plot that would have destroyed hundreds of ghosts. We can't just ignore that."

"Yes, you can," he insisted. "It's the last thing I'll ever ask of you, I promise. Just give me five minutes. Let me slip out of here, and you'll never see me again." He looked pleadingly at me, but found no help there, so he turned back to his sister.

The sirens were still wailing from the police units. McGoo and the others pushed toward the stage, fighting their way through a tangle of mummies and witches as they shouted for the ghosts to evacuate.

I glanced at Sheyenne. "If it were up to me, I'd strangle him. But it's your call. He's *your* brother."

Her expression softened. "Get the hell out of here, Travis—and do it before I change my mind."

Her brother bolted behind the Globe Theatre stage and fled; he was gone by the time the police reached us. Robin finally came up to the stage, her voice hoarse from yelling so much. "We did it! Everyone's safe."

McGoo was panting. "You sure know how to throw a party, Shamble—and don't you dare tell me it was a false alarm."

"If you check these speakers, you'll find two high-powered ectoplasmic defibrillators. One of Balfour's creeps intended to vaporize all the ghosts in the audience, but we stopped him in time. I tore out the wires."

"Did you catch the senator's man?" McGoo asked. "We can wrap this whole thing up if we get a confession!"

"He got away," Sheyenne said.

As McGoo's expression fell, I added, "We might have enough evidence here to nail Balfour anyway. Harvey Jekyll built and sold the defibrillators, and if we can tie these to him, find a purchase order, compare the serial numbers, you can bring charges."

"It's enough to cause a scandal, even if we don't get the senator in jail," McGoo said.

"Maybe we can still connect him with the bomb at the brothel," Sheyenne said.

"And I have dozens more suits and injunctions to file," Robin said.

"You keep filing your legal challenges. I'll take a more direct approach." I looked at Sheyenne. "Will you forgive me for going back to the Full Moon one more time?"

"Only if you promise me it's business."

"You know the answer to that."

CHAPTER 47

Nobody was surprised when gaunt and shadow-faced Senator Balfour gave an emergency press conference early the next morning. In his ponderous voice he denied any knowledge of the unfortunate plot during the Shakespeare in the Dark performance. His frumpy wife, looking equally lifeless and unenthused, stood at his side, supportive in the most minimal way possible.

I had no interest in listening to the speech. I didn't care about the man's excuses, nor did I believe him, although I did find it ironic that he somehow managed to label the accusations against him as "unnatural harassment."

I hoped I would get what I needed at the Full Moon and wrap up this whole mess.

Without a warrant, McGoo would never be able to see Madam Neffi's client records—and getting such a warrant would be problematic, since his own watch commander was one of her customers, as I knew from my previous glimpse of the files. I, however, had a close connection with the mummy madam, and I hoped she would cut me a break. Given Neffi's vendetta against

Senator Balfour, maybe she would let me look through her surveillance images and client files from the night of the bomb threat on the chance that I'd recognize one of Balfour's minions. Perhaps the guy-in-tie or one of the demonstrators who had marched on the adult novelty shop.

The withered madam was distraught when I arrived; her long, clawlike fingers fluttered about, showing her nervousness. "It's been one nightmare after another! Considering this is the world's oldest profession, you'd think we'd have the kinks worked out by now."

"Don't some customers want the kinks?" I said.

She turned her ember eyes toward me. "This isn't a time for jokes, Mr. Chambeaux. Both of my zombie girls quit this morning, said they couldn't take the pressure. Necrophilia's big business here in the Quarter—now what am I supposed to offer my customers?"

Yes, I thought she'd be inclined to help. "You heard what happened during the Shakespeare performance? I'm gathering evidence against Senator Balfour. One more solid nail in his coffin could take him down for good. If you let me look through your client files, I might find the clue we need."

She led me into her office. "So long as you do it in an unofficial capacity. I can't let these files go public. The Full Moon is very discreet, and my client list is confidential."

"Then why keep such detailed records in the first place?"

"Plenty of reasons: for protection, for possible blackmail use, and for occasional special coupon offers. Good business practices." She pulled out a thick stack of manila file folders from the metal cabinet. "These are the customers from two nights ago."

I took them out into the parlor and spread them on one of the red velvet sofas. "Looks like business was good."

Neffi followed me. "We had so many customers we could

barely log them in. Fortunately, we got good images from our lobby security cameras. In another week, I would have had a lot more footage. I'm setting up secret cameras for our subscription-only video service, Monsters Gone Wild."

I was surprised. "You film your customers and your girls?" Good thing I was not, nor did I intend to be, a Full Moon customer.

"They sign a waiver," Neffi said. "It's not illegal."

"Do the clients understand what they're signing?"

The old mummy shrugged. "Probably not. It's written in hieroglyphics."

Robin would have something to say about that, but I had a different purpose right now. The two vampire princesses and Cinnamon offered to help me go through the file. They used their sultry seductive voices; I doubted they knew how to talk in a normal manner.

"Please, ladies—I don't need the distraction right now."

"When you do need a distraction, be sure to call," said Cinnamon. "And ask for me."

"Or me," Nightshade and Hemlock chimed in.

Neffi leaned over the sofa, all business. "I've been through the photos myself, but didn't see anything out of the ordinary. No customers stood out more than usual."

"I'd think everything's out of the ordinary in a brothel in the Unnatural Quarter."

"Clients are clients."

I began to flip through the photos, a handful of humans and a wide assortment of monsters. "You didn't notice anyone . . . nervous?"

Neffi's chuckle was a dry sound like wind rattling through reeds. "A lot of our customers are nervous. It doesn't mean they planted a bomb."

Balfour's minions would be human, so I started there, hoping to connect a face with someone I had seen holding a GOD HATES UNATURALS sign or tacking up posters or marching in the demonstrations. But none of the faces looked familiar.

Quite a few customers were visiting the Quarter for a sporting-goods convention (judging by the name tags they had forgotten to remove). More tourism. I went through the entire file and began to lose hope that I'd find any clue connecting Senator Balfour with the bomb. Travis had insisted the senator was not responsible, but Sheyenne's brother wasn't the most reliable judge of character.

I flipped through the other files, monster after monster. Most didn't look familiar; I recognized some unnaturals I had met on the street. I was shocked by a few I *did* readily identify, but I won't mention their identities here; that's their private business, and it has nothing to do with this case.

When I opened the next two folders, though, I recognized the culprit immediately—and I knew for certain that Balfour wasn't involved after all.

Two of the brothel's customers on the night of the bomb were the fiery-eyed demons who had roughed me up only a few hours earlier. Big scaly thugs, hired by Missy Goodfellow for intimidation and muscle. I tapped the photos. "These two."

Neffi leaned over. "They like it rough. Don't tip," she said, as if that were enough of an accusation.

"They work for Missy Goodfellow and the Smile Syndicate."

The mummy madam recoiled. "The Smile Syndicate? Those bastards!"

If I'd been able to bottle the venom in her voice, I could have sold it to the Defense Department.

She continued, "I told you the mob has been trying to drive me out of business. I guess threats weren't enough. They wanted to blow up my brothel!"

"When you talked about organized crime moving into the

Quarter, I should have realized the Smile Syndicate was involved," I said. "I've already got a beef with those two demons. They owe me a new hat and jacket—and the price of a restorative spell." That reminded me I had to see Mavis Wannovich soon; she was becoming increasingly anxious to talk with me— she had called again that afternoon.

The phone in my pocket rang, and I answered it. Sheyenne said, "Hi, Beaux. Not having fun at the brothel, I hope?"

"You might call it fun. We just discovered who planted the bomb."

She sounded hopeful. "The senator?"

"No—looks like Missy Goodfellow."

"Hmm," Sheyenne said without any apparent surprise. "Speaking of which, Robin and I have been digging through municipal records. We located all those hearts and souls that Angela Drake bought from the pawnshop. Go collect them if you want to make Mrs. Saldana and Jerry happy."

I brightened. "Where are they?"

"At the Final Repose Storage Complex."

I grinned. "This has been a much better day than yesterday. I'll head right over there."

CHAPTER 48

Seeing me enter the front office, Maximilian Grubb rocked backward in his swivel chair behind the little desk. The former necromancer and former golem sweatshop operator immediately expected the worst—which is not an inappropriate reaction from a man with a guilty conscience and a very long rap sheet.

"Now what have I done? I already made it up to that escaped golem. I've got good karma now, but I swear you people won't rest in peace until you've destroyed my livelihood."

"I'm not going to rest in peace anytime soon, Mr. Grubb." I egged him on. "I'm puzzled by your reaction—worried about something?"

"No, no, I've walked the straight and narrow, I swear! I made amends wherever I could, and I sleep better at night, or during the day, or whenever it's convenient. I took the second chance to heart. I listened to what you and Officer McGoohan said. I'm a changed man."

His gaze shifted from side to side, but the eyeliner-painted third eye in the middle of his forehead stared directly at me.

"Just like you said—I filled out every form, crossed every *t*, dotted every *i*, applied for every conceivable permit, paid fees that even the clerk didn't know existed! I ransacked every single storage unit and spent hours with my clipboard, taking a complete inventory—and some of our customers were definitely not pleased. Kicked out a few homeless zombies, found a colony of feral black cats—*talking* ones, who were plotting to take over the world! Now, that was interesting. . . ."

I already knew that Max had filed his meticulous inventory of the storage units with the city clerk; Robin had obtained it through some legal somersault or other, and Sheyenne had pored over the listings until she spotted exactly what we were looking for.

He continued to ramble. "I properly disposed of any improperly stored items. I ensured legally mandated safety interlocks on all dangerous supernatural objects." The former necromancer finally ran out of steam. "I've done nothing wrong." He sniffled. "Honest."

I decided not to reassure him; better to keep him nervous. "I'm investigating a storage unit that contains a large number of packaged hearts and souls. I need you to take me there."

His eyes were bright and terrified, and even the painted eye on his forehead seemed to widen in fear. "I just *knew* those were going to be a problem! The clerk's office didn't know what to do with them. I think she wanted me to pay her a bribe to forget about the matter—but not me, no! Everything aboveboard from now on. That's my promise." Max sat up straight. "I spent hours with her looking through the books of regulations, and finally I got a permit for Dubious Sentimental Items. But I told her—I *swear* I told her—I said, 'If this is the wrong category, call me back, and I'll fill out the proper paperwork.' I did think those combo packs were highly unusual. Why would somebody store them here?"

"I want to see these hearts and souls, Mr. Grubb." From the

pocket of my sport coat, I withdrew a thick folded document, an imposing and frighteningly legal-looking brief. "One of them belongs to a client of mine, and he will sue to get his soul back." I looked around at the squalid offices. "Since you own the storage unit where the items in question have been hidden—perhaps illegally—you'll be named as one of the parties in the lawsuit."

Max held up his hands to ward off the document, like a vampire faced with a crucifix. That was fine with me, since I didn't want him to read the papers anyway. The document was just Robin's application for us to install a neon Chambeaux & Deyer sign outside our building, which had to be approved by the city council. The document had nothing whatsoever to do with retrieving the hearts and souls, but the former necromancer didn't know that.

"No need! I'll give you my full cooperation, but I'm not authorized to let you take any of the items away without a court order."

"Right now, Mr. Grubb, my first duty is to make certain my client's heart and soul are intact and undamaged."

Max pecked away with two frantic, shaking fingers on his old, dusty PC, calling up the records. "Yes, yes, there's the unit. It was rented by a Ms. Angela Drake, paid two years in advance." He looked up with a small forced smile. "She got a free month that way."

"I already know who rented it. Now please, take me out there so I can verify that my client's heart and soul haven't been harmed through any negligence of the Final Repose Storage Complex."

Max yanked open a drawer and rattled a copious number of keys until he selected the correct one. He led me out the door, his purple necromancer robe swishing from side to side as he took me between rows of low buildings, along gravel and mud driving paths, until he stopped at the third row. He unlocked the padlock and rolled up the segmented garage door. Tugging on a string inside, he switched on the single naked lightbulb, which illuminated an empty vault.

The unit contained only a single rack of metal shelves, on which rested a dozen Mason jars with rusty screw-top lids; the jars were held in place with stretched bungee cords. Each jar contained a hardened, twisted lump—the shriveled heart of some creature desperate enough to have pawned it at Time-worn Treasures. Each heart was surrounded by the faint blue aura of a barely visible soul. The preserved hearts beat slowly, restlessly, like a nightmare-plagued person twitching in his sleep.

Maximilian Grubb beamed with relief. "There you are! As you can see, the items are protected from the elements. Un-harmed. I've taken all necessary security precautions. No dam-age to any jar, no negligence whatsoever on the part of Final Repose . . . no need for your client to include us in the lawsuit."

"That remains to be seen," I said, hiding my relief. While the former necromancer pranced from one foot to the other as if he needed to go to the bathroom, I used my cell phone to call the Hope & Salvation Mission to tell Mrs. Saldana the good news.

She let out a delighted gasp. "Oh, bless you, Mr. Cham-beaux! Bless you! Can we come get them?"

"And bring Jerry. He'll have to identify which one is his. They all look alike to me."

"A person just *knows* when he looks into his soul," Mrs. Saldana said. "We'll be right down!"

Robin would get the legal clockwork moving, appeal for Jerry's rights as the legitimate owner. I didn't even know the le-galities of whether you *could* buy someone else's heart and soul.

After I hung up, the former necromancer looked like a little puppy dog, standing there. "So, it's all right? I have nothing to worry about?"

"There's a chance you may be off the hook, Mr. Grubb." I ran my gaze across the Mason jars sitting on the shelves. The stirring hearts looked dark and unattractive, nothing at all like what you'd see on a Valentine's Day card. In fact, they looked like Cupid's rejects.

I shook my head. "I wish I knew what Missy Goodfellow wants with all these hearts and souls. What does she intend to do with them?"

The necromancer blinked at me in surprise. "Oh, no, it's not Missy. It's *Irwyn*."

Chapter 49

My phone rang before Max could explain himself, and Robin started talking in my ear. I had never heard her so agitated. "Dan, get back to the office right away! You're not going to believe this—Mavis Wannovich is here."

I stifled a groan. "Today's not a good day for that."

"You have to see the new evidence about Snazz's murder! Mavis has proof of who killed him."

That wasn't what I expected. "Who? And how did Mavis get it?"

Robin was like a little kid holding an unpleasant surprise. "Just get over here! I'm calling Officer McGoohan." She hung up without telling me.

I gave Max a stern warning as I turned to rush away. "Lock this place up tight and make sure nothing happens to those hearts and souls until I get back. Guard them with your life."

The former necromancer groaned, "I don't have much of a life." But he promised anyway.

When I arrived back at our offices, I felt breathless. Or

maybe *disheveled* was a better word. I was putting a lot of mileage on these dead-tired feet today, but if I could wrap up a couple of major cases, then I promised myself I would take time off and reschedule that date with Sheyenne. We hadn't had very good luck so far.

The first thing I saw was the sow standing in the middle of our reception area. Mavis paced back and forth in her black dress. The sisters had brought the large crystal ball in its birdbath-sized holder that they'd purchased from the pawnshop liquidation auction.

When Mavis saw me, her expression melted into one of relief. "We've been leaving messages and messages for you, Mr. Chambeaux, but you wouldn't return our calls! We were going to call the police, but we wanted to talk to you first."

"I'm really sorry," I said. "I've run myself ragged all week."

The witch ran her gaze up and down my form. "Everything about you looks ragged, Mr. Chambeaux. We've got spells for that. We can spruce you up, just like we promised."

"I'll take you up on that, Mavis, as soon as we get a free minute."

Alma snorted with impatience. Robin and Sheyenne both crowded close to the large crystal ball. "I never would have thought," Robin said. "Dan, come here and watch."

"Allow me." Mavis went to the ornately carved stand, touching runes carved into the decorative moldings, and the crystal ball sparkled. Images floated inside the glass globe, flickering back and forth. Mavis clucked her tongue. "Sorry . . . I'm still learning how to tune this thing."

It turned out the crystal ball that Snazz kept at the pawnshop's front counter was not just a decorative item that he loved to polish. The crystal ball was also a full-fledged security camera, with its curved surfaces able to record all activities around the shop, 360 degrees. It had allowed Snazz to sit propped on his stool and observe everyone and everything in Timeworn Treasures.

I felt guilty that I hadn't called Mavis back right away—not just because we had missed this clue, which might have an impact on several pending cases, but because I owed it to her. I'd given my promise, and she had done me plenty of favors. After this, I would sit down with the Wannovich sisters and their vampire ghostwriter for as long as it took to give them all the background material they needed.

"Ah, there we are—the correct time stamp," Mavis said.

I leaned closer and realized we were about to watch the little gremlin get murdered.

In the crystal ball, we saw Snazz working alone, well after dark. I wasn't surprised he had no customers because by now most window-shoppers knew the gremlin couldn't bear to be parted from his treasures. With an old rag, he polished sparkling gems and a gold amulet; I saw a tarnished old Arabian lamp in the pile of treasures waiting to be polished, and I dreaded what might happen when the pawnbroker started to rub *that*. . . .

But Snazz didn't get the chance. The door opened, and a customer came in—the gremlin's *last* customer.

"Watch this!" Mavis said. "This is it." The sow snorted and leaned closer, rising up so she could peer into the crystal ball.

"I'm watching," I said.

The crystal ball had no audio, so we couldn't hear the gremlin's greetings, or the customer's response, the loud arguments, the shouted accusations, the escalating violence. The murder had happened some time ago, but it was real and immediate for us to witness it now.

I watched in horror as the poor, greedy gremlin was attacked and strangled, his furry paws clutching at his neck, beating at his assailant, kicking his little furry feet, all to no avail, until his strangled and broken body was tossed unceremoniously on the floor.

Irwyn Goodfellow looked annoyed, but not unduly disturbed, by what he had done. He used Snazz's own polishing rag to wipe his fingerprints from any surface he had touched, then he departed from the dark and silent pawnshop.

"Looks like Irwyn's not such a good fellow after all," I said.

CHAPTER 50

Murder is never a cause for celebration, but McGoo was thrilled when I told him we had found the killer. "I promised I'd solve the case, but I'll let you take the credit. Another gold star on your record, another major crime solved, another reason for your chief to be proud of you."

I let him know we were heading to the Final Repose storage unit so we could retrieve Jerry's heart and soul. Mrs. Saldana was already on her way over, and I wanted to be sure her zombie assistant got what he needed before the Mason jars were confiscated as evidence. Since the Goodfellows could afford the best lawyers, the trial was sure to get tangled in a nightmare of appeals and delays.

I also knew, however, that the Smile Syndicate might soon be short on funds, thanks to other legal troubles. And Missy had damn well asked for it!

I smiled when I thought of the wheels I had already set in motion. I was still pissed off—not to mention sore—that Missy Goodfellow had sent her thug demons to rough me up and threaten Robin.

While Sheyenne and the Wannovich sisters arranged to turn over the crystal-ball security-cam footage, Robin accompanied me out to the storage unit. Maximilian Grubb was already intimidated, but I wanted her along in case we needed to do a little legal bluffing so Jerry could be restored. She agreed. "As long as it's *legal* bluffing."

When the solution to a case is humming along and building momentum, I always get optimistic, but I should know better by now. We arrived at the Final Repose, hoping that Max had locked the storage unit and kept the hearts and souls safe—only to find the former necromancer murdered in the front office.

Very murdered.

He had been shot multiple times with silver bullets, including one through the third eye painted in the middle of his forehead. A wooden stake had been pounded through his heart, and a scribbled deanimation spell had been safety-pinned to his shirt.

I had seen this sort of thing before. As Robin stood there aghast, I said, "The murderer looked up how to kill a necromancer online and got conflicting information."

McGoo drove up in his patrol car and whistled a cheerful tune as he pulled open the office door and stepped inside, said hello to Robin and me, then stared at the body of the thoroughly murdered necromancer. He looked at me and said, "Damn, Shamble, why is it always complicated with you?"

Then the astonishment wore off enough that another piece clicked into place for me. "We'd better get to the storage unit! Mrs. Saldana might be in trouble."

That old woman had devoted her life to helping down-and-out unnaturals. She had been tireless in her dedication, saving brain-addict zombies like Jerry, handing out charity blood packs to starving vampires, giving monsters a second chance when they needed it, despite all of her difficulties in keeping the mission open. As her benefactor, Irwyn Goodfellow had seemed a godsend, providing new hope for all lower-class unnaturals. Now, though, I feared we would find her dead, just like Maximilian Grubb.

We bolted out of the office, ran between the rows of storage units. I drew my .38 as we approached, and McGoo pulled his service piece—the one loaded with normal bullets, not the silver-jacketed ones. Irwyn Goodfellow was not a monster in the traditional sense, just a very, very bad man.

The roll-up door to the hearts-and-souls storage unit was open, and I heard rustling sounds inside, clinking jars. We knew what Goodfellow was capable of. I couldn't forget his demonic expression in the crystal ball as he strangled Snazz, and the numerous wounds on the former former necromancer's body made the point more clearly than words. "Robin, you'd better stay back where it's safe," I whispered.

Her eyes flared. "Are you kidding me?"

"Okay, silly suggestion."

McGoo and I walked up to the open storage unit, guns drawn.

Under the light of the single naked bulb, Irwyn Goodfellow was grabbing Mason jars from the shelves, stuffing them into a black duffel bag, and packing dirty socks around the jars so the glass wouldn't break. He picked up one jar that contained a brown and sluggishly beating heart surrounded by the aura of a contained soul.

When we yelled "Freeze!" it was like a moment in a cop show.

Goodfellow froze, as he was told. His face looked haggard; his big once-understanding eyes had more of an edge now. His thick flattop haircut looked like a bristly doormat used for scrubbing mud from the bottom of your shoes. He showed no sign of the smile he had worn during his many benevolent speeches.

Mrs. Saldana and Jerry lay on the floor inside the unit, both of them tied up with the bungee cords Goodfellow had detached from the shelves. Both had also been gagged with dirty socks stuffed into their mouths—which was disgusting in its own way.

Goodfellow held the jar in his hand, dangling it above the hard cement floor in a clear threat.

Jerry mumbled something through the wadded sock in his mouth. Even when his articulation was unimpeded, Jerry's words were often incomprehensible, and I couldn't understand a single syllable now. But the conclusion was obvious—Goodfellow was holding Jerry's heart and soul hostage.

"Put the soul down, Goodfellow," McGoo said. "Gently. No sudden moves."

"I don't think so. I'm very sorry, but I have to think of the benefit of the whole Unnatural Quarter. And since I'm doing so much good work here, it's important that I stay out of jail." Now the sincere, warm smile returned to his face. "You understand."

He glanced at the old woman, who struggled against her stretchy bungee cords but made little progress. "Even Mrs. Saldana knows what I'm talking about. I feel very bad about having to kill her, because she's such a nice lady who has her heart in the right place, but I need to cover my tracks."

"We know what you did, Goodfellow," I said. McGoo and I both kept our weapons aimed directly at him. "We've got crystal-ball security camera footage that proves you murdered Snazz the gremlin, and we know you killed Maximilian Grubb in the office."

"Yes, I killed them, but it was for a good cause." Goodfellow blinked at us, apparently baffled that we didn't understand. "You aren't seeing the forest for the trees here."

I spoke for all of us. "I'm confused."

Still ready to smash Jerry's heart and soul on the cement, Goodfellow said, "The gremlin would have revealed that I'd bought all the hearts and souls if you tempted him enough. I couldn't allow myself to be in that position. The whole Quarter would suffer if people stopped thinking of me as a good person. Do you believe altruism, benevolence, and philanthropy comes *easy* to a person? What kind of freak do you think I am?"

Mrs. Saldana squirmed and tried to shout something through the sock. Her face was screwed up in an expression of distaste, either from the sour foot sweat or from the revelations Irwyn Goodfellow was making.

"You have to understand," he continued, "I'm really a rotten guy inside—bad blood, you might say—but I just didn't *like* myself. After the falling piano almost killed me, I vowed to change. There's no law against self-improvement. I should be commended."

Considering the murders Goodfellow had already committed, I was glad I'd never met the *unimproved* version.

"But I masked my predilections by buying up other people's hearts and souls, which gives me all the kindness and generosity I need. I'm an artificially good person, but a good person nevertheless."

Robin was appalled. "You can't just buy kindness and generosity from other people! That has to come from inside yourself."

"That's what the books say, but I didn't have time for that. I'm a busy, important man. I needed a shortcut. After my epiphany, I knew I needed to do good works—I really did!—but altruism and good intentions weren't enough. I needed to stack the deck." He snickered. "Missy was so embarrassed, she convinced me to use her assistant Angela as a proxy, a buffer so that I wouldn't put another white mark on our family name. And Angela didn't mind the overtime."

He gave us his warm-fuzzy smile. "After I bought the first heart-and-soul combo pack from the pawnshop, I felt so *positive,* so happy with a rush of kindness! I realized that was the key. And look at all the good I've done since then. I put in a standing order with Snazz and started buying all the hearts and souls I could get my hands on. That way, I truly felt the joy of giving."

McGoo kept his revolver pointed at Goodfellow as he stepped into the storage unit. "Well, the joy's over. You're under arrest for the murder of Snazz the gremlin, the murder of Maximilian Grubb, and kidnapping—for starters."

"I can come up with a lot more," Robin said. "Give me a few minutes."

Goodfellow let out an exasperated sigh, growing more impatient with how thickheaded we were. "But those other people didn't deserve their hearts and souls. They pawned them—they were practically new, barely used!"

"Jerry pawned his heart and soul so that *Mrs. Saldana* could do good work," I said. "And now he wants them back."

Goodfellow's face twisted with rage that we could be so dense as to continue threatening him. "Well, he won't get it back if I smash this jar on the floor! You are going to let me walk out of here, free. Give me a small plane so I can fly off to a small country that doesn't extradite . . ."

"Yeah, we'll get right on that," I said with a snort.

"Oh, never mind, that's too much trouble. I'll just use one of the Smile Syndicate travel agents to set it up. But either way, you can't stop me. I am getting out of here."

"Not gonna happen, Goodfellow," McGoo said.

"Then I'll shatter the jar—and you know what happens when you suddenly release a contained soul?" His eyes glittered. "There'll be nothing left of this whole storage complex except a giant glassy crater."

McGoo hesitated and glanced at me. "Is he right?"

I shrugged. "Hell if I know." I looked at Robin. She didn't know, either.

The corrugated metal wall in the back of the unit split open, and a large shape battered through as if the wall were no more than wrapping paper. Bill the golem, wearing his brand-new security guard uniform, lumbered into the unit. "Stop right there!"

Goodfellow whirled—and the glass jar slipped from his hands.

I was already diving forward. I sprawled on the concrete pad, scraping off patches of dead skin, but I didn't feel it. None of that mattered. Somehow, the Mason jar holding Jerry's heart and possibly explosive soul landed on my chest and rumpled sport coat. I caught the jar before it could bounce off and break.

Bill seized Irwyn Goodfellow in a firm clay grip. "I am making a citizen's arrest." He did look dashing in his new dark uniform, with a badge on his chest and a neat cap on his head. "And I *am* a citizen, just like any other unnatural."

"*This* is your new job?" I said.

"I patrol the grounds. All day long, all night long."

"I can't believe you'd work for Maximus Max after he kept all your people as slaves," Robin said as McGoo slapped handcuffs on Goodfellow.

"He was trying to atone. Offered me a job, a real job. Paid well." His clay face smiled. "Good benefits."

Robin and I unfastened the bungee cord hooks to release Mrs. Saldana and Jerry. They yanked the socks out of their mouths, gagging and spitting. Jerry said in a slurred voice, "Tastes foul."

McGoo regarded the half-filled duffel bag, the remaining jars on the shelves. "We'll have to confiscate these hearts and souls, log them into evidence." Mrs. Saldana and Jerry were both crestfallen, but McGoo plucked the rescued jar out of my hands and said, "Unfortunately, in all the commotion, maybe I didn't notice this one." He handed Jerry back his heart and soul.

Even though shamblers tend to have very bad teeth, it was good to see Jerry smile.

CHAPTER 51

Even with Robin's numerous challenges to the Unnatural Acts Act pending with the courts, and with Sheyenne's overwhelming workload just wrapping up the various cases we had finished, I made them follow me out of the Chambeaux & Deyer offices. I wanted us all outside of Smile HQ at the right time and place.

"I promise, this will warm your hearts," I said. "Makes all our work worthwhile." Maybe that was an exaggeration, but it did get them interested.

We waited on the sidewalk across the street from the corporate headquarters, pretending to be mere pedestrians. I glanced at my watch.

The Smile Syndicate was a mammoth business with tentacles extending throughout the Unnatural Quarter and the normal world. In order to defeat such an organization, I needed something even more powerful and more dangerous than they were—which meant I had to make a deal with the devil (metaphorically speaking, honest).

With a squeal of tires, five black unmarked cars pulled up in front of Smile HQ. Each had tinted windows, nondescript license plates, and all the glaring indicators that government agencies include on a "discreet unmarked vehicle." Men in black suits, white shirts, thin black ties, and black sunglasses emerged. They carried briefcases instead of weapons, but in this instance the briefcases could cause far more damage than a bazooka.

"Who are they, Dan?" Robin asked.

"Internal Revenue Service," I said, then added with grinning finality, "Auditors."

More vehicles surrounded the corporate headquarters, and auditors swooped in like vultures onto a bloated corpse.

"How did they know to come here?" Sheyenne asked. "And how did you know it was going to happen?"

I smiled again, feeling good inside. "Could be someone made a phone call."

After I had obtained Snazz's hidden ledger and confronted Missy Goodfellow with the second set of books, she had all but admitted to me that the Smile Syndicate used the same shady accounting practices. Normally, that wouldn't have been any of my business, but once Missy's demon goons had roughed me up and played Pass the Zombie, and then threatened to twist Robin's head off like unscrewing a lid from a jar, she had crossed a line.

Being a criminal is one thing, but playing dirty is another, so I felt justified in playing dirty as well.

The two demon thugs had also planted a bomb at the Full Moon (and probably smashed the windows and ruined two of Neffi's mummified pet cats). And Irwyn Goodfellow had used Angela's services and Smile Syndicate funds to purchase his stash of pawned hearts and souls. But that was all just icing on the cake.

I knew the inherent dangers of contacting the tax authorities, and it was action I did not take lightly. You've heard stories about ill-advised amateur wizards who invoke supernatural entities that invariably turn on them, and my phone call tip was like summoning a powerful and uncontrollable demon. But the IRS was the only thing I knew that was scary enough to take down the Smile Syndicate.

The men in suits locked down the entire building and held a perimeter. No one was allowed in or out. A larger crowd began to gather, watching the commotion. I bought coffee for us from a cart on the corner.

I assumed that the auditors would find some way to track down Angela Drake in Tasmania—if indeed that was where she'd gone . . . if she was even still alive. They would take her statement, get her to turn state's evidence on Missy Goodfellow. She would also be a helpful witness in Irwyn's trial.

The three of us watched as a group of clerical golems marched out of Smile HQ dressed in business suits, white shirts, and black ties. They had been hired as office workers from Irwyn Goodfellow's own Adopt-a-Golem program, and now the ten clay figures walked in perfect single file, each carrying a banker's box full of confiscated financial records.

"The Smile Syndicate is finished," I said. "I don't know what'll happen to all those souvenir shops. And I hope Stu ends up running the Goblin Tavern on his own. We'll have to wait and see what happens."

Sheyenne asked, "If Angela purchased those hearts and souls from the pawnshop using Smile Syndicate funds, then won't all the Mason jars be considered company assets during the tax proceedings?"

"If this turns out as I suspect, they'll have to liquidate the company in order to pay back taxes," Robin said. "I'll file an immediate claim on behalf of the original owners of the hearts and souls. We'll arrange to buy them all back."

"And what about his charity work?" I asked.

"Even though his reasons might have been corrupt, Irwyn knew what he was doing in the philanthropy department. Fortunately, all of his finances were locked into the nonprofit, shielded from Smile Syndicate operations. They should be immune from confiscation, no matter what the IRS finds in the audit." Robin had been looking into the matter since Irwyn's arrest. She had decided to join MLDW as a full member and legal advisor; Mrs. Saldana was the head of the board of directors and would be taking over the charities.

We stood there for hours, watching the proceedings and never growing bored. Yes, it was turning out to be a good day.

Now, when I take on a case, the job is all about getting the client what he or she wants, to solve a mystery or wrap up a crime. *Gloating* isn't supposed to enter into it, but I did feel a warm glow of satisfaction as we watched the squad of agents herding goldenrod-haired Missy, her hands cuffed behind her back, forcing her to do the perp walk to one of their unmarked vehicles. I took a few photos for my scrapbook.

As the men in suits pushed her toward the car, Missy's eyes met mine, and a flash of understanding crossed her face. Her lip curled down in vengeful fury—not at all like the smile the company sported on their logo. She tried to shout something at me, but one of the agents pushed her head down and strongly encouraged her into the backseat of the car.

Even though Missy couldn't hear me, I said, "We hope your day is a sunny one."

CHAPTER 52

The ghost of Alphonse Wheeler escaped from prison, to no one's surprise.

Instead of simply drifting between the bars or walking through the solid walls, the ghost bank robber went the extra mile and arranged a daring escape, as his reputation required. He had obtained a jeweler's file from somewhere (rumor had it that he slipped out one night and stole it from a hardware store, then sneaked it back into the prison) and patiently cut through the bars of a high window. He tied sheets together so he could drop down, even though he could just as easily float, then threw one of the sheets over a guard and tied him up so he could have enough time to slip away.

My suspicion was that Wheeler just wanted the attention, and he played by the rules to maintain his cachet of notoriety. During his bank-robbing career, Wheeler had been quite a showman, so his escape from prison couldn't be as simple as floating away after he got bored with unlife behind bars.

Unfortunately, the uproar caused by his escape reignited the issue of effective punishment against ghosts, even after what had happened during the Shakespeare in the Dark performance. Not surprisingly, Senator Balfour's supporters demanded widespread use of the ectoplasmic defibrillator in even the mildest cases.

Not one to miss an opportunity to speak out against unnaturals, Balfour called a press conference after Wheeler's escape. In the crowd, his determined minions carried scrawled signs rife with misspellings. Sheyenne insisted that we attend the press conference; she was still angry with Travis, but even more upset at how the senator had used him as a patsy.

Robin, who was still battling the defamation and libel suit Balfour had brought against her, came along with us, determined to show that she intended to go down fighting. (Of course, her preference was not to go down at all, but to be victorious.)

Balfour stood at the podium like a stick-in-the-mud with lips. Surrounded by so many followers who expressed innate hatred toward anything that was different from them, we felt distinctly out of place. After all, we were certainly *different*.

The senator fixed his gaze on Sheyenne as he said, "The violent escape of the convicted bank robber Alphonse Wheeler only demonstrates the inadequacy of our means to protect ourselves against these unnaturals. That poor prison guard whom Wheeler assaulted in his escape will suffer severe psychological problems from his traumatic experience. We are all at risk! The only way to ensure that good normal people remain safe is to give them access to ectoplasmic protection! Any unnatural— whether it be a ghost, vampire, zombie, werewolf, or any other *thing* that breaks the law—must know it will meet the ultimate punishment."

Balfour's minions cheered and hooted. I noticed that the media cameras and reporters paid more attention to the antics of his knuckle-dragging supporters than to the senator.

From the other side of the crowd, counter-protesters shouted,

"Ectoplasmic defibrillators are dangerous! They should be banned!" They had been rallied by MLDW in support of equal rights for the unnaturals.

"Conflict of interest! Senator Balfour is an investor with the defib manufacturer," another MLDW supporter yelled. "He's in this for the money."

Balfour looked mortally offended. "Anyone who makes such an accusation had better show proof, or I'll sue you for slander—just as I'm suing Ms. Deyer there." He pointed directly at us.

Robin lifted her chin and put on a brave face. "The truth is the truth."

The senator's slack face finally showed a small smile. "At last I agree with you, Ms. Deyer: The truth is what shields us all."

There was a stir in the crowd, and Balfour turned as a small man made his way to the stage, accompanied by a werewolf who cleared a path through the crowd. It was Harvey Jekyll. His pale and patchy skin suggested that he hadn't yet invested in a better embalming job, even though I'd recommended Bruno and Heinrich's parlor to him.

The senator looked uncomfortable to see the unexpected guest. "Ah, my . . . associate, Harvey Jekyll." He didn't want to say "friend." Since Jekyll was the inventor and sole manufacturer of ectoplasmic defibrillators, however, Balfour could not deny his connection to the man.

The crowd muttered and grumbled. Both unnaturals and unnatural-haters found common ground in reviling Harvey Jekyll.

Though he was a small man, Jekyll shouldered Senator Balfour aside, took the microphone at the podium. "Ladies and gentlemen, thank you for such a warm welcome." Jekyll must have heard something I hadn't. "I don't like to think of myself as a vindictive man, but . . ." He gave a small, helpless smile. "I am what I am. This man, however, is *not* what he seems." He jabbed his finger toward the senator. "Senator Rupert Balfour is a fraud, a complete and utter fraud."

The crowd exploded. "Security!" Balfour shouted.

While guards rushed the stage, Larry the werewolf bounded up next to the podium and protected his boss, muscles bulging, fur bristling, fangs bared. Jekyll needed only a moment to say what he had come to say. His voice carried over the crowd.

"Senator Balfour claims he hates unnaturals, but he is, himself . . . *a zombie!* And I am sick and tired of keeping his secret."

A simultaneous gasp of indrawn breath from the audience sucked all the oxygen from the immediate vicinity. Robin, Sheyenne, and I stared at the stage. Senator Balfour was a gaunt and cadaverous man, humorless, loveless. "I should have seen the signs before," I said.

"If it's true," Robin added, "he gives zombies a bad name."

In the immediate uproar, Larry managed to push past the guards and angry crowd members and whisk his boss to safety. Most of the howling masses, though, were charging the stage to demand answers from the senator.

Over the course of the afternoon, the rest of the story came out. The senator holed up and refused to answer questions, but soon enough his wife turned on him. Two of Balfour's personal doctors, as well as his illicit mortician, gave interviews with their sides of the story. They also hinted that they were currently shopping tell-all books to various publishers.

Senator Rupert Balfour, whom Robin had so aptly labeled an "ambulatory wad of phlegm," was a bitter, grim man who had died one night of a heart attack, alone in bed. He came back to life, thanks to the aftereffects of the Big Uneasy.

And nobody noticed the difference. Even his wife, an equally bitter and grim woman, had not remarked on the change for two weeks.

Since he was a man of considerable power and means, Balfour covered up his death and resurrection. No wonder his wife looked perpetually sour, although it was clear to most observers that she hadn't been satisfied—in any sense of the term—for some time, before or after her husband's death.

Upon hearing the news, Senator Balfour's minions, once so vehement and supportive, turned on him like a pack of rabid lemmings. All efforts to enforce the Unnatural Acts Act were "halted, pending review," and an emergency session was scheduled to repeal the Act, based on the highly unusual circumstances.

For a man once so outspoken against his philosophical rivals, Balfour limited himself to statements comprising only two words: "No comment."

Chapter 53

It isn't easy to tell when a mummy is nervous, but I knew Ramen Ho-Tep well enough that I could detect subtle indications of anxiety. He talked too quickly, fidgeted, and avoided what was obviously the point.

He shuffled into our offices on the pretext of "just stopping in to say hello"—which is never the real reason for a visit.

"You look spruced up," I said, remembering the first time he had dragged himself in to see Robin. His bandages had been brown, frayed, and loose, and he dribbled dust and moths everywhere. Now he had taken extra care to make himself presentable, with a few golden scarab baubles and one of those rubber support-the-cause bracelets for some charity or other. "What's the occasion?"

"Oh, nothing special, Mr. Chambeaux. I just like to look nice in case . . . well, you never know whom you might bump into," he said in his erudite British accent. "I *am* the Pharaoh of all Egypt. You might say I'm a trendsetter of mummy fashion everywhere. By the way, I wonder if you might be a good chap? Do me a favor?"

As I said, stopping by just to say hello is never the real reason. "Always happy to help our friends and former clients, Mr. Ho-Tep. What can I do for you?"

"I am in possession of a certain VIP ticket to my presentation at the museum tomorrow, and I'd like to hand it to you."

"We've got other plans on Saturday, Mr. Ho-Tep. Sorry." We were committed to going to Tiffany's comedy routine.

"Oh, you have already seen the show, Mr. Chambeaux. The ticket is not intended for you. I hoped you might consider delivering the invitation to Madam Neffi over at the Full Moon brothel?"

Now it made sense. "You could just deliver it yourself. Neffi would be happy to see you."

"I hope so." He shuffled his bandaged feet. "But I'm a tad nervous."

I was surprised. "The Pharaoh of all Egypt, who commanded great armies, who built gigantic pyramids, who ruled countless slaves . . . is nervous?"

He swallowed in a very, very dry throat. "This is *Neffi* we're talking about."

"I see what you mean." I reached out my hand. "I'll be heading over there to wrap up some matters on a case, and I'll deliver it to her in person." I had to bring our final bill, close out the account, and maintain goodwill; I had no doubt that Full Moon would need the services of Chambeaux & Deyer at some time in the future.

"Thank you very much. I hope . . . I do hope she's willing to see me again."

That afternoon, when I presented the special invitation to the mummy madam, a look of delight crossed the shriveled old face. "Why, Ramen Ho-Tep, that rascal! He sends you to do his dirty work? That man doesn't know how to perform the simplest actions without his minions."

"He'd be very grateful if you'd attend his presentation," I

said. "He's proud of the work he does, and I think it's interesting."

"Oh, I'll go and see him, although I think it might rattle the poor man." She giggled. "It's funny when a great pharaoh stammers too much to complete a sentence. If nothing else, I'll be there to correct any misperceptions he gives the audience. As a pharaoh, Ramen never knew how *real* Egyptians lived. He had his brain removed with a silver spoon up his nose."

She drew a deep breath and heaved a long, dusty sigh. "Oh, it'll be good to see him again." She took the invitation and tucked it into her bodice, where I knew for certain that it would be safe.

It was a night for celebration on many levels, and Robin, Sheyenne, McGoo, and I got together for a drink and a laugh. Yes, we had promised to see Tiffany's routine at the comedy club, but this was no mere duty dance. I was actually pleased to be at the Laughing Skull.

Tiffany made sure we had seats at one of the front tables near the stage. While there was no ticket charge for the open-mic night, the Laughing Skull did institute a two-drink minimum for all clientele, natural or unnatural. Since Sheyenne could nurse a drink but not actually enjoy it, McGoo and I manfully helped to meet her beverage obligations as well as our own.

Bill was already seated at the table, the big clay guy facing the still-empty stage with a broad grin on his face. He had been moistened and smoothed over for the evening, and he looked freshly molded. He did not wear his security watchman uniform; rather, he had donned a bright Hawaiian shirt.

"Are you done with your job at the storage complex?" I asked.

"No, got the night off. I wouldn't miss this!"

The emcee welcomed us all; it was the same wizard who had

acted as auctioneer for the Timeworn Treasures liquidation sale. The cocktail waitress brought our drinks, and we all sat back, ready to laugh as Tiffany stepped onto the stage. She was a solid woman, dressed in a too-tight pantsuit, possibly for humorous effect, or possibly because that was what she had in her closet. Tiffany wore very little makeup, didn't smile, and seemed all business—the last sort of person you would expect behind a microphone in a comedy club. We gave her a round of supportive applause.

On a stool near the microphone stand, she had a plastic bottle of water and a curved cocktail glass filled with what looked like a Bloody Mary but wasn't. Tiffany began rattling off her jokes and, oddly enough, she was hilarious.

"So, I just came back from dinner. Went to an all-you-can-eat restaurant." She smiled enough to show her fangs. "I had two waiters and a busboy."

McGoo laughed out loud, deep rumbling chuckles from his belly. "I'll have to remember that one. That sounds like a joke I would tell."

"I went into a bar with two of my vampire friends," Tiffany continued. "The bartender asked what we wanted to drink. My friends both ordered glasses of blood, but I just ordered a shot of plasma. So the bartender said, Let me get this straight . . . that's two bloods and a blood lite?"

She was on a roll, and the crowd was already loosened up. "Somebody asked me, How do you fit forty vampires into a Volkswagen Beetle?" Tiffany looked around the audience, saw us, and continued, "Easy, I said. Gather forty vampires out in the parking lot, wait until the sun comes up, and then put them all in the ashtray."

Tiffany finished her set with most of the audience in stitches—or in unraveled stitches. Bill shot to his feet, slamming his clay hands together with loud thunderclaps. She bowed to another round of applause.

Although McGoo had laughed throughout, now he looked perplexed. "I don't get it, Shamble. What am I doing wrong? When I tell the same kind of jokes, you never laugh. Well, *sometimes*, but only because we made a deal. What's the difference?"

"You know how it is, McGoo," I said. "She's a vampire. She's allowed to tell jokes like that."

I finally made an appointment to see the Wannovich sisters and their vampire ghostwriter at the Transfusion coffee shop to tell them everything they needed to know. I was no stranger to interviews: As a private detective, I knew how to pry information from suspects or witnesses. I wasn't accustomed to being on the other side of the questions, though.

I didn't know what I could say to make my work sound exciting. A detective's job is just a job, like a grocery store manager, or a cop, or an accountant—not necessarily interesting. (All right, maybe it is more interesting, or at least more hazardous, than an accountant's job.)

It remained a mystery to me, all detective work aside, why anyone would want to read the adventures of a zombie private investigator, but I'm not the arbiter of literary tastes. Chatting with Mavis and Alma Wannovich over a cup of coffee was the least I could do. Besides, thanks to Sheyenne's negotiating, I was even getting a regular restoration spell out of it. Mavis was so excited by the prospects that she had given me a bonus touch-up after my rough treatment in the past week, just so I felt fresh for the interview.

We met at Transfusion in the middle of the afternoon. The black-glass windows kept the hazardous sunlight out. Soft jazz played over the speakers—the annoying tuneless kind that no one except the barista seems to like. Only a few other customers sat at the tables: two sleepless vampires working on their laptops, a group of young wizards gathered around two pushed-together tables discussing well-highlighted copies of a thick book—a Necronomicon study group.

The large witch and the large sow were waiting for me, sitting next to a plump female vampire who wore cat's-eye glasses, and I recognized the Welcome Back Wagon volunteer. Mavis introduced us. "Mr. Chambeaux, thank you so much for coming! We'd like you to meet our friend and colleague, Linda Bullwer. She'll be writing the zombie detective series for Howard Phillips Publishing."

"Under the pen name of Penny Dreadful." The vampire woman pushed her cat's-eye glasses up on her nose before she shook my hand. "Primarily, I'm a poet, but so far I haven't been successful in getting published. This is a great opportunity for me."

"Happy to help out, Miss Bullwer. You'll have to do some embellishing to make sense out of my cases."

"Not a problem at all. I have my artistic license, fully paid for. It's valid for the next year." She took out her notepad, ready to get to work. She had already doodled in the margins.

I ordered my coffee, got another round for the three ladies; Alma's was chai tea served in a bowl. I sat down, cautioning the vampire ghostwriter, "Remember, you're not going to use my real name. These will be fictional exploits, right?"

"Everything will be dramatized, the names changed to protect the innocent and the unnatural," Linda Bullwer assured me. "But inspired by real events."

"Howard Phillips hopes to make this series a great success," Mavis said, accompanied by a succession of grunts from Alma.

"The cases don't solve themselves," I said. "And real cases don't always turn out as neat and tidy as in a novel."

"Novels don't write themselves either, Mr. Chambeaux," said the vampire, scribbling notes. "Don't you worry—a good writer improves on real life."

CHAPTER 54

"Another round, Francine." McGoo held up his empty beer mug. "Shamble's buying."

"I didn't agree to that."

"I didn't ask," McGoo said. "What are friends for?"

"Then give me another one, too, Francine," I said.

Two nights later, we met at the Goblin Tavern, glad the Quarter was finally getting back to normal—whatever that meant. Francine was back behind the bar, full of energy, chatting with the customers. Her black cobwebby dress had a lower neckline and a higher hemline than most customers would have preferred, but Francine seemed comfortable in it. In fact, she said it helped her fit in. Who were we to judge?

Stu was in his office, working on the accounts, punching keys on a calculator, making phone calls. Ever since the Smile Syndicate had been placed under investigation, all of the company's records and assets were frozen. I was worried that the Tavern might be shut down pending liquidation, but since the place was generating income with a renewed customer base, the tax authorities allowed it to stay open.

Every ten minutes or so, Stu came out to say hello to the customers, smiling to assure them that he appreciated their business. "Francine's taking care of you all?" he asked no one in particular. "Isn't she the best?"

"I agree," I said. "You should give her a raise."

Stu scuttled back into his office, pretending he hadn't heard the comment. I knew he had been working with the Trove National Bank on a business loan and was trying to find investors so he could buy the Goblin Tavern himself. I thought he just might pull it off. McGoo and I were doing our best to help by contributing to the nightly take in the cash register.

On the bar television, we watched a news report that showed harried-looking Senator Rupert Balfour, head down and covered with a newspaper, being hurried into his car as reporters and angry former minions shouted after him. The Tavern regulars let out a chorus of boos and catcalls.

McGoo planted his elbows on the bar. "Everyone in the Quarter can rest easy now."

"The senator won't," I said.

Despite his disgrace, Balfour had been defiant throughout the scandal. He had refused to resign as senator and vowed to fight on . . . but his colleagues removed him from office by unanimous vote. The senate rules stated explicitly that a senator was to be replaced upon his death. Even though no one had immediately noticed, Senator Rupert Balfour was indeed dead, and therefore could no longer serve in office.

The increasingly unpopular Unnatural Acts Act was repealed, not because of any deafening outcry among the citizens, but because of a minor legal loophole: Since Balfour had been dead when he proposed the Act, it should never have been brought to a vote.

Robin would have enjoyed fighting her challenges and striking repeated blows in the name of Justice, but Chambeaux & Deyer had other work to do. I convinced her to be satisfied with what we had accomplished.

That afternoon, I had gone to visit Hope Saldana and Jerry at the mission. She had baked a chocolate cake, and everyone from the mission had signed a homemade thank-you card for me. They gave me a round of embarrassing applause as Jerry presented the card himself, before going to the piano and playing a lively rendition of "Heart and Soul"—this time with the exuberance of a ragtime professional.

Yes, we had plenty to celebrate.

After McGoo and I had another beer, I made my way back to the office. Robin's door was closed, the lights off, and I was glad to see that she'd taken the night off; maybe she would catch up on her sleep for a change. Balfour's attorneys had quietly dropped the defamation and libel lawsuits against her, knowing they would never get a sympathetic jury. Besides, most of her contentions had been proved true.

I stood alone in our quiet, minimally decorated offices, just thinking, but at a loss. I looked at the potted ficus plant, Sheyenne's reception desk, the file cabinets, my office, Robin's office, the conference room, the kitchenette. Yes, this place felt like home, even though my actual one-room apartment was upstairs, rarely used.

Most of the cases were wrapped up for now; nothing seemed urgent. Having no desperate cases or clients in peril was a new situation for me. I didn't know what to do with myself: back from the dead with no place to go.

Sheyenne appeared, looking beautiful as always. "Working late again, Beaux?"

"Just being here late. Want to hang out?"

She rummaged in the top drawer of her desk and held out an envelope with a blurred postmark. "This came for you."

I looked at the return address and saw that Ruth had sent it. I felt a lump in my throat. Before I opened the envelope, I stepped closer to my girlfriend. "Read it with me," I said.

It was a short note, the succubus letting us know that she was all right. I was happy to hear that she had found a job working in a shop that specialized in dried floral arrangements. I knew how much Ruth liked flowers, and the company considered her to be a miracle worker. Any plants and flowers dried up immediately upon her touch, and, with a succubus working there, the shop could process five times as many floral arrangements, wreaths, and bouquets as before.

"Sounds like she's found her niche," Sheyenne said. "I'm happy for her."

The second part of the letter was even more surprising. Ruth told us that the ghost of Alphonse Wheeler had tracked her down after escaping prison. He had changed his identity, put on a spectral disguise, and pretended to live as an outlaw, although after the media uproar involving the Senator Balfour scandal, no one was really looking for him anymore.

"Why don't you take some time off," Sheyenne said to me. "Why don't *we* take some time off, together?"

"Sounds perfect, Spooky. How about a Mediterranean cruise? Alice could give us a recommendation."

"Let's just start with tonight," she said, with that tone in her voice, the one I could never resist . . . not when she'd been alive, not now that she was a ghost.

"Where would you like to go?"

She practically shimmered, and her blue eyes were intense. "How about upstairs? I got something for us, if you're ready for a little adventure. Did you know the adult novelty shop is open again? They have some very interesting merchandise."

I had no idea what a ghost and a zombie might actually *do*, since we could have no physical contact, but Sheyenne had my attention. All of it.

Upstairs, the door creaked open from long disuse. My room was dim and musty, with a distinct hint of mold. Some unnaturals preferred that for the ambience; in my case, it was strictly due to neglect. The dirty dishes in the sink had now become archaeological artifacts. The bed looked lonely and abandoned, and I realized that I should try to get rest more often. Even a zombie can't keep going and going without a little shut-eye.

"Let me slip into something more comfortable," Sheyenne said. "I want to make this a special night for us."

She flitted out of the small bedroom and passed directly through the door of my closet. I could hear her rustling around inside.

I went to sit down on the bed and noticed a plastic wrapper that had been wadded up and stuffed behind the nightstand—a bright label, a small zippered bag. So Sheyenne must have been planning this.

I heard her bumping and moving among the clothes in my closet, and I picked up the package she had been trying to hide, something she'd bought from the Unnatural Acts novelty store: *Inflatable Female Companion for the Lonely Gentleman.* The description insisted it was *100% Vinyl, and So Lifelike!*

"Spooky, I don't—" I said, but then the closet door opened, and she emerged in flesh-colored plastic. Sheyenne's ghostly image was superimposed upon it, and if I concentrated properly, I could see *her* and nothing else.

She moved forward jerkily and sat down beside me.

"I'm still getting used to this," she said. "It's like the glove I wore at *Macbeth.* This is just a doll, an inanimate object, a suit—I can move in it, live in it, but it takes a great deal of concentration. I don't know how long I can manage this." She lifted a hand and touched the side of my face. I saw her fuzzy spectral features. "It's fully functional, I think."

"I don't need that, Spooky. I just—" But it *was* good to feel her touch. The fingers were fake, the hands and arms just plastic, but the pressure and the presence behind it, those were real. "We don't need to see how functional it is," I said. I wrapped my arms around her, pulled her down onto the sheets.

It felt so good to relax, to be comfortable, to be beside her. The spectral image was smiling, and I saw translucent tears in her eyes. She was soft, squishy, rubbery . . . but it was *Sheyenne*. And it felt wonderful to hold her.

"This is nice," I said.

"Yes," Sheyenne said. "Yes, it is."

Don't miss Kevin J. Anderson's next
hilarious novel starring
Dan Shamble, Zombie PI

HAIR RAISING

Coming from Kensington Publishing Corp. in May 2013!

Turn the page to read an irresistible preview excerpt. . . .

CHAPTER 1

I've always been baffled by the things people do to amuse themselves, but this illegal cockatrice fighting ring was more bizarre than most.

Rusty, the full-furred werewolf who raised the hideous creatures and pitted them against each other in the ring, had hired me to watch out for "suspicious behavior." So, there I was in a crowd of unnaturals who gathered in an empty warehouse, laying down bets to watch chicken-dragon-viper monstrosities tear each other apart. What could possibly be suspicious?

No case was too strange for Chambeaux & Deyer Investigations, so I agreed to keep my eyes open. "You'll have a great time, Mr. Shamble," Rusty growled. "Tonight is family night."

"It's *Chambeaux*," I corrected him, though the mispronunciation may have been the result of him talking through all those teeth in his mouth rather than not actually knowing my name.

Rusty was a gruff, barrel-chested werewolf with a full head— and I mean a *full* head—of bristling reddish fur that stuck out in all directions. He raised cockatrices in backyard coops in a rundown neighborhood at the edge of town. He wore bib overalls and sported large tattoos on the meat of his upper arms (although his fur was so thick they were barely visible).

Cockatrice fighting was technically illegal and had been denounced by many animal activist groups. (Most of the activists, however, were unfamiliar with the mythological bestiary and had no idea what a cockatrice was, but they were sure "cockatrice fighting" had to be a bad thing from the sound of it.) I wasn't one to pass judgment; when ranked among unsavory activities in the Unnatural Quarter, this one didn't even make the junior varsity team.

Rusty insisted it was big business, and he had even offered me an extra ticket so that Sheyenne, my ghost girlfriend, could join me. I declined on her behalf. She's not much of a sports fan.

Inside a decrepit old warehouse, the spectators cheered, growled, howled, or made whatever sound was appropriate to their particular unnatural species. Even some humans had slunk in to place bets and watch the violence, hoping that violence didn't get done to *them* here in the dark underbelly of the Quarter.

In the echoing warehouse, the unsettling ambient noises reflected back, making the crowd sound twice as large as it really was. Previously, the warehouse had hosted illegal raves, and I could imagine the thunderously monotonous booming beat accompanied by migraine-inducing strobe lights. After the rave craze had ended, the warehouse manager was happy to let the unused empty space become the new home for the next best thing.

I tried to blend in with the rest of the spectators; nobody noticed an undead guy standing there in a bullet-riddled sport jacket. Thanks to an excellent embalming job and good hygiene habits, I was a well-preserved zombie, and I worked hard to maintain my physical condition so that I could pass for mostly human. Mostly.

The crowd hadn't come here to see and be seen. The center of attention was a high-walled enclosure that might have originally been designed as a skateboard park for lawn gnomes. The barricades were high enough that—in theory at least—snarling, venomous cockatrices could not leap over them and attack the audience (although, as Rusty explained it, a few bloodthirsty attendees took out long-shot wagers that it would happen; those bettors generally kept to the back rows).

While Rusty was in back wrangling with the cockatrice cages, preparing the creatures for the match, his bumbling nephew Furguson went among the crowds with his notepad and tickets, taking bets. Lycanthropy doesn't run in families, but the story I'd heard was that Rusty had gone on a bender and collapsed half on and half off his bed; while trying to make his uncle more comfortable, Furguson was so clumsy he had scratched and infected *himself* on the claws. Watching the gangly young werewolf now, I was inclined to accept that as an operating theory.

The fight attendees had tickets, scraps of paper, printed programs listing the colorful names of the cockatrice combatants—Sour Lemonade, Hissy Fit, Snarling Shirley, and so on. The enthusiasts were a motley assortment of vampires, zombies, mummies, trolls, and a big ogre with a squeaky voice who took up three times as much space as any other audience member. And there were werewolves of both types—full-time fully-furred wolfmen (affectionately, or deprecatingly, called "Hairballs" by the other type), and the once-a-month werewolves who looked human most of the time and transformed only under a full moon (called "Monthlies" by the other side). They were all werewolves to me, but there had always been friction between the two types, and it was only growing worse.

It's human, or inhuman, nature: People will find a way to make a big deal out of their differences—the smaller, the better. It made me think of the Montagues and the Capulets, if I wanted to be highbrow, or the Hatfields and the McCoys, if I wanted to be lowbrow. (Or the Jets and the Sharks, if I wanted to be musical.)

Rusty asked me to pay particularly close attention to two burly Monthlies, heavily tattooed "bad biker" types named Scratch and Sniff. Even in their non-lycanthrope form, and even among the crowd of monsters, these two were intimidating. They wore thick, dirty fur overcoats that they claimed were made of werewolf pelts—nothing provocative there!—coated with road dust and stained with clotted blotches that looked like blood. Known troublemakers, Scratch and Sniff liked to bash their victims' heads just to see what might come out. They frequently attended the cockatrice fights, and often caused problems, but Rusty allowed them to stay because they placed such large bets.

In recent fights, however, a large fraction of the money was disappearing from the betting pool, as much as 20 percent. Rusty was sure that Scratch and Sniff had somehow been robbing the pot, and I was supposed to keep my eyes open. But these two didn't strike me as the type who would *subtly* skim 20 percent of anything; my guess, they would take the whole pot of money and storm away with as much ruckus as possible.

Furguson wandered among the crowd, recording bets with a pencil in his notepad, accepting wads of bills and stuffing them into his pockets. As he collected money, he was very diligent in writing down each wager and recording the ticket number. For weeks, Rusty had pored over the notations, trying to figure out why so much money went missing. He counted and recounted the bills, added and re-added the list of bets placed, and he simply could not find what was happening to so much of the take.

Suddenly, the Rocky Balboa theme blared over the old rave speakers that had been left behind (confiscated by the warehouse owner for nonpayment). Eager fans surrounded Furguson in a frantic flurry, placing their last wagers, shoving money at the gangly werewolf as if they were over-caffeinated bidders on the floor of the New York Stock Exchange.

Now, I've been a private detective in the Unnatural Quarter for years, working with my legal crusader/partner Robin Deyer. We had a decent business until I'd been shot in the back of the head—which might have been the end of the story, but I woke up as a zombie, clawed my way out of the grave, and got right back to work. Being undead is not a disadvantage in the Quarter, and the number of cases I've solved, both before and after my murder, is fairly impressive. I'm very observant and persistent, and I have a good analytical mind.

Sometimes, though, I solve cases through dumb luck, which is what happened now.

While Rusty worked in the back, rattling the cages and giving pep talks to his violent amalgamated monsters, the Rocky theme played louder, and the last-minute bettors waved money at Furguson. They yelled out the names of their chosen cockatrice, snatched their tickets, and the gangly werewolf stuffed wads of cash into his pockets, made change, grew flustered, took more money, stuffed it into other pockets. He was so bumbling and so overwhelmed that bills dropped out of his pockets onto the floor, unnoticed—by Furguson, but not by the other audience members. As they pressed closer to him like a murder of carrion crows, they snatched up whatever random bills they could find. In fact, it was so well choreographed, the whole mess seemed like part of the evening's entertainment.

Scratch and Sniff had shouldered their way to the edge of the cockatrice ring, where they'd have the best view. Despite Rusty's accusations, the big biker werewolves had nothing to do with the money that went missing. As the saying goes, never attribute to malice what can be explained by incompetence—and I saw the gold standard of incompetence here.

I let out a long sigh. Rusty wasn't going to like what I'd found, but at least this was something easy enough to fix. His bumbling nephew would either have to be more careful or find another line of work.

The loud fanfare fell silent, and Rusty emerged from the back in his bib overalls; his reddish fur looked mussed, as if he had gotten into a wrestling match himself with the vile creatures. The restless crowd pressed closer to the fighting ring.

Rusty shouted at the top of his lungs. "For our first match, Sour Lemonade versus . . . Hissy Fit!"

He yanked a lever that opened a pair of trapdoors, and the two creatures squawked, hissed, and flapped into the pit. Each was the size of a wild turkey, covered with scales, with a head like a rooster on a bad drug trip with a serrated beak and slitted reptilian eyes. The jagged feathers looked like machetes, and their sharp, angular wings gave them the appearance of a very small dragon or a very large bat. Each cockatrice had a serpentine tail with a spearpoint tip. Their hooked claws were augmented by wicked-looking razor gaffs (I couldn't imagine how Rusty had attached the equipment). Forked tongues flicked out of their sawtooth beaks as they faced off.

I'd never seen anything so ugly—and these were the domesticated variety. Purebred cockatrices are even more hideous, ugly enough to turn people to stone. (It's hard to say objectively whether or not the purebreds are in fact *uglier,* since anyone who had ever looked upon one became a statue. Scientific studies had been done to measure the widened eyes of petrified victims, and a standard rating scale had been applied to the expression of abject horror etched into the stone faces, but I wasn't convinced those were entirely reliable results.) Regardless, wild turn-you-to-stone cockatrices were outlawed, and it was highly illegal to own one. These were the kinder, gentler breed—and they still looked butt-ugly.

One of the creatures had shockingly bright lemon-yellow scales—Sour Lemonade, I presumed. The other cockatrice had more traditional snot-green scales and black dragon wings. It hissed constantly, like a punctured tire.

The two creatures flapped their angular wings, bobbed their heads, and flicked their forked tongues like wrestlers bowing to the audience. The crowd egged them on, and the cockatrices flung themselves upon each other like Tasmanian devils on a hot plate. The fury of lashing claws, pecking beaks, and spitting venom was dizzying—not exactly enjoyable, but certainly energetic. I couldn't tear my eyes away.

The barbed tail of Sour Lemonade lashed out and poked a hole through Hissy Fit's left wing. The other cockatrice clamped down with its serrated beak, locking jaws on the yellow creature's scaly neck. Claws lashed and kicked, and black smoking blood spurted out from the injuries. When it hit the side of the pit ring, the acid blood burned and bubbled.

One large droplet splattered the face of a vampire, who yelped and backed away, swatting at his smoking skin. Scratch and Sniff both howled with inappropriate laughter at the vampire's pain. The spectators cheered, shouted, and cursed. The cockatrices snarled and hissed. The sound was deafening.

Then the warehouse door burst open, and I saw Officer Toby McGoohan in his full cop uniform standing there. "This is the police!" he shouted through a bullhorn. "May I have your attention—"

The ensuing pandemonium made the cockatrice fight seem like a Sunday card game by comparison.

CHAPTER 2

Shouting "Fire!" in a crowded theater is a well-known recipe for disaster. Shouting "Cops!" in the middle of an illegal cockatrice fight is ten times worse.

Officer McGoohan—McGoo to his friends (well, to me at least)—was taken aback by the explosion of chaos caused by his appearance. His mouth dropped open as he saw dozens of unnaturals—already keyed up with adrenaline and bloodlust from the cockatrice fight—suddenly thrown into a panic.

"Cops! Everybody, run!" yelled a vampire with a dramatic flourish of his cape. He turned and ran at full speed into a hulking ogre, which stunned him. The ogre reacted by flinging the vampire against the pit ring with enough force to crack the barricade.

Inside, the creatures were still hissing and thrashing at each other. Several zombies shambled at top speed toward the back exit. The human spectators bolted, ducking their heads to hide their identities. A bandage-wrapped mummy tripped and fell while other fleeing monsters stepped on him, trampling his fragile antique bones and sending up puffs of old dust. The clawed foot of a lizard man caught one of the bandages, and the linen strips unraveled as he ran.

At the door, McGoo waved his hands and shouted, "Wait, wait! It's not a raid!" Nobody heard him, or if they did, they refused to believe.

The skittish ogre smashed open an emergency exit door, knocking it entirely off its hinges. The door crashed to the ground outside, and fleeing monsters charged into the dim alleys, yelling and howling.

"We can work this out," I said, heading toward McGoo, who stood waving his hands and urging calm. He might as well have been asking for patrons in a strip club to cover their eyes. I saw that he hadn't even brought backup.

Gangly Furguson ran about in a panic, not sure what he was doing. He bumped into unnaturals and caromed off them like a pinball. Scratch and Sniff looked at each other and grinned. As Furguson came close, they grabbed the skinny werewolf and used his own momentum to fling him into the already-cracked pit wall, which knocked down the barricade. All the haphazard currency stuffed into Furguson's pockets flew up like a blizzard of money.

The cockatrices broke free and bounded out of the pit, still slashing at each other with razor gaffs but now taking a jab at anything that came near. They were like hyperactive whirlwinds, flailing, attacking. Sour Lemonade latched its jaws onto the shoulder of a zombie who did not shamble away quickly enough. Hissy Fit swooped down and attacked the vampire that had already been burned by acid blood; the vamp flailed his hands to get the beast away from his head and his neatly slicked-back hair.

Taking matters into his own hands, Rusty grabbed Hissy Fit by the scaly neck and yanked it away from the vampire, stuffed the cockatrice into a burlap sack, and cinched a cord around the opening. "Furguson, get the other one! We've got to get out of here!"

After being bashed into the wall, however, Furguson flew at Scratch and Sniff in a rage. He extended his claws, bared his fangs, and howled, "Shithead Monthlies!" Hurling himself upon Scratch, the nearer of the two, he raked his long claws down the werewolf-pelt overcoat, ripping big gashes. With his other hand, he tore four bloody furrows along the biker were-wolf's cheek.

Sniff plucked Furguson away from his friend and began punching him with a pile-driver fist. Scratch touched the blood on his cheek, and his eyes flared. The tattoos on his neck and face began pulsing, writhing, like a psychedelic cartoon—and then the deep wounds on his face sealed together. The blood coagulated into a hard scab that flaked off within seconds; the flesh knitted itself into scar tissue. The tattoos fell quiescent again, and I realized that it must be some kind of body-imprinted healing spell.

Very cool.

Amidst the pandemonium, I reached McGoo. He looked at me in surprise. "Shamble! What are you doing here?"

"I'm working. What about you?"

"I'm working, too. Just answering a disturbance call. Scout's honor, your friends sure have hair triggers! Did I catch them doing something naughty?"

Rusty tore a large two-by-four from the cockatrice barri-cade and waded in to Scratch and Sniff. He whacked each one of them on the back of the head, which sent them reeling, then pulled Furguson from the fray. He shoved the burlap sack into his nephew's claws. "Take this and get out of here! I'll grab the other one."

With the struggling, squirming sack in hand, Furguson bolted for the nearest door and disappeared into the night. As he ran, the poor klutz was still dropping bills out of his pockets.

The two biker werewolves shook their heads after being battered by the two-by-four. They both puffed themselves up, peeled back their lips, and prepared to lunge at Rusty, but the big werewolf swung the board again, cracking each man full in the face. "Want a third one? Believe me, it'll only improve your looks."

"We may need to intervene in this, McGoo," I said.

"I was just thinking that." He sauntered forward, displaying the arsenal of unnatural-specific weapons that he carried for defense in the Quarter.

The two biker werewolves snarled at Rusty. "Damned Hairball!" Thanks to the hypnotically twitching tattoos, the bloody bruises on their faces had already healed up and vanished faster than they could wipe the stains away.

McGoo stepped up and said to them, "Know any good werewolf jokes?"

Scratch and Sniff looked at his uniform, snarled low in the throat for a long moment, then they retreated into the night as well. Outside, I heard a roar of motorcycle engines starting.

The less panicky, or more enterprising, spectators scurried around to grab fallen money on the floor; then they, too, darted out of the building. Rusty managed to seize Sour Lemonade from the zombie it was still attacking and stuffed it into another cloth bag, which he slung over his shoulder, then loped away from the warehouse through the large doorway the ogre had shattered.

McGoo and I stood together, catching our breath, exhausted just from watching the whirlwind. He shook his head as the last of the monsters evacuated into the night. "This place looks like the aftermath of a bombing raid. Mission accomplished, I suppose."

"What mission was that?" I asked.

"One of the nearby residents called in a noise complaint. Some kind of writer. She asked me to stop by and request that they keep the noise down, said the racket was bothering her."

"That was all?"

"That was all." McGoo shrugged. "Should be quiet enough now."

McGoo is my best human friend, my BHF. We've known each other since college; both married women named Rhonda when we were young and stupid; later, as we got smarter, we divorced the women named Rhonda and spent a lot of guy time commiserating. I established my private-eye practice in the Unnatural Quarter; McGoo, with his salty and non-politically-correct sense of humor, managed to offend the wrong people, thus derailing his mediocre career on the outside in exchange for a less-than-mediocre career here in the Quarter. But he was a good friend, a reliable cop, and he made the best of his situation.

It had taken McGoo quite a while to learn how to deal with me after I was undead. He wrestled with his own prejudices against various types of monsters, and, thanks to me, he could honestly say, "Some of my best friends are zombies." (I didn't let him use that to get any moral high ground, though.)

As we surveyed the empty warehouse, he said, "I'd better go talk to the lady, let her know everything's under control."

"Want me to come along? I could use something a little calmer after this." I had, after all, solved the case of the missing money, but I decided to wait for the dust to settle before I tracked Rusty down.

I found a twenty-dollar bill on the floor and dutifully picked it up.

McGoo looked at me. "That's evidence, you know."

"Evidence against what? You were called here on a disturbing-the-peace charge." As we walked out of the warehouse, I tucked

the bill into the pocket of my sport jacket. "That's our next couple of beers at the Goblin Tavern."

"Well, if it's being used to buy beer, then I'll consider that
you were doing your civic duty by picking up litter."

"Works for me."

Behind the warehouse, we found a set of ramshackle apart-
ments; I saw lights on in only two of the units, though it was
full dark. A weathered sign promised UNITS FOR RENT: LOW
RATES! *Low Rates* was apparently the best that could be said
about the place.

McGoo led me up the exterior stairs to an upper-level apartment. When he rapped on the door, a woman yanked it open,
blinking furiously as she tried to see out into the night. "Stop
pounding! What's with all this noise? I've already filed a complaint—I'm calling the police again!"

"Ma'am, I *am* the police," McGoo said.

The woman was a frumpy vampire, short and plump, with
brown hair—and she looked familiar. "Well, you ought to be
ashamed of yourself. The noise only got worse after I called! It
was a mob scene out there."

She plucked a pair of cat's-eye glasses dangling from a chain
around her neck and affixed them to her face. "How can I get
any writing done with such distractions? I have to finish two
more chapters before sunrise."

I knew who she was, and I also knew exactly what she was
writing. "Sorry for the interruption, Miss Bullwer."

McGoo looked at me. "You know this woman?"

"Who's that looming out there on my porch?" The vampire
lady leaned out until she could see me, then her expression lit
up as if a sunrise had just occurred on her face (which is not
necessarily a good thing when speaking of vampires). "Oh, Mr.
Chambeaux! How wonderful. Would you like to come in and
have a cup of . . . whatever it is zombies drink? I have a few
more questions, details for the veracity of the literature. And

you can pet my cats. They'd love to have a second lap; they can't all fit on mine, you know."

"How many cats do you have?"

"Seven," she answered quickly. "At least, I think it's seven. It's difficult to tell them apart."

I had first met Linda Bullwer when she volunteered for the Welcome Back Wagon, catering to the newly undead. More importantly, she had been commissioned as a ghostwriter by Howard Phillips Publishing to create a series of zombie detective adventures loosely based on my own exploits.

She gave a sweet smile to McGoo, and her demeanor was entirely changed now. "And thank you for your assistance, Officer—I'm sure you did your best, especially with Mr. Chambeaux's help." She cocked her head, lowered her voice. "Was it another case? Something I should write about in a future volume?"

"I doubt anyone would find it interesting," I said.

"That's what you said about the tainted Jekyll necroceuticals, and about the mummy emancipation case, and the Straight Edge hate group, and the attempted massacre of hundreds of ghosts with ectoplasmic defibrillators, and the burning of the Globe Theatre stage in the cemetery, and the golem sweatshop, and . . ."

I knew she could rattle off cases for hours because I had spent hours telling her about them. She had listened carefully, taking dutiful notes.

"It's nothing," I reassured her. "And we don't even know if your first book is going to sell well enough that the publisher will want to do a second one."

"They've already contracted with me for five, Mr. Chambeaux. The first one is just being released—have you gotten your advance copy yet?"

"I'll check the mail when I get back to the office." I have to admit, I was uncomfortable about the whole thing. Vampires shun sunlight, and I tended to avoid limelight.

McGoo regarded me with amusement. "I believe we're done here, ma'am. Enjoy the rest of your quiet night."

"Thank you, Officer. And thank you, Mr. Chambeaux, for your help." She drew a deep breath. "Ah, blessed silence. At last I can write!"

A loud and anguished howl split the air, bestial shouts barely recognizable as words. "Help! Help me! Help!"

McGoo was already bounding down the stairs, and I did my best to keep up with him. We tracked the cries to a dark alley adjacent to the warehouse. A gangly werewolf leaned over a sprawled figure on the ground, letting out a keening howl. Beside him, two squirming cloth sacks contained the captured cockatrices; fortunately, the ties were secure.

As we ran up, Furguson turned to us, his eyes opened wide, his tongue lolling out of his mouth. "It's Uncle Rusty!"

I recognized the bib overalls and reddish fur. The big werewolf lay motionless, sprawled muzzle-down in the alley.

"Is he dead?" McGoo asked.

Bending over, I could see that Rusty's chest still rose and fell, but he had been stunned. The top of his head was all bloody, and it looked *wrong*.

Furguson let out another wail.

Then I realized that someone, using a very sharp knife, had *scalped* him.